MW00616962

A special thanks goes ⌐
project. It is my every inte
enjoyment and satisfaction. Extra special thanks to the ......
Ward, and the city of New Orleans in its entirety. The
experiences growing up in "tha boot" help mold me into the
man I am today, and is the inspiration behind Part One of this
saga. I welcome you all into my world, and I hope you find the
reading of this novel just as pleasurable as it was for me to
write it,

Clever Black.

ISBN: 13-978-0985350901

ISBN: 10-0985350903

THE HOLLAND FAMILY SAGA

Part One

THEY DON'T MIND DYING

A Novel

Created By

Clever Black

CHAPTER ONE

THE LITTLE GIRL FROM BENEFIT STREET

"Aahaa, Ms. Joyce, I tricked you! You thought I was gone!" Eight-year old Katrina Sanders yelled as she crawled from under Ms. Joyce's bed on a hot and muggy night in August of 1989.

The little girl, who stood about three and one-half feet tall, danced happily, kicking her legs from side to side in the hallway just outside of Ms. Joyce's bedroom after crawling from under the woman's sleigh bed. Katrina Sanders was a caramel-complexioned little girl with a thin face and body frame. She had almond-shaped, dark eyes, a slender nose, pointed chin and thin lips that were the same color as her caramel skin. Her eyebrows were thin, long and very dark; they curved downward on either side of her eyes. Besides the jet-black curly locks that hung just above her shoulders, her eyebrows were the one thing people noticed when they saw the cute and petite, perky little girl. Although she was only eight years old, Katrina had begun filling out. She had a firm round curvy behind and little buds had begun to sprout, although she didn't wear a training-bra.

"Girl, I been all up and down the sidewalk looking for you," Ms. Joyce said as she placed her hands on her hips and smiled at Katrina from the opposite end of the hall. "Come on so you

can take a bath, baby."

"Yes!" Katrina exclaimed as she ran to her drawer on the armoire inside of Ms. Joyce's bedroom and grabbed a fresh set of sleeping clothes.

Ms. Joyce was a thirty-two year old full-figured, big-breasted, thick-thighed, dark brown-skinned woman who often wore her honey-blonde-dyed hair in a French twist. As she walked towards the kitchen of her two-bedroom apartment inside the Desire Housing Project, a sprawling forty-four hundred acre urban housing complex, Ms. Joyce passed her son Manny's bedroom.

At fifteen years old, Manny was dark skinned like his mother. His eyebrows were thick, his eyes big, dark and round. He had a thin mustache that was neatly trimmed and sported long side burns. Manny also wore his hair in small dreads as he had just begun to try and grow long locks. Manny stood about 5'8" and had a muscular build. He played middle linebacker his freshman year in high school, but he quit the team in October of '88 when he tore his Achilles tendon. Two months later, during Christmas break, Manny dropped out of high school completely.

When he saw his mother pass in her tight-fitting white spandex outfit with a pair of blue and white G-Nike's on her feet, Manny jumped up from the bottom bunk bed in his room, turned down The Showboys's rap song *Drag Rap* (Triggerman) that was blaring on his stereo, and stood in the doorway of his bedroom. "Where you going with that outfit?" He asked his mother angrily as his eight gold teeth glimmered under the hallway lights.

"When you start buying my clothes, you can ask me that shit!" Ms. Joyce snapped as she turned around and walked back to the threshold of Manny's bedroom, paused, folded her arms and stared Manny down letting him know she meant business.

Manny said, "I give you money, ma! I just gave you two hundred on the rent yesterday!"

Ms. Joyce rolled her eyes. "Manny, this has nothin' to do with you helping me out from time to time. For the umpteenth time —you are not my man! And I'm not any of them little hussies you deal with out there! I'm your *mother*! I tell you what to do! It ain't the other way around, baby." She told her son matter-of-factly.

"I'm just sayin', brer! I always have to check niggas behind you and shit! For the simple fact they always be sayin' how much they wanna hit that. And when you wear stuff like that, I gotta hear that shit on the streets!"

"Manny, please! These men back here don't have nothin' I want!" Ms. Joyce replied as she headed towards the kitchen once more.

Manny and his mother had been living in the Desire Housing Project for nearly twelve years. They had moved there after the police raided their lavish thirty-five hundred square foot Lakefront home in June of 1977 and found one-hundred pounds of marijuana that Manny's father had hidden in the attic. The police held Ms. Joyce in custody and had threatened to turn Manny, whose real name is Manuel Lawson Taylor Junior, over to the state if Manny's father did not turn himself in to the feds.

Not wanting to see his wife go to jail and have his son taken away from his mother, Manuel Lawson Taylor Senior turned himself in to the FBI and freed his wife and son. Nevertheless, the feds took Taylor Senior's home, his three cars, all his money, and sentenced him to sixty years in the federal penitentiary. The money Ms. Joyce had stashed away had been exhausted on her husband's appeals, all of which he lost. The sixty years stood in court. Taylor, Sr. would be eighty years-old when he would be released, so Ms. Joyce and Manny were left on their own.

Ms. Joyce was a proud woman. She refused welfare and food stamps, but she did accept a public housing apartment as she had nowhere else to go at the time. Now, over twelve years later, Ms. Joyce was a licensed nurse with a college degree and close to being free of debt. Things were looking up for Ms.

Joyce and her son, Manny. The apartment was fully furnished. A white leather Queen Anne sofa set with white marble end tables decked the living room, and Manny had a black lacquered oak and brass bunk bed set in his bedroom. Ms. Joyce had a king-sized sleigh bed crafted out of pecan wood in her bedroom, and a washer and dryer, cherry wood breakfast nook, electric stove and Maytag refrigerator with an ice-maker laced the kitchen. Manny and his mother were close, too; Ms. Joyce was only seventeen years older than her son, and the closeness in their ages allowed the two to relate well to one another.

Ms. Joyce had come up in the game with Manny's father in the seventies; she was hip to the streets. Everyone in the Desire projects knew of Ms. Joyce and Manny; they were popular people. Ms. Joyce was popular through Taylor Sr. and her old hustling ways from back in the day. Manny gained his popularity playing high school football early on, and through his gangster ways of the present day and time.

Katrina Sanders lived in the apartments in the next porch over from Ms. Joyce. The apartments throughout the Desire Housing Project were all two story, light-tan, brick apartments that featured either four, or eight unit apartments consisting of two, three and four bedrooms. Katrina lived in the same courtyard on Benefit Street as Ms. Joyce and Manny in a two bedroom apartment with her mother, Faye, in an upstairs apartment on the porch to the left of Ms. Joyce's apartment, if you were facing the building.

Faye Sanders, unlike Ms. Joyce, had succumbed to the crack epidemic that plagued the entire city of New Orleans, Louisiana during the middle and late eighties. Ms. Joyce and Faye knew one another well, although Faye was eight years younger than Ms. Joyce. Faye used to look up to Ms. Joyce when she was running the streets back in the day. She was like a little sister to Ms. Joyce in the beginning; but crack cocaine had placed a serious and permanent rift in the two women's friendship.

The reason being was because Faye had broken into Ms.

Joyce's home one afternoon and had stolen two-hundred dollars in cash. Ms. Joyce learned Faye was the culprit when she mentioned to Faye that someone had broken into her home. Faye gave herself away when she asked Ms. Joyce who would break into her home and steal her money. Ms. Joyce knew that no one, not even the police, had known that the money was stolen out of her home. That day had become the same day the two women stopped speaking to one another. The funny part was that Ms. Joyce would have given Faye the money if she had only asked for it, but by stealing it, Faye Sanders had proven herself to be an untrustworthy individual who would do anything to get high—up to and including stealing from those who placed trust in her.

Ms. Joyce, although she felt sorry for Katrina, never intervened in the little girl's life; but it was for the better in Ms. Joyce's eyes at the time. Having been preyed upon by Faye, Ms. Joyce had been avoiding both daughter and mother at all costs, because if Faye ever tried to steal from Ms. Joyce again, Katrina would grow up without a mother; but unbeknownst to Ms. Joyce, Katrina was already living under that particular circumstance.

Ms. Joyce's avoidance of Katrina changed when Manny brought her home with him one evening a year ago. When Ms. Joyce came in from work that night, she noticed her living room smelled of urine. "What is that awful smell," she yelled as she opened her living room windows that warm August night in order to air out her apartment. "Manny!" She called out to her son.

"I'm right here with Oscar in the bathroom, momma!" Manny yelled back to his mother.

When Ms. Joyce walked into the bathroom, she saw Manny and the youth who had been Manny's friend since first grade named Oscar Henderson. Oscar was a black-skinned, 6'1" one-hundred and sixty pound, fifteen year old with a short, bald-faded haircut. He had a big nose, big lips, and droopy-like, dark eyes.

Manny and Oscar were kneeling beside the tub bathing

Katrina as she stood naked and crying inside the bathtub. She sobbed and heaved as the teenagers scrubbed her petite body and poured cold water onto her outstretched hands. The little girl looked as if she hadn't had a bath in a week. Ms. Joyce felt compelled to help the little girl at that moment.

"What happened to her?" Ms. Joyce asked Manny as she knelt beside her son and began scanning Katrina's body.

Manny answered, all the while washing Katrina's body, "She was outside in the courtyard playing with Jason 'nem until everybody went inside to eat. When she got home, Faye was passed out, high on the sofa. Katrina said she was hungry and she tried to fix some hotdogs. She went to move the pot off the stove and it burned her hands. Me and Oscar was on the porch when we heard her screaming, so we went up there and grabbed her and brought her down here."

Ms. Joyce sighed as Manny began relating to her how nasty Faye's apartment was kept. Manny described dirty dishes strewn about inside the unit and more, "She got dirty clothes all over the floor, momma. And it smell like shit in there because the toilet can't flush right. It's overflowing. They got shit on the floor in the bathroom! Piss stains in the mattresses with no sheets or nothin' on the beds to cover up with! How Faye let this li'l girl sleep in that filthy place?"

Ms. Joyce didn't answer Manny, but she knew very well the answer to Manny's question: crack cocaine. The place Manny had described sounded sickening; and the thought of having a child living under those conditions angered Ms. Joyce. The circumstances also compelled the woman to take care of the little girl. She looked at Katrina's hands and saw that they were reddened, but not burned. She wrapped them in ace bandages and sent Manny and Oscar to K-mart to buy Katrina some new clothes. While the two were gone, Ms. Joyce put a large T-shirt on Katrina and sat her down at her nook and fried a large beef hamburger.

The seven-year old ate the entire hamburger and politely asked Ms. Joyce to fix her another one. Ms. Joyce realized that the little girl was starving. She told herself that she would not

let that happen again. From that day forth, Ms. Joyce, Manny and Oscar made certain that little Katrina Sanders always had clean clothes and blankets along with a hot meal before she went home. Manny would walk little Katrina to school in the mornings after bathing her and fixing her breakfast, and he would pick her up and have a snack for her when she got back over to his mother's apartment. On weekends during the school year, and just about every night during the summer, Katrina often got to sleep over to Ms. Joyce's apartment; this hot summer night in August of 1989 would be one of those nights.

Katrina was grateful that someone cared enough to feed and bathe her, because when it got down to it, her mother was only interested in getting high at any cost; and even though she had some measure of care and stability, Katrina still had serious problems at home; but for the time being, whenever she was with Ms. Joyce and Manny, Katrina was always a happy child.

That night with Katrina and her scorched hands had transpired a year ago. Now, on a hot summer night in August of 1989, as she was preparing to eat and take her bath, eight year old Katrina Sanders stood at the end of the hallway dancing to Soul II Soul's song *Keep On Movin'* as it blared from Ms. Joyce's stereo inside her bedroom window whilst Ms. Joyce ran her bath water. Katrina could smell chicken frying in the kitchen and she had seen Ms. Joyce cutting fresh potatoes to make French fries. She was more than ecstatic. Katrina simply loved being over to Ms. Joyce's home with her and Manny. The Taylor family had given the little girl from Benefit Street something she hadn't received from her mother in years, something every child needs: tender loving care.

Under Ms. Joyce's care, little Katrina Sanders flourished. She loved school and was very intellectual. This was a happy time in the eight year-old's life.

CHAPTER TWO

BEN HOLLAND

"Henrietta, can I have some of my money you been holding for me?" Benjamin Holland asked his aunt politely.

Ever since his parents were murdered outside a motel room in Kenner, Louisiana, a small suburb of New Orleans, in 1984, Ben Holland had been living with his aunt, Henrietta Jenkins. Ben was the beneficiary of his parents' life insurance policy; but his young age prevented him from seeing any of the currency. His aunt was given power-by-the-attorney over the money, about fifty-thousand dollars in total, and she immediately began to run through the funds.

During the last five years, Henrietta Jenkins had bought a three-bedroom brick home in Ponchartrain Park, a quiet and predominately Black middle-class neighborhood just north of the Desire Project. Ben was also receiving a monthly stipend of five-hundred and fifty dollars from the government. Henrietta, however, was cashing the checks and keeping that fact hidden from Ben until he found out by accident one day while he was looking for an ink pen in one of Henrietta's desk drawers in her den. Ben had found check stub after check stub in his name going back almost five years; although he had never seen any of the money. When he asked his aunt about

the situation, Henrietta told Ben that he was too young to understand at the time. She also told Ben that his money was in the bank. Ben believed Henrietta until he asked her for some money to buy some clothes for the summer.

In March of 1989, Henrietta and Ben had a dispute and Ben had come to the conclusion that Henrietta believed that the money was hers to do with as she pleased for all the time she had been looking after him.

The forty-year old, tan-skinned slender woman with long brown hair told Ben that everything she did, she did for him. Benjamin didn't see it that way, however; the 6' one-hundred and sixty-five pound, yellow-skinned, fifteen year-old with long, jet-black hair that hung down to his shoulders, told his aunt he didn't remember asking her to buy him a three-bedroom house and put leather sofas and other expensive items in the house, including a china cabinet and a grandfather clock. Ben had tolerated his aunt's distant and lackadaisical emotions towards him for as long as he could remember; but he was quickly becoming annoyed with the way Henrietta was treating him. Ben often stated that the two of them were living in a "loveless house".

Deep down inside, Henrietta herself was beginning to view Ben as a burden; but she never expressed those feelings towards her nephew. But on a cool spring night in March of 1989, it all came to a head. As Ben stood in the doorway of Henrietta's den, rubbing the peach fuzz that was growing under his chin, he waited for his aunt's reply to his request for some of his money. As he stood awaiting Henrietta's reply, Ben came to the realization that he literally had to beg his aunt for things that he not only wanted, but very much needed. He focused his brown eyes on Henrietta and stared at her angrily as he lowered his thick, dark brown eyebrows and asked her again, this time with more passion. "Etta, I need my money! I ain't had nothing new since Christmas! It's fucking March!"

"I don't care what month it is, Benjamin! I'm barely making it as it is. I feed you and you have a bed to sleep in. That's good enough for now until things get better. You have clothes

in there from last spring and summer anyway, don't you? I know you want new items right now, but I simply can't afford it. I'm sorry." Henrietta replied in an apologetic tone of voice as she sat at her dining room table with a calculator adding up the monthly bills, never looking up at Benjamin.

"That's my mutherfuckin' money," Ben yelled. "You been stealing from me from day one! You ain't mean my momma and daddy no good from the get go!"

Henrietta removed her eyeglasses and stared at Benjamin with wide eyes, having been astonished by the disrespectful manner in which he was talking to her. "How could you talk to me in that manner, Benjamin," she asked. "And then you bring Gabriella and Samson into this discussion?" She probed further in a somewhat surprised manner. "I'm the only family member alive now that's willing and able to take care of you. I'm all you have left in this world and I'm doing the best that I can for you, son."

"Fuck you, brer!" Ben snapped as he walked out of the dining room.

"That's it!" Henrietta yelled aloud as she slammed her fists onto the table, damaging her eyeglasses in the process. She then stood up in frustration as tears of anger began to flow down her cheeks. The long-suffering woman's tolerance had just reached its apex. "Every day you find a way to disrespect me, Benjamin and I'm sick and tired of it! We both lost Gabriella! She was my *heart*! My baby sister! My *only* sister! How do you think I feel," she asked loudly through her tears.

Ben turned around and reentered the dining room and pointed at Henrietta with his right index finger, "I don't care how you feel! All I know is ever since my momma and daddy died, you been—"

"Let them be! Let *her* be! God I can't take anymore!" Henrietta yelled aloud as she franticly waved her arms in the air and stormed past Benjamin and opened the front door to the house. "Get the hell out!"

"This my house!"

"No, it's not!" Henrietta cried as she ran into the dining room and grabbed the deed to the house off the table and presented it to Ben. "This is *my name* on the deed! *I* own it! It ain't yours! So you get the hell out of here! I don't *have* any more money and I'm tired of you talking to me like I'm some trash off the street! And then you constantly, constantly throw Gabriella and Samson in my face every God-forsaken day of my life! Get the hell out of my house!"

Benjamin stared at Henrietta in disbelief. He came to believe that his aunt, his own flesh and blood, had taken all of his money and used it for her own personal gain. The young teen was devastated by what his aunt had done to him. He walked out of Henrietta's house that day in broken spirits and started living a hard life on the streets of New Orleans. He spent many nights in an abandoned house on Piety Street, just outside of the Desire Project in the Ninth Ward. Benjamin now found himself alone and hungry, without anyone in the world who cared about what was happening in his life—except for Anastasia Gordon.

Anastasia was a young teenager Benjamin had met at the Covenant House, which was a shelter for homeless teenagers nearby Louis Armstrong Park in downtown New Orleans. Anna, that's what Benjamin called her, was homeless as well. The day Ben walked into to the place, Anna helped him settle in and the two had become good friends. The brown-skinned voluptuous, bow-legged, round-faced sixteen-year-old-year had the most beautiful brown eyes Ben had ever seen.

Anna was 5' tall, and stacked with big breasts and a wide, soft behind. She was Ben's first and Anna had given her virginity to Ben as well one night inside the Covenant House as the other teenagers slept. It was fair to say that these two loved one another. Their circumstances, however, had prevented the two from being together the way they wanted. Anna always stayed at the Covenant House, a place Ben despised; therefore, he would leave her for three or four days at a time. During those times, Ben would return to the Ninth Ward and earn a few

dollars cutting grass and cleaning yards and fixing automobiles for the people who lived in and around the Desire Housing Project.

Ben had lived that way for months, popping in and out of the Covenant House, only returning to see Anna. When he returned one day in late August of 1989 after one of his solo adventures, Anna confronted him. "Why you keep leaving here?" She asked Ben with a look of concern.

"You know I hate this place." Ben responded nonchalantly as he plopped down onto his cot and picked up one of his World History books.

"It's all we got. You know that. Where do you go when you leave here? Is there somebody else?" Anna asked anxiously. "Shoot," Anna then said as she went and sat beside Ben and looked sadly towards the floor, "I wouldn't blame you if there is someone else. What person in their right mind really wants to be here anyway?" She asked somberly.

"Ain't nobody else Anna," Ben said as he sat up on his cot and placed his feet on the floor, "I be sleepin' in this old house in the Ninth Ward. That's where I make my li'l hustle. I'm too young to work, I mean we ain't got no money, I'm just tryna do something for us."

"So there's nobody else? You're not leaving?" Anna asked meekly as she looked Ben in the eyes.

Ben stared at Anna and smiled. He could tell she was fearful of his departing, so he decided to show Anna exactly what he was doing better than he could tell her. He took Anna with him that very same day and showed her the abandoned house he sometimes called home. Ben also showed Anna his lawnmower and mechanic's tools he had hidden under the house, along with a few clean clothes he had wrapped in a plastic bag.

Anna immediately realized that Ben was telling the truth and her fears went away. She also saw just how well-intended and thoughtful Ben was; Anna remembered the Gucci short set Ben

had bought her for her birthday a month ago and she now understood that what Ben did, he did for the two of them. "I'm sorry I didn't believe you, at first Ben." Anna said softly as she knelt beside him staring at all of Ben's worldly possessions, which amounted to much of nothing.

"Don't be sorry," Ben replied as he stared at what little he owned. "We both got it bad right now."

Anna's heart was moved. She leaned over, grabbed Ben's cheeks and kissed him, forcing her tongue fully into his mouth. "Show me what you do when you 'round here, Ben." Anna requested as she pulled back and stared Ben in the eyes.

Ben shrugged and began to oblige. He walked Anna through the Desire Project and pointed out a couple of teenagers around his age that he had intentions on doing business with. The two then walked over to a burned-out lot a couple of blocks outside of the Desire Project where Ben mentioned to Anna that he remembered a building being there, "I remember this alleyway beside this lot as a kid. I was watching my aunt Henrietta and my momma and daddy play with a turkey or something." Ben stated as he and Anna stared at the dilapidated, junked-out lot.

"Who owned this place?" Anna asked lowly as she looked up to Ben.

Ben told Anna he didn't remember. "Maybe Henrietta know, but I can't talk to that woman. She the reason I'm in the position I'm in now." He ended somberly as he grabbed Anna's hand and walked away from the lot. "Come on, let's go and get something to eat. I made a few dollars cutting grass earlier today."

Ben and Anna purchased hot sausage Po-boys from a sandwich shop on Louisa Street and returned to the abandoned house. Ben had convinced Anna to spend the night with him at the old house as it still had running water and working electricity. Anna was reluctant at first, but Ben told her that he'd been sleeping there for months and nobody had ever bothered him. He assured Anna that nothing would happen to her and they would return to the Covenant House first thing in

the morning. Anna agreed because she trusted Ben and believed he would keep her safe.

They entered the dark living room of the home, which had a musky smell, dingy walls and a worn roof with a hole in the ceiling. "I never stay in this room here. I got some blankets and a lamp in the back bedroom. The doors still lock in here and all the windows have screens on 'em. It's not home, but it's a place ta' chill." Ben remarked as he guided Anna to the back of the home where the carpet was clean, soft, and dry and the rooms were more habitable.

Ben showed Anna the bathroom he kept clean as he grabbed his three blankets from the closet. Anna saw a stack of books on the shelf inside the closet when he was removing the blankets and she asked Ben what they were about. Ben told her they were Science and History books, two of his favorite subjects. "Let's read them while we eat." Anna suggested.

Ben grabbed the blankets and books and the two went into the last bedroom of the three bedroom home and spread out their belongings on top of one of the blankets. The two teens ate, laughed, and read some of Ben's text books and talked more about the future.

"Where you wanna be five years from now, Anna?" Ben asked as the two now lay on their backs side by side on the blanket.

"Living with my momma in Seattle and about to graduate college!" Anna answered enthusiastically as she stared at the ceiling and smiled.

Anna's mother had been incarcerated for five years on an armed robbery charge. She had been locked up for three years so far and was scheduled to be released on Anna's eighteenth birthday. Anna had run away from a foster home in Slidell, Louisiana over a year ago because the people that were supposed to be her foster parents were physically abusive. They used to beat Anna over the slightest of things—talking on the phone, having the radio too loud, staying up late on a Saturday night just to watch TV. Anna was a typical teenager,

and she did all that her foster parents asked; but they were always angry over something and they often took out their rage on Anna. Because of that fact, Anna felt that her chances of survival would be better if she were on her own. She caught a Greyhound Bus back to New Orleans in June of 1988 and had been living at the Covenant House ever since.

Anna wrote her mother shortly after arriving at the Covenant House and told her of the situation and why she had run away from the foster home. She also told her mother she would stay at the Covenant House and go to high school and earn her high school diploma while waiting for her to get out. Anna had enrolled herself into NOCCA, (New Orleans Center for Creative Arts), a magnet school that took in students that were in the top percentile of their schools.

Anna's mother, having seen the determination and spirit within her daughter, had a complete change of heart in prison over her daughter's actions. She was planning on taking her daughter and move from Louisiana to the state of Washington upon her release so that the two of them could start life anew; that in itself gave Anna something to look forward to with great joy and anticipation.

"What about you Ben?" Anna then asked as she turned over onto her stomach, laid her head on Ben's muscular chest and looked him in the eyes.

"I want my own place, a car, and a good job," Ben responded as he smiled at Anna.

Ben once again reflected on what his aunt had done to him over the last five years and he vowed to never let anyone take from him again.

"What kind of job do you want?" Anna then asked.

"I don't know. Maybe a mechanic or something. My own business you know? Whatever it is, it's definitely gone be mine's. After what Henrietta done to me, I'm a make sure I look after what belongs to me."

"What about me? Do I belong to you?" Anna asked as she

nuzzled up against Ben's chest and closed her eyes.

Ben wrapped his right arm around Anna and said, "No doubt. I wanna take care of you, Anna. When I rise up, you rise up. And when we get on our feet I'm a do whatever it takes ta' stay there. Nobody should ever have ta' live like this."

"Amen ta' that, Ben. Amen ta' that." Anna responded as she stared at the carpeted floor and hoped for better days for both she and Ben.

Anna and Ben slept in the old house that hot summer night and made love on the floor. As they lay side by side on their backs, after a passionate love-making session, the two teenagers made a pact that they would always take care of one another no matter what. Even if they were no longer boyfriend and girlfriend, they agreed to help each other no matter where they were or whom they were with in life.

CHAPTER THREE

THE DAY THEY BECAME A CREW

"Manny throw the ball, brer! I'm open," yelled Jason Witherspoon.

Manny was out playing football on a hot summer afternoon in late August of 1989 with Jason, the skinny brown-skinned, dark-eyed, Afro wearing, and pearly-white teethed, nine year-old and the rest of Jason's friends, including Katrina, and three boys named Lamont, Cedric and Jermaine. Lamont was a little taller than Jason with more muscle and platted hair. The tan-skinned nine year-old had a square jaw and a broad flat nose. Cedric was a round-faced, short, light-tan ten year-old with short hair and brown eyes. He was the shortest of the bunch, but he had the most muscle tone. Jermaine was the tallest of the four children, an ebony-skinned nine year-old with long, lanky legs and arms. He had a slim face, pointed nose, and a short, faded haircut with an earring in his left ear.

The young boys loved playing football with Manny in the courtyard. Manny often called them his young "thugs-in training". They would often try to imitate Manny whenever they were around him.

The boys loved Manny; he was a lot of fun to be around.

While all the other teenagers were too busy playing "gangster" and had no time for games, Manny always had time for the kids in the courtyard. He was cool to them. So was his mother, Ms. Joyce. Their house was always open to the kids; it was the funhouse. The Taylor family would always have parties and bar-b-ques at their home and Ms. Joyce would often place her stereo speakers in the window and play it loud for the kids. You could often hear NWA, Too Short, Keith Sweat, The Two Live Crew, and other popular artists from the summer of 1989 blaring in the courtyard on Benefit Street.

Alicia Mason, a chubby, red-boned eight year-old with short curly hair, and Tanaka Romaire, a skinny, dark-skinned eight year-old with Chinese-looking eyes and Afro puffs, was Katrina's two friends. Together, the three little girls cheered the boys on as they played football in the courtyard. When Jason dropped a pass from Manny, Alicia and Tanaka began booing him.

"Man, you can't even catch!" Tanaka yelled.

"I can catch better than you!" Jason retorted loudly.

"No ya' can't! Sad ass!" Alicia yelled as she and Tanaka began throwing trash, including empty plastic soda bottles and old tennis shoes into the courtyard, intentionally disrupting the football game.

The four young boys took off running after the little girls, including Katrina, as they began running away from them while laughing and screaming. The boys caught up with the girls on side of Manny's building and held them down as they played 'cramp time', a game Manny and Oscar often played with them whenever the boys picked on the two teens. The boys hit the girls on their legs until they gave in by saying "you tha' man", and the young boys let them up.

The little girls walked off limping and dusting themselves off while still running off at the mouth. "Lamont, you hit like a girl, ya' punk!" Alicia yelled when the girls were far enough away that the boys couldn't catch them again.

"We gone get y'all again next time," Lamont yelled back. "And Katrina, you gotta come back in this courtyard because you stay here, ya' traitor," he yelled.

The game had abruptly ended, so Manny went and joined Oscar in the driveway to finish working on an old 1978 station wagon that his grandfather had left him and his mother just before he passed away. The two had been under the hood of the car for about an hour when they were confronted by nine year-old Jason.

"Man y'all idiots ain't gone never get that raggedly mutherfucka started!" Jason yelled from across the driveway as he and his boys walked towards the car.

"When I do li'l nigga, you ain't ridin' in my shit!" Manny replied as he looked from under the hood.

"I don't wanna ride in this piece of shit ass car anyway!" Jason said as he ran up and kicked the passenger side door of Manny's car.

Jason, Jermaine, Lamont, and Cedric then took off running down the driveway as Manny ran behind them in a futile attempt to catch either one of the little boys. "I'm a get y'all li'l mutherfuckas for that shit!" Manny yelled as he stood in the middle of the driveway searching in vain to find a rock to throw at the little boys.

Unable to earn payback at the present time, Manny returned to his car and he and Oscar began working on the station wagon again.

"Them some bad li'l niggas right there." Oscar said to Manny as he handed him a ratchet.

"I know. I like them li'l niggas, though, brer. They gone be hard when they grow up."

"Those li'l niggas always together, too." Oscar remarked.

"I know. Them my li'l thugs in training right there. They gone be straight later on down the road once we get our shit right, Big O." Manny replied as he went up under the hood of the car

once more.

Manny and Oscar were still working on the car three hours later and they still could not get the car's engine to turn over. Oscar had a 1980 four door, white Oldsmobile Delta 88 with chrome Tru rims and Vogue tires. The car didn't have the best paint job as it was rusting slightly near the trunk; but it was clean with an all-white interior, and two 15" sub-woofers in the trunk. It was a reliable, road worthy vehicle, and the chrome rims did turn a few heads at times. Oscar offered the keys of his car to Manny, but Manny insisted on repairing the old wagon. The reason being was because Manny and Oscar were armed robbers. Manny didn't want to use Oscar's car to commit any crimes because he felt it would be easy to spot by the police and anybody they robbed.

"It's probably ya' carburetor." A voice spoke out from a distance a little while later.

Manny jumped and hit his head on the hood of the car, and Oscar burst into laughter.

"Shit ain't funny, O! What happened, dog?" Manny asked as he came up from under the hood of the car and saw a light-skinned teenager standing near the rear bumper.

"Ya' carburetor. I been watching y'all work on that wagon for a while. I can fix it for ya' for a few dollars."

"Alright, homeboy. You fix this mutherfucka, you got forty bones in ya' pocket!" Manny said as he handed the young man the ratchet and backed away from the car.

"Nah, brer," the young man said. "I got my own tools."

The young man pulled out a shiny chrome ratchet set from a worn-out black canvas back pack and worked on the station wagon for about thirty minutes before he told Manny to try and start the car.

Manny turned the ignition, and the old wagon fired right up.

"How the fuck you do that, brer?" Manny asked over the roaring engine as he emerged from the driver's seat.

"I told ya' dog," the young man said calmly while pointing up underneath the hood, "it was ya' carburetor. It wasn't gettin' gas to the engine."

"Cool, dog!" Manny said as he handed the young man forty dollars. "I'm Manny. That's my homeboy, Oscar right there."

The young man dapped Oscar and Oscar asked him if he was from the Desire Project.

"I don't stay in the projects, but around the corner."

"What's ya' name, dog?" Manny asked.

"Benjamin Holland."

"Good looking, Ben. You smoke weed, dog?" He then asked.

Ben nodded his head to say yes and the three teens went and sat on Manny's front porch in the courtyard and smoked a joint.

Ms. Joyce walked out onto the porch a few minutes later and Ben tried to hide the joint and hold the smoke in when he saw the woman. Manny and Oscar, however, didn't budge because they knew it was cool to smoke weed in front of Ms. Joyce. In fact, Ms. Joyce would smoke with Manny and Oscar from time to time. Ben was unaware of that fact; and when he could not hold the smoke in any longer, he began to cough and blow the smoke out from his lungs

"What's wrong with you?" Ms. Joyce asked when she saw the thick cloud of smoke surrounding Ben's head.

"I had a frog in my throat," Ben responded while still coughing.

Ms. Joyce knew what the boys were doing, though; she tapped Ben on the head and told him not to tell a story in front of her door before she asked for the joint. "You can't smoke a frog, li'l boy! Manny, who is this dirty red child you got sitting on my front porch?" She asked before she took a toke.

"Huh, brer!" Manny yelled to Oscar as the two dapped. "We

got a nick name for 'em O! That's my dog, Ben Holland, a.k.a. Dirty Red, Ma. He just fixed grandpa's old station wagon for me."

"Oh, alright. You from the Desire, Dirty Red?" Ms. Joyce asked.

"No," answered Manny, "he stay around the corner on Piety Street."

"Damn! You know all about him, huh?" Ms. Joyce asked through light laughter.

"Yeah, that's our new dog." Manny said as he pushed Ben on the shoulder to loosen him up a bit. "Chill out, brer. Moms cool."

Just then, little Katrina ran out onto the front porch. Ms. Joyce passed the weed to Oscar without Katrina noticing, started towards the interior of her apartment and said, "Come on, Katrina. Ain't nothin' out there for you to see."

Manny saw Katrina peeking from inside the hallway out the corner of his eye and right away he knew she wasn't about to go inside just yet. "Oh boy," he said as he pulled down on his White Sox cap and leaned back on the porch and stared out into the courtyard, "she tryna come and see what a nigga doing just like moms just did."

"She gone blow a nigga high. I bet she got a thousand questions, too." Oscar said as he rubbed his chin.

"I know. She always tryna act like my momma, ya dig," Manny remarked just before he was bombarded with a slew of questions.

"Where y'all two been all day? Y'all ain't never hear me callin' y'all name out there? What's that smell? Who is that boy, Manny," Katrina asked quickly and loudly.

"There you go with all them questions. Go inside and I'm a talk to you later." Manny remarked.

"Okay then, but what's that smell?" Katrina asked.

"Somebody burning leaves in the other court. Come on inside so you can eat," Ms. Joyce said as she straightened the living room.

"That smell like weed! Which one of y'all li'l boys is smoking weed out here?" Katrina asked as she placed her hands on her hips and tapped her right foot on the ground repeatedly.

"Girl, bring your smart-mouth behind in this house!" Ms. Joyce snapped.

"Manny, is he your friend?" Katrina asked again just as Ms. Joyce walked back into the hallway and began pulling her inside the apartment by the sleeve of her shirt.

Katrina broke free of Ms. Joyce's grip and ran back onto the porch. "Manny! I said who is that new boy right there?" She asked inquisitively as she stared at Manny and pointed towards Ben.

"Damn, you nosy! That's my homeboy, Dirty Red. There, are you happy now?"

"That's all you had ta' say at first! I was just askin' you a question, man! Hello, Dirty Red. My name is Katrina Sanders." Katrina said as she extended her hand and did a cute but quick curtsy. "My teacher taught us that at school last year," she added.

Ben smiled and nodded towards Katrina and shook her hand. She was a relentless child in his eyes, but she was respectful, cute and had a set of manners.

"What's up, li'l Katrina? Call me Ben."

"Okay, Ben," Katrina responded as she place her hands behind her back and gave Ben a friendly smile.

"Katrina, come on inside so you can take a bath before you eat, sugar," Ms. Joyce exclaimed as she walked back onto the porch.

"Bye, Ben." Katrina said as she walked back into the

apartment.

"Make sure you get your sleeping clothes before you go in the bathroom, Katrina," Ms. Joyce said aloud. "Y'all boys hungry," she then asked. "Oscar? Dirty Red? Y'all hungry?"

Oscar and Ben nodded to say yes. Ms. Joyce then folded her arms and leaned against the steel door and scanned the courtyard. She also had a smirk on her face because she could see Manny looking back at her on occasion.

Manny was sitting on the steps waiting patiently. After several silent minutes had gone by, he turned to his mother. "Okay," he said as he rubbed his chin, "you asked Oscar if he wanted something to eat, you asked Dirty Red if he wanted a plate, when you planning on asking me, ya' own flesh and blood?"

"Aww shit! I guess you can eat too, Manny!" Ms. Joyce joked.

"That's cold, Ma," Manny remarked as he got up from the stairs and walked into the apartment with Oscar and Ben following close behind.

"I love you, Manny!" Ms. Joyce yelled happily as she walked into the kitchen.

"I love you, too, ma."

Ms. Joyce welcomed Ben into her home on account of Manny. Manny had only known Ben for a little more than an hour, but he thought Ben was cool. Manny, Ben, and Oscar began hanging together that very night; and over the next few weeks, they had gotten closer. They quickly became homeboys. Whenever you saw Manny, you saw Ben and Oscar. The little kids, Jason, Lamont, Jermaine, and Cedric, along with Katrina and her two friends, Alicia and Tanaka, all grew quite fond of the three young teens. They were fun to be around and they treated all of the children in the courtyard like little sisters and brothers. The three teens had become popular throughout the Desire Project as well. Everybody knew who Manny, Ben, and Oscar were. They were three cool teenagers

who hung in one of the liveliest courtyards on Benefit Street inside the Desire Housing Projects in the year of 1989.

CHAPTER FOUR

YOU CAN STAY WITH ME

A few months had passed and the weather was beginning to turn cold. Manny, Ben and Oscar had just returned from taking Katrina shopping for a new pair of tennis shoes and an outfit for Thanksgiving. They sat on the porch talking as Katrina sat on the bottom of the stairs, eating an ice cream cone. The little girl looked over to her left and saw Jason, Lamont, Jermaine and Cedric peeking from the side of the building and waving their arms trying to get her to come over to the side of the building where they were standing. Katrina looked back up the stairs and saw Manny, Ben and Oscar engaged in conversation, so she quietly stepped off the porch and headed towards Jason and the boys.

"We just wanted ya' out the way before we throw these at 'em!" Lamont stated with a devilish grin on his face.

Katrina looked down and watched as Lamont stretched out his shirt and showed her six eggs he had taken out of his mother's refrigerator. Katrina peeked back around the building and saw that Manny, Ben and Oscar were still on the porch.

"What y'all 'bouta do with them eggs?" Katrina asked as she continued licking her ice cream cone.

Jason and the boys had asked Manny to take them with him, Ben and Oscar when they were about to leave to take Katrina to the mall. Manny told the little boys to go ask their mothers first. When they walked back into the driveway prepared to ride, they noticed Manny had the car in the middle of the driveway. When the boys approached, Manny, Ben and Oscar jumped from the car and hit them all with water balloons and hopped back into the old station wagon and sped off. The boys chased the wagon, but Manny sped up quickly, leaving them soaking wet in the middle of the driveway. It was cold outside; the boys were freezing. They shivered back to their mothers' apartments, changed clothes, and waited for Manny, Ben and Oscar to return in order to pay them back.

They now stood on the side the building out of Manny, Ben and Oscar's sight. Lamont presented his out-stretched t-shirt to allow Jason, Jermaine and Cedric each to grab eggs. The boys then quickly jumped from behind the building and began hurling the eggs at Manny, Ben and Oscar. An egg smashed into Ben's back and one also hit Manny and Oscar each in the stomach. Katrina laughed as Manny, Ben and Oscar ran into the hallway and hid there, "Alright li'l niggas, y'all done fucked up now!" Manny yelled from the hallway.

After a couple of minutes, Manny stepped back onto the porch. Jason and the boys were not gone, however, and they hit Manny two more times in the side. The last egg crashed into the steel door on the porch.

"They out," Manny told Ben and Oscar. "We gone get y'all niggas today! Cramp Time," he yelled aloud as he jumped from the porch with Ben and Oscar following his lead.

"Manny called cramp! He called cramp!" Jermaine yelled as the boys all scattered with Katrina following closely behind, laughing at the top of her lungs.

That's how it went down in the courtyard on Benefit Street where Manny resided. It was always fun for the kids whenever he was around. There was always something for them to get into.

A week after Thanksgiving, Manny and Ben were sitting in the hallway on the front porch smoking a joint. Katrina, Tanaka and Alicia were quietly sitting at the bottom of the stairs. Manny had bought the little girls a bag of vanilla wafer cookies and the girls went and sat and watched as Oscar quarterbacked a game of football. The game had Jason and Cedric playing against Lamont and Jermaine.

Manny noticed a while back that Ben had been wearing the same clothes since the summer. Ben didn't even wear a jacket now, even though it was cold outside this time of year. Manny noticed that all Ben ever wore was a black polyester vest over a black and grey wool flannel shirt with faded black jeans and a pair of black worn out no-name leather shoes.

Manny and Oscar dressed fresh every day. Nike, Girbaud, Fila, Polo, Guess, Bally, Adidas, whatever was hot, Manny and Oscar had it or they went and got it. Manny felt compelled to look out for somebody he now considered a friend; because if he and Oscar were dressing fresh, then it was only right that Ben dress fresh right along with them. At least that's how Manny felt about the situation. "Here brer," Manny said as he handed Ben a hooded black Atlanta Falcons Starter jacket.

"What's this for?"

"I hate the Falcons, brer. Besides that, I know you be cold out here. I think you gone need that. See if it fit. Shit, I got about twenty of them mutherfuckas. I got a bunch of shit I can't even fit, brer. Brand new shit you can have, ya' dig?"

"How you get all that shit, man?"

"I told you, dog—me and Oscar be jackin' those niggas shit! We be catchin' niggas outside nightclubs, walking in they 'hood, coming from the mall with they ole lady with brand new clothes and jewelry and shit—we be stangin' licks all over this motherfuckin' city. " Manny said as he pulled out a black . 357 magnum and showed it to Ben. "Me and Big O been tryna put ya' down, brer. What ya' scared?"

"Nah brer, I just don't want lose Anna."

"You gone lose her anyway if you keep doing nothing. How you gone help her when she move to Seattle? Shit, you might can move with her when her and her momma go. We do shit right man, you could have a grip in ya' pocket, have some clothes and a car to start out with so y'all can get on y'all feet. "

"You might be right, brer," Ben responded. "But I ain't going to Seattle. Me and Anna already talked about that a while ago; but it'll be good to fly her in from time to time once she move out there when we get on our feet. I can get down with it."

"That's what I'm talking 'bout, dog." Manny replied seriously as he and Ben shook hands. "Let me ask you this though, brer," Manny then said, "where you stay 'round that corner? For real." He asked with concern in his voice.

"Why you care about that, brer?" Ben asked in a somewhat agitated manner as he bowed his head and began making small circles on the grit-covered steps with his fingertips.

"Look, I been knowing Oscar since the first grade. Jason and 'nem too young right now. I don't fuck with the rest of these niggas 'round here on that level. You cool, dog. You smart. And I know you got game in ya'. Big game! You my nigga and I'm just tryna help you out."

Ben rested his back on the stairs. "You know that old house 'round there," he asked embarrassingly as he looked at the wooden stairs and held back tears.

Manny knew Ben was about to say so he moved the conversation forward, "So that's your lawn mower and shit up under that house?" He asked.

"Yeah, man," Ben answered sadly while nodding his head up and down slowly. "I been sleeping there from time to time, doing shit like I did when I fixed the wagon that day to make a few dollars. But I know I gotta do more, I don't wanna be homeless all my life."

"You talk about a lot of different things that be going on in the world, dog. You be tellin' me shit that I never even heard of but it be all true when I look into it. How you get so smart?"

"I read a lot. I like World History. I study, and then take tests with Anna at the Covenant House. She take 'em to her school and have 'em graded. They come back—"

"All A's I bet." Manny said.

"All A's, dog. I shoulda stayed my ass in school."

"After I tore my Achilles, I said fuck it. LSU and Alabama was after a nigga hard. I woulda been a bad mutherfucka," Manny said as he reflected briefly on what may have been a promising football career.

"We ain't in school now though, might as well get paid while we out here, Manny dog. Make it worth our while, ya' dig?" Ben said.

"No doubt, no doubt." Manny responded. "Those your English and History books and shit in that closet in the back bedroom in that house?"

Ben laughed to himself.

"What's funny?" Manny asked.

"You ask more questions than Katrina."

Manny chuckled and said, "Alright dog, we done with the interview." He then reached behind his back and handed Ben the Science and World History books he'd taken from the abandoned apartment. "You got a new place to stay now, though." He told Ben.

"Where at?" Ben asked.

"You can stay with me."

"That's cool, but I gotta stay in touch with Anna."

"When we get on feet, dog, y'all two can move together. Let's just focus on this game and get paid. Anna ain't going nowhere no time soon."

"Your momma gone be cool with me staying here?"

"She already said you can move in. Come on let's go get set up." Manny said as he got up from the stairs and walked into the apartment with Ben following close behind.

Manny had been talking to his mother for about a week trying to convince her to let Ben stay with them. Ms. Joyce told Manny her hands were full with Katrina and she really didn't want to be responsible for another unwanted child; but when Manny showed her the abandoned house where Ben was staying, Ms. Joyce's heart was once again moved. She agreed, but she told Manny that Ben was his responsibility and Katrina would be everybody's responsibility. Manny agreed with the arrangement.

It's not often people open up their hearts and homes to strangers. Ms. Joyce and Manny was a rare breed. They were the kind of people who felt blessed when they helped someone else in need. Ms. Joyce and Manny would have been surprised to learn that in actuality, the people who were in need were the ones that felt blessed.

Amidst the violence and lovelessness that permeated throughout the city of New Orleans, there were still good, kind-hearted, loving people. Manny may have saved Ben's life this day, no telling, but one thing he did give Ben for sure was hope for the future. Ben Holland would be forever grateful for the love and consideration that his friend Manny and his mother Ms. Joyce had given to him on this day.

CHAPTER FIVE

HEAD FIRST

"Okay we heading in," Oscar said as Manny cruised past the Greyhound bus Station in downtown New Orleans.

It was just over two weeks before Mardi Gras in the year 1990 and Manny, Oscar and Ben were on the prowl on a Friday night, looking for people to rob so they could earn money to buy outfits for Fat Tuesday. Manny, Oscar and Ben had been using the station wagon to ride up on drug dealers in the Third, Fifteenth and Tenth Wards. The Third Ward was where the Calliope Project was located. The Tenth Ward held the St. Thomas Projects, and the Fifteenth Ward held the Fischer Project. This night, the crew was working the Third Ward.

As they rode up Earhart Boulevard, a wide four-lane boulevard with a large median in the center, they rode past the Calliope Project, which was on their left, and scanned the area for possible targets. No one worth robbing was out on the streets of Uptown during the wee hours of the night, however; Manny made a U-turn and headed back towards downtown. "We might have to shut it down for the night and hit something tomorrow, fellas," he said. "It's after three in the mornin, everybody done made it in tonight."

"Wanna go and see what's happenin' across the river in the Fifteenth Ward before we go in?" Ben asked from the back seat as the boys passed Booker T. Washington High School which was on their right.

Oscar, who was riding in the front passenger seat, was about to acknowledge Ben's remark, but he suddenly spotted a heavyset man in his forties walking towards a maroon, 1989 two-door Delta 88 with a white rag top, chrome Tru rims and vogue tires parked on one of the side streets just as they passed the high school. The man had on a blue silk suit and Oscar could tell that he was wearing jewelry from the way his wrists, fingers and neck twinkled under the street lights. "That nigga got a bunch jewelry on, and ain't no telling what's in that car. That's our lick right there. Make the block, Manny, dog," he whispered as he reached into the console and grabbed his pistol.

Manny turned right on the next side street. He made another right at the end of the block and then another right and was now headed up the block slowly approaching the crew's intended victim. They saw the older hustler, whose name was Tate, putting his key into the driver's side door to unlock it. Manny drove the station wagon up slowly and slammed the car into park and the three fifteen year-old teens quickly jumped out of the wagon and caught Tate off guard.

Manny had on all black—black Levis, black Bally tennis shoes, black Polo shirt and a black Raiders Starter jacket with the hood covering his head to shield his identity—and he was clutching a black. 357 magnum. Oscar was wearing a black suede-jogging suit with a pair of black Bally tennis shoes with a black handkerchief over his nose and mouth. Ben was dressed the same as Manny, except he had on a black and white 8-Ball leather jacket and black and white 8-Ball leather baseball cap pulled down low over his head to shield his face.

The three stood before Tate, Manny with his gun aimed directly at his head, demanding money. Tate, who stood about six feet and weighed two-hundred and fifty pounds, leaned back against his car, raised his hands and said calmly, "I ain't

got shit on me, young bloods."

The boys, however, still made Tate open the trunk; and it was there that they had found small leather Louis Vitton pouch containing two-thousand dollars in large bills and eight quarter ounces of rocked-up crack cocaine. Tate then realized that a bunch of what he viewed as amateurs, was robbing him. They couldn't have possibly known who he was or who he was working for. "Do you niggas know who the fuck I am? I been in this game since before you li'l mutherfuckas entered the nut sack!"

"Fuck you gone do about it, nigga?" Manny asked as he steadily held the gun on Tate.

"See y'all li'l young niggas with this jackin' and shit? Y'all the reason why the game in New Orleans is fucked up right now! You want the dope? Take it then! But when Damon hear's this shit—all three y'all li'l niggas is dead!"

"Fuck a nigga named Damon!" Oscar remarked angrily as he grabbed the pouch from Tate's trunk and began backing up.

"Hold up," said Manny. "That's Damon Dope?"

"Yeah, li'l nigga. And if y'all take that pouch, when Damon find this shit out, y'all ain't gone be able to walk the fuckin' streets. Not even in the day time. You know Damon shit don't get fucked with!" Tate replied as he stared the boys down while holding his hands in the air. "Your move, mutherfucka," he said coldly.

Manny, through his mother, knew some of the major players in the city. Damon was an older cat, around Ms. Joyce's age, and Manny knew the man was not a joke. Ms. Joyce told Manny about the things that went on between Damon and his daddy just before his daddy went to jail. Damon had killed one of Taylor Senior's best soldiers; and he had a posse behind him larger than the New Orleans Saints' football roster. Manny knew that even if he let Tate go, he would still tell Damon what happened. He and his boys would have a contract put out on their heads.

41

Manny felt he had no choice. He took two steps back and shot Tate in the stomach. The bullet exited Tate's back and shattered the glass in the driver's side window of his car as his body dropped to the ground. Manny then stood over Tate and shot him three times in the head at nearly point blank range. The three teens hopped into the station wagon, sped back to Earhart Boulevard, made a right turn and headed back towards the Ninth Ward.

"Fuck you doing?" Oscar asked in a panic-stricken state as Manny sped away from the scene.

"That's Damon dope, man! That nigga run uptown! Manny had ta' kill that dude!" Ben replied.

"I wasn't even talking to you, Ben! You still a rookie at this shit!"

"He right though, Big O! Damon really ain't to be fucked with! I had to do it so that nigga wouldn't tell!" Manny said lowly as he sped towards downtown New Orleans.

"How you know Damon?" Oscar then asked Ben.

"My daddy used ta' score from him, I think. I can't remember too good. But I do know the nigga woulda killed us if he woulda found out we robbed his boy."

Tate, a respected and feared enforcer for Uptown's biggest cocaine dealer, had become the crew's first murder victim. He was an enforcer for the big timer named Damon. No one ever found out who killed Tate that night, however; and the boys went on to split the two grand, bought an ounce of weed to smoke, and thus began a career in the treacherous, and more often-than-not, violent life style of the cocaine drug trade on the mean streets of New Orleans.

CHAPTER SIX

MY BROTHER, MY SAVIOR

It was now the middle of summer of the year 1990, and the courtyard on Benefit Street was packed. People were bunched up on the stairs and lined up along the sidewalk surrounding the huge courtyard. A couple of grills were going and Ms. Joyce had her stereo speaker in the living room window blasting Bel Biv Devoe's song, *Poison*. It was a sunny Saturday afternoon and there was a big football game going on. Four young boys from the back of the project had challenged Jason, Jermaine, Cedric and Lamont to a football game. Word had quickly spread throughout the project that Manny, Ben and Oscar had bet Haywood, who was another drug dealer that resided in the back portion of the project where the four young boys lived, five-hundred dollars a piece that Jason and his boys would win the game.

Haywood and a couple of his partners had put up fifteen-hundred dollars and Manny, Ben and Oscar had put up their fifteen-hundred. Manny explained to Jason, Lamont, Jermaine and Cedric what was on the line; and when he told the boys he would buy them all a new pair of Air Jordan's and a Polo outfit to go along with it if they won the game, they all grew excited and were even more determined to win.

The game began with Manny quarterbacking for his team and Haywood, the bronze-skinned bald headed 5' 10", one-hundred and seventy pound seventeen year-old from the back section of the Desire Project, quarterbacking for the four young boys on his team. As the game progressed, Katrina, Tanaka and Alicia stood on the sideline cheering for Manny and the boys. A little bit ways into the game, Faye stepped onto the porch and got Katrina's attention over the loud cheering and chatter emanating from the mouths of the scores of kids and teenagers, and even some adults who were out enjoying the game.

Manny caught a glimpse just as Katrina followed Faye, and a young man who appeared to be in his twenty's, upstairs to Faye's apartment. Manny had seen the man a few times before and he noticed Faye always had a task for Katrina just before or during the time the young dude showed up. Manny was thinking about the situation so deeply that he had thrown an interception to the other team. Ben and Oscar saw the play and told Manny to get his head in the game.

"Fifteen hundred dollars, nigga!" They kept yelling. "Keep ya' head in the game, brer!"

Manny walked over to the sideline and stood next to Ben and Oscar and they coached Jason and his boys on defense. Manny, however, still felt that something wasn't right concerning Faye, Katrina, and the dude who'd followed them upstairs.

Meanwhile, inside her apartment, Faye had just sat down on her dingy, grease-stained, white velvet sofa next to the man who was with her. Katrina was standing in the doorway with a nervous look on her face. Her mother told her to step inside and close the front door and lock it.

Katrina did as her mother requested and remained by the locked door.

"Come here baby," Faye said softly as she stretched out her arms to welcome Katrina into her bosom.

Katrina went and stood in front of her mother and hugged her as the twenty year-old young man, named Brian, looked on.

penetrate the little girl. He gave Faye a twenty dollar piece of crack cocaine to go along with the money he had given her as he stood up and smiled down at a frightened Katrina.

Faye quickly walked over the dirty clothes on the floor and entered the kitchen. She shoved dishes onto the floor, breaking them, hurrying to smoke the crack cocaine.

"Momma!" Katrina called out as Brian pulled her by the arm into the depths of the apartment.

Faye ignored Katrina's cries as she put the crack pipe to her lips and lit a fire to it.

"Momma, please! I hate this man, momma! Momma, help me!"

Katrina struggled as Brian dragged her into her bedroom, locked the door and quickly pulled down his pants. Katrina knew what Brian was doing to her was not right, but she was afraid to tell anyone because Brian always threatened to kill her. When Brian walked over to Katrina, she tried to unlock the door and run, but Brian grabbed her, ripped off her panties, and carried her to the bed. Katrina screamed and kicked as Brian got on the bed with her and put his hand over her mouth and said, "If you scream again, I'm a kill your momma!"

That was the wrong thing for Brian to say to Katrina because she had just lost a lot of feelings for her mother because she knew that Faye was okay with what Brian was doing to her. Katrina was going to fight Brian just so he would kill her mother because she now hated Faye just that much. Determined to scream, Katrina bit Brian's hand. He jumped up and grabbed his hand and Katrina scurried over to the window and began pounding on it, all the while screaming and pleading for help. Katrina could see the boys playing football and all the other people talking, laughing and cheering; but nobody could see nor hear her cries.

Brian ran and grabbed Katrina again, laid her down and began to slide his penis into her vagina. She screamed aloud as Brian's oversized penis pierced her hymen. She cried a loud

looking at Katrina in stunned silence as she lay on the bed with a small puddle of blood between her legs. Manny was dismayed by the sight that lay before his eyes. So much so that he couldn't speak. He went and knelt down beside Katrina, grabbed her head and shook her, whispering her name as his eyes began to fill with tears. Manny thought Katrina was dead but she jumped from her trance and screamed aloud as she reached out and hugged Manny.

"I'm sorry, Manny!" Katrina cried aloud. "I'm sorry!"

Manny rocked his body back and forth as he held Katrina in his arms, not understanding why she had apologized to him. "It's not your fault, baby girl." He said lowly as he wiped her tears and laid her back down on the bed before getting up to go after Brian.

"Manny," Katrina screamed through her tears. "Don't leave me!"

Just then, Cedric ran upstairs and yelled aloud from the living room, telling Manny that Ben and Oscar were beating up a naked man outside in the courtyard.

Manny had been telling Ben and Oscar about his suspicions ever since he'd thrown the interception, and when Ben and Oscar witnessed Brian run out the house into the courtyard butt-naked, they knew Manny was right about his assumptions.

Faye was so strung out and high, she just lay back in the chair, oblivious to what was going on. Soon, Jason, Jermaine and Lamont had made it inside Katrina's room. The boys looked at Katrina, saw her naked body and the blood on the bed and thought she was dead.

"She dead, Manny? Katrina not dead huh, brer?" The three kept asking Manny frightfully.

"No! Wrap her in this sheet and stay in here with her," Manny said as he pulled out his .357 magnum. "I be back!"

The people in the courtyard, meanwhile, were screaming as Ben and Oscar stomped Brian into the ground. They kicked

him repeatedly in the head, stomach and back. When Manny came out of the hallway with his gun, he jumped off the porch into the crowd. The people scattered and then gathered back and followed Manny as he walked up to Brian while checking to make sure his gun was off safety.

Ben and Oscar saw Manny coming and they egged him forward. "Yeah, that's right! Bring it on, nigga!" Oscar yelled towards Manny.

Ms. Joyce was on her porch yelling her son's name repeatedly once she had seen the gun in Manny's hand, but Manny had blocked out everything. It seemed like it happened in slow motion as Manny stood in between Ben and Oscar staring down at a pleading Brian.

"Shoot that bitch," yelled Ben and Oscar. "Kill that nigga! Kill 'em, dog!" They yelled repeatedly.

Everything then went deaf to Manny. He turned and saw his mother running towards him. He then stared at the crowd around him; they were looking directly at him, some whispering to one another while pointing in his direction. Manny then looked up at Katrina's bedroom window and saw Lamont, Jermaine and Cedric looking down at him.

Manny remembered what he saw in Katrina's bedroom and he imaged in his mind once more, Katrina, laying on her bed helpless and crying out in pain while bleeding from her vagina as Brian fucked her senseless and he grew enraged. With those thoughts and feelings running through his mind and heart, Manny turned back to Brian, who was still pleading for his life, aimed the gun at his head and squeezed the trigger six times, emptying the gun, releasing six shots that tore Brian's skull wide open.

Those who eyed the entire scene in the courtyard could now see bloody pieces of Brian's cranium and brain matter scattered in the grass where he lay. The gruesome scene that lay before their eyes sent many of the people running out of the courtyard gagging. Manny, Ben and Oscar were just staring at Brian seconds after the gunfire seized. They had just killed a second

person, but he deserved it the boys' eyes.

Ms. Joyce ran through those who'd stayed behind and quickly approached Manny and grabbed the gun. She then shoved Manny, Ben and Oscar towards her apartment.

"What the fuck is wrong with y'all? Why did you do that, Manny? There's over a hundred people out here." Ms. Joyce whispered as she eyed all the potential witnesses whilst walking her son and his friends back to her apartment.

Manny broke away from his mother and ran back up the stairs leading to Faye's apartment and grabbed Katrina off the bed and carried her down the stairs with Jason and the boys following him closely. When Manny stepped onto the porch with Katrina hugging his neck, the bloody sheet she was wrapped in came into full view. They could tell she was naked underneath the sheet as well. Everybody now knew why Manny did what he did on this day. Many of the people began to get angry, some cried or were shocked when they were told or realized that Brian had raped Katrina.

"Katrina! Katrina!" Ms. Joyce yelled aloud as she ran through the crowd. "What did they do? Manny what happened?" She asked through tears as she climbed the stairs quickly.

"That bitch nigga out there gave Faye some crack and she sold her to 'em. He fucked her and made her bleed." Manny answered angrily.

Manny stared at his mother, and without a word being said, Ms. Joyce stared her son in the eyes and nodded her head. *She* now understood why Manny had done what he did.

"You said she was our responsibility. I fucked up, but I handled that, momma." Manny said with watery eyes.

Ms. Joyce reached out for Katrina and the nine year-old jumped and hid her face in Manny's chest out of shame and fear. Her body was trembling, and she had a death grip on Manny.

Ms. Joyce pulled her hands back and held them together and

said in a loving manner, "Katrina, it's me. It's, it's momma Joyce."

Katrina peeked up from Manny's chest and Ms. Joyce gasped lowly when she saw the child's tear-stained face and bloody mouth.

"Katrina, let me help you." Ms. Joyce said lowly so that only she, Katrina and Manny could hear. "He won't hurt you anymore, okay?"

"I just wanna go home. But not home by Faye." Katrina whispered as she looked Ms. Joyce in the eyes.

Ms. Joyce and Manny took Katrina back to their apartment to take care of her. Being that she was now a Registered Nurse, Ms. Joyce was able to treat Katrina to prevent the police from finding out about the rape. As Manny, Ben and Oscar stood in the courtyard, many people, and a lot of the other hustlers came up and gave them their props. They would have done the same thing had it been their little sister or anyone else they cared about being treated in that manner.

The Medical Examiner's Office arrived to remove Brian's body while two homicide detectives nonchalantly walked through the crowd asking questions. The detectives were glad once Brian's body was tagged and bagged because they had grown apathetic towards the deceased. They'd asked everybody that was in the courtyard what happened to Brian, but nobody had anything helpful to say. The detectives didn't know exactly what happened to the young man, but they figured he'd gotten what he deserved; because out of more than one-hundred people, nobody had actually seen what happened to this butt-naked man lying dead with his head nearly blown off completely in broad daylight.

Court had been held in the streets this day; and the verdict for raping nine year-old Katrina Sanders was death. It would be years before Katrina would speak to her mother again. Ms. Joyce had become her mother and she would raise her. Manny, Ben and Oscar were her big brothers and they would protect her. Overtime, Katrina began to fully love and trust Ms. Joyce

and the boys. They had saved her life, and for that, Katrina would be forever loyal to them all.

CHAPTER SEVEN

SMOKING JACK MOVES

"Man, why you keep bringing that shit up, Haywood? That happened two years ago, brer!" Oscar snapped from the passenger seat of Manny's car.

It was now late summer of 1993. The boys had been in the game for over three years and they had amassed a substantial amount of money. Oscar, Manny and Haywood were riding in Manny's 1992 Park Avenue. The car was a four door ride with a navy blue paint job and all white interior. Manny had four twelve inch speakers in the trunk and had placed chrome Disc rims and Vogue tires on the car. It was a fresh whip.

Manny, Ben and Oscar had started out with the two ounces they had taken from Tate and slowly over time, they had worked their way up to two and one-half kilograms. They were scoring from a drug dealer from Kenner, Louisiana, but he was busted a month ago in Atlanta, having been swept up in a federal drug-trafficking investigation that was taking place there. Manny, Ben and Oscar had spent four weeks trying to find a new connection but could never find anyone that would sell them a quarter ounce, let alone a kilogram.

It wasn't as if no one in the game didn't have any cocaine at

the time—the fact was that many of the players in the game feared Manny. They didn't trust Manny, Ben or Oscar in the least bit. Besides that fact, a lot of people in the game were jealous of the boys, who started from nothing and had worked their way up to mid-level. The boys gained respect the day Manny killed Brian; but when some of the other drug dealers found out they were making big money, jealousy began to rear its ugly head.

Nearly two years earlier, back in 1991, a young man named Sebastian, who lived in the next driveway over from Manny, began to get angry that the boys were taking some of his customers. Even though they sold dope on opposite ends of the driveway behind Manny's building, Sebastian didn't like having the boys around because people were passing up his dope house in order to buy crack cocaine and powder bags of quarter ounces from the boys. The boys didn't see a problem, however; they didn't even know that the customers were pulling away from Sebastian and buying from them. They probably could've worked it out if Sebastian hadn't gotten out of line on a cold October night in 1991. When the boys walked into Sebastian's house to score a kilo, Sebastian began to talk down on Ben. The boys were seventeen at the time.

"You think you the shit now, mutherfucka?" Sebastian asked Ben in an aggressive manner as he emerged from the back of the apartment and entered the kitchen.

The twenty-four year-old, 6'2" slender, brown-skinned hustler stood in his kitchen trying to intimidate the boys as his twelve gold teeth glimmered under the kitchen's lights.

"Fuck you talkin' 'bout, dog," asked Ben.

"Y'all li'l niggas walk in here like y'all fuckin' kings, taking my customers, and disrespectin' a nigga! That's what the fuck I'm talkin' about!"

"Say brer," Ben replied, "we never set foot on your turf. We created that set ourselves. You know that. Now, maybe we can work some—"

"We ain't working shit out, bitch! Either shut down or get laid down! I ain't sellin' y'all li'l niggas no fuckin' dope! Y'all li'l niggas ain't shit! And Ben, you stand there in that brand new polo, ya' fuckin', ya' fuckin' Bally shoes and Girbaud jeans and shit? I remember when ya' was fuckin' broke and sleeping outside, li'l nigga! You think you gone take my customers and get rich? I'll send ya' back to the poorhouse before I let that shit happen! Manny, take ya' boys and y'all li'l niggas get the fuck from 'round here!"

Manny saw Ben reach for his gun and he stopped him just as four men came out of the back of Sebastian's apartment armed with Uzis.

"Nahh, let him pull that mutherfucka! And I'm a leave his bitch ass looking like some Swiss cheese in this bitch!" Sebastian said as he stared at Ben.

"Come on Dirty Red! O, grab the money!" Manny stated quickly.

When Oscar went to grab the money, Sebastian slammed his hands down on top of the duffel bag. "Where the fuck you think you going with my money, ole bitch ass nigga?" He asked coldly as he stared Oscar in the eyes.

One of the soldiers standing behind the boys cocked his Uzi and the other three quickly followed his lead. The boys, at that very moment, thought they were dead. Ben thought about Anna and how he might never see her again. Manny and Oscar both thought of their mothers. The three raised their hands in the air as one of the soldiers took Ben's Mac-10 and ordered all three to slowly walk out of the dope house backwards.

Sebastian let the boys live because he knew he had all their money and he believed that they would no longer be a threat. He meant what he said about sending Ben back to the poorhouse. It was the first time the boys had tried to buy a kilogram and they were robbed in the process. Manny and Oscar thought they had to start back from square one. Ben, on the other hand, had other plans. The boys knew where Sebastian lived. His house was in Covington, about an hour's

drive across Lake Ponchartrain to the north of New Orleans. The boys had been there for a party once before and Ben still remembered the way.

"You wanna go to this man's house, wait for him and then kill 'em, Ben?" Oscar inquired.

"That's the plan." Ben answered matter-of-factly.

"I don't know brer," Manny chimed in. "That's kinda risky. Plus he got them four dudes with 'em. We gone have ta' kill all five of them niggas if we do that." He said as he rubbed his goatee.

"Say brer," Ben responded lowly, "we worked hard to get to the level we was at. Now we sittin' on ya' momma porch broke just like in 1989. Just trust my plan and tomorrow we gone be back on top."

"You sure this shit gone work, homeboy?" Oscar asked with a hint of uncertainty.

"What other choice we got, O?" Ben asked. "Sebas took twenty-seven g's from us. Twenty-seven thousand dollars. We gotta rep ta' keep out here, ain't no way can let that shit slide. If we pull this shit off, ain't no other nigga out here gone try us like that again. Believe that, my nigga."

"And if we don't do that there," Manny asked as he rubbed his chin.

"I guess the game'll be over for us," Ben answered. "But I say fuck Sebas," he quickly snapped. "That nigga let us live. And that's where he fucked up. We gotta kill that nigga. That's the only way we can get back in the game—we gotta kill that boy."

"You right. You right in everything you sayin'. Fuck it, I'm down with it, Ben." Manny said seriously. "O, I know you down for poppin' a nigga, huh?" He then asked.

"Fuckin' right. Ben right man, we can't let that nigga Sebas play us like that." Oscar answered as the boys dapped one another.

Ben lit up a blunt and then shared his plan with his boys. The three then went to Haywood and shared their plan with him. Haywood listened attentively as Ben told him that with Sebastian out the picture, they could be the biggest dealers in the Desire Project.

"I killed a nigga last month," Haywood stated lowly as he held his hands in his jean pockets, "for talking stupid at the club. Caught his ass walking to his car and laid 'em out flat. Then took the fuckin' car and sold the rims. But Sebas, that's big, brer. If we go at that boy, we can't miss." Haywood said as he looked to ground in deep thought.

"You and Manny can catch his workers coming out the house and lay 'em out." Ben told Haywood.

"Fuck it, I'm in—but I think we need another trigger man," Haywood said as he dapped the boys.

"We got one," Ben replied.

"Who?" Haywood asked.

"Lil Earl."

Manny, Oscar and Haywood all knew Lil Earl. He was a fifteen year-old armed robber that lived up front in the project. Although he was only fifteen, Lil Earl was notorious. He often used to rob the pizza delivery and taxi cab drivers that entered the projects; he'd even gone so far as to rob ice cream trucks on several occasions. Lil Earl had a rep in the Desire of robbing anything that moved. It was because of his actions that the taxi cab and pizza delivery drivers no longer entered the Desire Projects, not even in the day time. The boys knew without asking that Lil Earl would be down and would not be scared to pull the trigger.

"You talked to him, Ben?" Haywood inquired.

"Yeah. He up front waiting on you and Manny. Me and Oscar gone head across the lake and wait on Sebas." Ben answered.

After the boys dapped and gathered their weapons, Ben and Oscar got into Ben's 1991 two-door Cutlass Supreme and

headed towards Covington. Ben's Cutlass was painted the same color as Ice Cube's Chevy Impala in his latest video, *It Was A Good Day*. The car was money green with a white rag-top and matching money green and white leather seats with gold Daytona rims, a gold grill and gold trimming.

Just as Ben and Oscar rode onto the Causeway, a twenty-four mile long elevated bridge that spanned the entire length of Lake Ponchartrain from north to south, headed towards Sebas's house, Manny and Haywood had just entered Lil Earl's driveway. They spotted him sitting on his back porch dressed in all black, including a black hooded sweatshirt. His gold teeth lit up as he cracked a smile and jumped off the porch with a pistol grip shotgun pump in his right hand. He trotted over to Manny's Park Avenue and jumped in the backseat. "That boy Sebas done stepped outta line, huh, fellas? I ain't never like that ole bitch ass nigga anyway." He said as he began loading shells into his twelve gauge.

Manny drove to the back of the Desire Project and parked his car in Haywood's driveway. The three then walked under the darkness of night back to Sebastian's driveway and hid in a dark alley in between two buildings directly across from Sebas' drug den. Manny had a M1 Carbine rifle, Haywood had a Mac-11, and Lil Earl was toting his chrome and black six-shot pistol grip twelve gauge shot gun.

By one 'o' clock in the morning Manny, Haywood, and Lil Earl had been waiting for Sebas's soldiers to exit the dope house for nearly three hours. Sebas had left over an hour ago, so Manny, Lil Earl and Haywood figured Sebas's soldiers would be coming out soon. They also figured that Ben and Oscar had already taken care of Sebas since he left earlier, but Ben and Oscar had been waiting for over four hours underneath Sebas's house themselves.

Sebastian's house sat three feet off the ground and was held up by concrete pillars. Oscar and Ben were crouched underneath the house hiding behind the concrete pillars. They knew somebody was in the house but it wasn't Sebas. Ben couldn't see the person clearly, but he could tell he was young;

if Sebas ever showed, whoever was inside the house wouldn't be a problem.

"Man, where this nigga at?" Oscar asked in a near whisper.

"I don't know," answered Ben. "We gone wait 'til just before the sun come up. If that nigga ain't here by then, we gone just go in and hit his stash."

Meanwhile, back in New Orleans, Manny, Haywood and Lil Earl were about to leave and head back to Haywood's house. They were about to call things off until Manny saw the lights in the kitchen of Sebas's dope house go off. The three quickly ducked back into the gap just as the backdoor opened. Sebas's soldiers stepped out the building with the same Uzis they had drawn down on Manny, Ben and Oscar with earlier. They were laughing and talking loudly amongst themselves.

"Let's go!" Lil Earl said lowly.

"Hold up. I know which way they going." Manny whispered.

Manny and his crew ran to the opposite end of the building on their right. They were now in front of Sebas's workers and their car, which gave them a much better angle to shoot. Manny peeked from the side of the building at Sebas's soldiers and watched as they descended the stairs with their Uzis in hand. Manny could hear the soldiers joking and laughing, talking about some females at a strip club they were headed to as they hopped into a navy blue four-door Cadillac Brougham sitting on chrome Tru rims and Vogue tires.

The car started up and N.W.A.'s song titled *Real Niggaz Don't Die* immediately began playing loudly.

"That's my fuckin' jam right there!" Lil Earl quipped lowly with a smile as the three watched the car pull away from the curb slowly, headed in their direction.

"Let's move!" Manny stated lowly as the soldiers' Cadillac slowly approached.

Manny, Haywood and Lil Earl simultaneously emerged from the alley and ran up to the car and opened fire on the car's front

right side.

Sebas's soldiers never had a chance. Manny and his crew released a heart-stopping and rapid torrent of bullets into the Cadillac, killing all four men in seconds. The driver fell onto the horn of the steering wheel and the horn blared loudly over the music in the dark of night. Lil Earl quickly walked around to the driver's side of the car and blew the driver's head off completely with his pistol grip. The horn went silent and the song continued to play as blood began to trickle down through the cracks of the doors and onto the concrete. Manny and his crew eyed the dead bodies inside the bullet-riddled Cadillac for a few seconds before they all took off running.

An old lady peeked through her bedroom curtains and saw three shadowy figures rapidly disappearing into the darkness of the Desire Project.

It was almost 5 A.M. when Ben and Oscar pulled themselves up onto the cold metal pipes underneath the house. They had waited six hours before Sebas had finally come home. He had been to the strip club where he was supposed to meet his boys, met a female, and had brought her home with him so she could spend the night. Ben and Oscar looked at one another seriously before they shrugged their shoulders at one another. Innocent or not, the female that was with Sebas was now a part of what was about to go down.

"Them niggas ain't even show up at the club tonight. Wonder what they got they ass into." Sebas stated as he and the female hopped off the motorcycle.

"Your boys were scared of my girls, that's all it was to that." The female remarked through light laughter.

"My niggas is straight up dogs! We all gone hook up in a minute. But tonight, you belong to daddy." Sebas said as he walked up the sidewalk leading to his front stairs.

"We'll see—daddy." The female replied as she grabbed Sebas's crotch from behind.

Ben and Oscar heard the conversation. They now figured that

Manny and his crew had taken care of their business so they knew they had to handle Sebas this morning. When Sebas walked up the stairs and unlocked the door to his home, Ben and Oscar rolled from under the house and drew their weapons —two chrome .44 Desert Eagles.

They rushed up the stairs and shoved Sebas into his living room, along with the female. Oscar closed the door and locked it; at the same time, Ben saw Sebas's little brother, Tevin, jump from the sofa and run towards the back of the home.

That's when the chaos began.

Sebastian never made a sound as Oscar blasted a gaping hole in the back of his head and Ben took off after Tevin. Ben caught the frightened teenager in one of the four bedrooms of the lavish home hiding in a closet. "I know you know where it's at, li'l nigga. Take me to it!" Ben commanded in a low tone.

The frightened thirteen year-old went to a safe in the master bedroom and unlocked it and Ben shoved the teen aside and quickly went for the items inside the safe. "Lay down on the floor, li'l nigga!" Ben said as he began stuffing drugs and money into a duffel bag.

The scared thirteen year-old complied and laid face down on the floor beside the bed. Ben zipped up the duffel bag, grabbed his gun from off the mattress, placed the barrel to the back of Tevin's head, and killed him execution style, shooting him two times in the back of the head and twice at the base of his neck at point blank range. When he walked back into the living room with the duffel bag containing Sebas's cocaine and money, Ben saw that Oscar was raping the female. Sebas lay on his carpeted living room floor bleeding from his head, his body convulsing from the bullet lodged in his skull. Oscar jumped off the high-yellow complexioned, big-fine woman when he saw Dirty Red and pulled up his pants as the woman pleaded for her life.

"You gone let my boy fuck, bitch?" Oscar asked her as he breathed heavily.

61

The woman slowly shook her head to say to yes and said, "I just met him tonight. I don't even know him like that. Y'all please, don't kill me. I got a baby. I got a baby."

"Go 'head, brer!" Oscar told Ben as he nodded towards the young woman, who was crying and repeatedly stating that she had a two year-old daughter.

Ben eyed the woman briefly and stared at Oscar before he made a trigger motion with his right hand.

"You missin' out, dog. Bitch had some good pussy." Oscar remarked before he calmly walked up to the female and shot her in the face two times, killing her instantly.

Ben didn't go to there to have sex, he was after the money Sebas had taken from him and then some; and he wasn't leaving any witnesses in the process. After Oscar removed a diamond bracelet and a diamond-crusted female Rolex watch from the woman's corpse, the two left and headed back across the Causeway and met up with Manny over to Haywood's house in the back of the project just before the sun rose over the horizon.

After tallying up the night's work, Ben, Manny, Oscar, Haywood and Lil Earl discovered they had made off with five kilograms of cocaine and seventy-two thousand dollars in cash, which was part of Sebas's re-up money. The boys had wiped Sebastian out of the game completely. And the hit they pulled had put the seventeen year-olds back on top of the game, just as Ben had said it would. Ben Holland's plan had worked to perfection. After that night, people rarely called Ben Holland by his real name. He was almost always known as Dirty Red.

Dirty Red, Manny, Oscar, Haywood and Lil Earl then went on a five-month rampage. The boys had robbed ten dope houses in that span and had killed eight more people. They had a total of eighteen bodies under their belts and pounds and pounds of cocaine to distribute. After Lil Earl was shot while running from the crew's last jack play, in March of 1992, the boys took him to Charity Hospital and dropped him off at the emergency room and fled scene in haste.

When Lil Earl came out of surgery, the New Orleans Police Department, or N.O.P.D. as it is commonly called, questioned him the following day about a triple murder that took place at a house in New Orleans East. Lil Earl told the homicide detectives that he was robbed and got shot at a park in Uptown while running from his attackers. The N.O.P.D. however, ran ballistics tests and had matched the bullet from Lil Earl's gunshot wound to a gun found in the house next to one of the dead men in New Orleans East. They tried to get Earl to confess to murder and tell who was all involved, but he stood solid. And since bullets from his gun matched none of the bullets lodged in either the walls or the corpses of the three dead men, they had no case for murder against Lil Earl; but the detectives planted a couple of ounces of cocaine in Lil Earl's jeans and charged him with possession of cocaine with intent to distribute. Lil Earl received a seven year sentence for that charge.

Manny, Oscar and Haywood reminisced about the night they killed Sebas as well as what happened to Lil Earl and how he stood solid back in 1992. Now, during the late summer of 1993, the boys had a new connection coming in through Haywood. They had just re-upped and the three of them were now headed back to the Desire Project after scoring a couple of kilograms. When they got there, they saw Ben and twelve year-old Katrina sitting in Ben's car in the driveway outside their dope house. The dope house was the old house where Manny and his mother once lived.

When Manny got on his feet, the first thing he did was help his mother buy a brand new home in Michoud, an upper middle-class neighborhood in the eastern part of the city. Ms. Joyce now resided in a luxurious and spacious four bedroom brick home in a tranquil neighborhood. The boys had taken over the house in the project; but Manny often told Ben how much he wanted a better place for his boys for the simple fact that the projects were becoming a little too crowded. The boys' dope house was easy to break into also. Manny remembered how he, Dirty Red, and Oscar used to kick in doors back in the day with Lil Earl and Haywood and he didn't want to be on the opposite end someone's trigger finger. When Manny stepped

out his of ride, Ben walked up to him holding a piece of paper in his hand.

"What's that?" Manny asked Dirty Red.

"A deed, nigga!" Dirty Red said smiling, his eight gold teeth shining in the bright sun.

"To what? I got two bricks in the trunk, nigga! What the fuck that is?" Manny asked in a low tone of voice whilst smiling at Ben.

"It's right 'round the corner brer, come see!"

When Manny, Oscar, Katrina and Haywood pulled up in front of the abandoned house where Ben used to sleep, Manny knew what was up.

"No! No you didn't nigga!" Manny said through laughter as he exited his car. "Fuck no!" He yelled again as he stared at the house.

"That's right, nigga. I done that shit ya' feel me? This our shit. You said we needed a better spot so I got us one." Ben said proudly as he and Manny dapped.

Dirty Red had bought the abandoned house he had slept in four years earlier for nine-thousand dollars. The house needed a lot of work, but it was located in a good spot just outside of the Desire Project. There was a front window inside a bedroom where someone could see the entire block from both directions. The house had a medium-sized front yard and a small alley down the right and left sides of the house. Behind the house was a large yard that ran back towards a wooden fence that bordered the project. Dirty Red had planned on cutting a door into the back fence so that customers could enter from the projects rather than walking up to the front of the house from the neighborhood just outside the project.

A small shed located just inside of the wooden fence could be used to serve cocaine. Trees lined both sides of the yard, so neighbors could not see what happened in the yard. Lookouts and soldiers could be placed up and down the back alley on the

outside of the wooden fence that ran along the projects. The spot was perfect. When Dirty Red showed the house to Manny, he knew it would work out well. The boys hired a professional renovating crew and roofers and within four months, the house was up and running. The last job was to have an alarm system and burglar bars installed by a top-notch security company.

When anyone first entered the house, a long black leather sofa was seen on the left. On the right was an entertainment center that held a Sony surround sound stereo system and a 32-inch TV. There was a bedroom to the right of the living room just pass the entertainment center that faced the street. Dirty Red spent most of his time here, seated in front of the window watching traffic. As one walked through the living room past the entertainment system and the door leading to the bedroom, straight ahead there was the dining room with a large, eight-seat cherry wood table that sat on top of polished cherry-lacquered wooden floors.

Just past the dining room to the left was another bedroom, but the boys had turned it into a den. It had its own private shower, laced with black ceramic tiles that lined the shower stall and trimmed the sink and floors. It also had a 57-inch screen television, a huge Panasonic stereo sound system, and a black leather c-sectional sofa that sat on top of thick, black, soft Georgia carpet.

Directly across from the den was another bedroom that featured a bathroom laced with white marble flooring and a Jacuzzi-styled oversized bathtub and ten karat gold accessories and handles on the shower nozzle, tub and sink faucets and the handle on the toilet. Ben and Anna spent many a night inside that bedroom, often reminiscing about the many times they had slept on the floor once upon a time.

Standing in the hallway facing the rear of the house, with the den on the left and the bedroom on the right, was a kitchen straight ahead. The kitchen had white ceramic tile throughout, a double door freezer, a large gas stove, and a small open-faced grill. There was a backdoor in the kitchen that led to a small deck. Here, Oscar would usually sit with his AR-15

assault rifle, keeping an eye on Jermaine who usually sat inside the shed while Manny and Lamont stood outside the fence with two lookouts, one on each end of the alley, and two soldiers they had hired for extra manpower. Jason was usually up at the front of the house sitting on the porch, or in the alley that ran along the right side of the house with three other soldiers from the project overlooking the block and watching traffic along with Dirty Red.

At the young age of thirteen, Jason Witherspoon, Lamont Charles, Jermaine Duplessis and Cedric Woodson, the four little boys who once played football in the courtyards of the Desire Project with Manny, Ben and Oscar, had been introduced to the drug game. Manny had waited for the day when they would come of age and it had finally arrived.

Manny spent a lot of time talking to the young teens, telling them all about the game. He taught them all how to use the different types of weapons the boys owned, how to count money at a fast pace, and how to cook crack cocaine. He also told them there might be a time that they would have to kill someone, but if they weren't able to kill, they might as well go back on Benefit Street and play football. The young teens remembered all that Manny had said and they had learned even more from Dirty Red and Oscar.

Although Manny, Dirty Red and Oscar, who were now all nineteen, never described what actually went on when they committed murder, the young teens knew that they had killed people in the past and would do it again if they had to. The image of Manny blowing out the brains of a man in their courtyard, forever impressed the young youths. Jason, Lamont, Jermaine and Cedric learned early on that murder, in the streets, earned one not only respect, but it put fear into the hearts of anyone that ever dared to test one's skills.

Thirteen year-olds Jason, Jermaine, Lamont and Cedric were each earning five-hundred dollars a week working for the boys. They were superstars at Carver Middle School. Other teens would gather in flocks whenever Dirty Red, Oscar, Manny, or sometimes all three, would pull up in front of the school and

let the boys out of their clean whips.

The girls at the middle school loved Jason and his boys. He and his friends dressed the way Manny, Dirty Red, and Oscar dressed—baggy Girbaud's, Polo shirts and two-hundred dollar Bally tennis shoes. They were fresh all the time; and whomever they wanted, they usually got. Females just wanted to be around the young teens. They would walk past the dope house after school just to look at them and to see what they were doing. They had even begun hanging with Katrina, now twelve, because they knew she was close to them.

Katrina enjoyed the attention she received as well, and Manny had always made sure she had the very best. At the age of twelve, Katrina was wearing Louis Vitton, Gucci, Girbaud, Ralph Lauren and other high end fashions. The boys had also bought the little girl bamboo earrings trimmed in half karat diamonds with her name engraved into them. All they asked of Katrina was that she brought home good grades from school. Katrina did just so, all-the-while turning down offers from numerous boys in middle school who tried to get inside of her panties.

Whenever Manny and his boys were not selling cocaine, they would let the young teens and their female friends use the den to kick back and chill. The young teenage girls would do anything to sit inside the dope house—*anything*. The house was laid out and all they wanted to do was be able to brag to their girlfriends in school that they were with the young teens the day before chilling inside the den.

Sex came at a rapid and easy pace for the young teens; but Manny, Oscar, and Dirty Red were off the chain and out the door with the amount of pussy they went through during 1993. To see two or more females fighting over either of the three in front of the dope house was a common sight for the crew. Dirty Red didn't want that kind of heat at the dope house, however, so the boys stopped allowing females to visit. Instead, they would take the females to hotels until they could find another house that could allow them to strictly have nothing but fun. Business was booming for the boys and over

the next three years or so, they grew richer and stronger.

CHAPTER EIGHT

AN UNWELCOMED VISIT

The year was 1996. Dirty Red, now twenty-two years-old, weighed one-hundred and eighty-five pounds and stood about 6' 2". His jet-black hair hung over his shoulders, but he always wore it in a single ponytail. He had a cleft chin with a thin goatee he kept neatly trimmed. He also now had ten gold teeth in the upper portion of his mouth.

Katrina, now fifteen, had grown into a beautiful young lady. The caramel-skinned teenager still had her curly black hair, only it had grown longer and hung just above her shoulders. Her behind was round and pert and her stomach was smooth and flat. Katrina Sanders resembled a young woman who portrayed a character named Laura Winslow on a popular sitcom in the nineties titled *Family Matters*. Katrina's full lips and dark, round eyes accentuated her beauty. The resemblance to the TV character was unreal, and whenever the show was on, the boys would tease her by saying that her twin was on TV.

Manny stood 5' 8" and weighed a solid two-hundred pounds and wore dreadlocks that hung just below his ears. He also sported numerous tattoos. Manny had his mother's and Katrina's name inside a heart on his right arm and a skull and

cross bones with his name in the middle on the left arm. NINTH was on his right forearm and WARD was on the left. Manny also now sported twelve gold teeth, his original eight at the top and four diamond teeth trimmed in gold at the bottom. Manny sort of favored the rapper Lil Flip, only he was a few shades darker than the rapper.

Oscar still looked the same although he had bulked up a little by adding thirty pounds to his 6'1" muscular frame. He now weighed one-hundred and ninety pounds and still sported a low-cut fade.

Jason now wore his hair in braids platted to the back. All the girls loved his smile. His six opened-faced gold teeth showed off his pearly whites beautifully and he had the "cutest dimples" the girls would always say. The girls all knew and believed, and even Manny and the rest of the crew, would always say that Jason Witherspoon, the 5' 8" one-hundred and seventy pound sixteen year-old was the lover of the crew.

Jermaine resembled Kevin Garnett, a power forward who played for the Minnesota Timberwolves during the mid-nineties. He stood 5' 10", and weighed around one-hundred and sixty pounds. He had four solid gold teeth at the top of his mouth and sported a tapered haircut with a neatly trimmed mustache and goatee.

Lamont had grown to be a rough-looking, square-jawed 5' 9" individual. At one-hundred and eighty pounds, he looked almost exactly like the rapper Xzibit.

Cedric was still the shortest of the crew at 5' 6", but he was a solid one-hundred and seventy pounds, browned-skinned and bald-faced, with a tendency toward the stocky side.

Three years had passed and the boys were deep in the game. They were bringing in serious loot now and were well-known throughout the city. Katrina was still in school, doing great, making straight A's; but Jason, Jermaine, Cedric, and Lamont had all dropped out of school a year earlier under the belief that no form of education they were receiving at the time could earn them over two thousand dollars a week. They had been in

the game for three years now, and they had seen a lot during that span of time. They had seen people killed by Dirty Red, Manny, and Oscar in the back alley behind the dope house. They had once even helped Manny, Dirty Red, and Oscar dump the dead body of an attempted armed robber into a dumpster inside the project. They were hardened by what they had seen, and their hearts were numb to the violence that Dirty Red, Oscar, and Manny perpetrated on the streets of New Orleans.

The crew all now resided at the dope house. They worked in shifts when they were slanging. Everyone slept with a pistol on his side in case something jumped off in the middle of the night. The crew didn't allow Katrina stay the night at the dope house ever because they didn't want anything to happen to her if ever they were hit. Katrina, however, would come over after school and spend time with the boys, do homework, and just chill for a while until one of them, usually Manny, dropped her off at Ms. Joyce's house in Michoud.

On a warm spring evening in early April, Katrina was lying across the bed doing her English homework in the bedroom with Dirty Red as he sat and looked out the window. "Look at this piece of shit comin' up the sidewalk." Ben said, unable to believe what he was seeing.

Katrina got up off the bed and walked over to the window. She peeked out and saw Faye, her mother, standing on the sidewalk talking to Jason and Cedric. Katrina looked at Dirty Red, curled her lips to one side, walked timidly into the living room, and slowly pushed open the screened burglar-barred door.

"See!" Faye yelled when Katrina came into view. "I told y'all she wanted to see her mother!"

Faye walked past Oscar, who was standing at the front gate, without saying a word, and made her way up the stairs and stood before Katrina as Manny and the rest of the boys stood on the sidewalk in front of the house. Dirty Red hung out of the window trying to get a better view of what was going on on the front porch. Faye stood in front of the doorway looking at

Katrina, who was the spitting image of her mother, smiling proudly. She was happy to see how beautiful her little girl had grown.

"How you been, baby?"

"Fine." Katrina said as she carefully backed into the threshold of the door.

"I, I got myself cleaned up. I got my own apartment! And I'm working, too! I mean, I'm a cashier at Burger King, but hey, it's something."

"That's nice, Faye."

"Faye? You *do* remember who I am right, Katrina? I'm your mother, baby!"

"No, you not!" Katrina snapped as she stood in the doorway. "And don't call me 'baby'. I ain't a fuckin' baby no more!"

"Katrina, I know the last six years or so I haven't been a good mother. I, I was caught up, ya' know? But I'm clean now. I come back to take you home."

"A good mother?" Katrina asked angrily as she began to cry. "Take me home? I am home! I been home for the last six years while you were out gettin' high!"

"Don't you curse at me! I'm still your mother!"

"Fuck you!" Katrina said as the tears ran down her face.

The boys all stood quietly in the yard as Katrina and her mother, who started crying as well, expressed their feelings towards one another. It had been a long time coming, and Katrina had to express to her mother all the hurt and anger she had accumulated towards Faye throughout her young life.

"I just want us to be a family again. The way we used to be when you were a baby." Faye said lowly.

"A family? A family, bitch? We were never a family! You left me on my own!"

"In the beginning I was always there for you Katrina! Always! You don't know everything that happened to me, baby. I loved you! This man, he—"

"A man!" Katrina yelled, cutting her mother off. "It's always been about a man! *I* needed you! And you let me down! Where were you when I burnt my hands? What about having a clean house? Clean clothes? Food on the table? The shit that mattered to *me*? Somebody else had to take care of me because you were never there for me!"

"I know I wasn't always a good mother, but—"

"You were never a good mother!"

"I am a—I was a good mother. I still am. And I care for you. I love you, Katrina."

"No you don't! They care for me! They love me!" Katrina responded through tears whilst pointing to the boys standing in the yard.

"Can we start over, Katrina?"

"Why, Faye? Why? So you can sell my pussy to your perverted friends again?"

"You don't know everything about me! Everything that happened to *me*! I'm sorry! And it's not about a man! Life fucked me over, Katrina. But God *knows* I love you!"

Faye reached out to hug her daughter, but Katrina pushed her arms away, backed into the house and pulled the screen door shut. Only then did she start to cry heavily. Katrina heaved as she thought about the things her mother had put her through. She couldn't believe that Faye actually had the audacity to show up and act as if nothing ever happened. It was not as if Faye went into rehab for thirty days and then returned home. She had neglected and misused Katrina emotionally and physically, and Katrina had never forgotten the things her mother had put her through when she was younger. The ultimate unforgivable act in Katrina's eyes was that Faye had repeatedly sold her for sex in exchange for crack cocaine.

Katrina knew she could never be a part of Faye's life again. The trust, and more importantly, the love, that Katrina once had for her mother had been forever lost.

"I'm sorry, Katrina." Faye said through the door as she hung her head low.

"I am too, Faye," Katrina said softly

"Please, baby!" Faye stated in a last desperate attempt to regain favor with her daughter.

"I'm not your fuckin' baby! Just, just stay away from me forever! You are not my mother! My mother's name is Joyce Taylor!" Katrina yelled. "I hate you, mutherfucka!" She screamed as she ran up and slammed the door in Faye's face.

Katrina ran through the house, she would have run out the backdoor and as far away from Faye as she could get, but she was stopped by Dirty Red in the dining room. Dirty Red wrapped his arms protectively around Katrina and the two stood in the den in silence in a warm embrace. Katrina hid her face in Dirty Red's chest and cried heavily as she pounded his muscular biceps with her balled fists.

"Why she come here? I never wanted to see her again in life!"

"We gone handle this shit. Just stay here. I know you ain't all right, you might wanna make a call." Dirty Red stated as he reached for the phone.

"Yea," Katrina stated as she backed away from Dirty Red and wiped lip-liner from his white t-shirt, "I'm a, I'm a call momma Joyce. Thanks, Ben." She said calmly as Dirty Red handed her the phone before walking onto the porch where he saw Faye sitting on the steps crying in her lap.

"Go your crackhead ass somewhere else and cry ya' lowdown mutherfucka! You gotta lotta nerve bringin' your funky ass back 'round here, Faye!" Dirty Red shouted.

"Dirty Red—everybody—I'm sorry!" Faye cried again.

"You ain't sorry!" Manny snapped as he walked onto the porch and got directly into Faye's face. "You only sorry we found about your nasty ass! That shit shouldna never happened! How the fuck you get it in your mind to pimp your own daughter, bitch? Get the fuck from 'round this camp!" Manny stated angrily as he grabbed Faye by the arm and dragged her from the porch towards the front gate.

Oscar happily opened the gate and nodded his head in agreement as Manny threw Faye down onto the sidewalk in front of the dope house. Lamont grabbed her purse and threw it to Manny, who slung it into Faye's bosom and told her never to show her face on the block again.

Faye got up heartbroken and embarrassed. She turned and walked out of the yard with her head hanging down. When she reached the end of the block, Faye saw Tanaka and Alicia, two of Katrina's childhood friends, who were both now the same age as Katrina.

"Hey Faye!" Fifteen year-old Alicia spoke cheerily.

"Fuck y'all li'l bitches! Every last one of y'all gonna get what's comin' to you! All of y'all gonna get exactly what you deserve outta life! Just like it happened to me!" Faye screamed aloud before she spat on the sidewalk and hurried off.

"What happened, bitch? Who in the fuck blew out your candle?" Tanaka snapped as she and Alicia laughed to themselves.

Faye didn't answer. She pranced up the sidewalk hurriedly, mumbling a host of inaudible curse words. Alicia and Tanaka laughed to themselves once more as they walked towards the dope house to visit Katrina, who was now sitting on the porch with the boys listening to Master P's hit song *I'm Bout It* blaring from Dirty Red's Cutlass that was parked in the driveway.

Tanaka Romaire and Alicia Mason had grown proportionally over the years. Tanaka was now 5' 7" and slim. She still wore her Afro-puffs, although, she now had long micro-braids in her

head to go along with the afro puffs. Alicia had shed her baby fat and was now a big-fine red-boned young woman with big grey eyes and short brown hair. Alicia also had a thin layer brown hair on her arms and legs that blended well with her high-yellow complexion. The girls walked into the yard dancing freely to the music coming from Dirty Red's car as Alicia told everyone she and Tanaka had just seen Faye.

Katrina relayed to them what happened a few moments ago and the girls had agreed with what Katrina had said and with what the boys had done. They all chatted for a while and then the girls asked Katrina to walk over to Tanaka's house with them to get their hair done. Katrina and her girls began to leave the porch, but not before Lamont began flirting with Alicia.

Lamont had been trying to get with Alicia for the past year, but Alicia wasn't giving in. The fifteen year-old prided herself on still being a virgin.

"Say, Alicia let me ask you something." Lamont said as he scratched his face.

"The answer still no, boy!" Alicia quickly retorted.

"There you go tellin' me no again, Alicia. Why you playin' the role, brer? Like you ain't fuckin'?"

"'Cause I ain't fuckin'—Mister Keith Sweat! And if I was fuckin', it wouldn't be with you! So...*there I go tellin' you no again...there I go...there I go*!" Alicia sang.

The boys all burst into laughter as Tanaka, Alicia, and Katrina walked out of the front gate and down the sidewalk. They sat and discussed which one of the young teens had slept with either of the three girls, and it had come out that Cedric and Lamont had slept with Tanaka once when they were thirteen. They had been Tanaka's first, but she quickly stopped sleeping with them when she heard how the young teens were fucking everything in a skirt at Carver Middle School.

Alicia was just straight up-tight with the pussy, they all agreed. All the young teens wanted her because she was a sexy red-bone and a virgin. The only problem was that they just

could not figure out how to get into her panties.

"Shit," Lamont remarked as he rubbed his chin, "I even offered that fine mutherfucka some money for some of that pussy! She *still* ain't with it!"

"Alicia just need a few more years, L-Dog." Dirty Red said to Lamont. "But when she do start fuckin', she gone be a wild one. I can see that there." He ended.

"Alright," Manny chimed in, "which one of y'all niggas fucked Katrina?"

"Damn!" Lamont, Jermaine and Cedric all snapped in unison.

"Come on, brer!" Manny said, smiling as he lit up a blunt.

Manny knew what the young teenaged females were doing in the projects and he wanted to see if Katrina was out there doing the same. Not that he would get mad or anything; in fact, Manny hoped that one of the young teens would claim Katrina as his ole lady. The young teens didn't think like that, however; they saw Katrina as a little sister. To everybody she was off limits—everybody except Jason Witherspoon. Jason had been sleeping with Katrina for the last four months and when he told Manny, Manny wasn't surprised.

"I figured it woulda been you lover boy." Manny said as he took a toke off the blunt and passed it to Oscar. "What happened, nigga," he asked Jason.

Jason told the entire crew that he and Katrina had been kissing and feeling on one another for about a month before it all went down. When January of '96 came around, the two were hot for one another; but they didn't have anywhere to go to be alone. Katrina didn't want to go to a hotel because she knew that was where all the boys took their playthings and she didn't want to be placed in the same category as the other females. The opportunity for Jason and Katrina, however, had finally presented itself on Martin Luther King's Day of 1996.

Jason told the boys that while everyone was at the parade on Canal Street, he stayed back and caught a cab out to Michoud

where Katrina was staying with Ms. Joyce. Ms. Joyce was going to a bar-b-que that day, so Jason and Katrina knew she would be gone for a good while. When Jason stepped into the house and locked the door, the two started French kissing passionately.

"Put this tape on," Katrina told Jason, in between kisses.

"What's this here?" Jason asked in a perplexed manner

Katrina loved Keith Sweat. Ms. Joyce would play his tape all the time when she was little and Katrina grew to like his music as well. When his song titled *Right and a Wrong Way* came on, Katrina let herself go. She stripped off her clothes and told Jason to make love to her as the two embraced and continued kissing.

"Don't fuck me." Katrina then whispered to Jason in between heated kisses.

"What?" Jason asked, confused by Katrina's request as he believed that that is exactly what they were about to do. "What you mean, Katrina?"

"Don't fuck me, Jason. Brian fucked me. I don't want to be fucked. I want you to make love to me. I want you to be gentle with my body. Even though it's not, I want this to really be like how I dreamt my first time would be. And I always wanted my first time to be with you. Ever since Benefit Street."

Jason then understood what Katrina was saying. He rewound the song as Katrina requested, slid on a condom and lay his naked flesh gently on top of Katrina's and made love to her off of Keith Sweat's song, *Right and a Wrong Way* as the two French kissed one another passionately. They repeated their act three more times that day, and each time they did, Katrina wanted Jason to play Keith Sweat's song.

"That's why your bitch ass kept singin' that stupid ass song for 'bouta fuckin' month, nigga!" Lamont yelled as he burst into laughter.

"That's a dirty mutherfucka," Cedric followed.

Jason just sat back and smiled to himself. He then told the boys not to mention what happened between him and Katrina because Katrina wanted to keep their personal business private. The crew understood. To them, Katrina wasn't a hoe in the streets. She was their home girl, and they would never make fun of her in that manner; especially when Jason told them how she wanted him to make love to her and not be fucked in the same manner in which Brian had violated her body.

Eventually, however, the word got out that Katrina and Jason were fooling around. Since no one made light of the situation, or passed an opinion, Katrina did not feel guilty about sleeping with somebody from the crew. She and Jason had become really close; and although they never actually became boyfriend and girlfriend, they did continue to sleep with one another for a while. They eventually began seeing other people, but both had ignited a flame towards another that would be hard to extinguish.

Katrina had experimented with lovemaking with Jason, Lamont, Jermaine, and Cedric by the end of 1996 because she simply could not bring herself to sleep with anyone outside of the crew. The crew was all she had ever known; on top of that, Katrina felt that if she slept with someone outside the crew, she would somehow be betraying them. Katrina felt in her heart that she could never repay the boys, especially Manny, for what they had done for her, so she willingly gave up her body to them. She had gotten wild sexually, but she would only have sex with the young teens because Manny, Dirty Red and Oscar all viewed her as off limits; but as far as the young teens were concerned, Katrina made sure they wore protection each and every time they had sex.

The crew had soon given Katrina a nickname they would use from time to time. They sometimes called her Kay Kay because Katrina Sanders was no longer "little Katrina". She had literally grown up overnight in their eyes.

CHAPTER NINE

MAJOR COME UP

It was now March of '99. Katrina Sanders was now an eighteen year-old senior at Carver High School at the top of her class and was as outgoing and wild as ever. Being around the boys for so long, Katrina had taken on some of their ways. She didn't take shit off anybody. She said what she felt when she felt it and was ready to fight if anybody didn't like it. The boys had taught Katrina a lot over the years, and she used her street savvy to begin playing games on the so-called players that she came across in the street. Katrina knew what real players and gangsters were supposed to be about; she had been around them all her life and she would be damned if she let any of the so-called players play her out for her pocketbook or her pussy. She was hip to the game. Manny had joked one day that he and the boys had created a monster, but they were all proud of the way Katrina had turned out. She could now fend for herself whenever they weren't around.

The crew was sitting on some major loot in March of '99. A year earlier, Dirty Red had begun leasing a hangar at Louis Armstrong International Airport to conduct business and to bring in extra revenue.

The boys also purchased a mini-mansion they called *Par 6,*

which lay in a gated golf course community on New Orleans' Lakefront. *Par 6* was the fun pad the boys had been waiting to score. They now had somewhere to parlay outside of the 'hood and no longer had to worry about running back and forth to a hotel whenever they wanted to kick back and chill.

They no longer had to sleep at the dope house with guns under their pillows either; but there was plenty of artillery at *Par 6*, whose location was known to only a privileged few. The crew was also able to store their cocaine safely at the dope house since Dirty Red had another security firm install a computerized security system, outdoor video cameras and impenetrable steel burglar bars on the windows and doors, along with a fireproof safe hidden in the floor.

The boys were excited the day they moved into *Par 6;* and were even more proud of the way they had laid the place out. Since the mini-mansion was sunk into a hillside on the golf course, the living room was on the second floor. The crew decked it out with a white leather C-sectional sofa facing a fifty-five inch screen TV. On either side of the TV were two French doors that led out to the golf course. There was an island counter in the kitchen which contained a large open grill pit. The appliances were all black. The floor, as well as the counter tops in the kitchen, was decorated with grey Italian marble.

The spacious dining room was laced out with a ten-chair black Italian marble dinette set imported from Sicily. It sat in the middle of the room, surrounded by ten black and white leather chairs, atop a white marble floor that had pea-sized specs of ebony flowing throughout. At the end of the dining room was a set of cream-colored marble stairs that led to the third floor, which contained five suites and a huge library teeming with World History books that had been personally selected by Ben Holland himself. Two suites were down the left of the hall, and three were to the right. They all had soft carpet and king-sized beds. Each suite also had its own balcony, shower-stall, a thirty-two inch TV, and surround-sound system complete with TV monitors to scan the premises.

An elevator that led to a four-car capacity garage was in between the kitchen and living room on the second floor. The garage area also contained a medium-sized soundproof office that the boys would often use to discuss business. The office was laced with a mahogany wood mini-bar, two burgundy leather sofas on either side of the room, and a huge burgundy-lacquered wooden desk that Dirty Red often sat behind as the boys talked business as he scanned the premises through the four monitors that sat atop the desk facing him.

They all had newer and fresher whips as well. Manny had a black on black '99 Ford F-150, Harley Davidson Edition pick-up that sat on 22" chrome Excursion rims. Oscar had a four-door '98 black Grand Prix. The car had black tinted windows, 19" chrome Giovanni rims and white and black leather interior. Dirty Red had purchased a pearl-white four-door '98 C class Mercedes Benz. He, too, had 19" Giovanni chrome rims with all white interior. Dirty Red had placed four 7" TV screens inside the car along with a killer Bose sound system. He didn't tint the bulletproof windows, however, because he felt the tint only detracted from the car's appearance.

Jason had a '99 black on black big body four door Sedan Deville Cadillac on 20" chrome Blades. He had the white interior with black trimming and three 15" sub-woofers in the trunk and eight 6x9 speakers placed in the doors, rear panel, and dash of the car. The two-thousand watt JVC amp literally shook the ground as Jason passed people on the streets of New Orleans.

Lamont had a '98 evergreen Lexus with evergreen and white interior. The car was laced out with wood grain that surrounded the four custom-made 7" screen TV's he placed inside of the car and 18" chrome rims.

Jermaine did not have his license yet, but when he did get it, he was planning to score a Navigator. Cedric, meanwhile, was locked up for having gotten busted at a picnic in City Park with marijuana.

The boys, despite Cedric's mishap, were doing very well for themselves. After being homeless and broke, Ben Holland, in

ten years, had built a tremendous amount of wealth for himself and his boys. He was at the height of his criminal career; becoming a lead member of one of the most respected and feared drug organizations on the Gulf Coast. If there ever was a time to back out, now was the time; but all Ben Holland and his crew could see ahead was more money and more power. The crew had been on a tremendous run. They had spent ten years eluding drug busts, and had been literally getting away with murder, armed robbery, and rape. Scores of stories would be told about the crew's ascension. Many people knew how they rose to the top of the game, but only a privileged few knew all the events surrounding the crew's torrid downfall.

It is said that many a great disaster has been caused not by one big event, but a series of small ones. Those seemingly insignificant problems tend to compound themselves, though. Alone, they mean nothing, but together, small problems can trigger big events that can have devastating and irreparable consequences and repercussions. The downfall of the entire crew would be a classic case in point.

Some believe the downfall started when Dirty Red, Manny, and Oscar were headed over to their supplier's house in Kenner, Louisiana in late February of '99 to pick up eight kilograms of cocaine when they were pulled over by two plain-clothed narcotics agents.

Gautier 'Swan' Swanson, a red-haired, pony-tailed, handle-barred mustached chief detective, and his longtime partner, Isaac Montgomery, a slightly balding, slim Italian, told Dirty Red and his boys that they were headed into an undercover sting. They also told the young men that their supplier had gotten Haywood and Cedric busted as well.

"Cedric said he had a marijuana charge." Dirty Red said through the cracked window of his Benz.

"Yeah, fifteen pounds worth!" Swan remarked.

"Why you think he didn't want you to bail him out? He thought you was gonna kill 'em." Montgomery added.

Dirty Red, Manny, and Oscar looked perplexed as they sat and contemplated what the two detectives were telling them. They didn't know what to exactly make of what the cops were saying and they began to wonder if they were actually telling the truth. The boys talked amongst themselves for a minute with the windows rolled up.

"What you make of this shit, Manny, dog?" Ben asked.

"Shit, I don't know. They might be for real, brer. I mean, how the fuck they know where we was going?" Manny replied.

"Them niggas might be settin' us up." Oscar stated from the backseat.

"Nah, Big O," Dirty Red replied. "If they was settin' us up, they woulda just let us ride to the party. I think they want something from us. Boy, if we get these police on the payroll..." Dirty Red's voice trailed off as he thought of the massive advantage his crew would have over other dealers if they had narcotics agents in their back pockets.

"Shit, let's see what they talkin' 'bout." Manny said.

Dirty Red rolled the window down and asked the cops how he and his boys could know for certain that they were actually telling the truth.

"Look," said Swan, "we know y'all killed a guy named Brian in one of the courtyards on Benefit Street ten years ago. We know about the dope house on Piety Street as well. Who do you think been keeping you guys from being touched by the local task force? This is not a shakedown fellas. It's a business proposition. We offer cleanup work, inside info, and we keep the heat from coming down on ya'—for a small fee, of course. How ya' know we for real? You got two-hundred thousand dollars in ya' trunk right now and you're on ya' way to score eight kilograms of cocaine from a guy in Kenner. You want more? I'm telling y'all, ya' supplier's wearing a wire. And I wouldn't be too fond of Haywood and Cedric if I was either of ya'. They been hangin' Uptown and workin' with another pusher whom you boys know and hate."

The boys talked it over and agreed to meet the two detectives at their airport hangar the following week. There, they paid the detectives ten-thousand dollars apiece and got a list of all the drug dealers in the city that were working for the local police. Dirty Red was surprised to see so many names, many of which he knew. Damon's name was even on the list. The game was now tainted. Until the boys could find a new and trustworthy connection in the city, they would have to get an out-of-town supplier. That move right there could be risky, however; drug dealers from New Orleans sometimes went out of town to rescore and returned home in body bags. Dirty Red, Manny and Oscar knew that to be fact because they had seen it happen on several occasions, one in which they were supposed to take a trip to Atlanta with three other dealers they knew out the Desire Project, but backed out at the last minute. The three men were shot to death inside their car and had it set afire after they were robbed out of their buy money in Decatur, Georgia, just outside of Atlanta.

Manny, however, had an idea—instead of going out of town to rescore, the crew could maybe pull off another jack-play to get them through the drought. Manny called his cousin Sherman Davis in Memphis, Tennessee and asked him if he could set something up for the crew when the boys got back to *Par 6*.

"I'm a call you back in a few days, cousin!" Sherman stated excitedly.

When Sherman called back two days later, he told Manny he had a sweet lick set up for him and his people. It had been a while since the boys had pulled off a home invasion, but Sherman said he knew for a fact that they had at least fifteen kilograms of cocaine stashed away in a house located in North Memphis. Sherman had been watching the house for a while, and Manny's call had come at just the right time. Sherman was a straight up dude, and he had been jacking people in Memphis almost as long as his cousin Manny was doing his thing in New Orleans. The two were just alike in some aspects, including looks. They could have passed as brothers instead of cousins.

The boys talked it over as they sat in the living room of *Par 6* sipping cognacs. "Fuck, we done ran up in niggas' shit before." Manny said as he poured a glass of cognac and lit a blunt. "Fifteen keys a do a nigga good right about now. Plus, they got this drought shit going on. We be the only established mutherfuckas with weight besides that bitch ass nigga Rico uptown. I don't know why Kay Kay even deal with that phony mutherfucka."

"Shiit," remarked Oscar through light laughter, "Kay Kay playing the fuck out that chump! Jason still taggin' that ass."

"Jason gettin' more pussy from Katrina than Rico—if he even fucking—and Rico paying for it! And Jason got a ole lady!" Dirty Red said through laughter. "I'm a have ta' get that punk ta' stop parking in front the fuckin' spot stuntin' with his li'l boom box he got in that fucked up Jaguar every time he come 'round the set too."

"So what's the deal niggas? We going up ta' M-town and do this shit or what?" Oscar asked just before he hit the blunt.

"Fuckin' right!" Dirty Red and Manny answered at the same time.

Three days later, the boys were on their way to Memphis. They had brought Jermaine along, but had left Jason and Lamont at *Par 6* with Kay Kay and Kim, Jermaine's girlfriend, and Dana, Jason's new beau. All the boys wanted to go, but Manny knew they would be loaded down with guns, ski-masks, and handcuffs. If they were pulled over and the police found all the paraphernalia they had, they would be dealt a serious blow. Jermaine was a true soldier, but Manny knew if something happened to him, Dirty Red or Oscar, he would rather have Jermaine take the fall with them.

Manny knew two things: one was that Jermaine thought with his heart, the other was the fact that Jay and L-Dog thought without conscience. The two of them were beasts. If anybody besides him, Dirty Red and Oscar could hold it down while they were off the streets, it would be Jason and Lamont. The game just came naturally to the two young gangsters. It wasn't

that Manny was using Jermaine; he just knew Jason and Lamont knew more about the ins and outs of the crew's daily operation than Jermaine.

The boys reached Memphis at about 2 A.M. on a cool spring morning early in March of '99. Oscar was behind the wheel of his Grand Prix and he yelled out for Manny to wake up and show him where Sherman lived.

"Stay on fifty-five, brer," Manny mumbled, still half asleep. "Just stay on fifty-five."

"If I stay on interstate fifty-five, we goin' up to Saint Louis, nigga! We in Memphis, homeboy! Wake your ass up quick-like so we can put this work in!" Oscar snapped as he shoved Manny's shoulder repeatedly.

Manny stirred himself awake and guided Oscar to their pre-ordained location, which was a rundown apartment complex in south Memphis. The neighborhood was still asleep as Manny walked through the worn-out orange-bricked complex and knocked on the door of a downstairs apartment. He tapped on the white wooden door repeatedly until it slowly opened. Sherman stood in the doorway in a pair of black silk boxers and a black silk wife-beater and greeted his cousin by pounding his chest with a balled up right fist. The bandanna he wore was twisted on his head. He, too, was still half asleep.

"What up cousin?" Manny asked as he gave Sherman a handshake and a hug.

"I'm chillin' dog. Y'all niggas ready to get paid today?" The husky twenty year-old asked in a gruff voice.

"Fo' sho' nigga. Just show us where it's at."

Just then, a little girl started crying and Sherman yelled for his girlfriend to come and get their daughter.

"How old my li'l cousin is now?" Manny asked with a smile as he peeked into the home to get a glimpse of the little girl, who was now sitting upright on the couch.

"She just made four last month."

"That's tight! I got a li'l cousin I barely know, man. We gotta kick it sometime, brer. Like back in the day ya' dig? Come hollar in the N.O. when ya' got time. I gotcha, cuz." Manny stated as he waved at the shy little girl.

The four year-old waved back at Manny as she rubbed her eyes and then extended her arms to allow her mother to pick her up.

"I'm feeling that! I'm a, I'm a do that, Manny. But this morning here, let's get this fuckin' money, cousin." Sherman stated as he handed Manny a paper with directions to the house.

Sherman told Manny that he had ridden through the area a couple of hours ago and everything looked good.

"This the play cuz—you gone see a cream-colored big body caddy with a white rag-top and triple gold rims on it. That's gone be the house. You can't miss the mutherfucka. Hit 'em up, drop my two bricks back this way, leave the guns so I can toss them in the river, and from there we straight." Sherman remarked and then stared at Manny waiting for a reply.

Manny nodded his head silently and dapped Sherman off. The two cousins then looked at one another without saying a word before they both cracked a sly smile.

"Fuck you laughing at nigga?" Sherman asked.

"You look like Aunt Jemima with that fuckin' head scarf on, nigga!"

"Oh, you got jokes early in the mornin', huh, bitch?"

"Have me some pancakes when I get back, mutherfucka!" Manny said as he walked off.

"Yea? You gone be a starvin' ass nigga waitin' for some dam pancakes! Y'all niggas be careful out there."

"We got this here ole pancake cookin' ass nigga!"

"Fuuuck ya'." Sherman said slowly as the two cousins

laughed at one another.

Sherman closed his door as Manny went and hopped into the back seat of the car and the crew was off to their final destination.

"Jermaine, you straight?" Dirty Red asked as the car turned slowly onto the street where the house was located.

"Yea, brer. I'm cool." Jermaine answered as he wiped sweat from his forehead.

The boys had their guns locked and loaded as they pulled down their ski masks. Oscar's black Grand Prix pulled up slowly and quietly in front of the house. They saw the cream-colored Cadillac, just like Sherman said, and they knew they were in the right spot. It was about 3:30 A.M. and the block was still and quiet. The upper middle-class neighborhood's houses were a little spaced out, and each house had a neatly-trimmed row of bushes or a chain-linked fence surrounding the entirety of the home. The boys exited Oscar's car, hopped over a row of bushes and quietly ran up to the front door of the spacious one-story brick house. They were each dressed in all black, wearing black ski masks, and black leather gloves.

Without hesitation, Dirty Red forcefully kicked down the wooden door, shattering the stain-glassed window in the process. The boys hurriedly entered into the house and saw two black men in their early twenties sit upright on the two leather sofas that were in the living room. The men had their hands in the air as Manny stood directly in front of them, clutching a calico automatic machine gun. An olive-complexioned man ran from the kitchen, but he was caught quickly by Dirty Red before he got to the end of the hall. Just then, a light-skinned female stepped into the hallway screaming loudly. Jermaine grabbed her around the neck, rushed her into the living room, and forced her onto the floor next to the two black men who were now kneeling on the carpet with a pair of handcuffs securing their wrists behind their back, courtesy of Oscar.

"What the fuck is this?" The olive-skinned man asked in an

aggravated manner as he stood in the living room staring down the barrel of Dirty Red's Mac-11.

"You know what this is bitch," Dirty Red yelled. "We want the yao, the money, the jewels, everything ya' got in this mutherfucka! Now bitch!" Dirty Red shouted before he punched the man in the face.

The man dropped to his knees, and spit blood from his mouth and told Dirty Red that they didn't have anything in the house. "Shit's been sold." He said in a nonchalant manner as he licked the blood from his lips.

The female and the two black men were intimidated by what was happening to them. The sight of four men, two of them with a bunch of gold teeth in their mouths, dressed in all black and wielding powerful firearms, had them frightened; terrified, in fact. They watched in silent fright as the intruders stood before them with their guns pointed at their heads.

"I'm a ask you one more time, nigga—where the stash?" Dirty Red asked the man calmly.

"Shit's been sold." The man said as he stared Dirty Red in the eyes.

Dirty Red, realizing the man was not going to give up the information easily, walked off. "Manny! Shoot that nigga right there!" He said as he pointed to one of the black men.

The man begged for his life in vain as Manny aimed the gun at his head and shot him multiple times with his calico automatic. The man's lifeless body lunged over onto his counterpart. After seeing what happened to his older brother, the second man immediately began to tell the boys where the dope was located in order to have his life spared. "It's in the bathroom behind the mirror over the sink! Pull the mirror out over the sink in the master bedroom!" The frightened young man yelled hysterically.

"You stupid mutherfucka! Now we all dead!" The olive-toned man yelled to the lone remaining black male as Dirty Red, Manny, and Jermaine rushed the two men into the master

bedroom.

Once inside the master bedroom, Dirty Red and Manny headed towards the bathroom to check behind the mirror as Jermaine pushed both men face down on the bed and held his gun on them. Oscar meanwhile, had remained in the living room with the female. After Dirty Red and Manny collected the dope, which was eighteen kilograms of cocaine neatly packaged in tightly wrapped plastic, and bagged up a couple of Cartier watches and gold bracelets they'd found inside a jewelry box on the dresser top, they turned back to the two men who lay face down on the mattress.

Dirty Red looked at Jermaine and nodded his head towards the two men who lay on the bed. "Waste one." He said through his ski mask.

The two men realized they were about to be killed. They told the boys they got what they came for and there wasn't a need to kill them. They promised not to tell and they even offered to leave Memphis. It didn't make a difference whether they stayed in Memphis or not, however; the boys weren't from Tennessee anyway. Jermaine stood at the foot of the bed and aimed his .45 caliber. Just then, Manny told him to hold up a second.

"Y'all bitches turn over!" Manny yelled aloud to the two men.

"Come on, amigo. There's no need to do this murder. You've gotten what you come for." The olive toned man said in a calm manner as he rolled onto his back. He then cursed the boys and spat at them when he realized no plea would spare his life. "I die like a man tonight!" He said as he stared Jermaine square in the eyes. "Send me on my way, nigger!" He yelled aloud.

"Jermaine! Handle ya' business!" Dirty Red hissed through his mask.

Jermaine walked up to the bed, pointed his gun at the olive-toned man and fired four rounds, the bullets shattering the top of the man's skull and leaving blood and brain matter splattered across the headboard and the wall behind the bed.

The second man tried to dodge the bullets coming from Dirty Red's Mac-11, but his body was riddled with at least twelve rounds of .9mm hollow tips. He died on the floor in between the bed and the dresser.

The boys then walked back into the living room where they saw Oscar raping the female. They could see the fear in the woman's eyes as she pretended to enjoy what was happening to her. She had been cooperative with Oscar the whole time. To save her life, she willingly offered herself to him. As she knelt on her hands and knees, she cried in silence, having been reduced to a mere sex object by a total stranger who now held complete sway over her life. The woman had a sexy body, and from the sounds emanating from Oscar's mouth coupled with the amount of force and speed that he drove into the young woman, she must have had some good pussy.

"Let's be out." Manny said as he started for the door.

Oscar pushed the woman off his dick and she fell onto her stomach and turned over onto her back. When she did, Dirty Red caught full sight of the sweet young thing Oscar had taken advantage of. Her pink nipples were rock hard and stood out about a half inch, she had smooth and toned, creamy thighs, pert titties and one of the prettiest pussies a man could lay eyes on. Dirty Red had to admit that she was a fine mutherfucka, but the rule was to leave no witnesses.

"Do the bitch so we can be the fuck out." Dirty Red told Oscar as he, Manny and Jermaine started towards the door.

"Look at me you sexy bitch you! I said look at me, mutherfucka!" Oscar yelled as he pointed his gun at the woman.

The woman laid back and spread her legs and called out to Dirty Red. "Papi! Papi," she said with tears in her eyes and her legs spread wide open. "Take turns on me, Papi," she requested. "You can, you can do anything you want to do to me, just don't kill me! Please, Papi! Don't make him kill me!"

All Dirty Red could do was shake his head in utter shame and

regret. He'd been here once before the night he and Oscar killed Sebas and the night Lil Earl got shot and he knew what had to be done. Dirty Red eyed the woman for several seconds, she was very much a pretty woman, innocent-looking, too, but she was in the game, or at the very least ran with some big time drug dealers that pushed a lot of weight. The bottom line was that there would be eighteen kilograms of cocaine missing and three people dead. There was no way on Earth this woman wasn't going to tell what all she knew and had seen. As innocent as she looked, and no matter how much she pleaded for her life, and all the pussy that she was willing to give away, it still could not stop what had to be done.

Dirty Red made a trigger motion towards Oscar with his right hand and walked off. Oscar turned and aimed his gun at the woman's head as she continued begging for her life while staring Oscar in the eyes. She began panting heavily and pleading loudly, her voice reaching a crescendo. "Papi, please! Please! Don't kill—" The woman's screaming voice was quickly silenced when Oscar fired two shots from a .357 magnum into her skull. Blood began to seep into the carpet from her cranium as she lay on her side, her body naked and limp.

In less than five minutes, the boys had made off with eighteen kilos, expensive watches, and fancy bracelets. They quickly paid off Sherman, handed over the guns for him to dispose of, and headed back to the Big Easy with enough cocaine to get them through the drought and move them up even further in the food chain.

CHAPTER TEN

HOW REAL NIGGAS DO

The boys had made it back to New Orleans early Friday morning and they were now sitting at the dining room table in the dope house preparing to repackage sixteen kilograms of cocaine while giving a few details about the Memphis job to Jason and Lamont. With the amount of cocaine they now had in their possession, the boys were indeed among the top-level dealers in the Crescent City.

Katrina was so worried about Manny and the boys that she had stayed home from school and left *Par 6* with Jason and Lamont to await their return. She was so relieved to see Oscar's Grand Prix pull up in front of the dope house early Friday morning. She ran out and greeted them all with a tight hug and followed them inside, happy they were all safe. When the boys began setting up scales and pulling out kilograms of cocaine inside the dining room, Katrina left them alone to handle their business. She was in the front bedroom looking out of the window watching what was going on outside, bobbing her head to Juvenile's song *Ha* when she saw Haywood and Cedric pull up in front of the house in a white '99 two-door Cadillac short. Katrina walked into the dining room and said, "Haywood and Cedric just pulled up."

95

"That bitch ass nigga Rico with 'em?" Dirty Red asked as the boys all grabbed a firearm and walked into the living room.

"No they by they self," Katrina replied as she ran into the den and locked the door at Manny's request.

"Jason, swing the door open, whoaday." Oscar commanded as he, Manny, Dirty Red, Lamont, and Jermaine stood in the middle of the living room clutching their weapons.

Jason swung the door open just as Cedric was about to knock. "Whoa, whoa, niggas! Don't shoot, mutherfuckas!" Cedric said as he stepped back.

"What up, dog?" Dirty Red asked Cedric, never lowering his Mac-10.

"Say, brer, you ain't gone let a nigga in?"

"I can't do that, Ced."

"What! Man, I help build this shit with y'all niggas and that's how you gone play me, Dirty Red?"

"Ain't nobody playin'! You knew the rules, nigga, and ya' broke 'em! Who the fuck told you ta' start fuckin' around uptown? Ya' got busted fucking with them niggas and now ya' wanna show up 'round here and make shit hot for us? Fuck that! You ask Rico and the resta' them 'morphadite mutherfuckas that's uptown to put ya' back on ya' feet! We through with ya' over this way, ya' dig?"

"That's how it is, brer?" Cedric asked as he rubbed both his hands together.

"Off top. Take Haywood with ya' and y'all two niggas stay the fuck from 'round this set right here. Feel me?" Dirty Red replied as the rest of the crew listened to what was transpiring.

Dirty Red figured that Cedric and Haywood were trying to play both sides of the coin. They were working for Rico, a big-timer from the Tenth Ward, while still trying to slang cocaine with the crew downtown. Dirty Red wasn't too concerned about Haywood, he wasn't a part of the crew, but when Cedric

went behind his back and then lied about it, he could no longer be trusted. To Dirty Red, it was easier to just let Cedric be on his own. Besides, he didn't want people from uptown trying to gain a foothold anywhere near his operation. That could get ugly since the boys weren't going to allow anybody, especially from uptown, to come downtown to set up shop in the Desire Project. Hoping to prevent a bloody feud, Dirty Red simply nipped that in the bud. Someone was bound to try it one day, sooner than later. The crew sent Cedric and Haywood on their way, finished bagging their cocaine, and opened shop for the weekend.

The boys had managed to sell four kilos over the weekend, mostly in twenty and fifty dollar pieces of crack cocaine and powder bags of quarter ounces, although Dirty Red did sell about sixty-four rocked up ounces at nine-hundred dollars a pop. The Monday following their big weekend, the crew was about halfway through their fifth kilo. It was early in the morning as Dirty Red sat in the window watching the elementary, middle, and high school children make their way to classes. Tanaka and Alicia had stopped by for Katrina, as she had spent the weekend at Tanaka's house but had returned to the dope house early that morning to change into her uniform. When the girls came out of the house without Katrina, Manny, who was in the front yard, asked what happened.

"Oh, she say Rico coming by ta' bring her ta' school today." Tanaka remarked.

"Fuck that shit! Make that buster ass nigga bring y'all too!" Manny said.

"Yeah, I know, ha?" Tanaka asked as she nodded her head in agreement.

None of the boys, Tanaka, or Alicia liked Rico. Katrina had met him in August of '98, while she was at the Esplanade Mall with Tanaka and Alicia. That day, Rico paid for Katrina's outfits and had taken her, Tanaka and Alicia to a nearby Red Lobster for dinner. Rico had spent over twenty-five hundred dollars that day and it was just the first time he'd ever met

Katrina and her two friends. He thought he was impressing Katrina, but he didn't know that she resided in a mini mansion with some of the biggest drug dealers in the city.

What Rico was doing did not impress Katrina. She had seen bigger and better. In Katrina's eyes, the 5'11", light-skinned twenty-two year-old, curly-haired Dominican was nothing more than a trick daddy. Everybody knew Katrina was playing Rico for his money—except Rico. He would come around the dope house in his metallic purple '99 Jaguar on 17" Giovanni rims with his music blaring and just sit there as if he was the shit. The only thing keeping Rico alive was the fact that he had a Colombian kingpin from Houston, Texas supplying him his cocaine.

Nobody knew exactly what the Colombians would do if something happened to Rico; so rather than take a chance on warring with a drug cartel, the boys let Rico stunt whenever he came around the house, because they knew each and every time, Kay Kay would expose him for the "buster ass nigga", as Manny was often heard quoting, that he truly was. This morning would be no different.

When Rico pulled up, he parked across the street from the dope house. He was playing *Balls and My Word,* an old school rap by the rapper Scarface, loudly as he stepped out of his car, walked over to the fence, and hollered out to Manny, who was under the window talking to Dirty Red, to call Katrina.

"Hold up, player. I'm a get her for ya'," Dirty Red remarked.

Dirty Red got up from his wooden chair and walked to the den where Katrina was with Jason. He turned the knob but the door was locked. He put his ear to the door, and over the music blaring from Rico's Jaguar, he could hear Katrina moaning Jason's name. He realized the two were fucking and he chuckled slightly and went back and sat in the window. Dirty Red told Manny what was going on and Manny started to laugh as well. Dirty Red then told Rico that Katrina was coming—his statement having a double and literal meaning that went unbeknownst to Rico. The Dominican went back and sat in his car as Manny dialed Jason's number on the cell

phone. Jason answered and Manny told him Rico was outside waiting on Katrina.

"That bitch gone have ta' wait 'til I'm through with her, dog." Jason said in a slow-pitched voice before he hung up the cell phone.

Manny burst into laughter and walked to the back of the dope house.

Five minutes later, Katrina lay under Jason's frame, breathing hard, as she had just experienced another intense orgasm brought on by her favorite lover. She hopped up quickly when Jason told her that Rico was outside waiting on her. She rushed into the bathroom, washed herself, sprayed perfume on her body, and slid her panties back on underneath her skirt. The two then laughed to themselves as they kissed passionately in the bathroom.

"One mo' time! Come on!" Jason said as he hugged Katrina tightly and then palmed her ass cheeks.

"No boy, I gotta go! I don't need him ta' get suspicious, Jay!"

"Fuck that nigga, brer! You know you for the crew! Shit, you with me more than you with that ole bitch ass nigga!" Jason replied, still copping feels on Katrina as he held her close.

"I know! That's why I gotta go so he won't figure out what's goin' on!" Katrina said as she tried to pry away from Jason's grip.

Jason grabbed Katrina around her small waist, pulled her close to him, and shoved his tongue down her throat hard. She moaned into his mouth and whispered that Dana, Jason's ole lady, and her friend, would be over in a little while.

"We got time for one mo'." Jason lamented as he picked Katrina up and sat her on the sink. He slid Katrina's panties to the side and slowly began entering her once more. The two each let out a moan of ecstasy as Jason began to thrust hard and fast.

Jason was thrusting into Katrina with so much force, and the

pleasure was so intense, she had snatched the towel racks that she was holding onto completely out of the wall. She dropped the towel racks and gripped Jason's back and held on for the ride as the two humped one another until Jason withdrew and shot semen onto Katrina's uniform shirt and inner thighs. They laughed at each other, panting and sweating, their faces tightly pressed together. Katrina had to take a complete shower and change entirely before presenting herself to Rico, who was getting more and more impatient.

Katrina was out of the house in fifteen minutes. She tapped Tanaka on the shoulder and told the girls it was time to go. As she walked out of the yard, Katrina looked over at Dirty Red, who was hanging out the window laughing uncontrollably right along with Manny, Oscar, Lamont, and Jermaine, all of whom had by now made their way back to the front yard, having been clued in along with Tanaka and Alicia about the things going on inside the dope house.

Everybody knew what was up now. Tanaka and Alicia just shook their heads. Tanaka told Katrina as they walked towards Rico's car that she did not believe it at first, but now she and Alicia both new that Rico was indeed a damned fool. He sat in his car the entire time waiting, while his so-called girlfriend was inside getting repeatedly fucked by a young hustler that could have the pussy anyway, anyhow, and anytime he wanted to have it. The three girls all hopped into the Jaguar sniggling as Katrina kissed Rico on the cheek. He blushed and pulled off slowly thinking he was the shit because he had one of the finest mutherfuckas the city of New Orleans had to offer.

"Damned fool!" Tanaka and Alicia thought to themselves from the backseat of Rico's ride.

Tuesday morning had rolled around and the boys couldn't wait to see what would transpire when Rico showed up. They were prepared for another good laugh until Rico pulled up into the driveway where Dirty Red normally parked his Mercedes. He had loaned his Benz to Lamont, who'd driven to Covington, Louisiana Monday night to visit his sick aunt. When Rico pulled into the driveway, Dirty Red leaned out the window and

said calmly, "Say Ree, do me a favor and park your ride on the other side of the street for me, my nig."

Rico thought that the boys were soft because they had been letting him come from uptown and roll up onto their set and pull one of their 'hoes', Katrina. The Dominican had it wrong, however; and on this morning he would cross the line. Dirty Red wasn't even paying Rico any attention until he stepped onto the sidewalk and said loudly, "Fuck you, ole bitch ass nigga! You might run these hoe ass niggas 'round here, but to me you ain't shit!"

Dirty Red jumped out of his chair, grabbed Manny's .357 magnum off the bed, and ran towards the front door. Katrina, dressed in her school uniform and holding her backpack, tried to stop him in the living room, but Dirty Red easily pushed her out of the way and made his way out the front door and down the stairs towards Rico.

The Dominican ran back towards his car, but Jermaine clothes-lined him, knocking him to the ground. Rico was then immediately surrounded by Manny, Oscar, Dirty Red, and Jermaine as Jason stood on the porch holding Katrina, preventing her from running down the stairs. She screamed at the top of her lungs for the boys not to hurt Rico as school children began to gather in the street in front of the dope house to see what was happening.

Manny went and searched Rico's Jaguar and found a loaded . 45 caliber handgun. "Oh, you was tryna shoot somebody, bitch?" He asked in dismay.

"Say Manny, brer, you know that ain't for me and you, dog. I'm just comin' for my girl, brer." Rico replied as he picked himself up from the grass.

"Your girl? Nigga, you come 'round here every other day stuntin' and shit! What you think we hoes or somethin' out the Desire?" Manny asked as he got in Rico's face.

"Nahh, brer, it ain't like that!"

Just then, Rico was struck in the head by Dirty Red with the .

357 magnum that he was holding. He fell back to the ground and the boys immediately began stomping and kicking him. School kids began laughing aloud at Rico as they stood in the street watching him get beat down.

Katrina broke free of Jason's grip and ran down the stairs, and pushed all the boys away from Rico. "Ben, don't kill 'em! He not worth it, brer! Let 'em go, man!" She yelled.

"I ain't gone kill 'em! But that bitch ain't welcome back 'round this mutherfucka no mo' ya' heard me?" Dirty Red said as he dapped his boys.

Katrina pulled Rico up from the ground and said, "Rico, just go on brer! I'm a talk to ya' later! Just go 'head before they change they mind," she insisted as she shoved Rico towards his car.

"I be back, mutherfuckas!" Rico said as he wobbled into the driver's seat of his Jaguar.

The boys rushed Rico again, but Katrina hurriedly slammed his door and told him to leave. Rico pulled off, but not before Dirty Red ran up to his window and jabbed him in the face again. The school kids scattered onto the sidewalks as Rico sped down the block with a busted forehead, a bloody mouth and a bruised ego. The boys sat on the porch all day, waiting with loaded AK-47's and AR-15 rifles. They waited for Rico to show up, but he never did.

Katrina called Rico at the corner store he owned as night fell, but Haywood answered the phone instead. She told Haywood that the boys had jumped Rico and Haywood replied by telling her that he heard what happened, but Rico had never come back to the corner store, let alone uptown.

"Rico in love with ya', Kay Kay. You cool with me." Haywood then told Katrina. "I ain't got nothing to do with whatever go down, either. I know Manny 'nem from back in the day. Them was my boys once upon a time. Shit different now, though. I'm uptown, they downtown, whatever happen, happen, ya' dig?" Haywood said.

Katrina relayed what Haywood had told her to Oscar, who was sitting beside her on the front porch.

"Yeah? Let them niggas come," remarked Oscar as he sipped a quart of beer. "Let 'em come. And we gone show 'em how real niggas do."

CHAPTER ELEVEN

HOW I MET MY OLE LADY

On the Saturday following the fight with Rico, the boys were sitting in the dining room of *Par 6* playing spades, sipping cognac, smoking blunts, and discussing a trip they had planned to take to Daytona Beach for spring break. Manny had seen a commercial on MTV and thought it would be cool for the crew to take a vacation and just kick back and relax. The boys were relaying stories about the different females they had slept with and they all grew quiet as Jason told the boys how he had slept with Dana Shelby, the high-yellow-skinned 5' 6", one-hundred and forty-five pound, big booty stallion with straight-pressed shiny black hair that hung down to her waist.

Dana was a mixed Puerto Rican. Her mother, who was Black, had met her father, a Puerto Rican, while attending the University of Miami. Dana came from an intact, upper middle-class family. Her mother and father were both medical professionals who ran a small health clinic and pharmacy in the Ninth Ward. They wanted Dana to be a part of the community, so they allowed their daughter to attend Carver High School instead of a private academy. She met Jason there after he dropped Katrina off one morning.

It had taken Jason nearly a year to get Dana from under the

watchful eyes of her mother and father. It wasn't too long after Jason had bought his Cadillac, in September of '98 that the two were in the backseat of Jason's ride, listening to a song off R&B singer's Rome CD titled *I Belong to You*. It could have been the music, the picturesque waves from the lake, or a combination of both, coupled with the fact that Dana had been kept in the house for so long, that when she finally got out, she went buck wild.

Since it was late at night, and she and Jason were the only two out on the Lakefront, Dana let herself go. She gave Jason head that night in the backseat of his Caddy, slowly humming the lyrics to one of Rome's songs titled, *I Wanna Be Down*. She asked Jason to eat her out a while later, but he told her no. When Dana revealed her sweet-smelling, clean-shaven, tan-colored virgin pussy to Jason, however, and told him he could have it anyway he wanted as long as he licked it, he couldn't resist. Jason said he was nervous at first, having never gone down on a female, but to his surprise and delight, Dana smelled and tasted good down there. He ate her to orgasm, then took Dana's virginity, and gave the then seventeen year-old virgin the fucking of her life, even though it was only her first time.

The music, the pretty car, and the handsome young gangster with money was all too real for Dana; she had fallen in love with Jason that very night on the lake when he had taken her virginity in the back of his Cadillac. Jason was fond of Dana as well; but he had his suspicions. He mentioned what happened between him and Dana to Katrina a few days after the event and told her that he knew Dana was playing the role.

"How could she be so freaky to say it was her first time?" Jason asked.

"Boy, is you crazy?" Katrina exclaimed as the two sat inside the living room of *Par 6*. "Jay, you know I be knowing! Dana ain't playing the role, man! You got her out the house. You got that big, pretty ass car. And you are a handsome nigga, a smooth talker, and a damn good lover if I do say so myself!"

Katrina had encouraged Jason to talk to Dana. The two made

a good couple in her eyes. Katrina was involved with Rico, but she and Jason would still hook up every chance they got.

"Huhh, brer," snapped Manny. "That's some player-type shit right there, nigga!" He concluded as he dapped Jason off.

"That is a bad bitch you got there, boy," remarked Dirty Red between sips of cognac.

Dana's parents had disapproved of her relationship with Jason at its inception; but since their daughter was now eighteen years-of age, they had to let her make her own decisions. They had cut off all financial assistance to her, however; and had even put Dana out of their home. The crew welcomed her into *Par 6*, and Jason took very good care of the sweet young thing. Dana's love for Jason was deep and unconditional. She knew Jason sold drugs, but to the optimistic Dana Shelby that really didn't matter. She actually saw a future for herself and Jason. When her parents realized she was not going to give Jason up, they allowed Dana to move back into their home, even though she would now spend most of her nights at *Par 6* with Jason and the crew. She would, however, call her parents everyday she was there to let them know she was okay. She kept her grades up and was in the running to graduate as the class valedictorian despite being somewhat of a disappointment to her parents.

Jermaine had met Kimberly Pollard at a block party in the Seventh Ward one Super Sunday in July of '98. Super Sunday was a day when many of the city's second-line jazz bands would gather in different wards and neighborhoods throughout the city along with members of different social clubs dressed up in Indian garb.

Good food, good music and second-line dancing would be the order of the day on Super Sunday. Orleanians would be out bar-b-cueing, eating seafood, drinking cold beer, and dancing in the streets. On Super Sunday, for a few hours, the outside world did not exist in New Orleans. Super Sunday was like one big family reunion for the entire city. People would see others that they had not seen in months or years; everyone would be in a festive mood. The gangsters would be out as

well, scoping some of the most beautiful women the south had to offer. Beautiful women of all shapes, colors, mixtures of races, and sizes abounded throughout the city.

Kimberly Pollard, a dark-chocolate complexioned, 5' slim, one-hundred and twenty-five pound nineteen year-old who often wore her black hair trimmed with brown highlights in finger waves in the front with a French twist in the back, was no different. She spotted Jermaine through the crowd leaning up against Jason's Cadillac. Dressed in a pair of navy blue Roc-A-Wear jeans with a white t-shirt and a pair of white Kenneth Cole casual shoes, the 5' 10" Kevin Garnett look-a-like had indeed caught her eye amidst all the ballers and players that lined the streets of Claiborne Avenue and walking the open field of Hunter's Park that day. She walked up to Jermaine and asked him if he was leaning against his own pretty car.

"Nahh, this my homeboy car," Jermaine responded as he pointed to Jason, who was under the Interstate-10 highway bridge with Dana and Oscar holding down the bar-b-cue grill.

Kim looked over towards Jason and saw him in his black Girbaud jean shorts, his three-hundred dollar white and black Howie Long throwback jersey and black "soldier" Reebok tennis shoes. She also noticed Jason's watch glimmering in the summer sun, along with his diamond bracelet. She admired Dana's white and black Gucci dress and matching white sandals, as well as her diamond wristwatch, and diamond studded earrings that were sparkling in the afternoon sun.

"All y'all together?" Kimberly asked as she eyed Dirty Red, who was sitting in his Mercedes, parked behind Jason's caddy talking to Anastasia, who had flown into the city, as she often did, to visit Dirty Red.

Ben Holland's first love and childhood friend had moved to Seattle to stay with her mom when she was released from prison. Anastasia's dream had come true. She was now a senior in college and working towards a degree in Mass Communications from Seattle University.

Kim then glanced over at Oscar's Grand Prix parked behind Dirty Red's Mercedes. JoAnne, Oscar's ole lady, was perched in the front seat bumping *Diamonds and Wood*, a rap song off the rap group UGK's album *Ridin' Dirty*. JoAnne was rolling a blunt as she rocked back and forth to the bass that permeated from Oscar's stereo. The 5' 11" black-skinned, slender, knock-kneed twenty-nine year-old with burgundy braids had been with Oscar for over four years. JoAnne Clemmons was the epitome of a gangster's bitch: never asking too many questions, knowing when to keep silent, but flip by the mouth at the same time, and always having her man's back at all times—right or wrong.

"Them all my peeps right there. Enough about them, though, who you be?" Jermaine asked, breaking the brief moment of silence.

"I be Kim from the Seventeenth Ward." Kim answered with a bright smile.

The two began conversing and had exchanged phone numbers that day. Kim locked Jermaine's number in her cell phone and the two hung out with the crew the rest of the afternoon. She had met the rest of the crew and they had even shared crawfish, shrimp and bar-b-cue with her. Dana complemented Kim on her outfit and Kim thanked her. Kim, however, thought Dana was being facetious since Dana was wearing Gucci and she had on an outfit purchased from Simply 6. Kim glued herself to Jermaine after being introduced to his friends, being careful not to let any other female push up on her future man. She knew she had a baller, and she wasn't about to let him go.

Jermaine had finished his story and the boys began teasing him as they sat at the table playing spades and just kicking back. It had been eight months since Jermaine had met Kim and the boys did not know for sure if he had sex with her as of yet. When Oscar posed the question, Jermaine told the crew that he had sex with Kim a few times, but each time he did so, it was like pulling teeth.

"I damn near have ta' rape that bitch ta' get a piece of pussy!"

Jermaine remarked frustratedly.

"What's wrong with that?" Oscar asked with a smirk on his face as he dealt out the next hand of spades.

"You did what I said, Jermaine, dog?" Manny asked.

"Man, that shit you keep stressin' don't work!" Lamont exclaimed to Manny as he threw out the ace of clubs.

"Like the fuck it don't! He just ain't do it right!" Manny replied.

Manny had decided to help Jermaine really wrap Kim up and make her his ole lady for good. He had been telling Jermaine the secrets to getting pussy and making women fall head over heels for you in the city of New Orleans—in his opinion. He called it "The Pussy Package"—a three piece, spicy, white chicken dinner with red beans and rice from Popeye's chicken, a large house special daiquiri with an extra shot of rum, and a dime bag of weed.

"Jermaine, you tried that shit Manny talkin' 'bout?" Dirty Red asked as he sipped his cognac while tapping Oscar on the leg and watching the hand unfold as he sniggled.

"Yeah, I tried that shit he recommended." Jermaine responded as he puffed on a blunt and then sipped his cognac

"What happened," asked Oscar, as he, too, began to sniggle along with Dirty Red.

Jermaine cocked his head to the side and looked at Manny and said, "That stupid shit don't work, nigga!"

The boys all burst into laughter.

"Hold up!" Manny yelled over the laughter. "Hold up! He ain't do it right!"

"Man," remarked Oscar, "a real bitch ain't going for that shit, nigga! A three piece from Popeye's, and a bagga' weed? That's G-Fab like a mutherfucka!"

"No it ain't! The shit work! How you think I got Shawonda?

That big-fine dark-skinned ass mutherfucka?"

"'Cause she not a real bitch and she G-Fab!" Jason responded as the boys burst into laughter once again.

"What tha' fuck y'all think we is? We all G-Fab 'round this bitch!" Manny stated loud and proud.

"You right," responded Dirty Red. "But it's good ta' have a little class every now and then, ya' dig?"

Manny gave two thumbs down and said, "Fuck class! Them hoes just wanna ride, get they belly full, get high and fuck. Period! They satisfied with a good dinner, a good drink, and a bagga' weed!"

"A good dinner is like Houston's, or Copeland's, man. Something like that, ya' dig? That's why your plan don't work —'cause you cheap." Lamont stated.

"Yeah that nigga cheap," added Dirty Red. "You right about Copeland's, L-Dog. That's a good dinner, and a good drink is like a' eight-hundred dollar bottle of wine or some shit. You know what I'm sayin', Jay?"

"Hell, yeah!" Jason answered. "And good weed is like this honey-dipped blunt I'm 'bouta blaze up right here, ya' heard me?" He asked aloud.

Just then, Katrina, having just awakened a few minutes ago from a long nap, walked down the stairs into the den. She spoke to the boys as she walked through the dining room and into the kitchen where she opened the refrigerator door to try and find something to eat.

"Say, Kay Kay, what's your idea of a night on tha' town?" Oscar asked.

Katrina rose up from the refrigerator and thought briefly as she eyed Oscar and wondered why he asked her this particular question. "A night on the town, Oscar? Shit. I guess a well-done steak, some wine and top it off with a li'l bit of dancing in the French Quarters, brer."

"See? That's a lady with class." Jason replied as he dealt out another hand of spades.

Katrina had caught the latter part of the boys' conversation as she descended the stairs. Now, fully realizing what the boys were discussing, she quickly gave another viewpoint concerning the matter. "On the other hand, though, I could easily go for a three piece spicy with red beans and rice and a daiquiri and a fat ass sack of weed right about now. That sound like a lotta' fun, Manny dog."

"I told ya', nigga! I told y'all!" Manny yelled as he jumped up from his seat.

The boys all stood up and remarked that Katrina didn't count.

"She seen both sides of tha' game, nigga! She know what's up!" Oscar yelled over Manny's taunts.

"Every woman got it in 'em, Oscar. It's a time to be classy, and a time ta' be nasty, ya' feel me?" Katrina remarked.

"Yeah, but them hoes this nigga right here deal with," Lamont said as he pointed to Manny, "them hoes don't have no class. Give them hoes a bagga' Lay's potato chips, a pig lip and a pineapple Big Shot soda and they gone be straight for the whole day! You won't hear a peep out them bitches! Nata!"

"I tell ya' what, mutherfuckas," Manny said as he threw on his New York Yankees baseball jersey over his white silk wife-beater and placed his white fur safari Kangol cap over his dreadlocks and smiled, revealing his twelve gold teeth, "I'm on my way ta' get tha' pussy package—and I guarantee I bust nuts all over that hoe—ta' night mutherfuckas! Y'all spend a couple of G's on them hoes! I drop fitty on them bitches and I'm good!"

The boys laughed aloud and talked for a few more minutes before they all dapped Manny off. Manny then hugged and kissed Katrina good-bye on the forehead and headed for the elevator.

"Don't forget we back at the shop Monday, nigga," yelled

Dirty Red, who by now was half-drunk off the cognac and buzzing from the blunt Jason had passed around. The rest of the boys were feeling much the same as well.

"I know, homeboy. I be there at six in tha' mornin' ya' heard me?" Manny said, just before the elevator closed to take him down to the garage to his Harley Davidson F-150 pick-up.

Dirty Red watched the monitor in the kitchen as Manny rode off from *Par 6*. He then reset all the alarms and the crew all turned in that night.

Katrina had Dirty Red drop her off in the Ninth Ward by Tanaka the following day. He then returned home to *Par 6* where he and the rest of the boys spent the remainder of the day inside watching NBA basketball and playing Resident Evil and Madden on PlayStation while getting high and sipping liquor.

CHAPTER TWELVE

NOT MY DOG

It was almost eight 'o' clock Monday morning following the weekend spent at *Par 6* and Dirty Red was growing worried about Manny because he was running almost two hours late. He called out to Oscar and asked him if he had heard from Manny.

"Not since Saturday, brer."

"*Fuck this nigga at?*" Dirty Red thought to himself before he spoke aloud, "Eh, take Jason with ya' and ride uptown on Martin Luther King and get that nigga from by Shawonda, brer."

Dirty Red and the boys knew whenever Manny hooked up with Shawonda, his timing would become highly unpredictable; but if he was running late, Manny would always call. On this day, however, Manny had failed to make contact with his crew. This never-before-seen occurrence with Manny worried Dirty Red so much that it had prompted the gangster to send two of his boys to go and check on Manny and make sure he was okay.

"That nigga better not be drunk," Jason stated to Dirty Red as

he walked towards the front gate. "Dana got a scholarship from Xavier University and we going out to celebrate. I ain't working that nigga shift today."

Oscar and Jason hopped into Jason's Cadillac and rode into the Tenth Ward and turned onto Martin Luther King Boulevard, or MLK for short, where Shawonda resided. Jason parked across the street from Shawonda's stoop, his Cadillac now facing the on-coming traffic, but out of the on-coming vehicles' right-of-way.

The two gangsters slowly exited the vehicle and scanned the neighborhood, which consisted of a four-lane street that only used two lanes as both outside lanes were used by residents to park either in front of the closely-built wooden shotgun house that they rented or owned, or several houses down from their place of residence. MLK was lined with thick oak trees that shaded a good portion of the boulevard. The close-built wooden shotgun houses also had narrow gangways on either side of the homes.

Oscar and Jason continued scanning their surroundings. School children were walking in groups of three or more on either side of the street. Some adults were out, mainly young mothers who were watching the kids walk to the elementary and middle schools two blocks down from where Shawonda's house was located. Oscar and Jason knew they were on someone else's stomping ground. They also knew that gangsters from the Ninth Ward weren't particularly welcomed into the Tenth Ward with open arms. Cocked pistols maybe; but never with open arms. Adversaries, ranging from killers-for-hire to heroin-addicted 'jack-artists' and low-ranking gangsters looking to earn stripes lurked about in the Tenth Ward like vultures circling a corpse.

Oscar made sure his white t-shirt concealed his nine millimeter as he stood on the sidewalk and eyed Manny's F-150, which was parked several houses down across the street on the same side as Shawonda's house.

Jason had just answered a cell phone call from Dana as he and Oscar jogged across the street, headed towards Shawonda's

stoop.

"We still on for tonight?" Jason asked Dana over the phone as he stepped onto the sidewalk and waited for Oscar to go and knock on Shawonda's door and wake Manny up from what the two of them believed was Manny's normal routine whenever he was with Shawonda, which was to run late.

Oscar took one long stride and jumped onto the top stair of Shawonda's low-lying stoop and knocked on the door and waited for a minute. When he got no response, Oscar knocked again and waited another minute; but he never got an answer. Oscar had seen Manny's truck parked several doors down so he knew Manny was inside.

"They probably walked to the store on the corner." Jason stated as he hung up the phone with Dana.

"Not with the door unlocked." Oscar responded lowly as he began to get anxious.

Oscar had decided to try the doorknob when neither Manny nor Shawonda answered his knocks and discovered that the front door had been left unlocked. Him and Jason pulled out their handguns, stood in the threshold, and yelled out into the home one last time for Manny, who never responded, before they cautiously entered the premises.

"Eh yo', Manny! Get off the pussy nigga! Time ta' go to work homeboy," Oscar yelled loudly with a smile on his face as he walked into the living room. "Manny!" He yelled again, this time a lot louder without smiling.

There was no answer. The house was dead silent.

Oscar and Jason stared at one another, the expressions on their faces could best be described like that of two soldiers who'd stumbled upon a battle that had taken place during a time previous to their arrival. They took a defensive mode, both gangsters cocking their .9mm Berettas as they began looking around for signs of a struggle.

Oscar and Jason had been to Shawonda's house on several

different occasions and the place had always been immaculately kept, just as it was on this day.

Noticing that nothing was out of place, Oscar and Jason walked slowly through the living room, and with guns pointed forward, they slowly entered the first bedroom and saw that it was empty. They then crept a little ways down the hall to the point where it made an L-turn. When they made the left turn, they paused at the foot of the hallway as they both had simultaneously discovered a trail of blood leading from the bathroom on their immediate left, to the bedroom down the hall, which was on their right.

"What the fuck happened here," asked Jason.

"I don't know, Jay-dog." Oscar replied in a low tone as the two approached the bedroom.

When Oscar and Jason reached the second bedroom, they found Manny lying face up with his head split open by what appeared to be gunshot wounds. His brains lay on the carpet and flies had begun to nest on the brain matter that had spilled from his open cranium.

Twenty-six-year-old Shawonda lay face down next to Manny with a large puddle of blood surrounding her entire head. The boys could see a large bullet hole in the back of her skull.

Jason backed out of the room and knelt down on one knee against the hallway wall opposite the bedroom as he shook his head and began to weep over the carnage his eyes had just gazed upon.

Oscar yelled Manny's name aloud and took a knee in between the two bodies as he scattered the flies away from the lifeless corpses of his deceased childhood friend and his dead girlfriend.

"Manny." Oscar said lowly as he rocked back and forth, watching tears drop down onto his chrome .9mm. "Not my dog." He whispered through tears. "Not my fuckin' dog!" He stated in disbelief.

Oscar and Jason stared at the two dead bodies in complete, stunned, and utter silence for several minutes. Jason watched as Oscar cried openly, staring at Manny's lifeless corpse, all-the-while wishing Manny would wake up. Jason knew all-too-well, however, that Manny and Shawonda were no longer apart of his world. The boys left the house and Oscar called Swanson and Montgomery, the two cops the boys had on the payroll, and relayed the information to them as Jason inconspicuously merged with the traffic flow.

Swan quickly informed his clean-up crew and had them ready their equipment and head over to Shawonda's house. He also told them to be on standby for more work coming down the pipe as he knew things were about to heat up on the streets.

When Oscar and Jason arrived back at the dope house in the Ninth Ward and stepped out of Jason's Cadillac without Manny, Dirty Red, who was still sitting in the window, laughed, and began teasing Jason, asking him if Manny had gotten drunk again.

"Yea buddy, Dana gone be pissed today if you miss that date with her, nigga! What? Manny got drunk again, huh?"

Jason never acknowledged Dirty Red's taunt. He put his head down and took on a defeated stance as Oscar went and sat on the porch, still clutching his .9mm. Beretta as he bowed his head into his lap and began to heave.

Dirty Red quickly discerned that Oscar was distressed. He then looked at Jason, who in turn, stared back at him with bloodshot, watery eyes. Jason shook his head from side to side as he stared at Dirty Red before he turned away and looked down the street aimlessly.

Dirty Red had an idea concerning what was going down, but he did not want to believe, let alone accept it. He walked out onto the porch and asked Oscar where was Manny. Oscar rose up, and with a face full of tears, he told Dirty Red that he and Jason had found Manny and Shawonda shot up in her house.

Dirty Red leaned back against the wall. "So, so you tellin' me

—you tellin' me my boy dead?" He asked as he slowly began falling into a state of shock and dismay.

Oscar looked straight ahead and nodded as he scratched his head, trying to grasp hold to what was happening on this cool morning in March of '99.

Dirty Red, after witnessing Oscar give an affirmative nod to his question, leaned forward and rested his hands on top of his knees. Reality had finally set in. Manny's death had caught everyone off guard. Oscar, Jason and Dirty Red could not believe it; and when Oscar and Jason broke the news to Jermaine and Lamont, they, too, were shocked to tears. The boys closed shop and sat at the dining room table inside the dope house with their guns locked and loaded. They all had a drink of cognac and smoked two blunts as they discussed potential suspects and exactly where Manny went wrong. The boys were sitting on the porch still grieving and plotting when Katrina arrived home from school.

Katrina noticed that each of the boys was clutching an automatic rifle. AK-47's, AR-15's, and M-16's were all over the front porch. "Damn what the fuck y'all niggas up to now?" She asked in a playful manner as she entered the front yard and approached the stairs.

As Katrina grew nearer the front porch, she began noticing the somber looks upon the boys' faces. They weren't smiling in the least. Katrina also noticed that Dirty Red was not in the window where he would normally be around this time of day; instead, he sat on the porch with his crew. When she looked at Dirty Red, he looked the other way, placing his hands underneath his chin. The boys were completely silent, as if in a trance on this day. No loud music playing from either car, no cracking jokes, no weed smoking, no drinking. They weren't even slanging cocaine. Shop was closed.

"What happened," Katrina asked, beginning to get worried. "Where Manny?"

No one answered. The boys just looked around into space, not wanting to have to break the news to Katrina, who loved

Manny dearly.

"Jason? Where Manny? Lamont." Katrina said, as her eyes started to well up. She looked around for Manny's truck but didn't see it, and that was when she became unraveled. "Somebody tell me what the fuck going on!" Katrina yelled aloud as she turned back to face the boys.

Jason placed his AR-15 over his shoulder and walked off the porch, shaking his head as he headed towards the back yard. Lamont and Jermaine looked towards Oscar as Dirty Red jumped from the top of the stairs with his AK-47 in his right hand and began to walk slowly towards Katrina.

The distraught eighteen year-old began to shake her head and cry when Dirty Red approached and stood before her in the middle of the sidewalk and tried to explain.

"Baby girl, Manny, Manny, umm, he—"

"What?" Katrina asked as she cut Dirty Red's speech short as she did not want him to tell her what she felt in her heart. "He went ta' jail? The police caught 'em?" Katrina asked through her tears.

"I wish that's what I was about to say." Dirty Red responded as he bit his bottom lip and held back tears. Dirty Red knew Katrina was hoping for the best-case scenario at this point; and he could also tell she knew what was really going down.

Katrina, in turn, knew the boys would not be so downtrodden if Manny had simply gone to jail; but still, she was holding on to the hope that Manny was still alive. "Tell me the police caught 'em, Ben! Tell me that's what happened!" Katrina yelled as she pounded Dirty Red's chest and repeated her request. "Tell me that's what happened to Manny!"

Dirty Red shook his head slowly side-to-side as he stared sadly at Katrina. The heartbroken eighteen year-old let go of her school bag and pulled on her hair as she leaned forward into Dirty Red's chest and screamed aloud. Her arms fell to her side and her body grew limp as she hid her face in Dirty Red's chest and cried out Manny's name before fainting.

Dirty Red caught Katrina before she hit the ground and he and Oscar quickly took her inside and laid her on the sofa. Oscar went and grabbed a cold, wet towel to place on Katrina's forehead while Dirty Red called Ms. Joyce to see if she was home. When Ms. Joyce answered, Dirty Red told her he was headed out that way shortly.

Dirty Red told Jason, Lamont and Oscar to stay at the dope house with Katrina and keep a careful eye out for anything and anyone looking and acting suspicious. He then had Jermaine gather up extra guns in preparation to ride out to Ms. Joyce's home. He had no idea if the person or persons who killed Manny would come after them during their trip, and he wasn't taking any chances.

Katrina was awakened by Oscar shortly after Dirty Red and Jermaine left and she was feeling worse than before. She thought she was dreaming at first, but when she saw that things were the same around the dope house before she fainted, she began crying nonstop. She was devastated having lost Manny.

Dana, who had received the shocking news from Jason, understood that he would not take her out that night, so she came over, as well as Alicia and Tanaka. The three girls sat with Katrina as she cried and rested her head in Dana's lap.

Dirty Red, meanwhile, had to take the longest ride of his life. He had to ride out to Michoud to tell Ms. Joyce that her son, the young man he had known for ten years, the one who had taken him in and had become a brother to him, was now dead. He shed tears in silence the whole way, listening to *Life Goes On*, by Tupac.

"...Bury me smiling...with G's in my pocket...Have a party at my funeral let every rapper rock it...Let the hoes that I used to know...From way before...Kiss me from my head to toe..." Tupac's lyrics were really hitting home for Dirty Red on this day.

Ms. Joyce had trashed her house when Dirty Red got there and broke the news. She had broken all of her vases and had thrown all of her dishes out of her China cabinet onto the floor

and up against the wall. The forty-two year-old woman lay on her back in the middle of the living room staring up at the ceiling, her hands wrapped tightly around a picture of her son wearing his football uniform when he was just fifteen years old as her lips trembled.

"My baby," Ms. Joyce cried aloud. "Why, Lord Jesus? Why?" She asked repeatedly.

Dirty Red and Jermaine helped Ms. Joyce up from the floor and she sat down on the sofa and listened to what Dirty Red knew about Manny's murder. He mentioned to Ms. Joyce that Manny was found naked, dead on the floor. "Look like he got caught off guard, Miss Joyce." Dirty Red remarked.

Ms. Joyce just stared at the floor. "You know," she said as tears fell upon the carpet, "his father always said Manny was strong, 'don't worry, he would be hard to kill', is what he would tell me. I would always reply, 'I know, but in this game, even the strong die'. I never wanted to be right about that, Ben." She stated through tears as she stared at Manny's picture. "He may have been a gangster to those who knew him on the streets, but he was always my son."

"And he was our brother, Miss Joyce. Don't worry 'bout nothin'. Whatever you need to send Manny off right, call me. I got my boy." Dirty Red ended as he and Jermaine sat with Ms. Joyce for a while and shared the good memories they had all created with Manny.

Manny's funeral was one of the largest funerals ever held in New Orleans. Players from every part of the city, including uptown and across the river, came to pay their respects to Manny and the crew. Rhodes Funeral Home on North Claiborne Avenue was packed on Friday afternoon, five days after Manny's body was discovered. The line to view Manny's black and gold marble casket with a raised, genuine ten karat gold and Diamond Bezel Saints football logo on top, stretched out the door and down the street as hundreds of on-lookers waited patiently to get a glimpse of the casket that held the remains of one of the realest gangsters to ever play the cocaine game in the city of New Orleans.

Manny's enemies, and there were many, were on hand this day as well. His death had come as a relief to the numerous big-time drug dealers who feared him. They actually came to make sure that Manny was really dead and not trying to pull some Machiavelli-type shit and come back and terrorize the dope game.

A pair of diamond-crusted Gucci shades covered Dirty Red's eyes. The dark shades were doing a fine job hiding the pain within as he stood by himself outside the funeral home to the far right-end of the building. From his point-of-view, Dirty Red could see everything and everyone. He stood silently and watched as friends of Manny, and enemies alike, poured in and out of the funeral home.

As he stood in his black Italian tailor-made silk suit and black gator shoes, Dirty Red eyed the people moving back and forth, eliminating suspects and taking note of people to keep an eye on. Just then, accompanied by Katrina, Ms. Joyce walked up to him. The woman felt she had to talk to Dirty Red at this moment because he had told Katrina earlier in the day that if it were not for him, he would not be burying his best friend. Katrina had sensed his guilt and had told Ms. Joyce. She grabbed Katrina's hand and they went over to the right side of the funeral parlor to comfort Dirty Red. Ms Joyce began talking to Dirty Red the way a mother talks to her son. In fact, Dirty Red was her son; she had taken him in and looked out for him for over three years. She had known him for ten years. Ms. Joyce explained to Dirty Red that she did not hold him responsible for what happened to Manny.

"I knew what Manny was into," Ms. Joyce said in a soft, caring tone of voice. "I know you have your mind set on revenge as well—but somebody has to say enough is enough. My son was no angel, Ben. A million Katrinas could never pay for the lives he's taken. That I know. But it's not your fault he's dead. You have to believe that, son."

Dirty Red really wasn't feeling Ms. Joyce's compassion at this moment. He knew she meant well, but what happened to Manny and his ole lady was something he could not just let

slide and say 'enough is enough'. If Dirty Red had to tell it, the shit was just hitting the fan.

"Me and Manny did a lot of dirt on these streets, Miss Joyce," Dirty Red said in a low tone of voice. "But we was always careful to cover our tracks. What happened to Manny wasn't over something we did in the past. This here just come up out the blue and I believe I know who dunnit." Dirty Red said as he continued watching the passers-by.

"Whatever you do Ben, don't let my child's death be the reason that you destroy everything that you and he put together. You have your whole life ahead of you. Use his death as a stepping-stone, and a lesson to never be repeated again. Otherwise he would've just died for nothing. I come up in the game, and I know what it's like to lose somebody you love— because it has happened to me twice now. I got a husband in jail, and a son now dead, like the song says, 'this ain't living'." Ms. Joyce stated in a loving manner.

Dirty Red reflected on Ms. Joyce's last three words, "this ain't living". She had played *Inner City Blues* by Marvin Gaye, which contained that phrase, repeatedly the day he and Jermaine broke the news. Dirty Red could hear the song once more as he thought of Manny and how much he would miss his boy.

"You right," Dirty Red replied as he stared at Ms. Joyce, "this ain't livin'. So you should understand the reasons why I can't let his killer continue livin'."

Ms. Joyce closed her eyes briefly and thought silently. She knew what Dirty Red was contemplating. She wiped her tears and eyed him with a look of love. "When will it all end," she asked softly. "Huh, Ben? When will it all end? When all of y'all are lying inside this very same building the way my son is laying right now? A closed casket? I had to put a picture frame of my son—*my son*—on top of his casket. A parent is not supposed to bury her child. But the path that you are planning on takin', is going to put all of y'all six feet under!" Ms. Joyce said through a waterfall of tears.

Dirty Red removed his sunshades and looked Ms. Joyce square in the eyes. "What about me don't you understand?" He asked bitterly.

"What you mean, Ben?" Ms. Joyce asked with a confused look on her face.

"If anything, after all I been through, for all that's happened to me early on in *my life*—shit! Right about now, I don't give a fuck about nothin'. Them niggas that touched Manny is dead!" Dirty Red remarked as he left Ms. Joyce and Katrina standing alone and went over to the front of the building where Oscar and JoAnne were standing and started talking to them.

Ms. Joyce grabbed Katrina's hand and the two turned and walked away. When she was younger, Ms. Joyce was all for Manny's father getting revenge on anyone who had wronged him or a member of his crew. Having lived a little longer and expanding in knowledge, however, Ms. Joyce knew that violence only begets violence; and she knew that Ben would be opening up a door that could have deadly repercussions for everyone involved. She told Katrina to focus on her education because she knew that's what Manny would want for her. As far as Ben, *"Well, that may have to play out until the last man is standing"*, Ms. Joyce thought to herself.

After Manny's body was placed into the ground, Dirty Red and Oscar went and stood over his grave. The rest of the crew had already gone to participate in a second line that was to take place on Benefit Street in Manny's old courtyard. Dirty Red knelt down over his friend's grave and smiled. "I never saw ya' lying flat on ya' back homeboy," he said through a painful smile. "Not even when ya' was fucked up. I think I know who done this to ya', gangsta. We might open up a can of worms on this next episode, too, but umm, we, we gotta do this for ya', my nig. We can't let this shit ride, ya' feel me? I know ya' do, nigga. Mom's gone be straight, brer, and Katrina, she, she gone be all right. I know how much she meant to ya'. We got her for ya', ya' feel me?" Dirty Red ended as he poured out an entire fifth of Courvoisier Cognac onto Manny's coffin and tossed a dime bag of weed into his grave.

"Missin' one thing," Oscar said as he stood with his hands inside his black silk suit slacks staring down at Manny's final resting place.

"What?" Dirty Red asked as he wiped his face with a black silk handkerchief.

Oscar chuckled as he reflected on the last conversation he had with Manny and said, "The pussy package."

Dirty Red smiled and looked down at Manny's casket and said, "A three piece spicy white with red beans and rice," as he smiled and nodded his head in agreement. "He woulda' love that shit. I wasn't even thinkin' bout it, O." He ended as he removed his sunshades.

"Don't worry 'bout it, homeboy. We gone make them niggas we send to 'em bring it when they get there, ya' heard me?" Oscar said as he dapped Dirty Red off and the two young men walked slowly away from Manny's grave.

"No doubt, brer, no motherfuckin' doubt!" Dirty Red stated matter-of-factly.

Dirty Red had discussed his suspicions about who may have killed Manny with Oscar during the ride to Manny's grave site. He noticed that everyone who knew and loved Manny, and even the people that feared and hated him as well, came to the funeral that day. Everybody except three people: Rico, Haywood, and Cedric.

While the second line was going on, Dirty Red and Oscar rode up on Jackson Avenue, outside the Magnolia Project to the corner store where Rico hung out. Dirty Red pulled his Mercedes up to the corner store and he and Oscar got out slowly and without fear. They were in enemy territory but remained unnerved; the people they were planning on talking to stared at them in disbelief as they stepped onto the sidewalk.

Dirty Red was clutching a hundred-shot Calico semi-automatic machine gun and Oscar held a tight grip on a fifteen shot twelve gauge automatic known as a "street sweeper".

The boys eyed Rico, Cedric, and Haywood as they approached the side of the corner store and began to ask questions about what happened to Manny.

"How the fuck I'm supposed ta' know what happened to Manny?" Rico asked in a nonchalant manner as he looked down the street.

"I know ya' know he dead, nigga. Y'all niggas ain't at the funeral, the second line or nothing. What the fuck I'm supposed ta' think, Rico?" Dirty Red asked angrily as he stood on the corner holding his machine gun in his right hand.

Dirty Red thought about just spraying the whole corner; but he wisely chose not to do so as he did not know for sure whether Rico had actually killed Manny. He and Oscar held the guns tightly, fighting back the urge to just kill Rico right then and there. Both men knew a move like the one they were fighting against could spark a huge war, however; so they let Rico talk, hoping he would reveal something.

"Man, I ain't got no beef with y'all niggas. What y'all did that day in front y'all house wasn't worth me killing Manny. Anyway, I'm still fucking y'all bitch, Katrina, so I could give a fuck less about who killed Manny!" Rico remarked as he stared Dirty Red and Oscar down.

"Nigga lying," Oscar remarked lowly to Dirty Red.

"Fuck you whispering for, Oscar?" Haywood asked angrily.

"Let me tell ya' something, bitch!" Oscar responded harshly. "First of all, I don't like ner' three you mutherfuckas! And if it was up to me, I'll kill all you bitches right here in broad daylight!"

"These niggas come 'round here like they workin' for Lucky Lucianno or some shit!" Cedric said just as Rico whistled and three gunmen stepped out of the corner store onto the sidewalk.

"You play the game well, Ben! I see why they call you Dirty Red." Rico remarked as he stood behind his henchmen and

threw down the blunt he was smoking, stomped it out, and scraped the bottom of his thousand-dollar Gucci shoes on the concrete to remove the ash from the bottom of his shoe. "But this time, my friend, ya' out numbered. Ya' won't make it off my block alive if ya' start shootin'."

"I don't mind dyin', nigga," Dirty Red said matter-of-factly as he scoffed at Rico.

"I know y'all li'l' sayin', mutherfucka. 'We from that nine and we don't mind dyin'." Rico sang as he looked towards Haywood and Cedric as they all began to laugh.

Rico then eyed Dirty Red seriously and said, "You can take that li'l downtown slang back to the Ninth Ward, whoaday, 'cause uh, to be honest, ya' not ready ta' die on no funky ass street corner. I told ya' I ain't had shit to do with whatever happened to Manny. Believe that, my nig'. Now, you got two choices—we could do this thing right now, you and me, we take each other out the game and that's it! But before you start blastin', I know this much, ya' not even sure who killed Manny so ya' wanna come fuckin' with me because we had a fight? I'm bigger than that, Ben. I think this all about me fucking Katrina and you hate the fact that it's a nigga from uptown that's taggin' the pussy on a daily basis."

Dirty Red and Oscar looked at one another and realized that Rico was stuntin' in front of his crew. They didn't travel uptown to discuss whether or not Rico was fucking Katrina. They were trying to figure out who killed Manny; but twice, Rico had shifted the conversation back towards Katrina. Since they had no solid proof, Dirty Red and Oscar, not wanting to argue with Rico over whether or not he was really fucking Katrina, something they could care less about anyway, decided to let the situation defuse itself this day for the simple fact that both men knew Rico was not going to reveal what he knew, if he knew anything at all, concerning Manny's death.

"We cool, dog," Dirty Red said as he walked back to his Mercedes, all the while eying Rico. "But I'm warnin' ya'—if ya' done it, ya' might as well kill me right now! 'Cause the next time I come at ya', you ain't gone even see me pimp! But you

damn sure gone feel me! Believe that shit, nigga!" Dirty Red ended before he hopped back into the driver's seat of his car and started the engine.

"Whatever, man!" Rico said as he walked back into the corner store, Haywood and Cedric following close behind.

"That nigga crazy huh, brer?" Haywood remarked to Rico as they walked behind the counter inside of Rico's store.

"Man, fuck Dirty Red! Nigga got a rep in the Ninth Ward for killin' this nigga and that nigga—but he ain't shit up here in the Magnolia! We got killas and real niggas too, fuck! Now, what he gone do is take his bitch ass back ta' the Desire and mourn for that bitch Manny with the resta' his hoe ass crew. Fuck a nigga named Ben Holland! And everybody that's with 'em!" Rico ended as he opened his cash register drawer and removed a stack of twenty dollar bills.

Dirty Red would not let up on Rico so easily. He had a gut feeling concerning what happened with Manny, but he also knew he could not touch Rico without repercussions from the cartel backing him. Dirty Red had an idea, however; he called Swan on his cell phone and told the narcotics agent to meet him at his airport hangar in an hour. Once there, Dirty Red discussed his plan with the detective and Swan readily agreed.

"It's an A-one plan. But that could get expensive." Swan told the two gangsters as they all sat at the bar.

"Manny was like a brother to us," Dirty Red replied. "If it wasn't for him, I wouldn't be here today. Whatever the cost, I'm willing to pay the price."

"We on it," said Swan. "Give me and Monty a few weeks to set it all up. I'll be in touch." He ended as he stood up and guzzled the remnants of a glass of J&B Scotch on the rocks.

Swan then shook Dirty Red and Oscar's hand and the men all exited the airport hangar.

As Dirty Red and Oscar rode in Dirty Red's Mercedes headed back to the second line in the Desire Project to celebrate

Manny, they both rode in silence and thought about the events that had transpired this day and what they were preparing to do in the near future. "Who woulda ever thought we woulda been in the game this deep?" Oscar asked Dirty Red.

Dirty Red chuckled as he looked straight ahead and spoke from behind the steering wheel, "Who you tellin', nigga," he responded somberly, over the song *Hand of the Dead Body*, (*Gangsters Don't Live That Long*) by the rapper Scarface. "Who the fuck you tellin'?" Dirty Red ended as he turned up the volume and headed back towards the Ninth Ward.

CHAPTER THIRTEEN

BAD GIRLS

"Where we going, nigga," Jason asked, while smiling from the backseat of Jermaine's brand new '99 Lincoln Navigator.

It had been almost a month since Manny's death, and it was now the first weekend in April. Jermaine had just purchased the SUV a few days earlier and he, Kim, Jason, Lamont, Dana and Katrina were out to celebrate his scoring the new whip. Jermaine's ride was a sharp one. It had a custom burgundy paint job and 26" chrome Sprewell spinner rims, three 18" sub-woofers, plush white leather seats and six 7" custom-made TV monitors placed in the visors and headrests of the seats.

"Let's go to the lake," Katrina responded to Jason's question.

"I said where we going, *nigga*. Not where we going, *bitch*!" Jason said, never dropping his smile.

"Don't talk to her like that!" Dana said as she slapped Jason's arm.

"Jermaine," Lamont yelled from the backseat, "let's go get somethin' ta' drink. A case of beer or some liquor ta' celebrate. Thissa clean ass whip dog!" Lamont ended as he looked around the jeep's interior.

133

"Thanks, whoaday. You right, brer. Let's get fucked up today. How 'bout it Jason?" Jermaine asked.

"For sho'! For Manny, homeboy, let's all get our head tight, ya' heard me?"

"How could y'all celebrate what happened to him?" Dana asked in disbelief.

"We gone celebrate every chance we get," remarked Katrina. "Believe me, if Manny was alive today, he'd be right along with us celebrating his homeboy new whip and getting just as drunk as we 'bout ta' get. There go the store right there, 'Maine, pull over."

The boys were gathering money and trying to figure out what to get when Katrina told them that she had money and was going to pay for everything as she exited the jeep. The store was down the block from Kim's cousin house in the Seventeenth Ward. The crew all knew the Chinese woman who owned the store pretty well, so their age did not prevent them from buying alcohol.

"Come on, Kim and Dana," Katrina said as she exited the jeep. "I'm a need for y'all ta' help me carry all this stuff."

"Tell Ma I said what up!" Jason yelled out the back window.

The girls walked into the small corner store and spoke to "Ma" as they walked down a short aisle towards the beer coolers in the rear.

"What y'all wanna drink?" Katrina asked as she stood before the coolers.

"Grab some wine coolers for me." Dana replied as she grabbed a lemon Hubig's pie.

"Alright. A four pack for Dana, uh, a case of beer for the fellas. Ma got the liquor behind the counter—grab that when we get up front. Kim, what ya' drinking, home girl? Liquor, beer or wine coolers?" Katrina asked aloud, but she got no reply from Kimberly.

"Kim!...Kim?" Katrina called out again in a now wondering tone of voice.

Getting no response, Katrina and Dana began walking towards the front of the store with the wine coolers and beer. When they got to the end of the aisle, they looked to their right and saw Kimberly surrounded by three men. A female was also with them. One of the guys, whose name was Stan, stood over six feet. He hovered over Kim's small frame.

"I mean, damn, a nigga can't get a phone number or nothing?" Stan asked.

"Man, I told you. I gotta ole man! He right outside in that clean-ass Navigator! And I'm 'bout to go call 'em so he can get yo' big, fat, nasty-looking ass up off me!" Kim remarked in an aggravated manner.

Stan turned and looked at his crew as if to say, *"This bitch don't know who I am"*. He was about to speak again but was interrupted by Katrina and Dana.

"Excuse me! Look, look out, brer! Step aside, chick!" Katrina said to the female who was with Stan. "I need to get two things —a bag of hot pork skins and my sister. Come on, Kim!"

"Who the fuck you supposed to be?" The female member of Stan's crew, named Tiffany snapped.

"Oh, I'm sorry, Miss Thang." Katrina replied nicely. "I'm the bitch that's gone prevent y'all four from dyin' today!"

Katrina knew how much Jermaine cared for Kimberly. She knew if Jermaine got into a fight with Stan, Jason and Lamont would jump in and help. She also knew she would have to whip the ass of the bitch that was with Stan. Katrina had a good day going; she was even willing to pay for all the drinks. The bottom line was that, just as much as Jermaine was celebrating his new ride, Katrina was celebrating being out with her people and she wasn't going to let Stan or anybody else ruin her day. "Now, can we three ladies pay for our merchandise and exit the premises," she asked in a sweet and innocent voice as she batted her eyes and smiled at Stan and

his crew.

"Not before I get your sister phone number!" Stan said boldly.

Stan then grabbed Kimberly's waist and pulled her close and tried to hug her while trying coax her phone number out of her. Kim pushed him away and screamed in frustration as she inadvertently punched him in the mouth. Stan stood back a little stunned as he eyed Kimberly. He then hauled off and slapped her in the face and knocked her down.

Dana, without thinking, closed her eyes, swung a wine cooler bottle and broke it on Stan's head and he took to one knee as he cussed aloud and grabbed his forehead, which was bleeding profusely. One of the people with Stan, an overweight black male by the name of Gary, grabbed Dana and began choking her. Katrina dropped the case of beer, jumped on Gary's back and began punching him in the head.

"Scooter" was the fourth person with Stan. He was not much of a fighter, so when the melee broke out, he ran out of the store. "Ma", who was working behind the counter, chased him outside. As "Scooter" ran up the sidewalk, the Chinese woman began to yell to Jermaine, Jason and Lamont. "Ma" was yelling in Chinese, but the boys knew something was wrong. The three hopped out the jeep and ran into the store. When they got in the building, what they saw surprised them. Jermaine had expected he might have to use the .45 Glock that was tucked in his waistband. Jason was ready to pull out his .357 magnum or maybe Lamont would shut the whole place down with his Mac-11. That was not the case, though. The boys simply started laughing.

"What the fuck they doin', brer?" Jason asked through laughter when he saw what was going down.

Lamont was laughing, too, but he decided it would be wise if he grabbed everybody's gun and hide them inside Jermaine's jeep. He grabbed his boys' heaters and quickly went and hid the weapons, ran back into the store, and continued watching the fight before him. Stan, the big tough guy, was out cold on

the floor bleeding from the forehead. Gary, the heavy-set male, was now on his knees. Dana and Kimberly were slapping him on his neck and back and kicking him while talking to him at the same time. Dana and Kimberly's actions were the things that had Jermaine and Jason bent over laughing. Gary was twenty-two years old and full-grown, but the two eighteen year-old females were slapping him like a little child and making antagonizing remarks towards him like, "that's why you can't get a girlfriend with your fat ass" and "you just big for nothing" as they kicked him in the ass.

Katrina, on the other hand, was dreadfully serious about her squabble. She had pulled some of Tiffany's weave out of her head, ripped off her shirt and bra, and had blackened one of her eyes. She was screaming for somebody to get Katrina off her.

"Uh, uhh! Don't cry for help now, bitch!" Katrina said in a high-pitched voice as she continued punching her opponent furiously, nearly jumping into the air as she swung.

Katrina punched Tiffany in the stomach and she dropped to her knees. She then picked her up by what little hair she had remaining and was attempting to ram her head through a glass freezer door. The boys rushed in, however, and stopped her before she could complete her task. Lamont grabbed Katrina and pulled her back as the girl fell head first up against the soft drink cooler, and then fell flat on her stomach. Katrina was kicking and pointing her finger, yelling loudly as Lamont pulled her away from the cooler.

"Yeah! What, bitch? Told yo' stupid ass! Don't fuck with us! Don't fuck with this here! *Now* look at you! *Look at you, bitch!*" Katrina yelled as she pointed back at the girl whilst being dragged by Lamont.

The boys rushed Katrina, Dana and Kim out of the store, leaving Stan on the floor out cold, and bleeding from the forehead. Dana and Kimberly had left Gary out of breath with welts on his neck and back. Katrina had left Tiffany with patches of missing hair, a blackened eye, naked from the waist up, and a concussion. "Ma" grabbed the telephone and told Jason to leave because she was about to call the police.

137

What Stan and his crew had failed to realize was that the boys were known in many parts of the city. On top of that, Kimberly's relatives lived in the neighborhood. The crew all knew and respected "Ma". And "Ma", in reality, did not like Stan and his crew because they caused trouble on the block on a daily basis. Stan had robbed "Ma" on one occasion, and in her eyes, she had received retribution this day for all the agony she had suffered at the hands of Stan and his petty crew.

Dana and Kimberly were now back inside the Navigator; but the boys were still trying to force Katrina into the jeep.

"She calling the police!" Lamont told her.

"Good! They can take that fat ass nigga with his head busted open, and charge him with attempted rape! That's right! The nigga tried ta' grab Kimberly! That's why the shit went down!" Katrina stated as she broke free of Lamont's grip and ran back to the store's entrance; she was quickly held back by Jason as he emerged from the building.

"What the nigga did?" Jermaine scoffed as he headed for the store's entrance.

"He tried to touch me, Jermaine," Kimberly yelled from the front passenger seat, "but Dana knocked him out with a wine cooler. Just let it go. The police coming. Get 'em next time, baby."

"Man, look," Lamont said to the group, "they got what they got. Let's get the fuck outta here, ya' dig?"

Jason agreed, but not before going in and giving "Ma" five-hundred dollars for the damage in the store.

"You come by anytime!" "Ma" said whilst smiling to Jason after he handed her five one-hundred dollar bills. "You are family *here*! You *family*! You beat up bad guy for *me*! Come by, I *cook* something for you! Bring friends. Especially female that hit with bottle!"

"That's Dana. That's *my* ole lady that did that shit right there!" Jason said proudly.

"Yeah. Bring her and other girl, and, and wild girl, crazy girl!"

"Wild girl—crazy girl?" Jason asked himself. "Oh. That's Kay Kay!" He then remembered out loud.

"Yeah, I know her. Her name Kay Kay! Kay Kay, Dana and Kim. Right? Kim?"

Jason was really ready to go, but "Ma" was so grateful and he did not want to be rude. "Ma" knew Jason had to go, however, since the police were on the way. Therefore, she thanked Jason again, told him she would take care of everything with the police, and told the boys to come by the store next Friday for lunch. Jason nodded and quickly ran out the store and jumped into Jermaine's jeep. Jermaine just drove for a while, aimlessly, while listening to the rapper B.G.'s song *Cash Money Is An Army*. Everybody was quietly listening to the CD until Jason asked, "Nigga, where we going?"

Katrina caught on to the scenario and replied, "Let's go to the lake!"

Jason could barely contain his laughter as everybody, including Dana and Kim, said at the same time, "I said *nigga*, where we going, not *bitch* where we going!"

Everybody then burst into laughter and began talking about what happened at "Ma's" as Jermaine turned down the stereo.

"I'm looking 'round and I holler 'Kim'...'Kim'? This bitch sittin' in the front seat was over in the corner back at the store 'bout to get raped, ya' dig?" Katrina said as she pointed at Kim. "So I jump in like, 'don't fuck with my sister—and let me get a bagga' them hot pork skins'!"

Lamont said, "Y'all don't look nothing alike."

"I don't care!" Katrina snapped. "That's my girl and I ain't gone let no *nigga* or *bitch*, fuck with her."

The gang had made another stop to grab a couple of bags of ice and a box of Swisher Sweets as they had forgotten to those items when they left "Ma's" store. They then went on to spend

the day at the Lakefront. Once there they drank and smoked as they reminisced about Manny. It had been a month since he was killed and no one ever really talked how he or she felt about his death.

"I just know when it's time ta' handle our business, we gone do just that." Jermaine said as he lit up a blunt.

"Really though." Jason replied.

As night fell upon the gang, they continued to talk, laugh, plot, scheme and plan. Kim, Dana, and Katrina were seriously drunk by now and it was time for Jermaine, Jason, and Lamont to make their move. That was their plan throughout the entire outing, to get the girls drunk, take them back to *Par 6* and have sex with them. Kim and Dana were somewhat naive about what was happening; but Katrina was well informed. After all, she had been with the boys her entire life. She knew their every move and she'd seen this one many times before. In fact, she had been a target for the boys several times. Not that she minded, she would have done it anyway, because that was just who she was.

It wasn't because the boys had money. It wasn't because they tricked Katrina or anything like that. The fact was, Katrina actually loved the boys. Sometimes, she would fantasize about her and Jason being married. She would have a little girl and she would name her Jarina. When Katrina found out that Dana Shelby wanted Jason, however, she let that fantasy fade away. She, in fact, encouraged Jason and Dana to see one another. She reasoned that someone just the opposite of Jason would be what he needed to grasp his attention and keep it, and she was right. Jason and Dana had been together ever since she told him that she knew for a fact that Dana wasn't playing the role.

To be honest, Katrina didn't think any of the boys would take her and call her his own, and she had reasons for feeling the way she felt. Katrina believed in her heart that she had crossed the line when she slept with the entire crew; and Jason himself had told her that she *belonged* to the "the crew" the day two of them had sex while Rico was waiting for her outside the dope house. Despite her somewhat whoreish disposition, which was

a temperament Katrina kept to herself, the boys all gave her love in ways she only wished she could have received from Faye because of the way they looked after her.

It was the boys who always gave her money so she could eat and have good school clothes, not just rags. The boys all spent untold amounts of cash on Katrina to keep her dressing nicely and well-fed. The boys were Katrina's only family in all actuality; and if she had to share her body with some of them from time to time, so be it. That was her reasoning. Things were changing however; Katrina realized that Jason and Dana was an item. Jermaine and Kim was a couple, so tonight she would be sleeping with Lamont, but that was cool with her. Lamont was a good lover, but it was Jason who really pushed her buttons. In Katrina's eyes, however, Jason was now off-limits. He belonged to Dana. Katrina liked Dana, and respected her as well; so sleeping with Jason on this night was totally out the question. As much as she loved and wanted Jason, it would be out of love and respect for Dana that Katrina would begin to relinquish her attraction to the young man; but still, Katrina knew deep down inside that that particular task would be a hard task to complete.

CHAPTER FOURTEEN

WELCOME TO CHINATOWN

The smell of bacon was lingering heavily in the air early Sunday morning inside *Par 6*, the day after most of the crew had celebrated on the Lakefront. Dana was the first amongst the sleeping to awaken this morning. She looked at the monitor on the nightstand beside her, which was focused on the garage, and saw Dirty Red's Mercedes, Oscar's Grand Prix, and the rest of the boys' vehicles. As she watched the screen, the monitor shifted to the second floor where Dana eyed Oscar in the kitchen, and Dirty Red sitting in the living room watching TV. She woke Jason up by saying, "Your boys are here," before she pulled the covers back over her head.

Jason got up a few minutes later and walked downstairs and grabbed a plate of grits and a few pieces of bacon.

"They showed it yet?" Oscar then asked Dirty Red.

"Showed what?" Jason asked as he searched for a fork.

Dirty Red told Jason that while he and the crew were out celebrating the night before, Swanson and Montgomery had busted Cedric for possession of three kilograms of cocaine. He was on his second strike for a major drug offense and he was

facing serious time. The stage was now set to allow Dirty Red to use Cedric to begin putting pressure on Rico to finally take him down, and at the same time, find out what really happened to Manny. Dirty Red went on to tell Jason if Cedric's drug bust made the news, the boys would have to find another way to get to Rico. If Cedric's arrest didn't make the news, however, the boys would know that Swanson and Montgomery were able to shuffle him out of Orleans Parish Prison without anyone ever missing him.

The three gangsters watched the television in silence as the morning's news unfolded. Three people, including a sixteen year-old female, were murdered inside a second floor apartment in the Fischer Housing Project in the Fifteenth Ward, and a tourist had been car-jacked in the French Quarters. A city council woman was also under investigation for allegations of drug use inside City Hall.

"I can't believe the amount of violence and corruption going on in this city. Somebody really need to do something about that shit." Jason remarked as he stirred his grits.

Dirty Red, Oscar and Jason looked around at one another and laughed lowly, knowing full-well they were more a part of the problem rather than the solution.

By 8:30 A.M. neither of the boys had seen anything on Cedric's arrest. At that time, the house phone began to ring. Dirty Red was expecting this call. He answered and said, "Talk to me."

"We got a bird in the cage," Swan remarked happily. "Feeding time is ten 'o' clock this morning."

The agent was talking in code, letting Dirty Red know that Cedric was willing to tell what he knew about Manny's murder. Swan was also indicating that he and Montgomery would meet the boys at the airport hangar at ten this morning.

"Get the resta the fellas down here so we can handle some business, J-Dog." Dirty Red requested of Jason as he hung up the phone and stood up and stretched.

Jason grabbed another helping of grits and bacon and headed through the dining room and up the stairs to awaken Lamont and Jermaine. He tapped on Jermaine's door, vaguely listening to the moans coming from Kimberly. "Eh yo', 'Maine! Time ta' go to work, nigga! Get off the pussy we got a meeting downstairs!"

"Alright, nigga I'm 'bouta bust a—fuckin'—nut!" Jermaine yelled aloud.

Jason laughed as he walked over to Lamont's suite and tapped on the door. Lamont cracked the door several seconds later and stuck his head out as Jason was walking off. "That's grits and bacon I smell?" He asked Jason.

"And ya' knooow iiiit!" Jason answered as he laughed again.

Lamont quickly closed the door to his suite and began to get dressed. He thought about the bacon Oscar had fixed, and he could not wait to grab a plate of grits to go along with it.

In some other place or time, Oscar Henderson could have been a Master Chef instead of a serial rapist, career drug dealer and killer. The crew all loved his cooking. Oscar was a wizard in the kitchen; and what made his meals especially delightful was the fact that he always took the time to prep his meals. Breakfast included.

Oscar had a special technique that he used to fix bacon, which allowed the quarter-inch strips to come out firm, but not too crisp. He first coated the entire slab of bacon in a sweet, honey-apple marinade and baked the slab in the oven until it glazed over and thickened to the point that he could slice it into the preferred size. Oscar would then place the bacon strips onto the open grill in the kitchen and grill the meat over low heat until the sliced strips could be pulled apart with tongs. He also made a special Swiss and sharp cheddar cheese sauce for his home made grits and trimmed the plate with cool, crisp, sliced tomatoes. The meal was not only tasty, but pleasing to the eye as well. Plainly put, Oscar knew his way around the kitchen.

The only problem the crew had when Oscar cooked was that he took a long time to prepare his meals. He would start eight hours ahead of time whenever the crew ate steak, stating that he had to marinate the meat first. Red beans and gumbo took almost an entire day to prepare. If one was patient, though, Oscar could prepare a dish that would satisfy any and everybody that ever picked up a fork; and when a meal came early like it did on this morning, it was indeed a pleasure to the palate.

Lamont, still in the bedroom dressing, and all-so-eager to get a plate of Oscar's breakfast dish, had just thrown on his diamond cuff-link bracelet, but he could not find his Rolex watch. He looked over at Katrina, who was fast asleep. *"The bitch got me!"* He thought to himself.

Lamont put on a pair of slippers and walked over to the side of the bed where Katrina lay in a peaceful slumber, and pushed her head down repeatedly into the pillows.

"Nigga, is you crazy? I'm fuckin' sleep, brer!" Katrina moaned with her eyes still closed.

"I can't find my rollie! I thought you probably picked it up last night while you was drunk and put in ya' purse by mistake."

"Man, I ain't got no Rolex watch in my purse!" Katrina snapped as she sat up on the bed rubbing her head, as she had a serious hangover.

Katrina had consumed a large bottle of Alize` and had smoked a total of four blunts the night before. As Lamont continued questioning her concerning the whereabouts of his Rolex, Katrina got up off the bed, ran into the bathroom, closed the door and knelt before the toilet and vomited all the liquor she had consumed. As she vomited in the toilet, Lamont started banging on the bathroom door.

Katrina finished vomiting and turned on the hot water to take a shower, all the while trying to ignore Lamont, who continued banging on the door asking about his Rolex. Katrina stuck her

head under the nozzle until the water grew warm and then removed her panties and stepped into the stall. She listened with disdain as Lamont continually banged on the door. She looked at the ceiling, then towards the bathroom door and moaned.

"Lord, please help this stupid young man!" Katrina said aloud as she stepped out of the shower, turned off the water, went to the bathroom door, and snatched it open. She now stood in the doorway, dripping wet. "Nigga, you don't even remember, huh?" She asked Lamont in an aggravated manner.

"Remember what?"

"See! You was so fucked up last night, talkin' 'bout I was drunk, you don't even remember ya' threw ya' fuckin' watch off the balcony, fool!"

"I did that shit?"

"Yeah, while you was imitating Tony Montana, but I don't remember Tony Montana throwing jewelry off the balcony of his own house!"

Lamont and Katrina had been lying in bed the night before smoking weed as they watched the movie *Scarface*. Lamont had gotten so psyched by the movie that he began bragging. He threw his watch away, saying he had money to burn. Katrina went and retrieved the watch off the golf course, but Lamont threw it away again. Realizing Lamont was acting like a total fool, Katrina went to bed, leaving him awake by himself as he quoted the movie word for word.

Lamont walked onto the balcony and looked down to the ground below and saw his watch lying in the lush green grass, shining in the morning sun. "Damn! I was trippin'!" He said as he scratched his head and laughed lowly.

"I know like the fuck you were!" Katrina replied as she joined Lamont outside on the balcony.

Katrina then had a moment of clarity. When she realized Lamont had been accusing her of stealing from him the whole

time, she slapped him hard on the arm and made him apologize. As Lamont and Katrina laughed over his silly antics the night before, they noticed two middle-aged white golfers riding in a golf cart off in the distance. The passenger was holding a pair of binoculars as his partner steered. Katrina noticed that the men were taking turns with the binoculars in order to get a close-up view of her naked body as she stood on the balcony beside Lamont.

Lamont laughed at the men as Katrina threw up her arms. "What?" She yelled aloud. "Y'all ain't never seen a naked black woman before?"

The men almost ran into a tree, an act that forced Katrina to erupt into loud laughter.

At that moment, Dirty Red stepped out onto the golf course and looked up towards the balcony. "I got a call from security sayin' they got a naked woman on the balcony. You know who they talking about?" He asked, looking directly at a butt-naked Katrina.

"Nah, brer. I ain't seen nobody naked out here this morning," Katrina replied with a smirk.

By then, a crowd was starting to form on the golf course about a hundred yards off as young and old men alike came to get a glimpse of the fine young sister on the balcony of *Par 6*.

"Look at those assholes!" Dirty Red remarked. "Look, y'all go on in before these white folk start tripping."

Lamont asked Dirty Red to grab his Rolex and they all went back into *Par 6*, but not before Katrina did a sexy dance as she backed into the suite. She was toying with the men on the golf course and they began whistling at her. Katrina was about to ask the men to come over and throw her some money, but Lamont hurriedly snatched her in by her hair and slammed the French doors shut.

Dirty Red, meanwhile, had walked back into the living room and removed his platinum bracelet, Cartier watch and white silk shirt. He then removed his .44 Desert Eagle handgun,

along with the shoulder holster. When the boys all came downstairs into the living room, he told them to put on some old clothes and leave all of their jewelry at the condominium.

The boys went and changed and headed towards the open garage and followed closely behind Dirty Red as he pointed out various tools for the boys to grab. They grabbed a mallet, two hacksaws, a chainsaw and a used car battery, and a pair of jumper cables.

"Fuck we doin'?" Lamont asked jokingly. "Fixing cars and building houses?"

Dirty Red looked at Oscar and the two twenty-five year-olds grinned at one another.

Both gangsters knew that the boys would see the game in a different light this morning. The tools Dirty Red had selected would not be used on inanimate matter, but on human flesh.

Jermaine had killed before, but Jason and Lamont were strangers to homicide. Although they had seen men killed by Dirty Red, Oscar, and Manny, they had never actually taken someone's life. Dirty Red prided himself on the techniques he used to kill other humans. He had taken death to a whole other level. He loved to torture other human beings, and, as long as he was in the game, he was going to make sure that the ones coming up behind him, and those who ran with him, were well-trained in the art of homicide.

As the boys loaded the tools into Jermaine's jeep, Dana had stepped off the elevator and called Jason over to her side. She began to get watery-eyed as Jason approached her.

"Why you cryin'?" Jason asked in a compassionate tone of voice.

"I'm scared that something gone happen to you out there. That somethin' might happen to us."

Dana knew what Jason was involved in, but on this morning she had a feeling that the boys were not just planning to slang cocaine in the Ninth Ward.

"What you mean by 'something might happen to us'?" Jason asked as they rode up to the second floor in each other's arms.

"I'm sayin', like if you go to jail or worse, like what happened to Manny. We could never have a family or get married."

"We had this conversation before, Dana. You know what I do. This our life right now, baby girl. Someday it'll change, but for now, it is what it is. You gone be down or not?"

"Jason, I'm more down with you than you could ever imagine." Dana replied as the elevator door opened.

"Now that's the Dana Shelby I know and love. I be back after while. Chill at the crib with Kim and Kay Kay until I get back. They ain't going ta' school today. Y'all just relax. Eat some of that bacon and shit Oscar fix and we gone hollar later." Jason finished up as he kissed Dana's lips and removed her dark hair from in front of her eyes and wiped tears from her face before he stepped back onto the elevator, and rejoined the crew.

Back downstairs in the garage, the boys were just finishing loading the tools into Jermaine's jeep.

"Damn, nigga," joked Oscar. "What took so long? Ya' had ta' check in before ya' leave, huh?"

Jason eyed Oscar and asked aloud, "You called and told JoAnne where the fuck you going this morning?"

"Fuck no! I'm a grown ass man. I don't check in with ner' bitch before I go no damn where!"

"Well, me neither then, nigga. I can't help it if my ole lady care about me and JoAnne don't give a fuck about what you do out here."

The boys all burst into laughter as Jermaine, Oscar and Dirty Red jumped into Jermaine's Navigator. Jason and Lamont would follow in Dirty Red's Mercedes. It was a quarter after ten when the boys reached the airport. The entrance to their hangar was to the far northwest end of the airport on Airline Highway. It was a gravel road shielded by a thick line of trees on the right and a huge levee on the left that held back the

Bonnet Carre` Spillway. The hangar faced away from the main runways of the huge airport and its terminals. It was used in the past as a private hangar for movie stars, musicians and athletes who wanted to sneak into the *Big Easy*, enjoy the night life, and sneak out without being seen by reporters and fans inside the main terminal.

The hangar was actually set up like a medium-sized house, complete with a gymnasium, a huge kitchen, a bar and dance floor and two huge bedroom suites, each with an over-sized Jacuzzi bathtub. Dirty Red and his boys leased the hangar and were now using it to hold meetings with the narcotics agents and to set up cocaine deals with Roscoe, their current kilogram connection who had ties to a Jamaican gang from Liberty City, down in Miami, Florida.

When the boys reached the small parking lot in front of the hangar, Lamont pulled alongside of Dirty Red as he sat on the passenger side of Jermaine's jeep looking around cautiously.

"What y'all need us ta' do?" Lamont asked Dirty Red from behind the steering wheel of the Mercedes.

Dirty Red continued staring at the surrounding area without answering Lamont's question. He arrived late on purpose in order to scope the scene out before he and his boys entered the premises. Satisfied that the front was clear, he looked over to Lamont and said, "Me and O gone walk around back and unlock the main door. Y'all get the tools out the back of the truck and meet us by the French doors in front. Don't touch the knob though 'cause you gone set off the silent alarm."

Dirty Red and Oscar grabbed their .9mm Berettas and exited the jeep and placed the guns in the back of their waistbands before they walked around to the rear of the building. They entered the hangar and saw Swan and Montgomery sitting at the bar to their right. The two detectives had each mixed Screwdrivers for themselves. They eyed Dirty Red and Oscar and Swanson nodded towards Cedric, who sat at a wooden table handcuffed to a chair in the middle of the dance floor. Oscar went and turned off the alarm to the French doors and let the boys in.

151

When the three eighteen year-old teens saw Cedric, their childhood friend from Benefit Street, handcuffed and gagged, sitting in the middle of the dance floor, their jaws dropped. They realized right then and there that Cedric would not be walking away from the airport hangar alive, let alone in one piece.

"Y'all 'bouta see some ugly shit." Oscar said seriously. "This shit here that's 'bouta go down—gone test your love for Manny, the game, and for each other. This nigga here," Oscar said as he pointed towards Cedric and continued talking, "he ain't gone make it through the day. So if ya' don't wanna know what's gone happen," Oscar said as his voice began to grow louder, "you need ta' turn around, walk out them mutherfuckin' doors, and keep going! Get the *fuck* from 'round us! Stay away from the dope house, Par Six, Dirty Red, and especially *me!*"

Oscar stared at the boys for a minute without saying a word. His nostrils flared and his chest heaved through the black silk wife-beater he wore. The teenagers shook their heads seriously and told Oscar that if Cedric had something to do with Manny's murder, then they were going to deal with him this morning, even if they did grow up together.

"That's what I'm talkin' 'bout! We got some real niggas in the building today!" Oscar hollered out to Dirty Red as he escorted the boys across the dance floor towards the table where Cedric sat in an intense state of fear.

When Cedric saw the boys, he shook his head in utter regret. The boys in turn, could not believe that Cedric had taken part in killing Manny, the coolest dude they had ever known. Manny had treated Cedric like a younger brother from day one. He taught the young teens many things about the game; and even though Dirty Red was indeed the mastermind behind many of the crimes the crew committed, it was Manny who had introduced Dirty Red to the game.

Dirty Red was always smarter than Manny, however, and Manny readily admitted that time and time again. It could be argued, however, that without Manny, there would be no crew. Dirty Red would not exist. But on the other hand, without

Dirty Red, there would be no *Par 6*, and no money for the crew. Even though the boys sold kilograms of cocaine instead of continuing on in high school, they had plenty to show for what they had been doing, and it all led back to Manny and the courtyard on Benefit Street. That's what the boys thought about as they watched Dirty Red intimidate and antagonize Cedric by waving a mallet in front of his face.

Cedric had seen all the tools that the boys had brought in; and he knew what the crew was capable of doing. He had seen, right along with Jason, Jermaine and Lamont, the murders that Dirty Red had ordered and participated in: Sebas and his four soldiers in the driveway, Brian, the body they helped place inside a dumpster in the project. Cedric knew the crew could get downright deadly, so rather than face prolonged torture, he decided to tell all that he knew concerning Manny's murder in the hopes that Dirty Red would kill him quickly and not make him suffer. Cedric knew he had fucked up; he was now sorry he left the crew and started hanging with some other game players he barely knew. He was more upset that it wasn't Haywood or Rico sitting in the chair this day, and the more he thought about it, Cedric wasn't even sure if Rico and Haywood would come looking for him if he was to up and disappear. He told Dirty Red he would tell his story willingly as he sat handcuffed to the chair.

"Talk to me." Dirty Red commanded as he sat on the table across from Cedric and gently placed the mallet on the table top.

Cedric sighed and bowed his head. "Manny stopped at Popeye's, then went to the liquor store," he began. "After that, he came up to the Magnolia and bought a sacka' weed. That's when Rico spotted 'em coming down Jackson Avenue. He passed right in front Rico store and Rico and Haywood decided ta' follow 'em to see where he was going. When he pulled up by this chick Shawonda house, they figured he was gone be in there for a minute. They waited about thirty minutes and rushed in through the back door with guns blazing. The li'l chick was in the kitchen pouring a drink when they busted in on her. She was so scared, man, she pissed on herself. They

asked her where Manny was and she pointed to the bathroom. Manny probably woulda had a chance if it wasn't for him being where he was. He couldn't hear what was going down because he was in the shower. Haywood walked behind Shawonda with a gun to her back, he said the li'l chick was faintin' and shit when they duct taped her mouth while they waited outside the bathroom for Manny. When Manny came out, Rico shot 'em in the forehead with a three-eighty pistol. Manny didn't die right there though. He stumbled down the hall to the bedroom, trying to go for his gun. He fell down in the bedroom and Rico grabbed Manny's forty caliber off the dresser and blasted Shawonda in the back of the head. She fell on toppa' Manny then Haywood kicked her body off of 'em. Manny was still alive, brer. He just shook his head from side ta' side, I guess ta' say 'no'. Then Rico hit 'em one more time with his own gun, right in the forehead again, then those niggas just walked out the front door. All that shit took maybe two minutes, but ta' Manny and Shawonda, I'm sure it was a lifetime. I told them they fucked up and they shouldna' done it, but they just kept sayin' 'fuck Manny'."

With tears of anger and sorrow in his eyes, Oscar asked Cedric why he didn't come to them the moment he heard what happened. Cedric responded by telling Oscar that he didn't think the boys would believe him.

"I believe the bitch." Dirty Red said in a low but angry tone as he stood up from the table. "I believe you all the way, Ced. Except I think you was with 'em when the shit happened."

"Say brer, I'm tellin' ya' brer—"

"Shut the fuck up!" Dirty Red yelled as he cut Cedric's plea short and reached for the mallet once more.

Dirty Red figured that Rico would not have told Cedric what he had done, knowing Cedric used to hang with Manny and the crew. He was convinced that Manny's murder was an initiation given to him by Rico to show that he was down. Dirty Red also knew that Cedric carried a chrome .380 pistol with him. He picked up the mallet and smashed Cedric's right hand without warning, nor giving it a second thought.

Cedric yelled aloud and begged Dirty Red not to hurt him anymore. He might as well been talking to a deaf man, though; Dirty Red was just getting started, and letting Cedric go was not a part of the mayhem that was about to be unleashed.

"I know you was in that mutherfuckin' house. You stole from me, Ced. You stole my brother from me, nigga!" Dirty Red yelled as he got in Cedric's face and clasped his hands around his neck. "In China, when you steal, they cut off ya' hands!" Dirty Red said as he slammed Cedric's head face first into the wooden table. "Welcome to Chinatown!"

Dirty Red then went and grabbed the hacksaw out of Lamont's hand and began to detach both of Cedric's hands. Swan and Montgomery, as well as the rest of the crew, watched in silence as Dirty Red sawed off both of Cedric's hands as the young teen screamed in agony. By the time Dirty Red got through using the hacksaw and jumper cables to administer low voltage electrical shots to his torso, Cedric was begging somebody to kill him and put him out of his misery.

"Jay! L-Dog—kill that mutherfucka'!" Dirty Red yelled as he walked towards the bar to pour himself a drink, his t-shirt, face, and forearms were splattered with Cedric's blood.

Dirty Red's hair hung wildly down his shoulders as he leaned against the bar next to the two agents who, by now, were half-drunk off vodka and orange juice. The three watched from the bar counter as Jason and Lamont blasted a total of sixteen holes into Cedric's body, literally tearing his insides apart. The young teens, with the aide of Oscar, then dismembered Cedric's body with the chainsaw and they each took turns hauling trash bags filled with his chopped remains out to the incinerator on the side of the hangar to dispose of his remains. It took all day to clean up the scene and by late evening, the crew was tired and hungry. They had done a gruesome thing, but it didn't seem to bother a great majority of them at all.

The boys had just tortured and murdered a childhood friend of theirs, but the price of betrayal in the game, according to the crew, is death. Cedric had to go. He was a traitor, a flip-flopper who had to be taken off the streets. Manny was much more

real than Cedric, Rico or Haywood combined. There was no way these three were going to be permitted to walk the streets. Cedric was the first to go, and now that Dirty Red knew the full story, he had his mind set on taking down the remaining two people responsible for Manny's death.

Dirty Red, however, knew the Colombian cartel was backing Rico. He knew he had to carefully plan his next move, which was to take Rico out and avoid a war. Before Cedric's body could burn completely, Dirty Red was conjuring up another plan to take over Rico's operation and earn favor with Rico's supplier, a man by the name of Damenga Lapiente`, a drug lord from Houston, Texas.

The two agents had told Dirty Red about Rico's supplier as his crew chopped Cedric's bloody, lifeless corpse into small chunks. His mind was steadily working. In the meantime, however, Dirty Red and the boys would enjoy a little payback for Manny's murder. The ultimate prize, however, still lay ahead.

CHAPTER FIFTEEN

YOUR TRUE COLORS

It was about 6P.M. when the boys finally finished discarding Cedric's remains. The crew had spent all day chopping body parts and cleaning up after they had completed their task. Swanson and Montgomery had left in their Lincoln town car after witnessing the crew murder, dismember and discard Cedric's remains. Dirty Red had paid the agents fifty thousand dollars for handing over Cedric; and after a hard day's work, the boys needed a break from the action. They all took showers and changed into their street gear and contemplated on what to do with the rest of the evening.

"Let's go get a bite ta' fellas. It's on me, ya' heard?" Dirty Red said to the crew as he sat at the bar smoking a blunt.

Lamont grimaced at the thought of eating after what had been done to Cedric; although it didn't seem to bother the rest of the crew in the least. After seeing what the human body looks and smells like on the inside, the last thing Lamont wanted to do was fill his stomach with food that he knew he was going to just regurgitate right back out of his system.

Jason, meanwhile, had decided to call Dana back at *Par 6* in order tell her, Kim and Katrina to meet him and the crew at

The Acme Oyster Company restaurant in the French Quarters. When he called, Katrina, recognizing his number on the caller I.D., scrambled past Dana and hastily answered the phone. "Will you please come and get this whining, in love ass young woman outta' my *god damned* ear!" She said in an aggravated manner.

For the last few hours, Dana had been crying to Katrina, repeatedly telling her that she was worried that something bad had happened to Jason. Jason laughed aloud when Katrina told him what was going on. He told Katrina to call a cab and head downtown to the oyster bar in about an hour. He then talked to Dana.

Jason's beau sat on the edge of the bed and immediately perked up when she heard his voice. "Where you been, Jason?" She asked softly.

"I was working, boo. Look, Kay Kay gone call y'all a cab and y'all gone meet us downtown at Acme's, ya' dig? Just relax, baby girl. I'm all right, ya' heard me? Let's just go out and have ourselves a good time ta' night! How 'bout that there?"

"Alright. I'm sorry Jay, I just, I just thought something happened to you out there. What we talked about earlier." Dana said in a relieved manner as she wiped away her tears.

"I'm good. I'm good. This me you talking to. You know I know how ta' handle my business. Get cleaned up and I'll see you in a li'l bit." Jason ended before he hung up the phone.

Dana quickly showered and got dressed and stood anxiously in the garage in her cream-colored Burberry dress with matching shoes and purse with her hair hanging down her back and covering the left side of her face.

Back in the mansion, Katrina grabbed her Louis Vitton ¾ length leather jacket that matched her leather Louis Vitton dress and shoes. She checked her twisted Afro in the mirror one last time and then headed towards the elevator as she called out for Kim, who was still in Jermaine's suite getting dressed.

When Kim walked down the stairs in her white silk Armani dress and white Manolo Blahniks, heading towards the elevator, Katrina noticed that she had a set of car keys in her hand. She kept quiet as the two rode the elevator down to the garage.

Dana was now calmly waiting for the cab at the foot of the driveway. When the two girls stepped off the elevator, Kim walked over to the driver's side of Jason's Cadillac and began searching the set of keys she held in her hands.

"What the fuck you doing, Kim?" Katrina asked in a shocked manner.

"I'm 'bouta drive this motherfuckin' Caddy!" The dark-skinned nineteen year-old announced boldly as she fumbled with the keys.

"You know you ain't supposed ta' touch that man shit when he not around, Kim! Not to mention you ain't got a mutherfuckin' license and you totally disrespectin' Dana!"

"You gotta lotta' nerve, talkin' 'bout disrespect!" Kim snapped as she curled her lips.

"What the fuck you said, bitch?" Katrina whispered as she jammed Kim up against the driver's side door of Jason's Cadillac.

Dana couldn't hear the conversation because she was still at the foot of the driveway waiting for the cab to arrive.

"The way I see it," Kim replied in a low tone of voice, "you more outta line than me by lovin' on another woman's man! Yea, I know 'bout that shit!" She said slyly as she eyed Katrina and twisted her lips as if to say, *now bitch what?*

Katrina couldn't believe what she was hearing and seeing from Kim. At the outset, she believed that Kim was a cool female because that's the way she presented herself. Katrina had even stood up for Kim when she was about to get assaulted in "Ma's" store; but on this night, Kim had shown a different side of herself. Yes, Katrina did love Jason, and she had told

Dana a while back that the two had slept together, but she understood how Dana felt for Jason. Dana had grown to be Katrina's friend and, no matter how much she wanted Jason, Katrina knew if Dana discovered how she truly felt about Jason, it would hurt her deeply and Katrina knew in her heart that Dana didn't deserve to have that happen to her.

Kim had shown her true colors to Katrina this night. She was a newcomer to the crew, though, and if Katrina had to tell it, Kimberly Pollard was at her core, a conniving, malicious and materialistic wanna-be. Katrina then made a mental note to keep an eye on Kim, because she wasn't about to let Kim play Jermaine out of his money the same way she was playing Rico out of his cash flow. Katrina snatched the keys from Kim's hand, when Kim tried to grab the keys back, the two girls began to tussle in the garage. Dana heard the commotion and quickly rushed back into the garage and stood between the two girls, asking what was the problem. Kim immediately began to tell Dana that Katrina had fucked Jason while she and Jason were just beginning to hook up.

Dana smiled and turned her head to the side and then burst into laughter. She then quickly jumped serious and said, "Kimberly, everybody know that Jason and Kay Kay used ta' mess around long before I even entered the picture. Until you know the whole story of why she stays here at Par Six, don't try and kick off something that's old news. If you want to remain a part of what's going on here, I suggest you keep your mouth closed and stop trying to break up friendships that were established long before you even got here. And give me my man keys, too! I ain't even much drivin'! And I be damn if *you*, or any other bitch gone sit they ass behind the steering wheel of this car!" Dana ended angrily as she snatched the keys from Kimberly's hands.

Katrina stood behind Dana bucking and pointing her middle fingers at an embarrassed Kimberly. Just then, the cab pulled up and Katrina and Dana started walking towards the car. Kim, not wanting to miss out on what the night had to offer, reluctantly got into the backseat of the cab and the girls rode to the French Quarters and met up with the boys inside the

restaurant and everybody, with the exception of Lamont, sat and ate a hearty seafood dinner consisting of deep-fried oysters, spicy boiled crabs and grilled shrimp.

Lamont had excused himself after having a quick drink, announcing that he had a rendezvous with a female he had been trying to hook up with for a long time. He took the keys to Dirty Red's Mercedes and slid him the keys to Jermaine's Navigator, exiting the restaurant alone, as the rest of the crew headed out to the Lakefront with two fat sacks of weed and four bottles of Cristal. It had been a while since the crew had hung out together. In fact, the last time they really hung out was a few weeks back, the night Manny was killed. All over again, they celebrated in memory of Manny. The boys now knew for certain what happened and they had taken care of part of the problem. They could now concentrate on Haywood and Rico, the two main people responsible for Manny's death.

It was about three in the morning when the crew had decided it was time to head home as they were all buzzing from the champagne and weed, and feeling pretty good. It was a very pleasant evening as the crew sat and chatted and joked with one another. Before they loaded into the Navigator, Dirty Red pulled Jermaine over to the side and talked to him about Kim. Katrina had told him about what had transpired between the three girls at *Par 6* earlier that night. Dirty Red told Jermaine to remember what happened to Manny, and not let a female be his weakness.

"Kim fine, brer," Dirty Red said to Jermaine as they sat side by side on the steps over-looking the lake. "She short, cute, and sexy, too, brer. But don't let that cloud your judgment about the type of person she is. She kinda' got outta pocket at the crib last night, ya' dig? Now, she welcome at the house, brer, but if she gone be with that foolishness, we gone have ta' cut her off. We don't need that shit, brer. You know how them white folks get ta' trippin'. Kay Kay told me, and now I'm telling you, this li'l broad ya' got here, she showed her true colors in front of Kay Kay when she tried to drive Jay-Dog's car. She gettin' outta pocket. You gotta' handle up, 'cause she a feisty li'l female."

"I know she gotta attitude, brer. But I ain't gone lie, I got feelings for her." Jermaine replied as he rested his elbows on his knees and looked out over the darkened waters of Lake Ponchartrain.

"I'm not sayin' you can't love her, 'Maine. I'm just saying make sure she the right one ta' love. Ya' feel me?"

Jermaine understood what Dirty Red was saying and he took it to heart. His love for Kim was overwhelming, however; and he could only hope he could keep his emotions in check and not let his love for Kim cloud his judgment.

"Let's ride people," yelled Dirty Red. "We gotta get these two love birds home," he said pointing to Dana and Jason, who were wrapped in each other's arms listening to *Voyage To Atlantis*, a classic slow jam by the Isley Brothers.

"Kim and Jermaine not in love!" Katrina answered, as she stood outside the rear driver's side door of the Navigator, deciding to complicate things as she was still angry with Kim for what she had done earlier back at *Par 6*.

"That's fucked up." Dirty Red replied, trying to keep from laughing. "I'm talking 'bout Jay and Dana."

"Oh, my bad!"

"You messy!" Kim snapped as she slid pass Katrina and hopped into the back row of the Navigator.

"And you a conniving bitch! Now what?" Katrina said as she got in behind Kim.

Before Katrina and Kim could pass any more words, Oscar turned up the stereo as loud as it would go and lay the front seat back. Oscar was high and drunk, and the last thing he wanted to hear was two females go back and forth calling each other names. The crew rode home and turned in for the night and began to prepare for their trip to Daytona Beach which was set to take place the upcoming weekend.

CHAPTER SIXTEEN

BE DOWN FOR ME

"Hundred! Hundred! Twenty! Fifty! Hundred! Hundred! Hundred! Twenty! Oh, yeah! Keep it coming! One line, mutherfuckas! One line! Straighten this shit up!" Jason yelled towards a jumbled line of at least thirty dope fiends that was steadily growing in length and numbers.

It was the Wednesday after the boys had done away with Cedric and the week before spring break. For the past few days the crew had been hustling steadily and readying themselves for their trip to Daytona Beach, Florida.

"Shit," Lamont exclaimed excitedly as he dropped a twenty dollar piece of crack cocaine into a fiend's palm, "we gone sell out before it get *dark*!"

Lamont and Jason had a system they used when they were selling product. With Oscar and Jermaine guarding the back of the house, and Dirty Red watching the block, from his favorite spot, the front window, the two came up with what they called the "Cash and Serve". One of the boys, usually Jason, would collect the cash and count the money real fast. Jason would then call out a number: 20, 50, or 100. That was the only way the boys served their product to the fiends.

Smaller dealers in the area sold nickel and dime and pieces; but they only got the scraps that fell off the boys' table. The crew had been hustling this same spot for years, and in that span of time, they had built up a large clientele. When the crack users came to score, they knew to have twenty, fifty, or a hundred or more dollars on their person. It depended on the day of the week it was, but on the average, the boys, made about three thousand dollars an hour, not including the money Dirty Red brought in from wholesaling his product. To make four hundred thousand dollars in a week's time was nothing to the crew—that was actually viewed as a slow week.

The plan was to hustle the remaining eight and a half months of the year then close the doors and go legit by throwing a city-wide bash on New Year's Eve. The next millennium would be crime-free and legal for the crew. Their run was slowly nearing its end.

The boys were on a pace to clear over fourteen million dollars at the end of their run in 1999. They would each walk away from the game with two million dollars each. Dirty Red had already taken two million dollars that was made early on and had put it away in an "expense account", so-to-speak. The monies that the crew was now spending was from the two-million dollars that Dirty Red had put aside for everybody to use. Dirty Red figured five young men should not spend four-hundred thousand-dollars apiece within a year, so the crew had plenty of money to play with.

The boys knew what Dirty Red had done, and they spent the money wisely. Everyone was looking forward to that last week in December, when they could all walk away from the game together, rich, and retired. What happened to Manny was like a bump in the road, because Dirty Red knew all-too-well that the venture the crew had taken on, one solid year of trouble-free hustling, would be a tremendous, if not impossible feat to accomplish without running into obstacles. Manny's murder had proved it. Still, the boys were keenly focused on their target date, in spite of losing Manny. That's what Dirty Red thought about as he sat in the window watching Lamont and Jason collect money from crack heads.

Dirty Red had also been talking to Swanson and Montgomery in the days following Cedric's murder. He discovered that Cedric's mother had filed a missing person's report the day after the boys had killed him, but the police weren't investigating the case because they had assumed Cedric was in jail under an alias name, something he'd done before. Dirty Red was happy to know that the law was not willing to get involved in Cedric's disappearance; and since Cedric's murder was not a problem, and the boys were planning to leave in two days to head out to spring break at Daytona Beach, he reasoned that now would be the perfect time to get rid of Rico and Haywood and set up a meeting with Damenga (the Colombian drug lord).

Dirty Red knew Haywood would be an easy mark because he always hung out on the corner of Jackson Avenue, where Rico's headquarters was located. Rico, on the other hand, moved around a lot, and Dirty Red didn't want to let on that he was plotting against the Dominican. Dirty Red wanted a plan that meant that the next time he'd see Rico, it would be for the last time. He decided the best way to pull off this particular job would be to hit Rico in his weak spot—so he sent Katrina back around to Rico's neighborhood.

Dirty Red told Katrina what Cedric had told him and the boys about what happened to Manny before they killed him and Katrina was shocked into silent tears. As she looked out of the windshield of Dirty Red's Mercedes a couple of days earlier, as the two sat parked outside of the hangar, Katrina was given the news and informed by Dirty Red that he really needed her help to take Rico down for what he'd done to Manny. As tears rolled down her face, Katrina took a deep breath, sighed, looked Dirty Red in the eyes and asked, "What you need me to do, Ben?"

Dirty Red explained to Katrina that she must be herself. No matter how mad she got at Rico, she must continue to be Katrina.

"Do I have to sleep with him," she asked.

"You ever slept with him before?" Dirty Red asked. "And be

honest about it." He added.

Katrina admitted that she had indeed slept with Rico the day after he killed Manny, but she didn't know Manny was dead, let alone that Rico was the one who had killed him. At that point, Katrina was angry. She didn't like to be played for a fool. All this time the eighteen year-old was under the impression that she was playing Rico, but she now knew that Rico had turned the tables by killing one of her friends and had turned right around and slept with her the very next day.

"He fucked me after knowing what he did to Manny?" Katrina asked as she wiped tears from her eyes.

"That's the kinda' game we in, Kay Kay." Dirty Red responded. "But I ain't mad at you, baby girl. I know you didn't know. Shit, we didn't find out Manny was dead until that Monday. That go to show you how much that nigga Rico care about you."

"You right," Katrina said somberly. "I got 'em!" She then said confidently, nodding her head. "I got that bitch!"

Dirty Red and Katrina hatched their plan to get rid of Rico on that very night. The Tuesday following their talk in Dirty Red's Mercedes, Katrina went over to Rico's house with Alicia. She made Rico take both of them out to eat and then to the mall to buy her a couple of outfits to wear for spring break. Rico tried to sleep with Katrina that night, but the thought of it made her sick to her stomach. She told him no and caught the bus home that Tuesday night with Alicia.

Now on this sunny Wednesday afternoon, Katrina was back over to Rico's house alone. She asked him to take her to the store so she could buy dinner and cook for him butt-naked. Katrina was throwing on her charm once more and Rico was steadily eating it up. As they were leaving Rico's house, Katrina told Rico that she had left her purse on his sofa. He went back inside to get it, and while he did so, Katrina remained seated in the passenger seat of his Jaguar. When Rico went into the house, Katrina removed two kilograms of cocaine from her school bag and placed them under the driver's

seat of Rico's car. Rico emerged from the house a few seconds later and got into the car, handed Katrina her purse and rode off to the grocery store; but before they got into the supermarket parking lot, they were pulled over by two plain clothes cops. The two cops just happened to be Swanson and Montgomery.

All day, Katrina had been teasing Rico about the good time she was going to show him. She told him she was going to cook him dinner butt-assed-naked and give him the best head he'd ever had in his life before she rode him to ecstasy. Rico's eyes lit up when she spoke those words. He had been with Katrina only one time; but he wanted so very much to be with her again, that he was willing to do anything, especially for a blow job. Nothing was going to stop Rico from freaking Katrina, except, maybe, Swanson and Montgomery. The two agents walked up to the driver's side of Rico's pristine metallic purple Jaguar and asked him to step out. Rico got out smiling to himself while asking the two agents what was the problem.

"Man, look," Rico told the cops before they answered his question, "I got this *bad* bitch! Katrina step out the ride so they can see what you look like, baby."

Katrina exited the car and struck a pose and smiled as she looked at Swanson and Montgomery.

Swanson had to keep his composure. He was tempted to laugh as he and Montgomery, along with Katrina, knew that they had Rico falling for their rouse. Rico was using his head to think with, but it was the one below his Prada jeans and not the one above his platinum-clad neck.

"See that fine mutherfucka right there? She gone cook for me —naked! Picture that shit!" Rico said whilst smiling.

"Yeah?" Swanson asked as he turned his attention to Rico and continued speaking. "That's nice. And she is a looker I must say. But we have reason to believe you are trafficking drugs in this neighborhood so dinner may be cut short, son."

Rico donned a look of disbelief. "What? Drugs? I ain't got no

drugs, man! You can look if you want. Go ahead! Look!" He replied as he extended his arms towards his car.

Rico was confident he didn't have any drugs in his car, so he willingly gave the agents permission to search. When Montgomery came up with the cocaine, however, Rico nearly fainted. He leaned against the hood of the car with wobbly knees, repeatedly stating that cocaine wasn't his and he didn't know where it had come from.

"Whatever! We heard it all before—playa! Turn your ass around and place your hands on the fuckin' hood!" Montgomery remarked without compassion as he shoved Rico forward.

Swanson handcuffed Rico and Katrina began her act once again. She was begging the agents not to take Rico to jail. Getting no reply from the agents, she ran around to the driver's side of the car. "Y'all bitches is wrong! We wasn't even fuckin' with y'all! Y'all put that in there! Rico don't say shit! They stopped you for nothin'!" Katrina said as she continued putting on a drama-filled performance worthy of an Oscar nomination.

Katrina had to play it that way so Rico wouldn't know he was being set up by her and the two agents. Swanson, adding to the stunt, pushed Katrina against the car and told her to, "get the fuck outta here". He then winked at Katrina, releasing a little smirk as Montgomery placed Rico in the back seat of the police car. Swanson then got behind the wheel of Rico's Jaguar and the detectives drove Rico to the police station and left Katrina, who caught the bus back to the Ninth Ward.

Inside the police station, the two cops began to apply pressure to Rico. They told him that he was looking at thirty years behind bars, but if he cooperated, they'd let him go.

"I can't! Them niggas gone kill me!"

"You got money," Swanson said. "You can leave town. Hell, you can leave the country! Anything's better than doing thirty years behind bars in the federal pen, right, my friend?"

"No, man," Rico said. "I can't rat. I just can't do that!"

"Alright," Swanson said as he grabbed Rico's folder. "Isaac, umm, forward everything to the D. A.'s office so we can get the ball rolling on this case. We got enough evidence to send this guy away for a very, very long time, partner."

Montgomery grabbed the folder and began to inquire, "Do the drugs go—"

"Put that in evidence. It's been tested already. Make sure those results are in with the product, too. When we go to trial, we'll need those samples to prove our case." Swanson said, cutting Montgomery's question short.

"It'll be an easy one." Montgomery replied as he headed for the door.

"Hold up, brer," Rico called out to Montgomery. "I'm a give you a name. I'm a give you a name."

Montgomery paused and turned around, "Go ahead. We're listening," he said as he walked back to the table and stood before Rico.

Rico paused for a moment, held his head down and said softly, "Damenga Lapiente`.''

"Ohh," Swanson remarked as he leaned back in his chair. "Damenga. That's, that's the umm, the big time drug pusher from Texas, right?"

"That's him!" Rico snapped. "Now let me out this fuckin' shit hole!"

"It's not that easy, Rico." Montgomery remarked.

"You think you can drop a name and we're gonna just let you vamoose?" Swanson asked with a chuckle. "You have to give us more than just a name, my friend."

Rico leaned back in his chair in a defeated state and said, "What y'all need to know about him in order for me to go free?"

Swanson lit a cigar and looked over towards Montgomery

and smiled. The two detectives couldn't believe how easy it was to corner Rico. They had no intentions of busting Rico, let alone Damenga. All they wanted to do was get Rico to say Damenga's name. Rico did that and more; and Swanson and Montgomery secretly recorded every word he had spoken. They applied more pressure, telling Rico that with the amount of cocaine they had discovered, he may very well be in violation of federal laws, which would allow the government to seize all his material possessions.

Not wanting to become dead broke, Rico gave in and told the cops everything about Damenga's connection to the city. He told when and where the Colombian makes his drops and pick-ups, how many people he had working with-in the city, and how much cocaine he moved for Damenga in a month's time. Rico had given the cops enough information to take Damenga down and put him away for life.

Around the same time Swanson and Montgomery were wrapping up Rico's confession, Katrina had made it back to the dope house. She spoke to Lamont and Jason, and went straight to Dirty Red. She entered the bedroom and sat on the bed and folded her arms and stared at him as he sat in the chair in front of the window. Just minutes earlier, Dirty Red had gotten a phone call from Swanson, informing him of the progress that had been made. "I heard what happened, Kay Kay," Dirty Red said to Katrina. "How ya' feeling?"

"I'm cool," she replied.

"That's good, baby girl. You did *damn good* out there today." Dirty Red remarked as he pulled out a wad of money.

"No need to pay me, Ben. That one was on me."

"You sure?"

"Yeah," Katrina said as she stretched. "That was for Manny. But I'm tired, brer. I need to get some sleep. I got a lot on my mind, too. It's been a long day."

It was unusually quiet out this evening and the sun had just begun to set. The boys were out walking back and forth around

the house, having offed most of their product, and people in the neighborhood were lounging in their yards drinking beer and washing their cars. It was quiet in the dope house as well when Dirty Red mentioned to Katrina that she would have to see Rico one more time, knowing full well that Rico would go into hiding for a while until he was able to sort things out with Damenga and straighten things out in his neighborhood without anyone finding out he had gotten busted by the police. Dirty Red and Katrina now had Rico's back up against the wall and they were preparing to finish him off. In the meantime, they would wait on Rico's phone call to Katrina, which was sure to come.

"He gone wanna make sure you didn't tell nobody what happened today, Kay Kay. Knowing the nigga like I do, he gone do either one of two things—kill you, or pay you off ta' keep you quiet. And knowing that he gone need every dollar he got ta' lay low, he probably planning ta' kill you. That's what I'd do if I was in his shoes." Dirty Red remarked to Katrina.

"But you not Rico, Ben. And Rico may ask me to do something else—a third option."

"What's that?" Dirty Red asked as he turned around and eyed Katrina with an inquisitive look.

"He might ask me to run away to the Dominican Republic with him. You forgot he from there?"

Dirty Red frowned at Katrina's remark. "You actually think this nigga gone ask you to run off with him? That's a fuckin' fantasy, Kay Kay! This shit here real! This ain't a fuckin' movie! Y'all ain't gone runoff and live happily ever after! This nigga ratted on the mob! He gone cover his mutherfuckin' tracks and make sure nobody speak about what went down— including *you*!"

"As long as he think I don't know it's okay ta' him!" Katrina retorted in an aggravated tone.

Dirty Red knew Katrina all-too-well; but on this day, she was not speaking like the Katrina he had always known.

"Why we even having this conversation, Kay Kay," Dirty Red asked. "I mean, you sound like you hoping he do some shit like that so you can runoff with the bitch!"

Katrina was having a hard time expressing herself. She knew she was in deep with Dirty Red and she also knew Dirty Red was going to kill Rico the first chance he received. The reality of the situation was weighing heavy on her mind; on top of that, Katrina was now feeling sorry for Rico. She had set the man up, and now he was near death. Katrina's heart was blocking her judgment, but she dare not tell Dirty Red what was troubling her, so she shifted the conversation so as to avoid expressing how she truly felt, which was to maybe rethink killing Rico. "I don't want to runoff with Rico. And why would you say that you would kill me, Ben?"

"I'm sayin'—if I was in Rico's *position.* You know I got much love for you. Now, what's the real reason you talkin' crazy?"

Katrina really did want to rethink killing Rico; but she knew that was not an option with Dirty Red. The frustration of the situation had suddenly made the confused young woman felt alone and vulnerable , to say the least. Eighteen year-old Katrina was now in need of comfort and reassurance. And she knew exactly the person who could give her what she craved, as she was staring right at him.

Katrina stood up from the bed and walked over to Ben, grabbed his hand and said, "Ben, understand this here, I'm risking my life for crew. Right now you and I are the only two who know what's going on with Rico. I could be spending my last days on earth. These last few days have been hard on me, man. I haven't been feeling no love. It's been 'Go here. Go there. Meet me over here.' I'm scared, real scared, and if Rico's face is the last face I see before I die, I wanna die knowing somebody loved me."

"I love you. You know I love you."

"That's 'hood love. I'm talkin' 'bout real love. I want you to make love to me, Ben. Here and now." Katrina said as she

stared at Ben and took a few steps back.

Dirty Red had never looked upon Katrina in the way she was presenting herself to him this day. He always thought of her as a little sister. He knew Jermaine, Jason, Lamont, and Cedric, when he was alive, had all slept with Katrina, but for Dirty Red, Manny, and Oscar, she was always the little girl from the courtyard on Benefit Street who was taken from her mother and raised by them and Ms. Joyce.

Dirty Red began to realize that Katrina wasn't a little girl anymore. She was preparing to graduate from high school and attend college. She had transported dope for him and helped set up a big time drug dealer. She had been having sex, smoking weed and drinking on a regular basis. Katrina wasn't a little girl anymore, she was grown up, indeed. As she stood in the middle of the floor, removing her high school uniform, Dirty Red eyed her smooth caramel skin, curvy hips and flat stomach.

Katrina bit her bottom lip as she lowered her dark eyes, and pulled her jet black curly hair up into a ponytail. Dirty Red eyed her with the full understanding that she was no longer the little girl from Benefit Street, but an eighteen year-old young woman who was in serious need of comfort and reassurance. He lowered the window so he could still hear what was going on outside and locked the door to the room he and Katrina were in. He walked up behind the sexy teenager, pressed himself firmly against her round bottom and placed his right hand on her stomach. He gently placed his left hand under the now heavy-breathing teenager's pointed jaw and pulled her lovely face around to his.

The two stood in the center of the room kissing passionately as Katrina turned around to face Dirty Red head-on. She ran her hands through his shoulder length hair and clung on tightly to his muscular light-skinned frame as she kissed him hungrily. Dirty Red removed her bra and panties and Katrina's pert c-sized breast and silky smooth hairy vagina revealed themselves. Her nipples stood erect and throbbed to the rhythm of her beating heart. He placed a hand on Katrina's soft fleshy

mound, rubbing its soft labia and inner lips gently.

Katrina moaned, placed her head on Dirty Red's shoulder, raised one of her fleshy thighs and wrapped it around his waist and ground herself on his hand, releasing low soft moans. Dirty Red removed his clothes and guided Katrina towards the bed and slid on a condom as Katrina stretched her arms and spread her legs wide, lovingly welcoming Dirty Red. He laid his body gently on top of hers and immediately mounted Katrina, as she was dripping wet from the intense passion that the two were feeling towards one another at this particular time.

The two made love slowly at first. Dirty Red wanted to savor the moment he spent inside of Katrina's warm, tight-fitting vagina. He relished the young woman's flesh, adoring the feel of having Katrina's soft, sweet smelling skin next to and underneath his body. Dirty Red then turned over onto his back and Katrina straddled him and leaned forward and the two kissed passionately again as Katrina moved up and down on her lover's rigid pole. He gripped her firm round bottom and thrust hard, Katrina meeting his every stroke in return as she moaned sexily.

The two were in perfect unison as they stared one another in the eyes, grabbing one another, rubbing tender spots ever so gently. Katrina was receiving so much pleasure from Dirty Red she began to call his name. Over and over she moaned Ben's name, telling him how much she needed him until she climaxed in a high-pitched moan of delight and slowed her motion. She closed her eyes in preparation of a second orgasm as she hugged Dirty Red's head, rested her chin atop his forehead, and let him stroke her in rapid motion. The two were no longer making love, they were now eagerly fucking one another with uninhibited lust, holding onto one another tightly and kissing hungrily. Katrina spread her legs wider and slid all the way down Dirty Red's dick in an attempt to make herself become fully impaled.

When she reached the base of his shaft, she clasped her vaginal muscles repeatedly, milking Dirty Red's pole until the

twenty-five year-old could no longer restrain himself. He pulled Katrina's hair and stared her in the eyes as he grimaced and ejaculated into the condom. Dirty Red let go of Katrina's hair as she released her grip and eased off Dirty Red's sweaty body, all-the-while kissing him deeply. The two then lay in each other's arms, their flesh hot and sticky, both gasping for air as they laughed lowly. Dirty Red and Katrina silently replayed in their minds what they had just done as they kissed passionately. It seemed as if they were the only two on the planet at this particular moment. Katrina wiped the sweat from Dirty Red's face as she lay in his arms and kissed him fully on the mouth again before she sat up on the bed and thanked him for relieving her anxiety.

"We may never do this again," she said while looking at Dirty Red in a loving manner as she stroked his chest, "but it's one time I'll never forget, Ben."

Katrina then got up and wrapped a sheet around her body and picked up her clothes and began to unlock the door and exit the room to go and take a shower. "If I knew you was that good," she said before exiting the room, "I woulda gave you some a long time ago."

"My sentiments exactly." Dirty Red replied as he and Katrina chuckled lowly.

Katrina blew a kiss to Dirty Red before she exited the room and walked through the dining room towards the bathroom. She saw Oscar in the kitchen smiling and knew right away that he'd heard the two in the room. Oscar looked at Katrina's body, what little she had showing and began to chuckle.

Katrina smiled back. "I needed that, Oscar. You think I'm wrong?" She asked.

"Wrong for what? Shit, y'all grown. Y'all not kin either. I mean, you know you like a sister to me and Ben, but still, y'all ain't related."

Katrina walked into the bathroom smiling to herself about what had just taken place between her and Dirty Red. Oscar

walked into the bedroom where he saw Dirty Red putting his Dan Fouts throw back jersey back onto his body and pulling up his Girbaud jeans and smiled at Dirty Red as he handed him the blunt he was smoking.

"After all that noise you had home girl making, I know you put in some work. I think you gone need this ta' getcha' wind back. That shit good, ain't it?" Oscar asked.

"I don't know yet. I even hit the weed yet, O."

"Not the weed, nigga," Oscar said laughingly. "I'm talking 'bout the pussy!"

"You see me 'bouta smoke this mutherfucka, huh? Yea, brer, Katrina got that comeback for ya' ass. I see why Jason can't stay away from her."

The two twenty-five year-olds sat in the room and talked for a minute before Oscar went back onto the front porch to watch over the block as Dirty Red sat in the window and quickly replayed the whole scene one more time between him and Katrina before getting back into focus to continue making money this warm Wednesday night.

CHAPTER SEVENTEEN

THE SNAPSHOTS

About an hour later, as Katrina lay in the bed asleep, Oscar escorted Derrick Burkman, a husky, bald-headed 5'10" two-hundred and forty pound, dark-skinned eighteen year-old hustler into the room to see Dirty Red. Derrick, sometimes called 'Big Derrick', scored a half of kilo from the crew on a weekly basis and was in tight with the boys. As he sat across from Dirty Red, Derrick offered to help count the huge pile of hundreds, fifties and twenties that he poured onto the table. Dirty Red declined, telling Derrick that he always counted his own money. As he placed the bills into $1000 stacks, Dirty Red noticed that Derrick kept looking over to the bed where Katrina lay asleep under the covers.

"Eh, nigga! Ya' money on the table, not up under them covers over there!"

Derrick snapped back around and told Dirty Red how fine Katrina was and he'd pay for a piece of pussy.

"You'll pay for it huh, nigga? Yea, you and about a hundred mo' mutherfuckas. Too bad though whoaday, she ain't for sale."

"I know player, but it's a li'l chick out y'all crew that is for sale." Derrick responded.

"You don't say." Dirty Red replied as he raised his head up from the stacks of money on the table.

Dirty Red knew Derrick from the 'hood. He also knew Derrick was a man of his word because every time he spoke something, it proved to be true. Derrick was real, so Dirty Red listened attentively as he began to speak on what he knew.

"Man, you know I'm straight, ya' dig? I'm cool with y'all niggas and shit. I been 'round for a minute and I know y'all tight. So when I see somethin' fucked up going on, I'm a let y'all know what the dilly. But this time I'm telling *you* and *you* only. That li'l broad Kim? One of the niggas that work for me told me him and his twin brother paid the li'l chick five-hundred dollars and they took her to the hotel and ran a train on her. That was Monday night, and I knew he wasn't lying 'cause we rode by Delgado College campus in City Park yesterday mornin' and the li'l niggas called her over. She came over to they Expedition and hopped in the back seat and told me ta' get out while she handled her business. She gave both of 'em head that mornin' in the school parking lot."

"You saw this?" Dirty Red asked as he leaned back into his wooden chair.

"I'm, I'm tryna' tell ya' now, nigga! I was there! The niggas took pictures of the shit!" Derrick exclaimed as he slammed seven Polaroid pictures onto the wooden table that showed Kim sitting on the leather seats of the Expedition.

Kim was sitting next to Burtell, the twin who had paid her. She was naked from the waist up, shamelessly revealing her apple sized breasts as she clutched his penis in one hand and held up a middle finger with the other. The pictures showed Kim bending over the back seat, revealing her thong underwear, she had her legs spread, pulling her thong to one side revealing her sex. They were explicit pictures of Kim in various poses; three by herself and three with Burtell and one with Jarell, his twin brother, in which she sat on his lap

completely naked, except for the thong she wore, with her legs spread open.

Dirty Red picked up the pictures and looked at the sexy nineteen year-old and shook his head. He wasn't too surprised to learn of Kim's affairs outside of Jermaine after what Katrina had told him what *she* thought of Kim. Dirty Red was upset, however, that Kim was making a fool out of Jermaine behind his back. He decided to tell Jermaine, but not before they pulled the hit on Rico and his crew. Since they were leaving for Daytona in two days, he decided to hold on to the pictures and show them to Jermaine in Daytona. He wanted Jermaine in the right frame of mind since the move they were about to make on Rico and his crew could be deadly and dangerous.

Derrick told Dirty Red that as far as he knew, those were all the pictures. He had taken them from the twins and told them to stop messing around with Kim. When they refused, Derrick knew that keeping the twins on his payroll would cause conflict between him and the boys, so he fired the twins and sent them on their way. Dirty Red understood and told Derrick that they were still cool, and he was going to let Jermaine deal with Kim on his own once he showed him the pictures.

"You think he gone kill her?" Derrick asked.

"I ain't gone let that happen, Dee. If she a hoe, she a hoe. A nigga gone fuck a piece of pussy or get his dick sucked every chance he get—no matter who the hoe belong to. Them niggas know Jermaine, but fuck, they ain't his boys. And if his bitch gone give head or whatever, they gone take it. Bill and Monica showed us that shit. If the President gone get head in the Oval Office, what ya' think a nigga on the street gone do? They know Jermaine a baller. I guess they gettin' a thrill outta fuckin' another nigga ole lady or some shit. We gone put a stop ta' that shit in due time though." Dirty Red concluded as he placed the pictures in his pocket and opened the safe and handed Derrick a half kilo.

He then gave one-thousand dollars back to Derrick for the pictures and for being straight up and exposing Kim for who she really was.

Derrick left the room with his product; and when he did, Katrina sat up on the bed. "Let me see them pictures of Kim sucking dick!" She said loudly.

Dirty Red chuckled and told Katrina not to say anything about what was going on between Kim and the twins.

"I ain't gone say nothing! Come on! Let a bitch see the snapshots, brer!"

As he put on a wide smile, Dirty Red pointed his right index finger at Katrina and said, "I'm not gone put her out like that. Plus I know yo' ass—if you saw these pictures you probably hit her when ya' see her."

Katrina lay back down in the bed and rested her head on her forearm and shifted the covers with her free hand and said, "Alright, I ain't gotta see 'em. But that's fucked up about her, Ben. I told you she was only with Jermaine 'cause he buy her clothes and shit."

"You like money, too, though, Kay Kay."

"Man, you offered me money earlier and I turned it down. I know I can get whatever I want from any one of y'all, but do I always ask? No! A lot of the things I do, I do outta love. Y'all took me in and looked out for me when I couldn't fend for myself. I owe y'all man, and no matter what I'm always down for y'all, right or wrong, ya' feel me?"

All Dirty Red could do was nod his head in agreement as he sat behind the wooden table. Katrina was by far the most sincere and one of the realest females he'd ever known. Amidst a house full of killers, she held her own. She wasn't overly impressed by cars, money, clothes and the like, far different from Kim, who seemed to be truly materialistic. Katrina reasoned that if you were in the game killing, robbing, and slanging cocaine, then you should have the finer things in life. She had been around when Dirty Red, Manny, and Oscar were living hand to mouth. *"She watched us grow,"* Dirty Red said in a low tone inaudible even to himself, *"And in that time, she grew to become just like us."*

"You know, you can be a bad bitch if you wanna be." Dirty Red then said aloud.

"I'm already that," Katrina said as she pulled the covers back on top of her to go back to sleep. "I'm already that, Ben."

CHAPTER EIGHTEEN

DO THE DAMN THANG

"Shop closed! Who want some fuckin' grits? Shop closed!" Oscar yelled loudly from the front porch of the dope house early Thursday morning.

"Man, I'm tired as shit." Jason said as he rubbed his eyes and yawned.

"But not too tired for some grits, huh dog?" Lamont asked as he shook Jason to keep him alert.

"And you knooow iiiit!" Jason responded as he and Lamont laughed and crept from the right side of the home, headed towards the front stairs.

The crew had been hustling all night making deals and were just about to close their shop for the week. Jason and Lamont had been out on the block the entire night and were tired and hungry, but not necessarily in that order. Oscar, who had been guarding the front door, had taken some *No-doze* so he was wide awake this morning.

Jermaine had been guarding the back of the house with two newly-hired soldiers. One of the newly-hired guns was named Torre` Spears. He was a young dude about seventeen years-old

183

who stood about 6' tall. Torre` sported an Afro and he was real skinny. Dirty Red thought he would be a good asset to the crew after he learned Torre`s story.

Torre` was once a thief; he used to steal cars in the beginning. He then began breaking into houses and stealing clothes, and jewelry; but he was always broke. Dirty Red thought it was because he was on drugs, but he found out later that Torre` had his own apartment and a baby boy. Torre`s son's mother was in jail. She was locked up five months ago when the police busted her trying to pawn jewelry that Torre` had stolen. She took the rap for Torre` and received a two year sentence. Torre` wasn't on drugs, he was just a young hustler trying to take care of his family. Dirty Red came to see that he was a hustler that was able to keep his focus so he put him on the roster.

Lil Earl was the other newly-hired gunman. He was now twenty-three years of age. He'd become a hardened veteran in the fields of armed robbery and car-jacking. Lil Earl had done a couple of jobs with crew, including the job the boys had pulled on Sebas back in '91. Dirty Red had never forgotten what Lil Earl had done the night he was shot. So when he asked Dirty Red for a job after he got out of jail, it wasn't a problem in the least. Lil Earl now had ten gold teeth in his mouth, six at the top and four at the bottom.

Jermaine talked all night about Kim and his feelings for her, and when Oscar yelled aloud that shop was closed, Lil Earl was damn glad. He walked away from Jermaine quickly, headed to the front of the house.

"What's on tap for today?" Jason asked Lamont as the two crossed the front yard.

"I'm glad you asked, brer. I got this li'l freak I'm a toss up this morning!" Lamont answered with enthusiasm.

"Yeah," said Jason. "She tight?"

Lamont just looked at Jason with a blank expression on his face as they walked toward the front porch.

"My bad, brer!" Jason snapped.

"You know how I roll pimp," Lamont said. "And you'll never guess who, Jay dog."

"Who?"

"Guess!"

"Who, brer?" Jason asked, never bothering to guess.

"Alicia!" Lamont said.

"Alicia?" Jason said as if he didn't believe Lamont. "Stuck up Alicia," he then asked.

"No doubt!" Lamont answered matter-of-factly.

"No ass-giving-up Alicia?" Jason stopped and asked.

"Yea that one right there!" Lamont said as he began laughing.

"Think she all that Alicia?"

"Yea, that's her!" Lamont answered as he and Jason laughed once more and resumed walking towards the front porch.

"Well," said Jason, "I ain't gone ask how ya' got her to go along with ya' shit, but I am gone ask how much you paying for it."

"I ain't paying nothing, brer!" Lamont snapped. "It was raining one day after school and I was coming from the gas station in Gentilly. I roll up on her at the bus stop on the corner of Higgins and Louisa Street, ya' dig? She had a plastic bag over her head and was tryna hold her books at the same time. She dropped her books and shit, ya' know? I'm watching the whole thing as I pull up to the red-light. I swerve up on side the curb, get out, picked her books up and threw 'em on the floor in the back of the Lex and told her get in and I'd drop her off. She looked at me like 'no, he didn't'! But I know she playing the role and shit you know? When she got in, I had some of that old Keith Sweat that Katrina used ta' like bumping and shit, the heat on, ya' dig? So she looking around now while we ridin'. She see a cell phone in the car, the TV's, white leather and shit. We pull up in front her house and she

asked if my phone work."

"No," said Jason as he and Lamont climbed the stairs and dapped Jermaine, Torre` and Lil Earl.

"Yeah, brer!" Lamont replied and continued. "So, I was like, 'yeah my shit work! You need to make a call'? She said she needed to call her li'l sister and tell her to open the door. So I told her, 'you know once you put that number in there I'm a hit redial and ask for ya'." Lamont said and continued on, "she said 'that's cool', and I been hollering for the past three weeks. She see the cars, the clothes, the jewels, the money a nigga making and all that shit, thinking she gone be a part of what's going down, ya' dig? I remember when a nigga was walking instead of pushin' a Lexus and she ain't wanna hollar. But now she ready to up the ass to a nigga on a moment's notice since he paid, ya' dig?"

"I hear ya', pimp," Jason said. "But ya' know it wouldna took me no three weeks to get her where ya' got her right?"

"Nigga! I gots that! Alicia is a big undercover freak I'm telling ya'!"

"Yeah," asked Jason, "run the train type of freak?"

"Ask Oscar. Alicia my hoe now. I'm tellin' ya' Jay." Lamont said smiling.

"You serious, L-Dog?" Jason asked lowly.

"Really though!" Lamont said laughing.

"Fuck that. I'm comin' this morning, nigga. Let me see what this hoe 'bout."

"Boy, Dana w-will k-k-kick your ass g-good and hard." Torre said.

Torre` sometimes stuttered when he talked. It was a condition he had developed when he was a baby.

"Stay outta this, young one!" Jason said to Torre`. "Ya' stutter-stutt-stutterin' bastard!"

Lil Earl, Jermaine, and Lamont started laughing as Torre` pointed both of his middle fingers at Jason.

"For real I'm coming this morning." Jason stated to Lamont just as Katrina walked out of the house.

"Speaking of freaks." Torre` said.

"Li'l boy," Katrina snapped, "I will smack your short ass on toppa' your head and push ya' chin in between ya' ankles! I told you about playin' with me!"

"Damn," said Torre`. "Y-y-you c-can't take a j-joke?"

"Damn! Y-you c-c-can't talk?" Katrina replied and started laughing. "Now go get ya' money so you can trick it off to me like you did last week."

"You trickin' to Katrina, Torre`?" Lil Earl asked.

"Don't you get any ideas, Lil Earl. I'm just playing with Torre`. We get down like that sometimes, but Ben do have y'all money ready," she said before Torre` and Lil Earl went inside to get paid.

Katrina then checked her appearance, looking down at her outfit. She had on a tight-fitting white Chanel leather pant suit that showed off her ample breasts and firm bottom. She wore an orange leather b-bop cap and had an orange three-quarter length leather Chanel jacket draped over right her arm with a pair of three-inch-heeled, orange Chanel leather boots on her feet. She also wore a diamond-crusted female Rolex and a pair of stunning 2 karat diamond-drop earrings. "Y'all like my outfit," she asked Jason, Jermaine and Lamont as they sat on the front porch.

"Yeah, that shit tight." Jermaine answered. "You going to church today?"

"No, stupid!" Katrina snapped. "I'm taking pictures for the year book! I am a senior ya' know!"

"You ain't graduating, Kay Kay!" Jason chimed in.

"You got me fucked up, Jay! I'm passing all my classes and I'm going to college in Arizona or Oklahoma! I'm gettin' far, far away from this mutherfuckin' place! Now nigga what? What college you going to? Oh, that's right, you quit school! Dumb ass!"

"Shiiit," said Jason, "before you graduate college I'm a been done retired somewhere chillin' in a big mansion in East Over and running a legit business. Now nigga what?"

"You got your way and I got mine, Jay. On the real though, y'all ready ta' drop me off at school?" Katrina asked.

"Yeah. Come on, Lamont, fuck the grits," Jason said. "We can take the pimp wagon this morning, brer. Jermaine going meet Kim over to Delgado." Jason ended as he, Lamont and Katrina hopped into his Cadillac whilst Jermaine vacuumed his Navigator shortly before heading out to meet Kim.

Torre` and Lil Earl were inside collecting their money from Dirty Red. He told the two that they wouldn't be back on duty until next week sometime and he would holler then. He gave Torre` and Lil Earl four-thousand dollars apiece because business had been exceedingly good the past three nights. The crew had made just over $240,000 dollars in only three days.

Dirty Red was tired and ready to go kick back and relax. When Torre` and Lil Earl left, he and Oscar cleaned up the house, grabbed their AK-47s, two duffel bags full of money and set the alarm to the house and hopped into the Mercedes and rode out to *Par 6* to divide the crew's share and go over their plan for tomorrow's hit. Oscar was also having a jet-black Lamborghini delivered to *Par 6* this afternoon. He'd paid $110,000 under the table, and was planning to bring it out for show over spring break. The remainder of Oscar and Dirty Red's day would be spent at *Par 6*.

Meanwhile, Katrina, Lamont, and Jason were pulling up to the high school.

"Damn, they added another building?" Jason asked rhetorically.

"Yeah," Katrina answered. "I'm surprised you still know where this place at, you ain't been in so long."

"Leave me 'lone! Leave me 'lone!" Jason said. "I be up here damn near every day dropping Dana off. I just never noticed that new building."

"Where Dana at anyway?" Katrina asked.

"She at home sick. She say she got the flu." Jason answered.

Lamont looked over to Jason and said, "That's why you said you was—"

Before Lamont could finish his statement, Jason cut him off. "Shut up! Shut it up," he snapped as he tapped the dashboard.

"Oh yeah! My bad, dog!"

Lamont had forgotten for a brief minute that Katrina was in the back seat, and if anybody couldn't hold water, it was Katrina. Not because she was a tatter-tail, but it was because of the fact that she liked Dana a lot. Lamont and Jason both knew that Katrina would rather see Dana and Jason split up rather than knowingly go along with Jason fooling around on her. After all, it was she that encouraged the two to start seeing one another.

"At home with the flu, huh?" Katrina asked, not believing Jason. "That girl might be pregnant."

"Will you knock it off?" Jason replied in an agitated manner. "Look, there go the li'l retarded dude that be tryna' touch your titties every day! Go fuck with him!"

"Stop making fun of people, ya' damn fool! Let me out right here, shoot! Dirty Red want me to come Par 6 quick-like tonight so come pick me up when school over this evening." Katrina said before she exited the Cadillac.

"Alright, bye!" Jason quickly replied.

When Katrina exited the car, Jason turned his stereo as loud as it would go. Some of the students watched him as he cruised

slowly through the high school's parking lot. Admiration was something the boys loved. Everybody in the Ninth Ward knew who they were, and from time to time they would get their stunt on, just like Jason was doing this morning. He flashed his open-faced gold teeth and let his diamond-clad wrist hang over the door while eyeing some of the girls as he cruised the parking lot bumping *Hell 4 a Hustler* by Tupac and The Outlaws. Jason was thinking that if Lamont was taking a female to the hotel, he should at least get one of the many females who liked him to do the same.

As they turned out of the parking lot, Jason looked out of the passenger side window and saw a young lady wearing a mid-thigh-high white silk skirt, with a tight-fitting orange silk top and orange stilettos. Her caramel skin glistened in the morning sun, making her thighs look like they were coated with flesh paint. Her hair was pressed down to her back, and the thin sunglasses she wore made her look like a star.

"Damn," Jason said. "Who in the fuck is that?"

Lamont leaned forward in the passenger seat and turned the stereo down, "Man, that's Tanaka ass," he said nonchalantly.

"Tanaka?" Jason quipped. "What the fuck? She, she had a makeover? Some kind of surgery or something? That bitch looks good!"

"Hollar then, nigga." Lamont remarked casually.

Rumor had it that Tanaka was now gay because she was reportedly caught at a basketball game French kissing another girl from the opposing team's school in the restroom inside the school's gymnasium.

"How old she is now?" Jason asked.

"She eighteen." Lamont replied. "She a senior, too. She probably dressed up like that for the year book pictures just like Katrina was."

Jason pulled over onto the curb and waited for Tanaka to pass the car. When she did, he got out and walked to the back of his

Cadillac. "Tanaka," he called out.

Tanaka turned around and took off her sunglasses revealing her slender, dark-brown sexy eyes. "Jason Witherspoon." She remarked through a smile, revealing her pearly white teeth.

Eighteen year-old Tanaka Romaire remembered all the times Jason had tried to seduce her and the numerous times she had brushed him off. She thought it was really flattering to be chased by a young man who could have just about any female he wanted to have. So when she saw him, she thought she would be polite and friendly, and hear what he would say this time.

Jason walked over to Tanaka and began telling her how different she looked, how beautiful she was. When he asked Tanaka about her plans after graduation and if she had any career goals, Tanaka quickly grew weary. "Enough of the idle chat. What you really want from me this mornin', nigga?" She asked with a smile as she placed her hands on her hips and cut her eyes at Jason.

Jason went on to explain to Tanaka that he would like to kick it with her one last time, for the first time.

"So you wanna just hit it and quit it?" Tanaka asked, not sure what Jason was getting at.

"Not really."

"Then what's your point? Come on now, 'cause I gotta go." Tanaka said, getting a little aggravated by Jason's vagueness.

"Alright this the deal—you know I'm with Dana, but I was dropping Lamont and Alicia off at the hotel and I thought I would find me a special friend that I can chill with from time to time, ya' dig?"

When Jason said Alicia's name, Tanaka's entire demeanor changed. She closed her slender dark-brown eyes, smiled and then let out a long sigh.

"What's the fuckin' smile all about? You comin'?" Jason asked.

191

Tanaka didn't answer right away. She merely stood still and silent, folding her arms as she thought. Truth was Tanaka wasn't outright gay, but she did like girls a little more than boys, and Alicia was one young lady that she would love to be in the same bed with. Tanaka had made sexual advances towards her friend, eighteen year-old Alicia Mason, from time to time. She would lick her lips seductively in front of Alicia and tell her romantic tales of how good it felt to make love to another woman. She quickly began to notice that, instead of cutting her off or walking away, Alicia would listen and sometimes ask a question or two.

One day in the gym's locker room, while Alicia was tying her tennis shoes, Tanaka walked up behind her and placed her hand on Alicia's rear end and began to rub her ass gently. Alicia didn't protest in the least. Tanaka was keenly aware that she and Alicia were the only two in the locker room so she dared to go further. She pulled Alicia's shorts to one side and tried to slide a finger in between her panties. It was then that she realized that Alicia had on a thong bikini. Tanaka moaned softly as she caressed the soft light skinned flesh of Alicia's rear end. She knelt down behind Alicia and rubbed her face across Alicia's soft flesh. She let her lips touch the left cheek of Alicia's behind. She kissed both of Alicia's cheeks and bit the left one gently and it caused Alicia to moan softly. Alicia placed her hands first against the gym lockers to steady herself, but Tanaka told her to grab her ankles so she "could see her beautiful ass up close".

Alicia spread her legs slightly and grabbed her ankles as Tanaka used her tongue and began rapidly flicking it up and down from Alicia's clitoris to her asshole. Tanaka's actions were soon beginning to force Alicia to moan in a soft voice.

"We gotta stop before we get caught." Tanaka suddenly said in a sultry tone.

"Please. Just lick me. Lick me anywhere you want to, Tanaka," Alicia replied in a low, husky tone.

When Alicia uttered those words, Tanaka knew she had her. She had been seducing Alicia off and on for the last month

now. When they tried again during lunch in an empty classroom, they were almost caught by a teacher who'd walked in just as Tanaka was removing Alicia's panties to go down on her. They were able to play it off as the teacher was never expecting to see such behavior unfolding on school grounds. She paid the two no mind as she walked into the classroom and began writing on the blackboard as they shuffled their clothes back into proper position. When they walked home that day, Alicia told Tanaka that the two of them should maybe rethink what they'd started. She was deathly afraid of being discovered; but Tanaka wanted to go further. She cared less what people thought.

Alicia, on the other hand, was reluctant to experiment any further with Tanaka. She had been avoiding Tanaka for the last two weeks; but Tanaka knew if Jason was telling the truth, a hotel would be the perfect place for her and Alicia to finish the sexual experimentation that they had begun a month ago. With the chance of finally having Alicia completely, Tanaka readily agreed to go to the hotel with Jason.

"I'm a give you some kitty cat today, Jason," she said. "But in order for you to fuck *me*, you have to help *me* fuck Alicia."

Jason stared at Tanaka with a puzzled look on his face.

"Just do it my way." Tanaka said as she laughed at Jason's cluelessness. "I'm a show you somethin' you ain't never seen before, Jason. Not in real life anyway I don't think. With you ain't no tellin' though," she stated in a sexy voice as she pressed her index finger to Jason's chest.

"Let's ride!" Jason said as he and Tanaka walked towards his car.

When Tanaka hopped in the back seat of Jason's Cadillac, Lamont turned the stereo up loud and leaned over and whispered to Jason, "I don't wanna know what ya' said to get her to go along with ya' shit, but I am gonna ask how much ya' payin' for it!"

Jason laughed out loud, his six open-faced gold teeth shining

in the morning sun as he drove off. The gang of three rode over to Alicia's house, and by the time they'd arrived, Lamont was clued in on Tanaka's desire for Alicia. The three were eager to see Alicia's reaction when she saw Tanaka in the car. The boys hoped she would go along with the program. To see the two females together would be a new adventure for the both of them. To heighten the experience, it was Alicia Mason, who'd always pretended to be stuck up, and Tanaka Romaire, a female Jason had been trying to seduce for months. It would indeed be a memorable episode in their young lives. They pulled up in front of Alicia's house and Lamont called her to tell her to come on out. "We outside waitin' in the car," he told Alicia when she answered the phone.

"Who is we?" Alicia asked with an attitude.

"My boy Jay in the Caddy. He just gone drop us off." Lamont answered.

"Ummhmm." Alicia replied, her voice hinting that she did not really believe Lamont. "Y'all two wanna do the same thing you and Oscar did, huh?"

"Well, if it's all good with you then it's for damn sure all good with us." Lamont remarked.

"I don't know man," Alicia replied in an unsure tone of voice. "I can't let what I'm doing get out, Lamont."

"Nobody ain't sayin' shit!" Lamont snapped. "We been kicking it for a minute and nobody still don't know. If you wanna get down, get down and be a part of the crew. You know we some real niggas, brer! Let's just go have some fun, ya' dig?"

Alicia thought for a moment. Jason wasn't ugly at all. The boys did have money, and they were all fun to hang out with. Besides that fact, she knew all of them personally. If she wanted to get her freak on, who'd be better than some cool ass niggas she knew and was packing that paper? "I be down in a minute," she said, still a little unsure about her actions.

"My boy can come or what?" Lamont asked.

"If he want to!" Alicia replied in an aggravated manner before she slammed the phone down.

Alicia felt as if she was being forced to go along with what Lamont and Jason were planning; still, she grabbed her purse and walked out of the house a few minutes later wearing a pair of tight, white Prada jeans, a silk orange blouse, and a pair of orange leather Chanel boots. Her brown hair hung down to her shoulders, and her high-yellow skin glistened in the morning sun.

"She wore orange and white like me!" Tanaka said happily as Alicia approached Jason's car.

"Why wouldn't she?" Jason asked. "Ain't that part of the school colors?" (orange, white and green).

"Yeah," said Tanaka, "I'm just saying... that's a sign...a good sign."

"Well, we 'bouta find out." Lamont remarked just before Alicia approached the car.

Alicia opened the back door to Jason's Cadillac and sat on the back seat. She didn't even notice Tanaka until she reached to close the door. Tanaka was sitting opposite of her with her shades on smiling from ear to ear looking directly at Alicia.

"Tanaka!" Alicia said surprised.

"Hey, chick!" Tanaka replied with a shit-eating grin on her face.

"See Lamont, brer! I told you I didn't want nobody to know what we doing!" Alicia snapped as she opened Jason's back passenger door and jumped out of the car.

Lamont tried to stop her, calling out from the front passenger seat, but Alicia continued walking angrily up the sidewalk back to her apartment building, never looking back.

"I'm a go talk to her!" Tanaka said as she got out of the car and ran towards Alicia.

"Alicia!" she called out loudly. "Alicia wait! Hold up! Why you tripping, girl?" Tanaka asked as she caught up with her friend. "I thought you woulda been glad to see me!"

"What we did," Alicia said as she paused and faced Tanaka, "what we did was between us. The same thing goes for what me and Lamont do—it's between us! I come out and see y'all two and Jason in the same damn car! It's like y'all just had it all planned out for Alicia!"

"You was going with Jason and Lamont anyway right?" Tanaka asked.

"And?" Alicia asked as she leaned back and stared Tanaka down as if to say "what that has to do with you"?

"What's the difference if I go, Alicia?"

"The difference is you a girl that wanna sleep with me in front of a bunch of people!"

"A bunch of people? That's Jason and Lamont! *Two* people! Two cool ass niggas from back in the day that's tryna' put ya' down but you too stuck up to have a li'l fun because you worryin' about what people gone say! Fuck 'em! You know ya' wanna come, Alicia!"

"I do! But I don't want anybody to know!" Alicia stated as she stomped the ground in frustration.

"Know what? That you like what I did to you in the locker room and that you want me to do it again? What? You scared to make love to another woman? Or is it just this woman? 'Cause I'm feelin' you, chick." Tanaka replied softly.

Alicia felt as if she was getting in over her head. The thought of her, Tanaka, Jason, and Lamont in the same room naked frightened her. As bad she wanted to experiment with Tanaka, it just seemed too freaky for her to have to go through with what her three friends had planned.

Tanaka reached out and touched Alicia's hand and Alicia jumped. "Damn, Alicia. You shaking." Tanaka stated in a caring manner. "Girl, calm down. It's all in good fun. You only

live once, ya' know? Let's just go and see, and if you don't like it we'll leave. Okay?"

"Promise?" Alicia asked coyly.

Tanaka grabbed Alicia's hands and pulled her back towards the car. "Stay close to me," she said as she walked backwards, pulling Alicia along gently. "I promise...you won't want to leave. Forget about Jay and Lamont. Act like they're not even there. I'll take good care of you, baby. I promise."

With those words spoken, Alicia eased up a little and grabbed Tanaka's hands a little harder. "I'm nervous." Alicia whispered.

"Me too. But you know just as well as do that it'll feel so good," Tanaka replied sexily as she continued pulling Alicia towards Jason's car.

When the two girls walked back and got into the backseat of Jason's car, they started giggling. Tanaka had game, serious game, and once again she was able to seduce Alicia. This time, she got Alicia to go along with her, in spite of her protests at the out-set.

Alicia in turn, decided to let herself go for one day. Tanaka turned her on, she had to admit, and she was uncontrollably curious to know what it would be like to make love to another woman, *this* woman, named Tanaka Romaire, her best friend. Today Alicia's fantasy would be fulfilled. Looking back on everything, she was glad Tanaka had come this day. She also began to see that Jason and Lamont were really cool and they could be a lot of fun to hang out with.

"Let's ride before I change my mind!" Alicia said as she began to loosen up.

Not wanting Alicia to abort the mission, Jason leaned over and whispered to Lamont over the music as he pulled away from the curb, "I don't know what Tanaka said, and I don't wanna know, but I am gone ask that bitch how much she paid!"

"You stupid, nigga!" Lamont said laughing.

"I was gone say it out loud yeah! But I ain't wanna fuck it up!" Jason remarked.

"I know!" Lamont responded. "Let's go do the damn thang!"

CHAPTER NINETEEN

ROOM FOR FOUR, WITH A TWIST

Katrina walked hurriedly down the breezeway of Carver High School headed towards the front office. She had gotten a call from someone saying he was her brother only a few minutes earlier. She was anxious that it would be Dirty Red on the telephone with bad news. She silently prayed that everyone was safe this day as she did not want to have to go through with what she gone through the day Manny died.

When Katrina answered the phone in the school's office, she was surprised to hear Rico's voice on the other end.

Rico told Katrina that he had to see her that night; but Katrina knew she couldn't see Rico without first letting Dirty Red know the two had talked. She figured Dirty Red would want to pay Rico a visit, the only problem was, no one knew where Rico was hiding out. Katrina began talking nicely to Rico, telling him how much she missed him and how worried she was about him. Rico took Katrina's bait and within minutes, she was able to get him to tell her where he was staying. Katrina in turn, told Rico that she would come and see him later that night. Rico told her to come by herself and Katrina agreed; although she knew off top that she would dare not go and visit Rico by herself. She got on her cell phone after

hanging up with Rico and contacted Dirty Red.

When he heard the news, Dirty Red figured now was the time to hit Rico, "Make sure Jay and L-Dog bring you out this way right after school." Dirty Red stated calmly.

Katrina agreed and snapped her cell phone shut and walked back towards her Trigonometry class whilst wondering where Jason and Lamont were since it was almost 2:30 and school was to be over at 3:15.

Jason and Lamont, meanwhile, had just finished their sexual encounter with Tanaka and Alicia and were on their way out of the room headed to the lobby of the Knight's Inn in Gentilly, a suburb of New Orleans not too far from Carver High School, to buy a couple of sodas from the vending machine. Tanaka and Alicia lay sprawled across the king-sized bed beside one another. Tanaka had asked the boys to order a pizza as they walked out the door, stating that she and Alicia were hungry.

"We can order something when we get back." Lamont replied.

When the two young men exited the room, they walked a little ways down the hall and burst into laughter.

"Can you believe that shit?" Lamont yelled.

"Huh, brer," responded Jason. "That was some straight outta *porno-type shit* that went down today, L-Dog."

Tanaka had indeed shown Jason and Lamont something they had never seen before with their natural eyes. She had sex with both young men at the same time in the beginning. Tanaka gave head to Lamont while Jason sexed her doggy-style. The boys then switched positions and repeated the act. Alicia sat in a chair and stroked herself, becoming more and more aroused as she watched her friend pleasure two males at the same time.

When she was done satisfying Jason and Lamont, Tanaka went and took a shower and emerged from the bathroom and turned her full attention to Alicia. She fell onto the bed on her left side and used her right middle finger to beckon Alicia onto

the huge mattress. Alicia got up as if in a trance. She never took her eyes off Tanaka as she walked over to her and stood beside the bed awaiting orders from her friend, who seemingly had her under a spell. Tanaka stretched forth her left hand and grabbed Alicia's left hand and pulled her onto the bed and laid her on her back and began to kiss her softly on the lips. Alicia reciprocated with lust-filled hunger by placing her tongue deep into Tanaka's mouth. Alicia was beside Tanaka with her right arm gently rubbing Tanaka's back and Tanaka quickly took charge. She moved forward and lay on top of Alicia. The two females' breasts meshed together and Alicia gasped in delight as she savored the new-found sensation of another woman's breast having been placed atop hers touching nipple to nipple.

The ecstasy that coursed through both females had their finger tips and toes tingling. Tanaka stared down at Alicia as the two gyrated in unison. Her fantasy was coming to fruition. Tanaka had wanted Alicia for so long, and now that she had her under her spell, she was going to do all she could to make Alicia's experience as unforgettable as possible so as to have her wanting more and more. Tanaka, wanting to please, began to make love to Alicia slowly and methodically. The two were gyrating in a lust-filled rhythm that had the both of them calling one another's name and kissing each other in an animalistic-type hunger as Tanaka began using her fingers to stimulate Alicia's clitoris as she kissed her passionately and ground her body against Alicia's sweet-smelling, smooth creamy flesh.

Jason and Lamont, meanwhile, walked around the bed watching what was to them, one of the sexiest sights they had ever seen: two females, one slender, sexy and dark-skinned, the other, thick, yellow-skinned and sexily voluptuous, go at it in an uninhibited manner that most males would only witness on video.

Tanaka was right. She was indeed showing the boys something they had never seen before with their naked eyes; and even though Jason and Lamont had received more than an eyeful, they could not get enough of the scene. And not only did they want to watch, they wanted to participate. The two

were taking in different angles of the two females making love, touching them on occasion as they waited for Tanaka's cue.

Alicia ground her body against Tanaka and shuddered in ecstasy, having accomplished the best orgasm of her young life thus far. Tanaka then sat back on her heels and spread Alicia's legs and began lapping at her soaking wet vagina. As she pleasured Alicia orally, Tanaka motioned the boys over to the bed with her left hand.

Alicia was so caught up in the pleasure she was receiving from Tanaka's tongue that she didn't even care that the four of them were now in the bed together. She opened her eyes in surprise when Jason knelt beside her, grabbed her right hand and guided it towards his erect member. Tanaka had Alicia so turned on, she couldn't resist even if she wanted to. She grabbed Jason's member and slowly stroked it before guiding him into her moist, warm mouth. She moaned as Jason's tool slid back and forth in between her lips as Lamont got behind Tanaka and sexed her doggy-style once more.

Jason then moved his member down Alicia's body and placed it before Tanaka's waiting mouth and she licked him like a woman possessed as Lamont pounded her ferociously from behind.

Tanaka then moved aside, encouraging Jason to "fuck her good", in reference to Alicia.

Alicia was beyond redemption at that point. She put up no resistance when Tanaka moved away from Lamont and knelt over her head and grabbed her legs and pulled them back towards her and held them open to allow Jason easy accesss to her friend's vagina.

Alicia moaned loudly as Jason penetrated her and began pounding her tight pussy relentlessly. Tanaka, as she held onto Alicia's out-stretched legs, straddled her and sat upon her face and placed her vagina onto her lips. Alicia lapped at Tanaka's juices as Jason fucked her hard. She repeatedly asked what was happening to her as she began writhing about uncontrollably. Tanaka looked down at Alicia's soaking vagina and could see

her pussy foaming and spurting clear fluid as Jason stroked her. Alicia had begun having multiple orgasms. She pushed Tanaka off her face, nearly throwing her from the bed. Tanaka only laughed, thinking of how reluctant Alicia was in the beginning, now here she was, coming nonstop and grabbing Jason's ass whilst bucking on his member. She was out of control.

Jason and Lamont then took turns on Alicia. The boys sexed both girls repeatedly until neither of the four could stand another round of sex. For over four hours, the gang of four enjoyed hot, mind-blowing sex that stretched from mid-morning well into the afternoon. As the four lay across the bed gasping for air and fanning the sweat to cool their bodies, Alicia asked them, practically begged Tanaka and the boys not to tell anyone. She did not want people to know that she went both ways, that the four of them had raunchy sex, and she had gotten downright freaky with the three of them. Tanaka assured Alicia that what they had done would be "their little secret".

Jason and Lamont, at the same time, knew they had turned Alicia out and they weren't about to spoil what they had going on with neither of the two females. Quiet would be kept.

The boys were discussing what had taken place as they stepped off the elevator into the lobby of the inn when they saw Kim walking past the front desk with Burtell and Jarell, the twins Derrick had mentioned to Dirty Red the day before. Kim saw Jason and Lamont and she tried to hurry and leave the lobby with the twins without being seen, but it was too late, she had already been spotted. The boys followed Kim into the parking lot and began asking her what she was doing coming out of a hotel with the twins. Kim began stuttering and told the two that she was helping the twins "do something".

"Fuck you was doing?" Jason asked in a disgusted tone. "Helpin' 'nem bust a nut?"

"How the fuck you gone play my boy like that? You know Jermaine still lovin' on you!" Lamont chimed in.

Kim took a defensive stance at that moment, believing she had something on at least one of the boys this day. "Why y'all standin' there tryna' check me?" She asked angrily and continued her protest. "What the fuck y'all two doing here? Now, unless y'all fucking each other, which I wouldn't put it past y'all two nasty asses, I know y'all got some bitches in y'all room! So you need ta' be tryna' figure out what ya' gone tell Dana when she hear this shit!" She said in complete sureness of herself whilst looking directly at Jason.

Jason charged at Kim, but Burtell jumped in between the two. The slender, dark-skinned, bald-faced, thin-eyed nineteen-year-old stuck his arm out and pushed Jason in the chest and told him to stay out of his and Kim's business.

Jason pounded his right fist into his left hand and looked to the sky and said, "Say, whoaday, you touch me again, and I'm a bust ya' fuckin' nose. Get the fuck out my way and take ya' punk ass twin with ya'! This bitch here off limits ta' y'all from here on out, brer! She for crew and she know that there. The only way she go is if she get let go and my dog ready ta' let her go! And right now, my nigga 'Maine ain't ready ta' let her go! My car right there, Kim. Let's go!" Jason ended as he ushered Kimberly towards his car.

Burtell reached out to grab Jason's arm as he shuffled Kim towards his Cadillac. When the twin grabbed him, Jason turned around and punched Burtell in the nose, breaking it. His brother, Jarell, tried to swing and hit Lamont, but Jason grabbed him and put him in a choke hold as Kim began screaming for Jason not to hurt the twin.

"Get the fuck in the car right now before I kill this nigga!" Jason yelled aloud as he tightened his grip around Jarell's neck, causing the twin to gasp for air and flail around helplessly.

"Alright, alright! I'm a go, man!" Kim yelled as she ran towards Jason's Caddy.

Jason let go of Jarell and shoved him forward towards Lamont, whose left fist quickly connected with the twin's forehead before he unleashed a torrent of rapid jabs to Jarell's

face that dropped him to his knees. "Let's kill these bitches!" Lamont yelled as he began kicking Jarell until he lay motionless, flat on his back.

Kim stood screaming next to Jason's Cadillac and watched as he and Lamont repeatedly stomped Jarell in the face and kicked him in the side as he lay motionless in the parking lot beside his brother, who had been knocked unconscious by Jason and lay on the concrete face down with a broken nose.

Jason then grabbed Jarell by his silk navy blue wife beater and pulled him up from the concrete and looked him in the face and said, "Ya' feel me now, huh, mutherfucka? Tell ya' brother when that bitch wake up—if I see 'em with this ho' again I'm a kill 'em," before he flung Jarell's limp body back to the concrete.

Jason then looked over to Burtell, who hadn't made a sound since he was punched in the nose. Realizing Burtell was still out cold, he looked around the parking lot and commanded Kimberly to get into the car. Kimberly was frightened out of her mind. She listened to Jason's command and entered the back of the car while Lamont went back into the lobby to pay the hotel clerk to keep him quiet about what happened in the parking lot.

When Lamont returned, Jason ran back up to the hotel room and gave two hundred dollars to Tanaka and Alicia so they could order their food and catch a cab home when they were ready to leave. He also told them that he and Lamont would get back with them later on down the road. Jason and Lamont then left the hotel and headed towards the high school to pick up Katrina.

During the ride to Carver High School, Jason and Lamont spoke not a word to Kimberly. They had visualized what they had done with Tanaka and Alicia, and they could only imagine what Kim had been doing with the twins. Kim didn't say anything during the entire ride either. Lamont would look over the backseat at her from time to time and just shake his head in disgust; and whenever he did so, Kim would just look at Lamont with wide eyes and pop and roll her neck as if to say

"nigga, what"?

Kim knew that Jermaine was weak for her, and all she would do is make up a story, make love to him once more, and everything would be back to normal. She hated the fact that the boys looked out for one another the way they did, though. If she could just get the rest of the crew to stop interfering, she could have her cake and eat it too. She liked Jermaine's money. She liked *Par 6* and all the pretty cars and the fun the boys had on a daily basis, but Jermaine, if Kim had to tell it, was not a good lover. Kim loved to have kinky sex, rough sex, and Jermaine was a lame lay for her. The twins turned her out a while back and she couldn't get enough of what they had to bring to the bedroom.

Kim loved Jermaine's money, but she loved how the twins' put it down when it came to sex. She was torn, and rather than make a decision, she played all three of the young men. She began to realize that she wasn't going to be able to pull off her act for much longer if she didn't sharpen her skills. That's what she thought about as the boys pulled into the school's driveway to pick up Katrina.

When Katrina got into the backseat of the Cadillac, she noticed the look of aggravation displayed upon Kimberly's face. When she asked Kimberly what was her problem, Jason jumped in and told her what he and Lamont had witnessed at the inn and Katrina merely shook her head. She wasn't surprised in the least because she had already heard about Kim and the twins a day earlier.

Kimberly decided right then and there that the more the crew interfered with what she had going on, the more she would just fuck over Jermaine. Kim was getting under the crew's skin and she knew it; but she also knew that if Jermaine wanted her around, the crew would have to respect that fact. *"I just have ta' be more careful how I deal with Jermaine."* Kim thought to herself.

The crew had arrived at *Par 6* just before five in the evening. Jason had stopped to pick Dana up from her parents' home and had dared Kim to tell her what happened before Dana entered

his Cadillac. Kim realized that Dana would not believe her, especially after what happened between her and Katrina in the garage the week before, so she kept her mouth closed the whole ride. When the five of them stepped out of the car in the garage over to *Par 6*, they noticed an extra car in the garage covered with a tarp. Lamont and Katrina were preparing to raise the cover, until Oscar came over the monitor and told them not to touch the vehicle.

"That's for Daytona! Step away from the fuckin' vehicle!" He laughed over the P.A. system.

The five looked at the tarp and tried to guess what was underneath as they stepped onto the elevator to head upstairs.

"Whatever it is, I know it's sweet," remarked Jason.

"No doubt," added Lamont. "You know Big O always gotta out do the next man. But he gone keep it covered up ta' keep a nigga guessin'."

"You cover ya' shit up and try ta' hide it when you don't want nobody knowing what ya' got goin' on." Katrina said as she stared Kim down, referring to what had taken place earlier with her and the twins.

When the elevator door opened, everybody stepped off, Kim was the last person, and as she walked behind Katrina, she purposely stuck out her leg and tripped Katrina as she walked off the elevator. Katrina turned around after she caught her balance and charged at Kim, but Jermaine stepped in and greeted Kim with a hug before Katrina could get to her.

Jermaine then asked Kim where she had been, as he had been up to the college campus looking for her. As she looked Katrina in the eyes, Kim kissed Jermaine on the cheek and told him she went to the downtown library to finish a term paper she needed to complete for the semester at Delgado College. The boys had a meeting with Dirty Red and Oscar, so Kim immediately kissed Jermaine fully on the mouth and walked past him.

"Go ahead and handle your business, baby," Kim remarked

devilishly as she eyed Katrina, "I ain't going nowhere."

Katrina rushed Kim again; it hurt her to see this female play with Jermaine's feelings in such an uncaring manner. It reminded her so much of the way she was playing Rico, and Katrina knew exactly where Rico was headed. Dirty Red stopped her and told her Kim would get hers in due time.

"Just be cool," he whispered. "You know what we 'bouta do. We gone handle that shit right there, but now ain't the time." Dirty Red whispered as he hugged Katrina and backed her into the kitchen.

"That's a lowdown bitch! I'm tellin' ya', if something happen to Jermaine, I'm a bury that bitch. She ain't like us, Ben, and you know that shit! I hate that hoe!" Katrina hissed lowly to Dirty Red.

"I know, but we gotta let Jermaine know and then let him deal with that. But now ain't the time. You and Dana just chill out. We gone have this meeting and then we gone go see what's up with Rico. Fuck Kim!"

Katrina wiped the tears that began to flow from her eyes and walked over to the dining room table and poured herself a glass of cognac as Dirty Red and the boys stepped onto the elevator to ride down into the garage to enter the office in order to review some information that had been obtained from Swanson and Montgomery earlier in the day.

CHAPTER TWENTY

ONE IN THE CHAMBER

When the boys were all settled into the office, Oscar turned on the projection screen that was behind Dirty Red's desk and handed him the remote control before he rested up against the mini bar. Jason, Lamont and Jermaine all took a seat on the leather couches lining the walls of the room as Dirty Red sat behind his desk, turned and faced the video screen, and told the crew that they were now watching the video of Rico ratting out Damenga.

Dirty Red and Oscar had deconstructed the video earlier in the day and the two of them wanted to hear the boys' opinion of the footage they had reviewed before they went any further with the plan they were putting together.

The boys watched the video intently as they listened to Rico tell all he knew over a period of thirty minutes.

"What y'all think?" Dirty Red asked as he picked up the remote, turned off the video and turned around in his huge leather chair and faced his crew.

"Man," answered Jason, "when Damenga hear this nigga telling this man whole operation, he should wanna pay us for

doin' him a favor." He remarked as he and Jermaine dapped one another.

"I'm thinkin' that too, Jay," Dirty Red replied, "but if it's as good as we all think it is, and if we play it right, Damenga should wanna fuck with us on the strength of what we done for him. Plus we get payback for Manny without repercussions from the cartel, ya' dig?"

Lamont listened, and when Dirty Red finished speaking, he posed a question to him. "What if Damenga don't give a fuck about what Rico did and decide he just gone come after us for touching one of his soldiers?"

"Good question, L-Dog." Dirty Red replied as he poured himself a drink. "The li'l bit I do know about Damenga? If he don't agree with what's going down—then we just killed ourselves. But I been in this game long enough ta' know that nobody likes a rat, ya' dig? Damenga's a business man—first and foremost. The nigga love *money* and we *makes* money. Now, I ain't never been wrong about a nigga all this time we been in this shit, and it's my gut that's tellin' me that we gone be some rich hustlas if we go through with what we 'bouta do. I love y'all niggas—ever since Benefit Street. We been down for each other from day one. Like family ya' dig? And if I thought for a split second that this move right here would get my family killed, I wouldn't do it. I'm asking y'all ta' trust me and Oscar on this move right here and in less than a year, we can all walk away from the game rich and retired. We can come out with way more than just that two million apiece we pushing hard for, ya' feel me?"

Jason, Lamont and Jermaine nodded in agreement and Dirty Red told them what he needed the boys to do. The following day, at around 12:30 in the afternoon, they were to ride up on the corner outside the Magnolia projects and shut the whole block down with the heavy artillery stored away at *Par 6*. He then gave the boys a firm order, "I want Haywood dead. If nobody else get hit, make sure that nigga Haywood get took out when it's all said and done."

Dirty Red wanted Haywood dead not only for participating in

Manny's murder, but also for the fact that he knew that Haywood was a strong enforcer for Rico. If anybody in the city could step in and block him and the boys from connecting with Damenga, it would be Haywood. Dirty Red also knew that Haywood could wage a war with the crew. Not that he would win, but Dirty Red knew that by killing Haywood right away, he would eliminate a bloody feud and an unnecessary step towards the crew's ultimate goal, which was to do business with Damenga. Dirty Red then called the boys over to his desk, and as he sat back down in his chair, he poured each of the boys a glass of cognac and stood up in order to propose a toast.

"I want y'all ta' be careful out there tomorrow," he said seriously as the boys all held their glasses in the air. "I want y'all ta' make it back unhurt, and then we gone party in Daytona for Manny. For Manny!" He said as he picked up his glass of cognac.

"For Manny!" The boys all said in unison as they touched rims and downed their drinks.

The boys began to unwind as Dirty Red called Katrina down to the office from the monitor on his desk. Oscar turned on the stereo and the boys sat and talked about the upcoming job. As Dirty Red sat behind his desk nodding his head to the *I Got Five On It* remix by The Luniz, he reached into his desk drawer and pulled out a fat ounce of weed and a pack of Swisher Sweet cigars.

"Somebody come help me roll these blunts!" Dirty Red yelled aloud.

Jermaine got up off the sofa and went over to the desk. "This that fire?" He asked as he unwrapped a cigar.

"'Maine, this that killa weed, ya' heard me?" Dirty Red said over the music as he and Jermaine laughed.

As the boys began smoking, Katrina knocked on the door and Oscar buzzed her in. "Damn, it's cloudy in here!" She stated as she fanned the smoke.

Dirty Red beckoned Katrina over to his desk as he sat back in

his chair and asked her to braid his hair into a ponytail. The two were getting ready to pay Rico a visit at the hotel he was staying in just outside of Hammond, Louisiana, about a forty-five minute ride northwest of New Orleans. The crew knew what Katrina and Dirty Red were planning that night and as the time grew close for them to leave, the tension in the room began to mount. They began asking Katrina if she was nervous or scared.

Katrina told the boys that she was cool and she knew exactly how to play Rico. It would be dangerous, indeed, because nobody knew for certain what Rico would do once Katrina entered the room. Somehow, she had to unlock the door to allow Dirty Red to enter the room without raising suspicion. For several minutes, Katrina and Rico would be alone in the room. As the two exited the office and got into Jermaine's Navigator, the only vehicle the crew had that Rico wouldn't recognize, the boys all hugged Katrina and told her they loved her.

"I know y'all don't want me and Ben ta' do it like this, but it's the only way ta' get next ta' Rico. We gone be straight. Y'all just make sure y'all handle up on Haywood tomorrow uptown." She concluded as Dirty Red backed out of the driveway, but not before telling Oscar to call Swanson and Montgomery to let them know that the two cops should get their clean-up crew ready.

The ride towards Hammond was calm and quiet. Katrina sat in the leather passenger seat sipping on a glass of cognac to relax her a little more, and then took a few tokes off the blunt that Dirty Red was smoking as the two cruised down a lonely stretch of Interstate-55 that crossed a body of swampland. She glanced out into the dark, murky waters of Lake Ponchartrain and the ghostly images of bald cyrpess trees cutting into the star-lit sky as she removed her 2 Karat diamond earrings and placed them in the console of the Navigator. She then placed the switchblade that Dirty Red had given her into her white Reebok jogging suit pants and laced up the shoestrings of her black "soldier" Reebok tennis shoes. Her dark, round eyes hung low as she removed her lip gloss with a napkin and

pulled her hair back into a French twist. When they reached Hammond, about an hour later, Dirty Red parked the Navigator in a Winn Dixie parking lot, out of sight of the hotel, just in case Rico was watching.

Katrina grabbed her cell phone and smiled a beautiful, but deadly-looking smile at Dirty Red. "Let's go get this bitch." She hissed.

Dirty Red smiled and nodded and told Katrina he would be outside the door no more than two minutes after she entered the room, so she could unlock the door whenever she was ready. While watching Katrina cross the busy four-lane street and enter the sparsely-filled and dimly-lit parking lot, heading towards the stairs leading to Rico's room, Dirty Red placed a silencer on the .45 automatic he had brought along to finish the job. He tucked the gun into his waistband just as the door Katrina was now standing before slowly opened.

When Katrina entered the room, Dirty Red saw Rico stick his head out quickly and scan the area. He knew Rico was making sure Katrina was alone. The decision to use Jermaine's jeep and park out of sight was a smart move on Dirty Red's part. Had Rico seen any car he recognized from Dirty Red's crew, the mission would have been severely compromised. When the door closed, Dirty Red exited the SUV, crossed the street and walked slowly up the stairs and stood beside the door as he waited for Katrina to unlock the door.

Meanwhile, inside the hotel room, Rico had grabbed Katrina and kissed her passionately. His breathing was heavy as he held on to Katrina for dear life. Katrina was caught off guard by Rico's affection, but she returned the gesture because she still had some feelings for the guy. The two hugged one another for a brief moment until Rico broke their embrace. Katrina then began looking for a way to let Dirty Red into the room, but every time she went towards the door Rico would stop her, saying that he didn't know if Damenga or anybody else was looking for him and they may burst in at any time. Rico then hit Katrina with a bombshell. "Katrina, run away with me."

"What?" Katrina asked as she eyed Rico with a look of disbelief.

"Yea, baby, me and you? We can go anywhere in the world. But I'm thinkin' we can go to my homeland in the Dominican Repub', ya' dig? We can buy a huge condo for ourselves. Chill on the beach, maybe have some kids, ya' feel me?"

Katrina did not want to hear those words come out of Rico's mouth. She had the same conversation with Dirty Red earlier in the week, and Dirty Red said he wouldn't bring it to the table. Katrina had reservations at the out-set; she knew Rico, but she trusted Dirty Red. She also had a gut feeling this situation would arise in spite of what Dirty Red had told her earlier in the week. Katrina was silently kicking herself because she didn't press Dirty Red for further advice about this particular scenario should it present itself.

She had trusted Dirty Red's words; but Katrina now knew that Dirty Red was wrong that day. She would have to wing it, and still find a way to unlock the door; even if she was able to do so, Katrina wasn't sure if she would even open the door for Dirty Red now. After all, Rico was prepared to give her a ticket to a new life. A new life outside of the game in an entirely new setting. The offer was becoming tempting to Katrina.

"I love you," Rico said, breaking Katrina's train of thoughts. "I know what happened with Manny was fucked up, but he embarrassed me in front of you. I can't be your man going around lettin' nobody disrespect me, disrespect us like that! I'm sorry for Manny, but Katrina, believe me, if I didn't care for you, baby, I would've left you alone, but I want you to be mine."

"So you killed him? You really did kill Manny?" Katrina asked as tears filled her eyes.

"Katrina trust me, baby, I wouldn't have never done that shit if I didn't love you. The day we got into that fight, when it was said and done, I felt, I felt—"

"Embarrassed?" Katrina asked.

"Yeah. Somebody made me look like a bitch in front the woman I love. You mean so much to me, Katrina. I think about you all the time. My world ain't right unless you in it. Please, come on home with me."

Katrina was now torn. No man had ever claimed to love her as much as Rico. She could tell that he was sincere in what he was saying, and when he put a ring on her finger and promised to make her an honest woman, she began to cry. As much as she wanted to run away with Rico, however, Katrina knew she was committed to her crew. Her crying was now more out of shame rather than happiness. Shame because she had briefly entertained the thought of running away with Rico. *"What the hell was I thinking? Runaway? With Rico? Really?"* Katrina asked herself as she stared at the three karat diamond and platinum ring that had been placed on her left index finger.

Katrina, in her heart, couldn't get past the fact that Rico had killed Manny, the young man that had saved her life, protected, clothed and fed her through the rough years. To run away with Rico would mean betraying Manny, Ms. Joyce, and the entire crew. That act would be too hard to swallow for Katrina. And the thought of her and Rico walking side by side on some beach in the Dominican Republic holding hands and lovingly smiling into one another's eyes as the waves lapped at their feet was the very thing Dirty Red had told her days earlier—a fucking fantasy.

Katrina could never love Rico completely after knowing what he had done to Manny. To love Rico, if Katrina had to tell it, would be just as if she had pulled the trigger and killed Manny herself. The thought not only sickened her, it now angered Katrina.

Rico began to notice Katrina's reluctance to give him a definite answer concerning the two of them running away together; and it hadn't crossed his mind the moment he laid eyes upon Katrina because he was so happy to see the woman he loved—but Rico was now wondering just how in the hell did Katrina make it out to Hammond all by herself when she

didn't have a car of her own. He didn't see any car that he recognized from Dirty Red's crew when he surveyed the parking lot, so he posed that very question to Katrina.

Katrina in turn, had no answer to Rico's inquisition; but her decision against him was final. Trusting that Dirty Red was waiting outside, Katrina broke and ran towards the door and quickly unlocked it.

Rico was stunned by Katrina's actions; but he was even more shocked when he witnessed Dirty Red now trying to enter his room. Katrina and Dirty Red would have caught Rico by surprise and would have been at an advantage had the top latch not been placed on the door. Those few seconds allowed Rico to quickly analyze the situation and at the same time it prevented Dirty Red from rushing into the room and swiftly overtaking Rico.

Rico immediately slammed the door shut and began slapping Katrina in the face ferociously once he realized that she was trying to set him up to be killed by Dirty Red. "How could you do this shit ta' me, bitch? I loved your ass!" Rico yelled in dismay as he attacked Katrina.

Katrina shielded her face with both her arms for a few seconds before she began fighting back to maintain her existence. "You killed Manny! What the fuck I'm supposed to do? I could never love you like that!" Katrina yelled as she tried the best she could to defend herself from Rico's powerful fist jabs and body blows.

As the two fought inside the room, Dirty Red was trying desperately to kick down the door. The door was solid, however, and he could hear Katrina inside the room engaged in the fight of her life. Rico slammed Katrina down onto the bed and straddled her chest and began choking the life from her lungs. She scratched his face and Rico, in turn, punched her in the face and knocked her unconscious just as Dirty Red penetrated the door and charged at him full force.

Rico pulled out a .9mm, jumped from the bed and the two young men began to struggle over the gun. The .45 that Dirty

Red held in his waistband fell onto the floor when he penetrated the door and he lost sight of his gun in the process. He now had to try to wrestle the gun away from Rico in order to save both he and Katrina's lives.

As the two struggled in the room, the noise they produced went unheard as the hotel had only a few guests on that side of the building and the two rooms on either side were empty. The door was still open, however; but the day to day hustle and passing cars kept the few people that were walking down the sidewalk that lined the parking lot from hearing any unusual sounds coming from the hotel room off in the distance.

As the two young men wrestled over the gun, Katrina stirred awake and witnessed the battle unfolding at the foot of the bed. Rico was getting the best of Dirty Red. The light-skinned Dominican was cock-strong. He began to gain control of the . 9mm the two wrestled over. He squeezed the trigger but Dirty Red had his hand on the gun as well. He had placed his hand in between the hammer of the gun and the gun's barrel. The hammer slammed forward into the flesh in between Dirty Red's thumb and fore finger and prevented the gun from firing. Dirty Red cursed at Rico, calling him "mutherfuckas" and "bitches" in various forms as Rico continued to squeeze the trigger repeatedly, tearing Dirty Red's flesh as he did so.

Dirty Red was able to slide the clip out of the gun. He now had a few seconds to catch his breath and continue to battle this formidable foe who was much stronger than he'd anticipated. Dirty Red let the gun go, and Rico took charge of the .9mm and aimed it at his skull as he stood before him.

Katrina screamed when she realized Rico had gotten the ups on Dirty Red. Dirty Red knelt on one knee as Rico squeezed the trigger, but the gun didn't fire. As he slid the clip out of the barrel, without Rico knowing, Dirty Red had placed the .9mm on safety, thus preventing the gun from firing. Dirty Red had taken a serious gamble; but he was being over-powered by Rico so he had to come up with a plan to for a counter attack against this spirit who would not go away easily. His ploy worked. Rico looked at the gun when it didn't fire and Dirty

Red seized the moment. He leapt to his feet and swung and hit Rico in the chin, knocking the muscle-bound Dominican back onto the dresser. The gun Rico held landed on the bed and Katrina quickly scrambled across mattress and picked it up. She looked at the side of the .9mm to see if she could see the red button on the side that would let her know that the gun was ready to fire just as Manny had shown her a while back. Katrina didn't see the red button, so she fumbled with gun and was finally able to push a lever down to release the safety latch. The red button was now in view.

Rico, meanwhile, had ripped the twenty-five inch TV from the wall and had thrown it at Dirty Red. Dirty Red caught the TV in his chest and stumbled back against the wall with the TV in his arms. He quickly regained his footing and raised the television above his head and threw it back at Rico, but Rico moved out of the way. The TV landed back on the dresser and shattered the huge glass mirror mounted on the wall before sliding across the top of the dresser and crashing to the floor in broken pieces. Rico quickly grabbed a piece of broken mirror glass and began charging towards Dirty Red again.

Dirty Red was almost out of breath. He told Katrina to shoot just as Rico charged at him with the broken mirror glass. Dirty Red was cut in the side by the broken glass that Rico held. He jumped back, Rico's second swing missing his stomach by mere inches. Rico went in for another swing, but before he could bring his arm forward, Dirty Red grabbed his wrist. Rico stuck out his leg and used his free hand to push Dirty Red backwards. He tripped over Rico's foot and landed on his back. The two were locked again as Rico began applying pressure to the broken glass he held, trying to penetrate Dirty Red's chest as he lay flat on his back.

"Shoot the fuckin' gun!" Dirty Red yelled to Katrina as he lay on the floor with Rico kneeling over him trying to drive the broken mirror glass into his chest.

"Go 'head and shoot bitch! It ain't loaded!" Rico yelled as he got up off of Dirty Red and kicked him in the face, incapacitating him. "I was gone give you the fuckin' world!

But you and this punk mutherfucka gone come here and try and kill me? Fuck that! I kill y'all bitches instead!"

Katrina just stared at Rico as he picked up the gun clip from beside Dirty Red and walked towards her. Emotions within Katrina were spinning out of control. She looked at Dirty Red as he lay in a daze and felt alone and helpless all of a sudden.

"I got the clip right here in my hands, bitch!" Rico said through heavy gasps of breath. "You gotta empty gun," he said matter-of-factly. "Give it to me and I'll let you live. But the nigga who you think you down for life with? I'm a have ta' kill homeboy! Now, we can still do us. I can kill 'em right now and we home free. I got over two-hundred and fifty thousand dollars under that same bed ya' kneeling on! The gun you got ain't loaded. If you squeeze that trigger and that burner don't fire like I know it won't 'cause I got the clip right here? I'm a kill both of y'all. It's your choice, Katrina. Ride with me, or die, bitch!"

Katrina thought hard about pulling the trigger. She remembered Manny telling her something about how a gun could still fire without a clip in it. It was not ride or die for her as Rico had said seconds before, it was do or die. Katrina then remembered a song Manny used to sing. *"I always keep one up in tha' chamber...ta' blast onna nigga whenever I'm in danger"*.

Manny had told Katrina once upon a time to never take a clip out of a gun and squeeze the trigger afterwards because it still had one live round in the chamber. He said the gun would still fire, but only once. As Rico stood at the foot of the bed, Katrina, now fully remembering the lesson Manny had given her, stepped off the side of the mattress and aimed the gun at Rico's chest. When he realized Katrina was about to fire, Rico lunged forward and tried to grab the gun from Katrina, but she quickly squeezed the trigger and blasted him in the chest. He fell forward, landing inches away from Katrina's feet and trembling legs.

The gunshot brought Dirty Red back into focus. He sat up and searched for his gun as Rico, with a bullet lodged in his

chest, crawled towards Katrina, grabbing at her legs, repeatedly telling her he was going to kill her. Katrina climbed back onto the bed and watched as Rico pulled himself up, using the covers for support. Rico's head came into view and Katrina could see the rage in his eyes as she rested upon her knees atop the mattress. "You's a dead mutherfucka!" Rico spoke angrily through his bloodied mouth as he began to climb onto the bed.

Katrina moved off the bed and stood opposite Rico as Dirty Red moved beside her and took the gun that she held in her hands and tucked it inside his waistband. Dirty Red had located his .45 seconds earlier underneath the bed. He grabbed Katrina by the hand to guide her towards the door with his .45 in his left hand as he eyed Rico, who was now standing at the top of the bed beside the head board.

"Ben, you ain't shit! Your bitch saved you!" Rico yelled as he and Dirty Red stared one another in the eyes.

"See, that's what you got you in trouble the first time, nigga —that big ass mouth of yours. Katrina close the door so we can finish this shit." Dirty Red said as he stood at the foot of the bed and aimed his silencer-tipped gun at Rico.

Rico eyed Katrina with a disappointed and heartbroken look displayed upon his face as she shut the door and went and stood beside Dirty Red. It was at that moment that he realized he should have killed Katrina the day after he killed Manny in order to eliminate the only person out of Ben's crew who could've ever gotten close to him. The love he had for Katrina, however, had fogged his thinking, and in the end, it would cost him his life.

"Katrina, fuck you and that bitch Manny! Suck a dead man dick!" Rico yelled aloud just before Dirty Red shot him four times in the chest.

Rico screamed in agony as he fell over the nightstand onto the bed. Sparks flew from the busted light-bulb as his body convulsed on top of the mattress. Dirty Red then walked and stood over Rico's body and shot him four more times in the

neck, nearly detaching his skull from the rest of his body. Rico's bloody corpse was left trembling violently on the bed. Dirty Red unplugged the lamp and he and Katrina hurried out of the hotel room, closed the door and fled unseen.

The two crossed the highway and disappeared into the grocery store's parking lot, hopped into Jermaine's Navigator and rode away calmly and quietly. Dirty Red's white t-shirt was torn and covered in blood. His left jaw was swollen, he had a slight cut on his side and the inside flesh of his right hand was ripped. Katrina was bruised as well. She had bruises in her face and around her neck where Rico had choked her. Her mouth was bloody and her Reebok jogging suit was nearly ripped off her body. The two breathed hard as Dirty Red called Swanson and Montgomery, who were on standby at a nearby hot dog stand, to clean up the bloody crime scene the two had left behind.

Dirty Red then turned on the air and turned the stereo up loud as he sipped cognac directly from the bottle. He passed the bottle to Katrina and she, too, gulped down a shot of cognac. Katrina then lit up the blunt she and Dirty Red were smoking before they went to the hotel to accomplish their mission. The two looked at one another and just stared for several seconds before they both burst into laughter as they smoked the marijuana, realizing they had pulled off a classic murder, toppling one of the biggest drug dealers in the city of New Orleans. It wasn't text book, but the job was done. Katrina thanked Manny in silent prayer, realizing that the things he had told her earlier in life had saved both her and Dirty Red.

"That was gangsta' shit right there. How the fuck you knew ta' pull the trigga' when I had done took the clip out that bitch?"

"Manny said he always kept 'one in tha' chamber'." Katrina answered as she took another toke off the blunt. "His spirit was in the room with us and I heard him talkin' to me." She ended proudly as she blew smoke through her nostrils.

CHAPTER TWENTY-ONE

STOP PLAYING

It was after midnight when Katrina and Dirty Red, both bruised and aching from their episode with Rico, arrived back at *Par 6*. When they got there, they saw that the house was quiet and only a few lights were on. The two exited the vehicle and headed up the elevator to the second floor of the condo. When they stepped off the elevator, they saw Jermaine sitting on the sofa smoking a blunt all by his lonesome. They could see that he had been crying, and as they walked towards him, asking what was wrong, they noticed a set of Polaroid pictures on the table.

"I was going upstairs to get in the shower with her right after y'all left. She left her clothes outside the door so I went ta' move 'em out the way. I picked 'em up and these fell out," Jermaine said as he picked up the pictures and threw the photos in Dirty Red and Katrina's direction.

Dirty Red picked the pictures up off the floor and looked at them and saw that these photos of Kimberly were a different set of pictures than the ones Derrick had given to him the day before. The pictures showed Kim on a bed, naked, lying next to Burtell. Katrina looked at the pictures and just shook her head, realizing that Kim was fast becoming a nuisance.

Kim had taken the pictures earlier that day when Jason and Lamont had caught her at the hotel with the twins. Dirty Red couldn't believe that Kim would be stupid enough to walk around *Par 6* with pictures of herself naked with another young man, knowing that the pictures may be found.

"Ya' need ta' let that hoe go 'bout her business, brer. For real." Dirty Red remarked lowly.

"I'm telling ya'," Katrina added. "She been a hoe from day one."

"Yea, but at least she ain't fucking the whole crew." Jermaine replied as he looked to the floor.

Katrina leaned back and stared at Jermaine with a look of shock displayed across her face. She placed her hands on her hips and rolled her neck. "Fuck you, Jermaine," she remarked angrily. "You lovin' on some wanna-be ass trick bitch that don't mean you no fuckin' good? Now, I'm a let what ya' said about me slide this time 'cause I know ya' hurtin' right now and ya' not thinking straight. But I'm a tell ya' to your face—that bitch right there don't give a fuck about you! Okay?" Katrina ended matter-of-factly in a high pitched voice as she held her hands up against the sides of her body and stared Jermaine down.

Dirty Red stepped in before the confrontation between Katrina and Jermaine heated up further. As he sat on the sofa next to Jermaine and began to bandage his hand, and while Katrina stood in the living room removing her tennis and half torn jogging suit to prepare for a shower, Kim walked down stairs through the dining room and kitchen and entered the living room. Jermaine saw her and immediately jumped off the sofa and ran in her direction.

Katrina grew excited as she watched Jermaine repeatedly slap Kim in the face while calling her names.

"Fuck you do that for, Ben," she asked when Dirty Red stepped in and pulled Jermaine off of Kim. "You shoulda' let 'em beat the shit out that bitch!" She said as she headed out the

living room towards the third floor to take a shower. "Too much drama around this get-up." She added just before she ascended the stairs. "And that bitch Kim is the main cause of it all."

Dirty Red shoved Jermaine down onto the couch and went and stood before Kim and stared down at her angrily. He was almost to the point of choking the life out of her; but he kept his composure. Still, he let his position be known, "I'm a tell ya' like this, Kim, 'Maine my dog, but the shit you pulling, gotta stop! You causing way too much trouble at par six! None of this shit, fighting, arguing, fucked up pictures and shit, didn't show up 'til your li'l stankin' ass came along! Now, I'm a say this and end mine, 'cause I'm ready for ya' ass ta' go, but ya' welcome on the strength of Jermaine! But I want you ta' hear me, and hear me good—you got one mo' mutherfuckin' time ta' show ya' ass 'round here—be it on pictures with the twins, or some other bullshit you bring to the table. Jermaine ain't gone have a fuckin' say so—I'm a throw you out this mutherfucka personally!" Dirty Red ended as he pushed Kim out of his face and walked into the kitchen to pour himself a drink.

Kim really didn't understand the type of people she was running with. She never knew that Dirty Red and Katrina had just come from killing somebody, and they would gladly do the same to her. She thought that the manipulation of Jermaine was just a game she could play without any repercussions. She was fast learning, however, that the crew didn't play games too often. She thought long and hard about what she was doing to Jermaine and the reasons behind why she acted the way she did.

"I don't want a nice boyfriend." She said as she walked around to the sofa and got down on her knees in front of Jermaine.

Dirty Red, realizing what was about to take place, turned down the living room lights and headed upstairs to his suite to clean up and turn in for the night.

"I got love for you Kim, but you keep fuckin' over me, brer."

Jermaine said lowly, nearly shedding tears over the drama Kim was putting him through on this night.

"I'm sorry Jermaine, but you a gangsta on the streets. Why you can't be one for me?" Kimberly asked, her voice cracking as if she were about to burst into tears.

Jermaine had always treated Kim with respect and adoration, but it was something that she didn't want at this point and time in her life. She knew Jermaine was a gangster, and she wanted him to be a gangster at all times. She didn't care about romance or passion; she wanted to know if Jermaine had killed somebody, how much dope he sold. She was infatuated with the lifestyle, and she wanted to be a "gangster bitch". Kim admired Katrina, and secretly, she wanted to be just like her.

Kim was in way over her head, however; the life she wanted to live beside Jermaine was a life she was not equipped to lead, let alone live. Katrina, on the other hand, had learned from some of the best. She came up in the game. She was raised by gangsters and her life was not an act; nor was it something to emulate or aspire to, the way Kim so desired. Katrina was surviving the best way she knew how, all the while striving towards a better day. That was the one thing about Katrina that Kimberly did not understand.

Kim, unlike Katrina, came from a well-to-do family. She had a good up-bringing like Dana, but she wanted so desperately to be a part of the street life; but she had no clue as to how to be down. She wanted Jermaine to teach her, but when Jermaine gave her love instead of game, Kim resented that and turned towards the twins. She explained everything to Jermaine before she pulled his silk pajama pants off and went down on him. Soon the pictures were forgotten and Kim and Jermaine sexed each other almost into a coma the entire night.

The next morning, the smell of bacon permeated throughout *Par 6*. Jason had awakened on this warm spring day and looked forward to some of Oscar's cooking. He was still half asleep as he reached over to his right side to put his arms around Dana. He crept across the length of the king-sized bed searching for Dana, but he did not feel his beau next to him.

He sat up on the edge of the bed and ran his fingers through his braids as he sucked on his gold teeth. He and Dana had gotten high and drunk off two bottles of Alize` and a blunt the night before and the two of them then had a wild time in their suite playing 'Boss and Secretary', a game in which Jason would put on one of his silk suits and have Dana, who was dressed in a business suit and wearing wire-rimmed eyeglasses, take 'dicktation'.

Jason smiled to himself as he replayed last night's episode with Dana as he got up from the bed and picked the used condoms up off the floor and threw them into the trash bin. When he did, he saw the hotel receipts from when he and Lamont took Tanaka and Alicia to the hotel. He also saw Tanaka's phone number that he had written down on the back of a business card, "Oh shit!" He yelled aloud in a desperate manner as he looked around the room for signs of Dana's belongings without success.

Jason began to think that Dana had found the hotel receipts and Tanaka's phone number and realized that he was messing around. He assumed that she had packed her belongings, and left *Par 6* to return home for good. He searched all around the room and saw that all of Dana's clothes were gone. He threw on his silk robe and rushed out of his room and headed down the stairs through the dining room into the kitchen. When he got there, he saw Oscar in front the open grill doing his thing.

Dirty Red was sitting at the counter reading the morning paper which featured a story about an unidentified male being found mutilated and shot to death in a hotel room in Hammond, Louisiana. "What up, Jay?" He asked, not getting an answer.

"You hungry, brer?" Oscar then asked Jason as he placed strips of bacon onto the grill.

"Nahh, brer! I can't find Dana! She found Tanaka phone number and that hotel receipt from yesterday! She took all her shit and left! You saw when she left?" Jason asked hysterically.

"Yea, she left with Jermaine, Katrina and Lamont in his Lex. They might still be in the garage though, 'cause they just went down the elevator, li'l whoaday. You might still can catch 'em, brer." Oscar said with a smirk on his face as he eyed Dirty Red, who was also smiling.

"Thanks, dog!" Jason replied as he jumped on the elevator and rode it down to the garage.

When he got to the garage, Jason saw that Lamont's Lexus was gone. "Mutherfucka!" He yelled.

"What's wrong, baby?" Dana asked in a soft, pleasant voice as she rocked happily to an Outkast song that blared on the radio in the garage.

Jason's heart skipped a beat when he realized that Dana was still in the house. "I thought you was gone!"

"No, silly! I'm washing my clothes so I can have something so fresh and so clean ta' wear to Daytona, 'cause...ain't nobody dope as me I'm just so fresh so clean!" Dana replied as she sung the chorus to *So Fresh and So Clean* by Outkast whilst gyrating happily to the song.

When Jason asked the whereabouts of Jermaine and Lamont, Dana told him that Jermaine and Lamont were on their way to drop Katrina off at the beauty salon in the Ninth Ward and then were headed over to JoAnne's house to pick up Manny's old station wagon. When Dana told Jason what was taking place and had not a hint of anger in her voice, he began to rationalize that she may not have seen the receipts and phone number.

"You know how ta' work that washing machine?"

"Yea, Oscar had showed me earlier."

It was then that Jason realized that Oscar was playing a trick on him. He rode the elevator back up and headed to the kitchen. When he got there, Oscar yelled aloud, "Gotcha," as he and Dirty Red burst into laughter.

"Y'all niggas play too much, brer!" Jason said as he sat down to eat a plate of grits and bacon, but not before returning

upstairs to hide Tanaka's phone number and to flush the hotel receipts.

Meanwhile, Lamont and Jermaine had dropped Katrina off at Kantrell's Beauty Salon in the Lower Ninth Ward and had made their way over to JoAnne's house in the Eighth Ward to pick up the station wagon that they would use for the hit on Haywood later on in the day. When they got to JoAnne's house, they saw the 5'11" skinny, dark-skinned, twenty-nine year-old sitting on her short stoop.

JoAnne brushed her burgundy braids over her shoulder and down her back as she eyed Jermaine and Lamont walking up the sidewalk. The boys spoke to her and she merely cocked her head to one side and blew the smoke from the marijuana blunt that she was smoking into the air, never speaking a word. The boys played around a lot with JoAnne; but since she was older than everyone in the entire crew, she wasn't always in a playing mood. It was usually because Oscar would stay gone for days at a time before he would return home.

Oscar, however, had always paid the bills and kept JoAnne with a pocket full of money. His not being around all the time was just a "side effect" of their relationship. At least that is what JoAnne told herself and her friends. Still, it bothered her sometimes. This morning was no different. "The keys in the wagon," she said. "Y'all niggas ain't been around in days, now ya' just pop up."

"You talked ta' Big O?" Lamont asked.

"Yea, that bitch called me this mornin' for the first time in four days. I don't know if he dead or not until he call my black ass. I keep looking ta' see that hoe on the news, but I guess he too smart for that shit ta' happen. Y'all get that mutherfuckin' raggedly ass station wagon out my yard so I can finish smoking this blunt by my damn self!"

"Let me hit that blunt!" Jermaine said as the two teens stood in front of JoAnne's stoop.

"Bitch, didn't you hear me say I'm a get high by my

mutherfuckin' self? Now y'all get y'all black asses in that mutherfuckin' car, start it up, and drive ya' black asses away from here!"

"Damn, brer! It's early in the mornin' and shit and you with all that fuckin' cursin' and shit! Fuck!" Jermaine said as he and Lamont began to sniggle to themselves.

"See, y'all li'l niggas now-days, y'all like ta' play a lot," JoAnne announced casually as she grabbed a chrome .380 caliber pistol from her backside and cocked it.

"What ya' gone do, JoAnne? Shoot me in the pinky toe?" Jermaine asked as he waved his left foot in front of JoAnne. "Come on, JoAnne! There it is! Shoot me in the pinky toe!" Jermaine chided as he imitated actress Della Reese's role in the movie Harlem Nights.

"Nahh, nigga, I'm a shoot ya' in ya' skinny black ass! That's where I'm a shoot ya'!" JoAnne said as her composure began to crack. "Man, y'all play too damn much, brer!" She finally said just before she burst into laughter. "I love that movie."

JoAnne loved all the boys unconditionally. They could always make her laugh, even when she didn't feel like laughing. She eased up at that moment; and as they chatted for a minute, JoAnne passed the blunt around and the three got high before Jermaine and Lamont got into the station wagon and drove back to *Par 6*.

When the two teens pulled into the driveway of *Par 6*, Dirty Red and Oscar were in the garage checking out Oscar's new whip. Oscar hurriedly pulled the tarp back over his Lamborghini when he saw the boys pulling up and he and Dirty Red walked out to the station wagon where Oscar quickly asked what happened to the car.

"What's wrong with it?" Lamont asked as he and Jermaine exited the station wagon and began to laugh to themselves.

"Look at that shit!" Oscar replied in high-pitched voice of disbelief.

Oscar had given JoAnne four-hundred dollars to tint the windows and place new hubcaps on the wagon; instead, she bought cans of black and white spray paint. She had spray painted the side and rear windows on the car black. She had found some old, rusted, aluminum mix and match hubcaps underneath her house and had placed them onto the vehicle. She also spray painted the word "GOD" on the rear window with white spray paint after the black spray paint had dried.

A few hours later, as the boys loaded their guns into the wagon, Oscar still couldn't get over what JoAnne had done; but he couldn't deny the fact that she had disguised the car really well. No one would ever suspect that a gang of killers would be riding in a black station wagon with the word "GOD" spray painted on the back.

Dirty Red, meanwhile, was headed out to the airport to meet Montgomery to pay the cops off for covering the crew's tracks after they killed Rico the night before. At the same time, Oscar, Jason, Jermaine and Lamont got into the station wagon and were preparing to ride uptown to deal with Haywood. As Oscar backed out of the driveway, he noticed that JoAnne had placed a bible on the dash and had opened it and circled Proverbs 24:8 which read, *"As for anyone scheming to do bad, he will be called a mere master of ideas."*

Oscar reflected briefly on the passage from the bible and closed the book and looked at Jermaine, who was sitting in the front seat. "What the fuck she put this shit on the dash for? That woman of mine need ta' stop playing with me, brer." He remarked as he looked over to Jermaine and put the car in reverse.

"I know what ya' mean, my nig," Jermaine said as he reflected on his and Kim's unstable relationship. "I know what ya' mean. These bitches just need ta' stop playing!"

CHAPTER TWENTY-TWO

PAY THE PIPER

As the boys rode across town in the station wagon, they turned on the radio just as a song by a local rapper, whose name was *Non-Stop*, was being played for the very first time. *Non-Stop* was from the same neighborhood as the boys; he knew them well as he often played football with Manny in the court yard on Benefit Street back in the day. When the boys heard the song, they grew exuberant. The name of the song was titled *From Day One*, and the boys all grew quiet as the rapper began to speak about Manny's murder, and also spit rhymes about Dirty Red and the boys, without using their names.

Katrina was sitting in the salon chair when she heard the song and she jumped up from her seat when she heard Manny's name. "That's my nigga, he rappin' 'bout," she said proudly as the room full of women looked at her with wide eyes and shocked expressions on their faces. "That's that boy Non-stop! He kickin' some real shit right there! That's *my people* he talking about!"

"Did somebody really get found shot up in a house?" A female asked inquiringly upon hearing one of the verses.

233

"Yeah." Katrina replied as she sat back down in the chair calmly.

Katrina began to realize that what *Non-Stop* was rapping about wasn't really anything to brag on, let alone be proud of. He glorified Manny's murder and boasted on how "them ninth ward boys" ran and controlled the neighborhood through violence and intimidation.

The boys, on the other hand, felt good about what *Non-Stop* was saying. "We out there, nigga," Oscar yelled as he continued to listen to the song blaring from the station wagon's radio as he turned into the drive-thru of a Popeye's.

"What the fuck you doin', brer?" Jermaine asked Oscar as he pulled up to the drive-thru menu.

"Huh? Oh! This here for Manny. Me and Dirty Red talked about this shit at his grave site. Let me get a three piece spicy white with red beans and rice!" Oscar yelled into the speaker.

"Well, fuck it then! Get another box for us!" Jermaine requested.

"Look," Oscar said to the cashier, "add a sixteen piece all spicy to that order, baby girl! And some fuckin' jalapeno peppers, ya' heard me? Eight of 'em!"

Oscar drove up to the window, paid for the order and left the drive-thru. Within minutes, he, Jermaine, Jason and Lamont were approaching Rico's old corner in search of Haywood. As they drove up Martin Luther King Jr. Boulevard past the house where Manny and Shawonda were murdered, Oscar stated in a somber tone of voice that he missed Manny.

"I ain't gone never forget that day, or what I saw in that house, brer." Jason said in a serious tone as Lamont and Jermaine nodded their heads in agreement.

The boys drove several more blocks past the wood-chipped boarded up houses that lined the busy four-lane avenue and made a right turn onto LaSalle Street. The narrow side street had cars parked on both sides of the curb in front of narrow

shotgun houses.

Kids would usually be out playing and hanging around, but it was just past noon, so the children were still in school. The neighborhood was somewhat void of people, except for a nearby Sewerage and Water Board crew that was preparing a broken water main a few blocks up.

Oscar drove several more blocks and made a right turn onto St. Andrew Street. As he rode, he looked to his left for signs of Haywood as he crossed over streets leading to Jackson Avenue. Oscar then made a left turn onto Magnolia Street and pulled onto the side curb in the middle of the block, two blocks east of Jackson Avenue.

He parked the station wagon in front of a vacant lot, which was overgrown with high weeds, piles of discarded appliances, and junked out cars. The mood in the station wagon was surreal as Oscar put the car in park and leaned over the front seat to look back at Jason and Lamont.

The inside of the station was a little dark as the sun wasn't able to penetrate the spray paint on the windows thoroughly. The whole ride the boys ate chicken, laughed, plotted, and reminisced about Manny as they rode through the city in the misfit looking black on black station wagon with "GOD" spray painted on the back. Now they were just two blocks away from Rico's neighborhood store and they began to take their guns off safety and prepare for the task at hand.

Jermaine placed his Calico machine gun in between his legs and rolled down his window completely. He swallowed hard, wiped sweat from his eyes, grabbed a pair of binoculars and leaned out of the window of the station wagon and aimed the binoculars towards the corners of Magnolia Street and Jackson Avenue where Haywood usually hung out.

"What ya' see?" Oscar asked as he bit into a piece of chicken.

"Not Haywood." Jermaine replied as he grabbed a piece of chicken and re-aimed the binoculars. "Hold up! I see two niggas out in front the store, and …" Jermaine then paused

briefly before he spoke once more, "Okay! I see Haywood Hummer parked across the street from the store, so he must be out here somewhere." He ended as he sat back down in his seat.

"Let me see them binoculars." Oscar requested.

Jason and Lamont sat in the back seat of the station wagon, both of them biting into a piece of chicken and trying to find a comfortable position to be able to fire their weapons when they approached their target. Lamont stood up on one knee as Jason knelt down on the wagon's floor. Neither could get into a position that felt comfortable enough to fire their weapon so they sat back on the seat, looked at each other and shook their heads as they ate their chicken.

Oscar peered through the binoculars and quickly recognized the two young men who were standing in front of the store. They were two of the three soldiers who came out of the corner store when he and Dirty Red confronted Rico, Haywood and Cedric the day of Manny's funeral. It was beginning to get hot in the station wagon and the boys were getting anxious.

"Man, let's move before those niggas leave, or somebody see us!" Jermaine said with a hint of frustration.

"Be cool, brer." Oscar remarked. "I wanna know where that nigga Haywood at before we go ride down there. Ain't nobody gone fuck with us right here."

"But I'm sayin', if Haywood ride out there, he out there!" Jermaine replied.

Oscar lowered the binoculars and stared at Jermaine. "How you know he ain't take one of them niggas shit and took a ride somewhere? Just be cool and trust me. I waited under a nigga house for six hours 'til he came home and I killed him. A few minutes ain't gone hurt, be chill!" He ended as he sat back and aimed the binoculars towards the corner.

After about five minutes, Oscar finally saw Haywood walk up onto the corners of Jackson Avenue and Magnolia Street from the opposite side of the building. Haywood whispered

into one of the soldiers' ears, and then walk back towards the opposite end of the store out of Oscar's line of sight just as the third of Rico's soldiers stepped out from the store and stood beside the other two soldiers.

"Alright," said Oscar, "they all down there. Look like Haywood on the other side on Jackson Avenue, but all of 'em outside the store now. Ain't nobody else out there either. Shit right for a nigga."

Oscar told the boys that it was about to go down. His plan was to let Lamont out with the AK-47 and approach the corner from Magnolia Street on which they were parked. Oscar would then ride off and turn right onto Josephine Street, one block before Jackson Avenue, go down two blocks turn left, go up another block, turn left again and approach the corner from Jackson Avenue. Jermaine would jump out in front of the store and open fire with his Calico, and Jason would let loose with his AR-15 from the back seat behind Oscar. "I'm a be bussin' the four-five until she empty. Everybody know they job, right? Remember what Dirty Red said, Haywood gotta go down today, homeboys." He said as he looked back at Lamont and Jason.

The boys all nodded before Lamont exited the car. Once Oscar placed the car in drive, he crept up slowly beside Lamont and said, "L-Dog, cross the street and stoop down some when you get on they block. When you hear us start bussin', you run towards the corner and hit any one of them niggas that run your way. Ya' got me?"

"I gotcha!" Lamont replied, his eyes wide open and breathing heavily.

Lamont quickly grabbed another piece of chicken, crossed the street, and began crouching low behind the parked cars that the lined Magnolia Street. Oscar then drove up one block and then turned right. He then drove down two blocks and made a left and began heading towards Jackson Avenue.

By that time, Lamont had made it onto the same block that Haywood and his crew were standing. He crouched behind a

parked car and raised a black bandana over his nose and mouth. He leaned his A-K 47 against the car and tightened his laces on his Reebok "soldiers", and rolled the cuffs up on his black Girbaud jeans. The oversized black tee shirt he wore, along with the assault rifle in his hands, gave Lamont the look of a soldier who was entrenched in urban warfare. In fact, at this moment of his young life, that it is exactly what he had become.

Lamont wasn't the only one transforming himself. Jermaine and Oscar both had ski masks on, too. The boys all wore black gloves, black t-shirts, black jeans and black shoes. Jason didn't have a bandana or black ski mask, however; he wore a pair of dark shades with a black skull cap that had a gold New Orleans Saints emblem on the front of it.

When Oscar made the left turn onto Jackson Avenue, heading towards Rico's store, the boys' adrenaline began to flow. They could see Haywood outside talking on his cellular phone. They could also see one of his soldiers standing next to him. The young man had on a jacket so the boys figured he had a gun or guns on him. They knew two more soldiers were on the other side of the store where Lamont was waiting. This was the point of no return for Oscar, Jermaine, Jason, and Lamont. It was about to go down; unprecedented violence in Uptown New Orleans was just seconds away.

"When I see that bitch Rico, I'm fuckin' 'em up on sight!" Haywood stated in a disgusted manner.

Haywood was upset because he believed Rico had him hustling out there by himself for the last three days. He was unaware that that Rico had been killed the night before and that Dirty Red and Katrina had had him in a trap since Wednesday. So here it was Friday afternoon, and Haywood was pissed off because he felt that Rico had him out there on the block by himself while he was laid up with some female. "Remind me to call that bitch Damenga tonight," was the last thing Haywood said to his soldier before the black station pulled up and stopped in the front of the corner store.

As Haywood chatted on his cell phone, he heard gunfire

erupt. When he saw his soldier fall to the ground and begin to leak blood from his skull, he knew a hit was being pulled and he was the intended target. The two soldiers on the other side of the store heard the gunfire and reached for their guns in order to return fire at the black station wagon, but Lamont, who was halfway down the block behind the two soldiers, began spraying his AK-47 and immediately got their attention.

One of the two gunmen turned around and his stomach was ripped open by the bullets that came from Lamont's AK-47. Two soldiers were down now and the gunfire was only escalating. The third soldier panicked and dropped his weapon and ducked down beside the store.

Haywood, having lost his back-up and fearing he would be hit with the hot lead that was raining down upon his set, dropped to the ground and rolled several times, dodging bullets as he rolled behind a parked car. He jumped up a few feet away and began shooting a .44 Desert Eagle as he ran down Jackson Avenue in the opposite direction of the station wagon.

The other soldier broke and ran in the direction opposite Haywood, but when he tried to cross Magnolia Street, Jermaine, who had hopped out of the front driver's seat, shot him in his legs. The soldier laid out in the middle of the street screaming in pain.

"Jay, get Haywood! Get Haywood!" Oscar yelled.

Jason jumped out of the back seat from behind Oscar and began to run after Haywood. Haywood would turn around and shoot from time to time, but his bullets never came close to hitting Jason. Haywood's soldier lay in the middle of Magnolia Street screaming in pain from the gunshot wounds inflicted upon him by Jermaine, but his battle wasn't over just yet. Oscar made a wide U-turn in the street. When he did, he purposely rolled over the soldier's legs, crushing them in the process just as Lamont jumped in the front seat of the station wagon amidst the wails and pleas of Haywood's last remaining soldier.

"I'm going down and make the block," Oscar told Jermaine, who was standing on the corner. "Run back down Magnolia

and turn left on Josephine! We gone trap Haywood on one of those blocks!"

Jermaine began to take off and run down the same block that Lamont was posted up on previously.

"Say,' Maine!" Oscar suddenly yelled.

Jermaine stopped and turned around. "What, bitch," he yelled towards Oscar in disgust as he was eager to catch Haywood.

"Do me a favor and kill that nigga behind the wagon and then go!"

Jermaine ran back past the wagon as Oscar sped off and stood right over the fallen soldier, "Hold up, brer," the soldier pleaded. "I ain't have nothing to do with Man—"

The soldier was silenced by the bullets from Jermaine's calico as they penetrated his skull, neck, and chest. He then took off down Magnolia Street, headed towards the next corner to trap Haywood.

Haywood by now had reached the corner at the opposite end of the block, and, as he made a right turn onto the next street, Jason opened fire with his AR-15 and shot him in the back. Haywood was so scared he didn't even feel the gunshot wound that Jason had inflicted upon him.

As he approached the middle of the block, however, pain and numbness began to set in from the bullet that went through his back and exited his stomach. Blood began to drip from the inside of Haywood's pants legs and onto the sidewalk, leaving a trail of blood on the concrete as he tried desperately to flee his attackers. Haywood began to stumble a little, getting weak from his wound. With the gun in his right hand, he ran along a wooden fence which implanted splinters his left arm, causing him more pain. Haywood made it to the end of the block, which was Josephine Street, and stepped into the middle of the intersection. When he did, he was greeted by the black station wagon. He fell to his knees at that moment, severely weakened from losing so much blood.

Oscar exited the driver's side of the station wagon and walked in front of the car and stood over Haywood.

Haywood looked Oscar in the eyes and spat blood from his mouth. "Say Oscar, brer, I ain't have nothin' ta' do with Manny, brer!"

"How tha' fuck you know this shit here 'bout Manny, nigga?" Oscar asked as he stood before Haywood.

Haywood realized that he was not going to walk away from this episode alive unless he used a little diplomacy, which was, by now, his only hope. He'd grown up with Oscar and tried to play on his emotions, relating how they use to hang together. "Come on, man! We, we fuckin' played ball together and shit back in the day! Made money together, dog! Remember, remember Sebas and, and, and all them licks we pulled and shit? And this, this how you gone do me?" Haywood asked through gasps of breath.

"Nigga, that's black history! What's good now, mutherfucka?" Oscar asked mercilessly as he aimed his weapon at Haywood.

When he realized his tactics were not going to work, Haywood cursed aloud, "Fuck you and that bitch Manny!"

Oscar kicked Haywood in the chest and he fell flat on his back. "No, fuck you, nigga! You know what time it is! Pay the piper, mutherfucka!" He yelled aloud as he snatched Haywood up by his shirt, placed the barrel of his .45 caliber pistol against Haywood's forehead and fired a single shot that blew the back of his skull open and sprayed brain matter onto the concrete, Oscar's shirt, hands and face.

Oscar flung Haywood's lifeless corpse onto the middle of Josephine Street and wiped the blood from his face with his t-shirt and quickly walked over to the passenger side of the car and took the three piece chicken dinner from Lamont's hands and threw it down beside Haywood. "Give that ta' Manny ya' ole bitch ass nigga!" Oscar said before he ran and hopped into the driver's seat of the station wagon just as Jermaine and

241

Jason made it to the intersection.

The two teens looked at Haywood's body and the chicken dinner beside him and laughed aloud as they headed towards the station wagon.

"Hurry up, brer!" Lamont yelled to Jason and Jermaine from the front seat as he looked around for any witnesses.

Jason and Jermaine hopped into the backseat of the station wagon and Oscar sped away, banging his hand on the steering wheel in exuberance as the crew sped down Josephine Street. Oscar then grabbed his cell phone and called Swanson, who was monitoring the dispatches that went out this day. The detective answered his phone and told Oscar that he had heard the reports of gunfire in the uptown area.

"Where y'all at?" Swanson asked quickly.

"Headed towards Saint Charles Avenue!"

"Well, get the hell outta' there fast! We got calls from a Sewerage and Water Board crew and a lady inside the store. They saying it's a war zone up there!"

"They know the car?" Oscar asked as he turned onto St. Charles Avenue and headed towards the interstate.

"All they know is a black four door was seen speeding up and down Jackson Avenue at the time of the shooting. Get rid of ya' soldiers, the guns and that fuckin' car now! Two of my guys giving a report that they were about to question two males in a black four door car nearby the river to the west. Most of the patrols headed that way. That should allow y'all time ta' get from around there and head east. I'll talk to you later." Swanson ended as he hung up the phone.

"Lamont, you left your Lexus by JoAnne right?" Oscar asked after hanging up the phone with Swanson.

"Yeah it's still over there."

The boys conversed as they rode calmly down St. Charles Avenue, and took the on-ramp leading to Interstate-10. The

station wagon bounced fiercely as Oscar veered onto the on ramp and floored the car. He told the boys that he would drop them off by JoAnne's house in the Eighth Ward and he would take the station wagon to the junkyard and scrap the vehicle.

The boys now rode in silence, and without remorse for what they had done. For them, it was just another day in the game and the boys were in it to win it. This day, like many other days, the boys had won. A necessary job was completed. Enemies were eliminated and everybody came away unhurt, just as Dirty Red had wished.

"Meet me out by the scrap yard after y'all hide those guns." Oscar said anxiously, breaking the silence as he pulled in front of JoAnne's house whilst looking to see if any police were around.

The car was hot and Oscar knew he had to get rid of it quickly. He made it over to the scrap yard on Almonaster Avenue within ten minutes and Jason, Jermaine and Lamont met him there fifteen minutes later, just as the car was being driven into the crusher.

Even though he was dead, it seemed as if Manny was with the crew the whole time they were exacting revenge on Cedric, Rico, and Haywood and Rico's soldiers. The boys watched as the old wagon, the wagon that Manny had first driven, the wagon from the 'hood that had given the crew its start, was flattened and discarded into a pile of scrap metal.

Meanwhile, Dirty Red had paid off the cops and had mailed the video he had of Rico talking to the cops, to Houston, Texas. It was addressed to a Porsche car lot owned by Damenga Lapiente`. In a few days, the crew would know if they had just moved themselves into position to become the lead players of the New Orleans cocaine drug trade, or if they had made a deadly mistake.

The entire gang met over at "Ma's" store where they all ate lunch and left town, headed towards Daytona Beach to relax for spring break. The streets of New Orleans would now be safe, at least for a few days.

CHAPTER TWENTY-THREE

SOUTHERN SWING

It was a beautiful Saturday afternoon when the crew arrived in Daytona. The sky was clear blue without a cloud in sight. The weather was near perfect, sunny and eighty degrees. The city of Daytona Beach was filled with spring-breakers from all over the South, Midwest and Northeast. People were everywhere; as well as the whips. The women were riding on the backs of motorcycles, walking down the main drag in large groups, hanging out of sunroofs of cars and sitting on the backs of drop tops. The fellas were all perched alongside their whips, enjoying the mixture of females of all shapes, sizes, colors and various ethnic backgrounds parading their "stallion status" as they searched out the top dogs that were hanging out along the Atlantic Sea's shore line.

It was a sight for everybody to behold when Dirty Red and the crew turned off Silver Beach Avenue onto South Atlantic Avenue. They made all heads turn and look their way as they cruised down the crowded avenue in full force. The sun beat down on the beach goers as they parted like the Red Sea to let the unfamiliar but stylish caravan parade down the heavily packed four-lane strip, commanding attention in the process.

Dirty Red led the way with his '99 Mercedes C class on 19"

245

Giovanni's with all white interior. His TV monitors were running a porno flick as he and Katrina eyed the people who were eying the crew.

Oscar followed in his black Lamborghini on 19" chrome spinners and the crowd gave him his props, emanating whistles and "chucking the deuce" as they nodded their heads. The interior of the "lamb" was black alligator skin trimmed in white leather, and the dash and steering wheel was laced-out in white oak. Oscar leaned forward and he encouraged JoAnne to do so as well. As he and JoAnne received props, Oscar pointed out to on-lookers that he had his name, as well as JoAnne's, engraved into the headrests in crushed diamonds and pearls. He and JoAnne rode down the strip with the top down and the doors up on the Lamb as they sipped cognac; enjoying the admiration they were receiving this day, stopping from time to time to take pictures with the partiers.

Jason followed Oscar in his "big body Caddy" with the killer sound system. He had the music crunk to the max as he played *Down for My Niggas* by C-Murder, Mr. Magic, and Snoop Dogg. The beach-goers rocked to and fro and bounced to the music, enjoying the heavy bass that permeated from Jason's Cadillac. Jason looked over at Dana and laughed when he saw she had covered her ears as the music and bass were just that loud and hard-hitting.

Jermaine and Kim followed Jason and people admired the burgundy Navigator on 26's with the TV screens lit up with the movie *Goodfellas* on clear display. Kim enjoyed the attention a great deal. From time to time, she would holler out the window to various on lookers that "the real niggas done made it to Daytona!"

Lamont was bringing up the rear in his evergreen Lexus. He, Tanaka and Alicia were riding together. It had taken some arm twisting to get Alicia to go along with the crew, but Tanaka had come through again; persuading her childhood friend to hang out with the crew in Florida. As they rode down South Atlantic Avenue, Tanaka, who was sitting in the back seat, began to grow horny as she watched all the sexy girls who

lined the street. She yelled Alicia's name, and when Alicia looked over the back seat, she saw that Tanaka had raised her New Orleans Saints Jersey skirt up over her waist and was shamelessly displaying her neatly trimmed thin-lipped vagina.

Alicia smiled and said, "Girl, you is nasty."

"Wait until we get in the yacht. It's gone really go down, home girl. In the meantime though, I gots ta' get off," Tanaka remarked. She rubbed her clitoris hard and fast as Lamont pulled into the parking lot of the Marina where the crew had leased two yachts until Monday morning.

Alicia watched as Tanaka brought herself off in two minutes. Lamont had witnessed the whole thing through his rear view mirror and had gotten Alicia to give him head in the front seat of the Lexus. While she was giving head to Lamont in the parking lot of the marina, Alicia heard a tap on the window. She raised her head up and stared at Oscar somewhat shamed, but Oscar told her it was cool. "Damn, he saw me sucking Lamont dick!" She giggled with her right hand over her lower face.

"That ain't nothing to be ashamed of, girl! Watch this! Oscar, let me suck ya' dick!" Tanaka exclaimed, much to Oscar's surprise and excitement.

Tanaka had traveled to Daytona to get the party started. She loved sex and she didn't care who she did it with nor did she pay any attention to what people thought, or said about her. She was a party girl, to the fullest extent.

"You gone give me some head? Right here, right now?" Oscar asked in disbelief.

"Yea, nigga! Get in the back seat!" Tanaka replied as she slid over to let Oscar enter the vehicle.

Oscar looked around and saw that JoAnne had boarded the ship with Katrina, Kim, Dana and the rest of the boys. He told Jermaine to keep watch as he hopped into the back seat and let Tanaka perform fellatio on him.

When she was through with Oscar, Tanaka sent him to the yacht to call Jason so he could get his turn. Tanaka was on a roll this afternoon. Being far away from home and surrounded by gangsters who were balling, she was having the time of her life acting like a total slut on purpose.

"Hey yo', Jay! Let me get that Scarface disk out ya' ride, pimp!" Oscar yelled towards Jason as he boarded the yacht.

When Jason stepped onto the deck of the 120' yacht, Oscar clued him in on the fact that Tanaka was in a giving mood. Tanaka had given head to Oscar, Jason, and then Jermaine. As she was going down on Jermaine, she saw Alicia giving head to Lamont once again as another person tapped on Lamont's window. This time it was Dirty Red, and he, too, wanted to join in on the action. "Y'all mutherfuckas got a freak nik goin' on and didn't invite *me*?" Dirty Red asked in mocked disbelief.

"Man, my fucking jaws hurt! Alicia, take care of Dirty Red while I finish Jermaine. We need ta' hurry up before they ole lady come back out!" Tanaka stated before she went down on Jermaine once more.

When Lamont was finished, he relinquished his seat to Dirty Red and the twenty-five year-old got into the front seat across from Alicia. Alicia looked at Dirty Red with wide eyes. The sexy, light-skinned eighteen year-old had always secretly admired Dirty Red from afar and she gladly accepted the opportunity to be with the well-renowned Ben Holland.

Within a minute, Alicia was down on Dirty Red. She savored the length of his pole and moaned as she slid her mouth back and forth over his shaft. When he climaxed, Dirty Red lifted Alicia's head and spilled his load onto her face. She had never had that done to her before, but she loved the way it felt. She wanted more of him.

Dirty Red knew Alicia wanted to go further, so he waited until Tanaka and Jermaine were through and he and Alicia got into the back seat. He slid on a condom and Alicia quickly raised her tennis skirt, slid off her thong bikini, and mounted him reverse cowgirl style. Dirty Red, if Alicia had to tell it,

was a good lover, just as Katrina had said a couple of days ago. The young teen gripped the seats tightly as she grunted and moaned in utter delight, grinding her ass down onto Dirty Red's shaft. Lamont's Lexus bounced up and down like it had hydraulics underneath its frame.

Dirty Red slapped Alicia's soft ass, turning the light-skinned female's flesh light pink as she continued to slide up and down on his pole. He cupped her breast and drove into her with so much force, he knocked Alicia's earrings from her earlobes. She began screaming in delight and then came with tremendous force. Her soft, creamy thighs quivered as she laid back into Dirty Red's chest and thanked him for making her come like never before. The two lay still for a few minutes, breathing hard, Alicia smiling to herself, thinking back to the day Tanaka turned her on to the crew at the Knight's Inn. She was glad she had made the trip. Dirty Red stirred her from her thoughts when he announced that they should join the rest of the crew aboard the yacht. Alicia dismounted Dirty Red and began looking for her earrings while Dirty Red straightened his clothes. The two then walked back towards the yacht, making light conversation about the boats they were using.

The crew had rented two yachts, a 120' yacht titled, *Sun and Fun*, which had three suites, a large playroom with a Bose sound system, fully loaded bar, two bathrooms and a huge deck. The other was an 80' foot yacht named, *Hard At Play*, which had two bedrooms, two bathrooms and a nice indoor lounge area with a large sun roof, but it had a smaller deck.

As Dirty Red and Alicia stepped onto the deck of *Sun and Fun*, they saw that the crew had already settled themselves in to enjoy the trip. JoAnne and Katrina had changed into bathing suits the moment they boarded and were now lying out on the deck in the shade, sipping strawberry daiquiris.

Alicia made her way over to the ocean side of the yacht where Dana, Kim, and Tanaka were standing as Dirty Red went to shower and join the boys in the playroom. Alicia smiled at Tanaka as Tanaka handed her a daiquiri. She sipped through the straw of the frozen drink as she and Tanaka turned

to face the huge Atlantic Ocean.

"How you feel?" Tanaka asked Alicia.

"Like a total fuckin' slut!"

"Me too!"

"You think JoAnne 'nem know what happened out there in the parking lot?" Alicia asked in a low tone as she watched Katrina walk towards the playroom.

"Fuck no! If they did, they woulda threw our asses off the side of this big ass boat!" Tanaka replied in a near whisper as the two girls burst into laughter and continued to drink their drinks.

Kim had spent over sixteen hundred dollars on a two piece Gucci bathing suit and two Tara Grinna one piece bathing suits; she had regretted the fact that she had done so as she stared at Dana, who looked stunning in her two piece silver silk bathing suit she had bought from Dillard's for only forty dollars. "I shoulda went where you went, Dana. Tara Grinna don't look good on me." Kim said as she looked down at the tiger-print one piece bathing suit she wore.

"You shoulda went and gotcha' own style," Katrina said as she walked back onto the deck with a fresh strawberry daiquiri. "You wanna be like me. You wanna be like Dana. Who next? Tanaka? Alicia?"

"No," Tanaka answered. "She can't do what we do."

"I don't wanna do what y'all do." Kim answered casually as she fanned Tanaka off.

"Nobody don't wanna do what they do, Kim." Katrina remarked.

"Don't knock it to 'til ya' try it, Katrina," Alicia stated just before she sipped her drink.

"Alicia, I'm shocked at you. Tanaka I been knew about, but you shocked me, girl. I never thought you woulda went that

route." Katrina said matter-of-factly.

"Me neither." Alicia smiled.

"Why then?" Katrina asked inquisitively.

"I was curious. I got seduced, I guess."

"Ohh, I got seduced too!" Dana said, in between sips of daiquiri, as the girls all huddled on the yacht's deck, leaning up against the rails.

"You did?" Tanaka asked happily. "Why you ain't been say nothin'?"

Katrina and Kim burst into laughter at that moment as they both knew that Dana didn't know what the rest of the girls were actually talking about.

"What's funny? Ain't nothin' wrong with gettin' seduced by a man. Shoot, Jason took my virginity on the lakefront. I always dreamed I'd be married when it happen though."

The girls burst into laughter again.

"Oh shit!" Tanaka said through laughter. "I thought we had a potential threesome, Alicia! Dana, we ain't talkin' about male seduction."

"Then what y'all talkin' 'bout?"

"They talking about girl on girl sex. Being with another woman." Katrina answered on behalf of Tanaka.

"Oh! No, umm, nahhh. I ain't never done that! I was on another subject. Sorreeeeee!" Dana stated as she tip-toed away from the girls and headed towards the playroom.

The girls had a good laugh about what had transpired and they then went off into different areas of the boat. Katrina walked away from Tanaka, Alicia and Kim, and went and sat next to JoAnne.

JoAnne heard the conversation. She knew Katrina and Dana, right along with Kimberly, were treading dangerous waters by

engaging in sex talk with Tanaka and Alicia. "Y'all gone let them two girls get y'all caught up if y'all ain't careful." She told Katrina.

Katrina was silently asking herself what was so exciting about being with a female just seconds before; and after hearing JoAnne speak on the matter, she now had a question. "You ever been caught up like that?" She asked JoAnne.

JoAnne looked to the wooden deck of the yacht then out to the ocean as she smiled. What she told Katrina early on, about getting caught up, was stated from experience. To make Katrina aware, JoAnne told Katrina the truth. "Yea. I was nineteen. A year older than you. Too much alcohol, too much weed and wilding out at college and shit. Hangin' around with girls just like Tanaka and Alicia. That's why I said what I said. They remind me of that li'l clique I used to run with back at SUNO. (Southern University of New Orleans)" JoAnne remarked as she looked over to Tanaka and Alicia. "Yep, I'm tellin' ya', Kay Kay, they smooth. You better watch 'em."

"How you felt about it, though?" Katrina then asked.

"Shit," JoAnne said as she sat up in her lounge chair and pulled up her shades, "At first I thought it was cool. It felt different, but it felt good at the same time. We fooled around— but then I decided I'd much rather have a man put his arms around me instead of a woman. It is a choice, ya' know? And it won't happen unless you allow it to. Just be careful not to put yourself in a situation where you can get overly excited or lose control to the point of no return. No matter what happens, though, remember this, whatever happens here in Daytona— just leave it all behind, right here in Florida! Have fun shit!" JoAnne ended as she placed her shades back over her eyes and leaned back into the lounge chair, leaving Katrina alone with her thoughts.

CHAPTER TWENTY-FOUR

A BLACK AND WHITE THANG

It was about eleven 'o' clock at night when the crew began to head out to enjoy Daytona Beach's nightlife. They were all rested up and ready for a fun night on the town. After eating bar-b-que prepared by Oscar, the crew all got dressed and headed out. Katrina had put on the outfit that Rico had bought. It was a black silk short set with a black silk tank top and a matching short sleeve silk jacket. She had also gotten Rico to buy her a pair of thousand dollar black Manolo Blahniks with a three inch heel. She had on all the jewelry Rico had bought her, which included a thick, platinum herringbone chain and three Princess cut diamond rings. She also wore a seven-thousand dollar platinum and diamond-bezzled Cartier watch and a five thousand dollar platinum bracelet that Dirty Red had given her shortly after he and the boys returned from Memphis. Katrina looked into a full-sized mirror and knew that she would be the best dressed woman in whatever club the crew went to tonight.

As she checked her appearance in the mirror, Katrina began to reflect on the fact that nearly everything she had on was bought by Rico: the shoes, the outfit and most of the jewelry. She was wearing clothes and jewelry bought by a dead man.

253

She added it all up and figured in the short span of time that she knew Rico, he had spent at least seventy-five thousand dollars on her, and all he got in return was a few rounds of sex and a busted skull. *"He shouldna killed Manny!"* Katrina thought to herself as she popped her collar and walked out of the bedroom, down the hall, and onto the ship's deck. When she stepped out into the opening everybody complemented her on how beautiful she looked. From her hair to her toenails, Katrina was blinging. Her entire ensemble was worth forty-nine thousand dollars.

Everybody was looking good. Tanaka had on a bubble-gum blue tank top, a pair of white, tight-fitting daisy duke shorts and bubble-gum blue stilettos. Alicia wore a white, tight-fitting all-into-one dress and white stilettos, while Kim wore an orange Gucci short set with matching Gucci sandals. The shorts were high and tight-fitting, leaving Kim's butt cheeks and navel exposed.

JoAnne sported a pair of Prada jeans with a white silk tank top and a pair of custom-made, white Prada stilettos. Dana wore a burgundy Burberry sundress with a pair of burgundy Burberry sandals with her initials on the buckle in diamonds. The boys all sported Girbaud jeans with throwback football jerseys and Kenneth Cole casual shoes.

They all hopped into their rides and headed south on South Atlantic Avenue towards the night clubs. The crew stopped at a red-light a few miles away from the marina, and a white-stretched navigator limousine pulled up next to Oscar and JoAnne. The window rolled down and someone hollered, "Bang! Bang! That's how it's gone happen to ya', nigga!"

"Where ya' at, pimp!" Oscar yelled back at Non-Stop, the rapper from the same neighborhood as the crew.

"What you doing way out here, boy?" JoAnne asked, quickly following Oscar's remark.

"I got a record deal, Jo! I'm out here celebrating! Shootin' some footage for my video and shit, ya' dig? Say, say, Oscar, follow me to the Bahama House down the street a bit on the

left! I'm a get y'all niggas in on the V.I.P. ya' heard me?"

The light changed and people behind Non-Stop began to blow their horns in frustration.

Non-Stop stuck his head out the rear of the limousine, faced the traffic and yelled aloud, "Shut up, bitches! I'm talkin' ta' my nigga, Big O! What? We rich, bitch! Go y'all asses around!"

"Go 'head, brer," Oscar said as he looked back at the traffic. "I don't wanna have ta' fuck—"

"I know! Don't fuck 'em up! Look, just walk through the line pass all them bitches and ask for me, brer! Y'all get in free! I'm a roll out and catch y'all later." Non-Stop ended as the vehicle pulled forward through the light.

At the next light, Oscar got out his Lamborghini and ran past Lamont's Lexus towards Dirty Red's Benz, which was at the front of the pack.

"Let's follow Non-Stop in the stretch Navie up to the Bahama Club and get in on V.I.P. It's gone be on the left."

"That's him in that ride right there? What happened? That boy done blew up overnight, huh?" Dirty Red asked over his sound system.

"Yea. That li'l nigga got a record deal. Say, brer, you smoking?"

"Let's wait 'til we hit the club before we blaze up. Kay Kay got the weed in her purse."

"Fo' sho! Fo' sho!" Oscar replied as he tapped Dirty Red's door and trotted back to his car.

When Oscar got back to his Lamborghini, a group of young white men in a 1996 black Impala SS on twenty-six inch chrome wheels pulled alongside of him and JoAnne. One of the young men, the one on the passenger side yelled out, "You stupid nigga! You holding up the traffic!"

"Aww fuck, no!" JoAnne yelled aloud as she raised the door on the Lamborghini, exited the vehicle and walked around the front of the car and stood next to a stunned Oscar.

"Who the fuck you callin' a nigga?" She asked as she stood beside Oscar with her arms folded, staring at the passengers inside the Impala.

"He need to move that pieca shit ass car out tha' way!" The passenger yelled angrily.

"A pieca shit? This ain't a pieca shit! What *y'all* riding in is a pieca shit! This is a mutherfuckin' ninety-nine Lamborghini! That *nigga* you talkin' 'bout done bought your mutherfuckin' pieca shit ass car five times over—cracker!"

There were four white men riding in the Impala. The young man sitting behind the driver got out. At the same time, Jason hopped out of his Cadillac, and Jermaine exited his ride, with Kim following close behind, hoping to see a fight. Dirty Red, Katrina, and Lamont had gone on through the light, so they were unaware of what was about to go down.

"What the prob?" Jason asked as he walked towards the Impala with his arms extended.

"The problem is ya' boy holding up traffic in his funny looking car!" The passenger in the front seat of the Impala stated.

"What ya' mean by boy?" Jermaine asked with a frown on his face.

"You know what I'm sayin', man."

"Oh now we men! A few seconds ago, I was a nigga!" Oscar snapped.

"He called you a nigga?" Jason asked hysterically as he began to walk towards the passenger with his fists balled up.

Just then the young man who had gotten out of the back seat intervened on behalf of his friend. "Hold up, man, hold up! He drunk and high, he just got some false courage, dude." The

young man stated to Jason.

"Dude!" JoAnne said through laughter. "Did that nigga just say dude?"

"Now you said it!" The young white man intervening on behalf of his friend remarked as he pointed towards JoAnne.

"Said what?" JoAnne asked.

"Nigga!" The young man snapped.

"*I* can say the word nigga! You *can't* say the word nigga!"

"Why?" He asked.

"'Cause it's an insult when white people say it to black people!"

"How come everything gotta be a black and white thang? Where we from, we call each other niggas all the time!" The young man replied through laughter as he dapped the passenger in front seat of the Impala. "Ain't that right, nigga?" He asked his friend in the front passenger seat.

"You right, my nigga." The young man in the passenger seat responded as the two dapped one another again and laughed aloud.

JoAnne took ease at that moment, not because of the young man's last remarks, but because she realized they meant no harm. Still, she took it upon herself to drop a little knowledge on the Caucasian youngsters. "They don't have white people in the 'hood where we from. And the ones we do see, when they say nigga, they mean nig-ger like a slave or some shit. When we say nig-ga, it's like saying dude or something like that. It's not meant as an insult."

The four young white men, who were all from Union City, Georgia, just outside of Atlanta, understood what JoAnne was trying to say. They apologized sincerely and offered the crew an unopened bottle of cognac as a token of their sincerity.

Oscar grabbed the bottle and just like JoAnne, he gave a little

insight to the youngsters. He told the young men to be careful whom they said the word *nigga* around because the group of "niggas" might not be so understanding.

The white boys agreed and they began pouring themselves shots of Absolute Vodka right in the middle of the street. When people behind them began to blow their horns in frustration, the white male standing outside of the Impala blurted out, "What, bitch? We rich! Go around, nigga," in imitation of what Non-Stop had said a few minutes earlier.

Oscar laughed. "These white boys crazy." He said to the crew, who unanimously agreed.

The white boys offered a blunt to the crew as the youngest got back in the Impala, but not before he insisting on following the crew to the club where Non-Stop had invited the boys. The crew realized that these were just a bunch of fun-loving young men, much like themselves, except they were white. That night, for the first time, the crew decided to kick it with some white dudes.

They all met up in the parking lot and walked up the aisle towards the V.I.P. door, white boys in tow. Oscar had introduced his new-found friends to the rest of the gang in the parking lot and they all welcomed Kirk, a short, black-haired twenty-two year-old and his cousin Geoffrey, a twenty-three year-old, freckled faced red head. Jamal was a twenty-three year-old Georgia Tech College grad who was also celebrating his birthday. Benny, who was the youngest, was a tall, slender eighteen year-old who was just as wild as the boys. He was the one who had jumped out of the car and gotten into the argument with JoAnne at the red-light over use of the N-word.

The rowdy group walked pass the scores of youngsters waiting impatiently to enter the large, extravagant night club, and approached the security at the doors and asked for Non-Stop after Dirty Red tipped the guard a hundred dollars.

When Non-Stop came out, he dapped Dirty Red off and handed the boys a bottle of Cristal. He then noticed the white boys with the crew. "Who the fuck them niggas is?" Nonstop

asked with a look of reluctance displayed on his face.

"These our white cousins. They wanna hang with the brothers ta' night ta' see how it's done." Oscar remarked as he laughed.

Non-Stop looked at the white boys, figuring they could maybe enhance his video and give him a new target audience. *"White and black people partying together in my video? That shit would be hot!"* Non-Stop thought to himself. "Alright then!" He said aloud as he stepped aside to let everyone enter the club. "Y'all niggas don't bring none of them racial slurs and shit in here with y'all! Y'all outnumbered one-hundred to one up this piece!" He then said to Benny and his crew.

Benny turned around in the doorway and eyed Non-stop and said, "Man, we just come ta' hollar at the sistas in this joint. The white man ain't gonna hold y'all down ta' night! And if they do, they gone have ta' come see me!"

Non-stop laughed aloud right along with the boys and said, "Alright! Y'all some cool mutherfuckas look like. Come on in and make ya' self at home right here in V.I.P. Player."

Non-Stop bought the crew another dozen bottles of Cristal and disappeared into the crowd as the music continued to pulsate throughout the club. It was a festive atmosphere. The crowd was vibing, a mixture of races and both sexes, everybody drinking, laughing and dancing. The music was on point as well. The club was playing the latest jams, too, from Nas's *Hate Me Now* to B.G.'s song *Bling Bling*. The crew sat with the white boys and they talked for a couple of hours, telling stories about life in their respective cities.

The girls all soon got up to dance and Benny followed. He and Katrina danced with one another, enjoying each other's company. The white boys were cool; they sat and drank and talked just as much shit as the crew, even more. It was fair to say that the crew liked the white boys from Union City, GA.

"Damn, looka them two!" Benny yelled loudly towards Katrina as they danced face to face.

Katrina turned around to see Tanaka and Alicia with a crowd

of people around them as they danced with one another.

"Aww shit! They 'bouta get it crunk in this muther!" Katrina said, just as Alicia raised her skirt above her waist and put her hands to the floor and began bouncing her rear end feverishly while Tanaka stood behind her and pretended to smack her behind.

Alicia and Tanaka were getting the crowd worked up to Lil Jon and the Eastside Boy's southern hit *Bia Bia.*

Benny left Katrina and got in between Tanaka and Alicia amidst cheers from the other club goers, yelling, "Go white boy! Go white boy!"

The club was jumping, everyone was having a good time until four black males, jealous of Benny, walked up to the eighteen year-old and ripped off his medallion and punched him in the face, knocking him out cold.

Kirk saw what happened from the V.I.P. stage and he, Geoffrey, and Jamal ran from their booth fighting their way through the crowd towards the ruckus.

Tanaka, Alicia, and Katrina had jumped in as the four black males continued to stomp on Benny. Patrons in the club headed for the doors screaming as the boys jumped from their booth to help their new friends, who were in serious trouble. Soon, there was a big brawl on the dance floor.

Tanaka, Alicia, and Katrina had gotten the best of one of the boys and Dana and JoAnne immediately jumped in to help the three girls take down the six foot, muscle-bound man when they reached the dance floor. The young man was knocked unconscious by the girls as the boys beat up on the other three young men until they broke and ran for the door leading out into the parking lot. The four aggressors believed Benny was by himself; but when they realized he had back-up, the three remaining perpetrators retreated, leaving their fallen comrade out cold on the floor.

The fight continued outside, however; Geoffrey, still angry over what happened to Benny, had grabbed one of the young

men and pinned him against the side of a car and started repeatedly punching the young man in the face with his left hand as he gripped his neck with his right hand.

The police had apprehended the young male whom the girls had knocked out, along with Katrina, Alicia, Dirty Red, Jamal, Oscar, Jermaine, Nonstop and Jason.

Lamont, Kim, JoAnne, Kirk, and Tanaka had picked Benny up off the floor and had left the club through the V.I.P. exit and had made their way to the parking lot before the police arrived. The authorities were still in the club trying to piece together what happened when the owner yelled that they were still fighting outside.

As they ran outside, the police, along with Lamont, Kim, JoAnne, Kirk, Tanaka, Benny and scores of club goers, scattered through the parking lot, some taking cover as gunfire erupted. Oscar, who was in the back seat of a police car, looked up after the gunfire subsided to see Geoffrey fall against the hood of a car and slide down face first onto the asphalt of the parking lot. One of the young men that had jumped on Benny had come up from behind and shot Geoffrey in the back.

The three black males then tried to run from the parking lot. The one with the gun was killed by the police when he opened fire on the officers and the other two were quickly apprehended. The four black males would later be charged with attempted second degree murder, attempted murder of an officer, aggravated assault, and attempted armed robbery.

The night ended with the boys being taken to jail, although they were later released without being charged. Geoffrey survived after being in surgery for two hours. The boys went to see him in the hospital after they were released as the girls headed back to the yachts in Jermaine's Navigator, but Jamal and Kirk did not want to talk to them, nor did they allow them to see Geoffrey.

As they walked out of the hospital, Benny ran up behind the boys and told them that Kirk and Jamal were mad because, in

Kirk's words, "Some jealous, ignorant niggas had ruined a perfectly innocent party."

"They blamin' all black people, man." Benny stated softly. "They say it's the same shit with black people everywhere they go. They through with it. But I just want y'all ta' know…I don't think y'all like them dudes that shot Geoffrey. If you don't mind me saying, I think y'all some real niggas that's just cool like that. Later, man." Benny ended as he dapped the boys and walked off with his head down.

It was almost three in the morning when the boys made it back to the marina. Dirty Red looked onto the deck of *Hard At Play* as he and Oscar walked towards the yacht, and could see one lone figure. He thought it was Katrina at first, but as he got closer, he smiled happily when he realized it was Anastasia, his childhood friend.

Dirty Red had called Anna and invited her down a week before the crew left. He didn't think that she would come to Daytona since she stayed on the west coast up in Seattle, but she made the trip cross country to see her friend and long-time lover. After all that transpired that night, she was a welcome sight for Dirty Red. He, Oscar, Anastasia and JoAnne settled down onto the smaller 80 foot yacht to relax over a blunt, some music and a few drinks as the teens all piled onto *Sun and Fun* to continue enjoying themselves the rest of the night.

CHAPTER TWENTY-FIVE

GIRLS JUST WANT TO HAVE FUN

It was after four in the morning by the time all the teens had showered and settled into the playroom of *Sun and Fun*. Jason, Lamont, and Jermaine sat at the bar enjoying a game of dominoes while Katrina, Tanaka, Dana, and Alicia entertained themselves with daiquiris and danced to the music blaring from the yacht's stereo atop the soft carpet.

"Say, man, I been waitin' for my turn on the dominoe table! Y'all done played twice already!" Katrina yelled over the music as she walked towards the bar.

"You up right now. I'm the low man," Lamont yelled back.

As Lamont moved from the stool, Katrina snatched the blunt he was puffing on out of his hand. "Leave the cognac, too, nigga! You lost everything! The weed. The drink. *And* the seat!"

Lamont iffed at Katrina as if he was going to hit her and Katrina threw up her hands. "What's hatnin'? I done knocked one nigga out tonight! What's hatnin'?" She asked as she bounced up and down.

Lamont laughed and turned around and shuffled over towards

the rest of the girls with another blunt that Jason had given him.

"Lamont, let met blow Alicia a shotgun!" Tanaka yelled aloud.

"Bitch, you don't even smoke weed!" Kim chimed in laughingly as Lamont handed Tanaka the blunt.

"You don't know what the fuck I be doing, Kim! Stop licking ya' lips and shit, bitch! Ya' know ya' wanna try this fire ass weed we got going. Here!" Tanaka said as she took a long toke and passed the weed to Kim.

Kim took a toke and began coughing and choking. The girls laughed as she bent forward, steadily choking off the marijuana smoke she inhaled. Tanaka took the blunt from Kim and blew Alicia a shotgun and the three girls formed a circle and began smoking the blunt, passing it back and forth amongst each other, along with Lamont. Tanaka was soon full of giggles. She was talking about a white girl whose phone number she had gotten inside the club before the fight when Dana tapped her on the shoulder.

"What, mutherfucka? What? You been over there in a corner the whole time now ya' come fuckin' with my high and shit! What?" Tanaka asked, pretending to be agitated by Dana's sudden intrusion.

"I wanna try it. The weed I mean." Dana replied softly.

"Ohhh, you do?" Tanaka answered in a surprised manner. "Not miss sweet and innocent! Church-mouse-Dana wanna smoke a blunt y'all!" She said through laughter.

"Hold up now, she did help whip ass at the club earlier." Lamont remarked. "Give her some." He then stated.

Tanaka blew Dana a shotgun and the eighteen year-old inhaled the smoke and covered her mouth and coughed lightly before taking another shotgun. Unlike Kim, Dana held her smoke in. After thirty minutes or so, the room was filled with the aroma of marijuana, and Black and Mild cigar smoke. The

crew was all feeling a good buzz. There was a good game of dominoes going, the music was just right and the liquor flowed freely and heavily. When R Kelly's song, *Half on a Baby* came on, Tanaka, who was a huge R Kelly fan, began to gyrate sexily in front of Lamont and Alicia. She then ran to the girls' room and retrieved a black 10" rubber strap on dildo and returned to the center of the playroom.

"What—the fuck—is that?" Lamont asked.

"It's a dick, nigga, what it look like? I call this here the Black Mamba." Tanaka replied as she stroked the rubber phallus.

Jason, Jermaine, and Katrina turned around when they heard Kim, Dana and Alicia bursting into laughter as they watched Tanaka play with the dildo.

"I ain't never seen one of those before!" Dana snapped.

"Let me touch it!" Kim said excitedly before she laughed aloud and grabbed the dildo away from Tanaka. "Who you use this on? Alicia?" She then asked.

"Uh, uh! I use it on Lamont!"

"Like the fuck you do, bitch! I'm doing the fucking here! Me, not you! Me! Ya' heard me?" Lamont retorted as he gripped the crotch area of his silk Polo shorts and hit the blunt.

The girls played with the dildo for about ten minutes until Tanaka took it away from Dana and put it on over her bikini bottom. She told the girls the different things she would do with the dildo and how girls would practically beg her to use it on them whenever she brought it out to use.

"Alicia go crazy when I put the Black Mamba on her! Huh, girl?" Tanaka asked.

Alicia blushed slightly and turned her head and sipped her daiquiri without saying a word. She was a little embarrassed that Tanaka was telling some of their bedroom secrets, but she remained quiet when she noticed Kim and Dana were listening closely to Tanaka as she described in vivid detail the way her and Alicia made love. Kim and Dana's behavior reminded

Alicia of herself, the way she used to try to ignore what Tanaka was saying; all the while her curiosity was steadily being aroused until she reached a certain point to where she had to see if what Tanaka was saying was true.

Between all of the alcohol, the weed, and Tanaka's explicit talk, the mood inside the playroom had shifted from one of festivity, to that of erotica. The others had not a clue; but Alicia knew exactly what Tanaka was doing at this particular juncture. Tanaka had earlier shared her desire for Katrina with Alicia back at the club. Alicia quickly realized that Tanaka was not only going to try and seduce Katrina, she was going to try and seduce the entire crew. Tanaka Romaire was a highly sexual and very seductive person; and, if given the opportunity, she could lead a person down a sexual path he or she would normally avoid. She was in rare form on this night and Alicia knew it.

Tanaka began her seduction by walking towards Alicia holding the dildo. Alicia playfully screamed and began running around the huge playroom pretending to be scared as everyone sat around the lounge laughing at the scene. Tanaka caught up with Alicia behind the bar and backed her up against the counter facing away from the crew. She kissed her on the lips fully and then whispered something into Alicia's ear. Alicia turned around and giggled towards the crew as she slowly sunk to her knees and disappeared behind the counter.

"Come on, Alicia! Let's go on the carpet!" Tanaka remarked a couple of minutes after Alicia had sunk to the wooden floor behind the bar.

When Alicia stood up, she was completely naked. Her thick thighs and pert breasts bounced to and fro as she and Tanaka headed towards the middle of the room. Tanaka had let her micro braids hang freely as she, too, removed all of her attire, revealing her slender, dark-skinned 5' 7" one-hundred and thirty-five pound figure. Tanaka had turned the lights off before she left the bar; the only light that now illuminated the room was the red neon Budweiser sign and the light from the moon that was shining through the moon roof of the yacht. As

266

the music from R Kelly's CD continued to play on, Tanaka and Alicia created an erotic scene for the crew. They put on a show for them by grinding their silhouetted bodies together sexily as they French kissed slowly in the darkness whilst slow dancing to R Kelly's song titled *Suicide*.

The two girls, through their sexual gyrations and lust-filled moans, had gotten the crew sexually stimulated and they all now wanted sexual relief. Kim was the first to move; she backed Jermaine up to the bar and sat him in a stool. After removing his clothes as well as hers, she went down on Jermaine, imitating what Alicia was now doing to Tanaka's "Black Mamba".

Jason and Dana went and sat on one of the huge soft leather sofas and began to kiss passionately as they stripped each other of their clothing. Katrina looked at Lamont and her eyes grew low. She looked around the room and saw Alicia on her knees uninhibitedly licking the tip of the rubber phallus as Tanaka stood before her giving her own breasts a personal massage. When Tanaka looked over to Katrina and licked her lips and smiled, Katrina looked away; but her eyes fell upon another erotic scene.

Katrina now saw Kim going down on Jermaine. She also witnessed Jason and Dana off in the distance locked in the sixty-nine position on the sofa. Katrina grew moist at the sight of Jason and Dana. She actually wished she were in Dana's position, straddling Jason's head as she rocked gently. Since that was by no means possible at the moment, Katrina shifted her attention to the only person who was not partnered-up. She grabbed Lamont from the bar and guided him towards the other sofa, pushed him down onto his rear end and removed all of her clothing. Lamont, eager for another round of sex with Katrina, stripped in the blink of an eye and waited in anticipation.

Lamont grew rock hard as he gazed up at Katrina's lovely physique whilst bobbing his head to R Kelly's song *Ghetto Queen* that was now playing in the background. He had seen Katrina naked many times before but, on this night, as the

moonlight shined down on her naked jewelry-clad body and apple-sized breasts and flat stomach, she looked stunning. With her vagina throbbing, Katrina began rubbing her breasts as she peered down at Lamont's erection and licked her lips. As wild and outgoing as she was, Katrina had never given oral sex to anyone except Brian, and that was against her will. This night, however, as the horny eighteen year-old looked around the room to see all of her peers engaged in various stimulating sex acts, she let herself go.

Katrina pushed Lamont onto his back and straddled his head, placing her round curvy bottom and moist, sweet smelling vagina over the nineteen year-old's face. Lamont grabbed Katrina's hips and began to kiss and lick her inner thighs and the soft folds of her womanhood. Katrina, in turn, gently grabbed Lamont's shaft and inserted it in between her lips and began to move her head up and down slowly, while stroking his rod.

Tanaka noticed what was going on and she patted Alicia on the top of her head and pointed to each of the couples around the room. "We got 'em going, girlfriend," she said with a sly grin. "Let's see what else we can make 'em do."

Alicia got up off her knees and hugged Tanaka from behind as the two walked slowly and quietly around the playroom peeking in on the couples. When they got nearer Katrina and Lamont, they paused. Katrina was moaning in a raspy voice as she gyrated her hips back and forth across Lamont's eager tongue. As she lay her head on his right thigh, Katrina would occasionally place her mouth on Lamont's penis to suck it; but the pleasure she was receiving was too intense. She relinquished her attempts to pleasure Lamont orally and she just laid there, moaning in ecstasy as she half-heartedly stroked his penis.

Tanaka felt Katrina could use a little help, so she and Alicia walked over and knelt down beside the sofa. Tanaka's heart was beating fast now; the eighteen year-old was nervous. She wanted Katrina all-so-badly, and now she was only inches away from the young woman she had been secretly admiring

for a long time. She wanted so desperately to reach out and grab Katrina, but she wasn't sure how Katrina would respond to the touch of another woman.

Alicia looked into Tanaka's Chinese-looking eyes and saw her nervousness and also her desire. She made the first move, assisting Tanaka in her seduction by licking the side of Lamont's penis as Katrina stroked him slowly. When Alicia licked Katrina's fingers, Katrina moaned and removed her hand as she looked at Alicia with half-closed eyes, half-closed eyes that Alicia could see were full of lust from the pleasure she received from Lamont.

"Suck his dick...And I'm gone suck it with you." Alicia said in a low sexy voice as she smiled at Katrina.

Katrina now knew fully the two girls' intent; but she had never been in a situation as erotic as the one she now found herself in on this particular night. She was close to losing control of her sexual desires. She didn't want to do what her body was telling her to do; but she just didn't have the willpower to resist. She moved her head forward and began licking Lamont's penis, opposite Alicia. When Lamont moaned aloud, it spurred Katrina on even more. She also noticed Alicia getting closer and closer to her face as the two girls gave oral pleasure to Lamont.

"She tryna kiss me!" Katrina thought to herself as her body temperature increased slightly, causing her to perspire uncontrollably.

Katrina knew exactly what was happening to her; and whether she wanted it to happen or not, she couldn't stop herself. She had reached the point of no return—the very thing JoAnne had warned her about. Her body had just betrayed her. Alicia licked Katrina's lips gently, and when she didn't resist, Alicia slid her tongue into Katrina's mouth and the two young women found themselves kissing one another passionately. Sweat trickled down Katrina's temples. Her body was becoming slickened by her perspiration and the pleasure had begun to course through her body, causing her to tremble slightly.

Katrina was enthralled in one of the most passionate, soul-stirring kisses she had ever received when she suddenly felt a pair of hands on her behind. She swung her head around to see Tanaka standing behind her. Tanaka's eyes were closed as she rubbed Katrina's ass slowly and methodically.

"What y'all doing to me?" Katrina asked in a soft, raspy voice.

"You have one of the most beautiful asses I have ever seen in my life, girl. I just gotta do it, Katrina." Tanaka replied in a sultry voice.

Before Katrina could respond, Tanaka breathed hard, moaned, spread her ass cheeks and knelt down and began to rapidly flick her tongue over Katrina's anus. Katrina's eyes widened and then closed tightly as she savored the feel of Tanaka's tongue rimming her behind. She moaned lowly as she ground her ass into Tanaka's face while clutching Tanaka's head to hold it firmly in place so as not to be relinquished of the intense sexual pleasure she found too enthralling to resist. Katrina had never had a tongue placed inside the crack of her ass before; but she loved the feel of Tanaka's tongue darting in and out of her anus.

Lamont realized that he was in the way of the two girls so he calmly slid from under Katrina and got on the floor behind Alicia and began sexing her doggy-style while Tanaka and Katrina got better acquainted with one another on the soft leather couch.

"Turn over, so I can do it good for ya', Katrina." Tanaka said while breathing hard with excitement.

Katrina lay on her back on the sofa and Tanaka pushed her legs up high, and as far back as they would go and returned to licking Katrina all over. Katrina had her fists balled up on either side of her breasts in a state of pure ecstasy, thoroughly enjoying what Tanaka was doing to her body. Never had she felt so good in her young life. She moaned Tanaka's name repeatedly until Tanaka stopped and rose up and the two locked lips in a heated kiss.

Katrina wrapped her arms around Tanaka and Tanaka held her face ever so gently with one hand as the other moved in between Katrina's legs. Katrina moaned loudly into Tanaka's mouth when she felt something hard and fleshy penetrate her inner lips. She looked down and saw Tanaka's "Black Mamba" slowly sliding into the tight folds of her vagina. She widened, then raised her legs higher to allow Tanaka better entrance to her moistened vagina and placed her hands around Tanaka's waist to pull more of the slender dark-skinned young woman into her.

When Tanaka began to thrust firmly in and out of Katrina's vagina as she placed her hand on Katrina's clitoris and began rubbing ther fleshy knob swiftly, Katrina thrashed her head from side to side and repeatedly asked Tanaka what she was doing to her body.

Tanaka didn't answer. She merely stopped stroking Katrina and let her tongue trail from Katrina's soft lips, to her breast, and down to her clitoris, an act which caused Katrina's thighs to uncontrollably quiver in delight. Katrina heaved as her entire inner being was rocked into a state of pleasure that was so intense, the young woman began to cry as she climaxed. She was now spent. Clasping her thighs together, Katrina held Tanaka's head in place and stroked it gently while Tanaka rested her head in between her legs, kissing and licking Katrina's thighs softly, all-the-while smiling to herself.

Tanaka was overjoyed that she had fulfilled her fantasy this night in Daytona. Her dildo, as well as her face, was covered with Katrina's creamy come. She savored the taste of Katrina one last time by licking her outer lips and pulling them lightly through her closed lips before she sat back on her heels. "Thank you," she then said as she smiled at Katrina.

"No, thank you. I never knew a woman could make me feel like that." Katrina replied as she gently placed her quivering legs back onto the carpeted floor.

The two girls smiled at one another and Katrina beckoned Tanaka to her with her middle finger. Tanaka knelt into Katrina and the two females' sweaty bodies meshed against

one another as they breathed heavy into one another's mouths. "I may never do nothin' like this again," Katrina said as she looked deeply into Tanaka's eyes, "but I'm glad it happened with you this night."

The two kissed passionately for a couple of minutes, enjoying the feel of their bodies against one another until they broke their embrace. "You made my dream come true tonight. I been fantasizing about you for a long time, Katrina. I'll never forget this." Tanaka said as she got up from the floor, backing away from Katrina slowly, letting the young woman's hand slip from hers.

"You satisfied me and my curiosity completely," Katrina responded. "Thank you," she ended as she lay back on the sofa, smiling at Tanaka before she closed her eyes.

Tanaka brought Katrina a glass of cognac and the two sat side by side on the sofa sipping their drinks, watching, until the rest of the crew were finished with their sex session. Before the night was done, all the girls had participated in a little girl on girl play, but not to the extent that Tanaka and Katrina had gone. The girls mainly played around with Tanaka's dildo, taking turns sliding the rubber phallus in and out of each other's vagina while French kissing as they smoked another blunt.

It was agreed among all that what happened on *Sun and Fun* this night would stay between only the people on the yacht. No one would ever come to know what had taken place in Daytona on *Sun and Fun*, not even Dirty Red and Oscar.

The Monday before the crew left, Dirty Red announced that he and Anastasia were making plans to be married in the future —if and when they finished their business with Damenga. The crew all knew Anna and they liked her. Out of all the women Dirty Red had ever been with, Anna, his childhood friend, was indeed the coolest and most down-to-earth woman he'd ever dealt with on a personal level. They all congratulated Ben and Anna as they hopped into their cars and headed back to Louisiana early Monday morning.

CHAPTER TWENTY-SIX

DAMENGA LAPIENTE`

At about 10 A.M. Monday morning, a black Learjet landed on an airstrip just outside of Houston, Texas. As the plane rolled to a stop in front of its hanger, two silver Hummers and a black jaguar on 22" chrome rims pulled up along its side. Four soldiers exited each hummer and the driver of the Jaguar exited his vehicle. Alphonso, the driver of the Jaguar, was twenty-seven years-old, standing about 5' 8" and weighing about two-hundred and ten pounds. He had dark brown eyes, short, curly black hair and a goatee. He removed his grey silk suit jacket and waited eagerly for the door of the jet to open.

When it did, a twenty-nine year-old, 6' Columbian, weighing about two hundred pounds, with short, straight black hair and a thinly-trimmed mustache and beard appeared. The man's name was Damenga Lapiente`. He was Alphonso's brother. The two tan-skinned men greeted one another with a hug and kissed each other's cheek. "Good to see you again, little brother." Damenga stated with a smile as he nodded towards his soldiers.

"How's Carmella? Can she talk? Can she tell us what happened?" Alphonso asked quickly, eager for answers to his questions.

273

"Slow down, slow down, 'Phonso. Carmella's awake now. Doctors say she'll be able to talk again by the end of summer. Let's let her heal up in Denver and then we'll get to her story." Damenga responded as the group walked back towards their cars.

Carmella Lapiente` was Alphonso and Damenga's baby sister. She was in Denver, Colorado, living as an inpatient at a rehabilitation center for traumatized paraplegics. Doctors said her brain injuries were serious and it may take a couple of years for her to fully recover; but she should be able to talk in a few months or so. Damenga told Alphonso what the doctors reported and the two men got into their Jaguar. Alphonso drove as the two brothers rode in between the two Hummers.

Damenga and Alphonso controlled the largest cocaine operation west of the Mississippi river. The brothers imported uncut white powder from Bogota, South America, and distributed the refined powder throughout the western half of the United States from Texas to Missouri, all the way to Seattle, Washington. Their reign was vast and violent. The two brothers, namely Damenga, could be very brutal at times.

Damenga sat on the passenger side of the car and opened a briefcase that Alphonso had given him. In the briefcase was the video tape and a letter from Dirty Red explaining what was on the tape. As Damenga read over the introductory letter, the slender Columbian looked over towards his brother and laughed aloud. "Is this guy serious?" He asked as he reread the letter which mentioned that there was a traitor within his operation and the video tape was all the proof he needed.

"He's very serious." Alphonso answered as he drove. "When you see the video, you'll understand. If nothing else, I think we should meet with this Mister Holland guy in person and listen to his proposal. It could mean a lot of money for all involved, and we could eliminate a mounting problem in the city of New Orleans at the same time."

"You watched the video?" Damenga asked seriously, realizing that this was not a joke, but a matter worthy of his undivided attention.

"Yes. There is no doubt that Rico was a stoolie. I would've done the same thing if I was in Mister Holland's position. He saved us a lot of trouble, if nothing else." Alphonso answered as he merged onto Interstate-10 and headed west.

Later, as the brothers sat in Damenga's office on the first floor of his thirty-two thousand square foot mansion on the west side of Houston watching the video, Damenga couldn't deny what he saw on the tape. He heard and saw Rico, his top man in New Orleans, repeatedly saying his name. He saw and heard Rico disclose his entire operation to two unknown narcotics detectives. The drug lord grew angry at the whole scene as it unfolded before him, and he agreed with his younger brother. "You think this man, this Ben Holland, is capable and trustworthy, Alphonso? We have many more markets in several major cities. Why not just leave the city of New Orleans alone all together?" Damenga asked as he turned off the video.

Alphonso stood up from his seat and released the leashes on two Doberman Pinchers. "DeAngelo, take them outside and feed them." Alphonso remarked to one of his enforcers.

When DeAngelo left the room, Alphonso stood before his brother and answered his question. "I love the city of New Orleans. I have fun every time I go there for Mardi Gras and the Bayou Classic. That's where I met Rico. I used poor judgment in recruiting him, I admit, but I did build a large operation down there and I want to keep it running. There's a lot of money down there in that Bayou City. There is no sense in letting the Miami boys, or some other cartel take over, hermano. I think Mister Holland is exactly the person we need to run the operation in New Orleans. With Rico out of the way, we can forge a new operation with a much stronger crew."

Damenga stood up and went to his bar, and, as he poured himself a glass of Captain Morgan's Spiced Rum, he thought hard about the situation that was thrust upon him all-of-a-sudden. Alphonso had a lot of influence in the organization the brothers ran. Although Damenga was the boss, it was Alphonso who was responsible for the day to day operations of

the cartel. He knew all the hot spots in every city in which he and his brother operated. The two brothers prided themselves on knowing everything that went on within their operation. Dirty Red, however, had impressed the brothers, especially Alphonso, by remaining under the radar as he took down Rico, and provided evidence that he was a snitch, and doing it all without word getting back to Damenga.

It was enough to convince Damenga to meet with Dirty Red and discuss matters further. He gave his approval by lighting a large Havana cigar and walking back towards his leather chair and sliding his custom-made 10 carat gold phone across the desk. "Make the call." He stated as he sat back at his desk and turned around to stare at the herd of mustangs that feasted upon the wild grass growing in the vast plain that was his backyard.

Alphonso smiled as he got on the telephone and dialed the number that was in the letter.

Dirty Red, riding with Anna beside him enroute to New Orleans, answered his cell phone.

"I'm looking for a Mister Holland."

"Speaking?"

"You know who we are and what this phone call is about. Your offer has been accepted. Wednesday. Eight in the morning. Hangar twelve at Sugar Land Regional Airport on the west side."

"Eight 'o' clock Wednesday. Me and my family will be there." Dirty Red responded.

"You must know, Mister Holland, we are very distrusting and suspicious men, but because I think you and your people are for real, we will see you on the strength of your previous actions. You handle things right, and we will make a lot of money, my friend. We think highly of you, Mister Holland. Don't you dare disappoint us. Comprendez?"

"I understand. See you Wednesday." Dirty Red replied just

before the phone went silent.

"It's done." Alphonso stated to Damenga.

"Good. Let's lay out our plan for our upcoming guest." Damenga replied as he turned around to face his desk.

Dirty Red, meanwhile, had pulled into a rest area and informed the boys of the meeting they were to have with Damenga on Wednesday before they continued on to New Orleans.

The boys arrived back in New Orleans late Monday evening and went their separate ways as they dropped off their girlfriends and checked on the dope house. As Jason was dropping Dana off at her parents' house, Lamont, who was at the dope house with Tanaka and Alicia, dialed his cell phone and asked him to come around the corner. Jason kissed Dana good-bye and headed towards the dope house. When he got there he saw Lamont standing in the driveway with Torre`, Lil Earl and Derrick.

"What the prob?" Jason asked as he walked through the front gate.

Torre` explained to Jason and Lamont that Roscoe, the young man whom Dirty Red scored kilos from, said he was taking over the Ninth Ward; and if anybody, including Dirty Red, wanted to sell cocaine, they needed his permission to do so.

Jason contacted Dirty Red and the boys met at *Par 6* early Tuesday morning to discuss the situation. Roscoe had picked a bad time to try to pull rank since Dirty Red was about to make a new connection with Damenga. Dirty Red wasn't too sure how things would turn out with Damenga, however; he told the crew that he would talk to Roscoe when they got back from Houston. "Let's just chill at Par 6 until we get back. I want everybody to stay from 'round the dope house until then. Jay, get on the phone and tell Derrick, Torre` and Lil Earl to lay low at the Sheraton downtown on Canal Street. Tell 'em get some suits from Rubenstein Brothers, too, because we gone need 'em when we go to Texas. I want everybody rested up and

looking professional for this here trip. Making this connect is our top priority as of now. Then when we get back, I'm a have a li'l meeting with Roscoe." Dirty Red stated as he poured himself a drink and dialed his car dealership connect to make a small purchase.

The crew was waiting in front of hangar twelve at eight 'o' clock sharp on Wednesday morning. The Colombians arrived twenty minutes later with a caravan of four silver hummers. The crew waited patiently in three brand new burgundy Denali's on 24" chrome wheels that Dirty Red had purchased the day before for the drive to Texas. Dirty Red wanted everybody in his crew to be riding clean back in the city once the connect was made. He would give each of the vehicles to Derrick, Lil Earl and Torre` once they returned to the city. Dirty Red knew this rendezvous was a real power move. He wanted his crew to look like the top dogs they were and the kingpins they were going to become if everything went right with Damenga.

When Damenga and his crew pulled up to the hangar, the boys hopped out of their rides. Damenga exited his Jaguar and was impressed with what he saw. Dirty Red had asked that the crew be dressed as professionals and they had done just so. All of them, Dirty Red, Oscar, Jason, Lamont, Jermaine, Torre`, Derrick, and Lil Earl, were dressed in five-thousand dollar Armani suits, two-thousand dollar shoes and all were sporting Cartier and Rolex watches worth between six and ten-thousand dollars. They were dressed like CEO's of major corporations, if Damenga had to tell it.

Surrounded by a dozen armed Colombian bodyguards toting AK-47 assault rifles, the tall, slender Columbian and his shorter, stocky-built brother walked towards the boys. The boys all pulled back their silk suit jackets to reveal chrome, Desert Eagle .44 automatic pistols tucked away in holsters. Damenga's soldiers stopped and aimed their weapons and Damenga quickly turned and spoke some words in Spanish. His soldiers immediately lowered their guns upon hearing him speak.

Damenga and Alphonso then walked towards the crew and stood directly in front of them. As he stood in his brown double-breasted Italian tailor-made silk suit and stared silently at the crew, Damenga removed his sunglasses and began to speak. "I would not have invited you here if I had plans to kill you, Mister Holland. I would do it on *your* home turf. Not mines."

"I just came prepared for anything, Mister Lapiente`. How did you know I was Ben Holland?"

"I didn't. I addressed all of you as Mister Holland since it was the only name I knew. Now that I know who *you* are, it's time we all greet one another and get to the gist of today's meeting."

The crew all introduced themselves and Damenga introduced Alphonso to the crew, along with several of the Colombian soldiers, including a man by the name of DeAngelo Spires, the cartel's third man in charge. After all of the handshaking was done, Oscar came forth with a briefcase and handed it to Damenga.

"What's this?" Damenga asked Dirty Red inquisitively as he stared at the package.

"Open it." Dirty Red stated calmly.

When Damenga opened the briefcase, he saw stacks of rubber-banded hundred dollar bills and a plastic bag filled with hot ice and a meaty object lying on top of the money. "That's the tongue of the man who ratted you out. Along with the two-hundred and fifty-five thousand dollars that he tried ta' leave the country with. No charge." Dirty Red remarked seriously as he stared Damenga in the eyes without flinching.

Damenga stared at Ben with a stoic look on his face. "*This guy is good.*" He thought to himself before he slowly began to smile and announce his approval of the boys. "'Phonso? You may have been right about this gang, hermano." He remarked as he shook Ben's hand.

Damenga, in a matter of seconds, had decided that this gang was indeed serious about the business they were in; and they

were also very courageous and ambitious. He thought that if any gang would come to Texas on such short notice and have all of their ducks in a row, and show no nervousness or fear, they were very capable of advancing to the next level of the cocaine drug trade. The tongue and cash was the icing on the cake for Damenga. He took the boys to his strip club in Pearland, Texas, just south of Houston. Damenga and the boys all sat at a large marble conference table at the back of the empty strip club and went over the setting up of their operation. Damenga first had to know what happened to Haywood.

"We knew that Haywood would be a problem for us." Dirty Red stated. "With Rico out of the picture for ratting on you, Haywood would've tried to do too much too fast. Between looking for who killed Rico and still trying to push ya' product and watching out for the feds, Haywood would've made a mistake somewhere."

"Uptown would've been ruined," added Oscar. "Not only for you, but for everybody involved. The last thing *you*, or anybody else woulda needed was for the feds to get involved and start asking questions."

"So we took the risk *and* the heat, did the hit, and used the police we got on the payroll to cover-up the hit on Rico and the job on Haywood." Jason added.

The more the boys spoke, the more impressed Damenga was becoming. "I have contacts on the inside, too, Mister Holland," he replied. "My connections run all the way up to Washington D.C. The Attorney General for the state of Texas is one of my closest allies. I give each captain of my organization freedom to operate as they please. All I ask is that they don't say my name if they are apprehended. I have powerful friends that can get them out of jail on a moment's notice. What you young men did in New Orleans was tactical, practical and, to be honest, brilliant. I hate to think what would've happened to me had that tape gone public. I don't understand how a man could handle fifty kilos a month and not put the police on the payroll. Rico wanted to ride fancy cars and spend money on women

when he didn't even have sense to buy his own home. A good earner, but a dumb business man. Had Rico not said my name, instead of becoming partners, Mister Holland, we very well may have become enemies. But, what's done is done. Rico is no longer in power. But I think your gang, Mister Holland, is ready to be in power."

"We been ready, Damenga." Dirty Red replied.

The men chatted for about an hour, discussing shipping plans and strategies for the future. Dirty Red told the brothers that within a year's time he would like to go legit.

"The game is like a stepping stone for us," he stated as several soldiers placed shrimp cocktail platters before each of the men along with a freshly poured glass of champagne. "Me and my boys wanna retire young and rich. We wanna open up clubs and invest in real estate. You give us a year of your time and we'll make you richer than what you are. More millions for you means more millions for us. Afterwards, we close down and move on."

"One year, hermano (brother)?" Damenga asked Dirty Red with a puzzled look.

"You seen our work. The people coming behind us will be more than ready to take over operations when we step aside. If you don't agree, we keep rolling until you feel comfortable. All I ask is that you be fair when the time arises. But the transition gone be so smooth, you won't notice the difference." Dirty Red answered.

Damenga leaned back from the huge table that he and the crew were sitting at and looked over to the bar towards his brother. Alphonso nodded his head in agreement with Dirty Red's request.

"You got a deal, Mister Holland; but I must warn you, amigo, it's rare that I like and trust a person so quickly. I would hate to wage a war with you and your gang, but I will if I must. You do as you say and we will not have any problems. But if you should fall short, or sway to the right or the left, I swear on my

beloved little sister that I'll come down the middle and terminate everything in sight. Understand?" Damenga asked seriously.

"Si," Dirty Red replied.

The men all shook hands and had a glass of spiced rum, Damenga's favorite, in celebration of their new venture. Damenga agreed to ship one-hundred kilos a month to New Orleans for starters, to see how well and fast the crew would distribute and move the product.

"I crown you the boss of New Orleans, Mister Holland. May your family, as well as mine, grow wealthy and enjoy longevity of life!" Damenga yelled aloud over South Park Mexican's song titled *Power Moves*.

The crew spent the entire day with Damenga in Houston, enjoying dinner and entertaining a few of the strippers later that night. They left for New Orleans the following morning. Damenga would be shipping the first load of cocaine before week's end so the crew had no time to play around. They had to visit "Ma's" store to get her to allow them to use the upstairs apartment to count money and prepare their product, and they also had to deal with Roscoe. That's what Dirty Red was thinking about as the gang rode east on Interstate-10 headed back to Louisiana in preparation to become the lead players in the city's vast cocaine drug trade.

CHAPTER TWENTY-SEVEN

I AIN'T YA' FRIEND

When the boys got back in town Thursday afternoon, they sat in the office of *Par 6* discussing their new set up. Jason and Torre`, along with Big Derrick and Lil Earl, were to handle things at the dope house back in the Ninth Ward. Lamont and Jermaine were to hire two new soldiers and operate out of the small apartment above "Ma's" store. Jason, Lamont, and Jermaine were eager to get out and began to run things. They had watched how Dirty Red, Oscar, and Manny, when he was alive, ran the shop and handled problems when they arose. They had been in the game for over five years and were well trained by Dirty Red, Oscar, and Manny.

Two hours after the meeting held inside *Par 6*, Jason, Torre` and Derrick were standing in front of the dope house with Alicia, Tanaka, and Katrina, observing the traffic going to and fro. A few crack addicts and several people looking to score ounces rolled through the neighborhood. Jason told them all that shop was closed, but the crew would be back in power Saturday morning. They were all just hanging out in the front yard chatting amongst themselves on this hot April afternoon when Burtell and Jarell pulled up in front of the dope house.

The twins got out of their navy blue Expedition with pistol

grip pumps in their hands and walked directly up to the boys. Alicia and Tanaka ran up the stairs, Katrina, however, walked over and stood behind Jason, Torre` and Derrick. The four eyed the twins as they walked through the fence and stood in front of them. Jason raised his shirt to show he was toting a .44 Desert Eagle automatic, as Torre` cocked his Mac-11.

"No need for the guns, Jason dog, we just came to deliver a message for Roscoe." Burtell said.

"What message?" Derrick asked.

"First off, I ain't talking to you! Second, Roscoe said when y'all open back up, the dope y'all pushing better be his. If not, the next time, it won't be a fucking message or a warning!"

Jason saw that the twins had their guns lowered as they continued to talk, so he quickly pulled his .44 and aimed it directly at Jarell's head. "If ya' raise ya' arm, I'm a blow ya' fuckin' head off! Ya' know I ain't playing!"

"Jason, don't shoot 'em!" Alicia yelled from the porch.

"Shut the fuck up! This man talk!" Jason snapped. "You tell Roscoe, from the whole crew—fuck him and everybody that's with 'em! And if y'all two niggas had any sense, y'all would stay from around here, and from around that nigga Roscoe."

The twins backed away from Jason slowly as Burtell announced that they were in business with Roscoe and before long, the crew would be working for them.

"Y'all must be the two stupidest niggas in New Orleans! These real niggas over here! We die before we bow down ta' bitches!"

"You can get it any way ya' want it, pimp!" Burtell remarked.

"Burtly, Butell, whatever, whatever the fuck your name is— take ya' twin, get the fuck in ya' ride, and keep going, brer! I'm through talking! My trigger finger getting restless, too," Jason stated angrily.

"You threatenin' our life?" Jarell asked.

"Nigga, I will *take* you and yo' brother life!" Jason replied as he spit on the sidewalk.

The brothers knew Jason was for real. They hadn't forgotten what happened in the hotel parking lot the week before. Burtell was thinking that he should've killed Jason on sight, but Roscoe hadn't ordered a hit on any members of the crew as of yet.

The twina backed out of the yard and got back into their Expedition and rode away, promising that things were not over between the boys and Roscoe. Alicia and Tanaka, along with Katrina, had decided to leave, just in case the twins or Roscoe came back and a shoot-out ensued. Jason then called Dirty Red on his cell phone and told him what had just transpired.

"That boy Roscoe tryna pull rank." Dirty Red told Oscar as the two sat at JoAnne's dining room table eating red beans and rice and fried chicken.

JoAnne asked the boys what they were planning as they began to load bullets into their .44 Desert Eagle clips. Oscar told her they were going to have a talk with Roscoe. JoAnne had grown accustomed to seeing Dirty Red, Oscar, and Manny come to the house to collect, drop off, and/or load weapons. Where most women would become nervous, JoAnne took on the role of sister to Dirty Red, and wife to Oscar, assisting the men as best she could without dipping too much into their business.

As Oscar kissed JoAnne good-bye and headed out the door, she asked was he coming back later on. "I'm a be busy the next few days, but I'll call you later." Oscar remarked.

"Alright then. Be careful, y'all," JoAnne said as she closed the door behind the young men, locked it and placed her .380 on the sofa next to her as she sat down to watch TV.

As the two young men pulled up onto Roscoe's block in Oscar's Lamborghini, they saw that the street was full of people. They were sitting on their stoops drinking beer, playing football in the streets and listening to music. The

houses on this particular block in the Seventeenth Ward were close together and lined both sides of the narrow street. Dirty Red looked at all of the narrow row houses and knew that people would hear gunshots. No way would they miss two men jumping into a black Lamborghini with chrome spinner rims riding off from in front of Roscoe's house after gunfire had erupted.

The boys then went to their back-up plan. Oscar reached under his seat and grabbed a switch blade knife and handed it to Dirty Red. The two young men then exited the vehicle and walked through the front gate towards Roscoe's front door. Dirty Red tapped on Roscoe's door as he shifted the .44 automatic he had hidden under his Raiders throw back jersey. Roscoe snatched the door open, clutching a blue steel .38 caliber revolver in his left hand.

"Fuck y'all niggas want?" Roscoe asked angrily.

If Roscoe was trying to intimidate Dirty Red, he'd just failed. Dirty Red was laughing on the inside. Roscoe wasn't the least bit hard to him. He knew not how to show force.

"Be cool, pimpin'!" Dirty Red replied as he play fought with Roscoe a bit by tapping him on the sides lightly in order to loosen him up. "I just came ta' find out why ya' trippin' with the 'hood and shit. We been in business a long time, brer. I'm just tryna keep everything on the up and up between you and my people ya' feel me?"

Roscoe opened the door to let Dirty Red and Oscar in and peeped outside to see if anyone else was with the two young men, "Ain't nobody out there, dog. We just came ta' holler at ya' ta' see why ya' gettin' all hostile all of a sudden." Oscar said jokingly.

"You'll be hostile, too, if you was gettin' cut outta twenty-six kilos a month, Oscar, dog."

"Who told you that?" Dirty Red asked as the three men walked through the living room towards the kitchen.

"Nobody ain't have ta' tell me shit, Dirty Red! I been in the

game long enough ta' know when a nigga got a new connect!"

Dirty Red rested his hands on the table and eyed Roscoe as he stood before the refrigerator. "I been dealing with you for a few months now, dog. I never asked you for shit! I pay ya' prices even though ya' over charging a nigga! I buy twenty-six kilos a month. Two-six. And never once did you cut me and my people a deal. Now, what can you possibly bring to the table that would make me change my mind about getting a new connect? If I was even thinking about goin' that route?"

Roscoe sat down in one of the chairs at the kitchen table and began to think. The 5' 9", brown-skinned, one-hundred and seventy pound twenty-four year-old, who had short, faded hair, and brown, cat-like eyes contemplated hard on what Dirty Red was asking.

Roscoe really was a cool dude, but he was weak-minded and big-headed. He knew he needed the money that the crew was bringing in on a monthly basis because he was only pretending to be the big man in the Seventeenth Ward. He might have had other people fooled, like the twins, but he didn't have Dirty Red and Oscar fooled at all. They knew the whole time that it was the Miami boys who were running things behind the scenes. Roscoe was lucky to make five hundred dollars off each kilo he sold. He was getting pimped and was too stupid to realize it. Rather than be the man, Roscoe was satisfied with pretending to be the man.

Dirty Red knew Damenga had agreed to split everything with the crew 50/50, a deal too sweet to pass up, and when Roscoe finds out that Dirty Red would no longer be making deals with him, he, Roscoe, would become a problem; but Dirty Red had figured out a way to dissolve the mounting tension and make everybody involved happy at the same time.

Dirty Red sat down at the table and laid out a plan for Roscoe. "Look, brer, we cool, ya' dig? With you running things behind the scene and us out there on front street, we can be bosses of the city, brer. It ain't no need ta' pull rank in the Ninth Ward when ya' got us out there handlin' business. Just let us run that shit down there, and when you get in touch with

your people, you can bring us to the table and we can work a new deal when we score the next package. I can score two, three times more than twenty-six birds and you know that. With that kind of buying power, we can move up in the game. Make money together, ya' dig? But in the meantime, player, I'm a need at least two kilos to hold me over for the weekend. I mean, if it's cool with you, big man." Dirty Red stated as he leaned back in the chair and waited for Roscoe's reply.

Roscoe, at that point, was beginning to ease up a little bit more. He placed his gun on the table and lit a blunt as he got up from the table and walked over to the refrigerator and grabbed three Heineken beers from the shelf. He handed one to Oscar and one to Dirty Red as he sat down excitedly and chatted for about ten minutes with the two young men about their new venture. He told Dirty Red that he was looking forward to running the city alongside the crew. He could finally get from under the Miami boys and break out on his own with Dirty Red.

In the meantime, he would continue to sell the crew kilograms at a reduced price since they were about to join forces. Dirty Red sent Oscar to the car to retrieve a brown grocery bag full of cash from the trunk. "Oscar gone get the money for them two bricks, brer. Let's get ready ta' make this deal." Dirty Red told Roscoe.

"The bricks ain't here. I gotta go get 'em."

"I know, pimp, but we gone count this money and leave it here while you go and pick those up. You can drop 'em off at the hangar whenever you ready." Dirty Red replied and then asked Roscoe for a bottle opener.

Oscar returned and placed the grocery bag on the table as Roscoe sat back down and passed the bottle opener to Dirty Red, and the blunt to Oscar, who was standing beside him as he sipped his beer. Oscar looked at Dirty Red and grinned as he took a pull off the blunt and handed it back to Roscoe.

"Let's count this money, brer." Dirty Red said.

"No doubt." Roscoe replied, as the blunt hung from the corner of his mouth.

When Dirty Red reached for the brown grocery bag, he knocked it over onto the kitchen floor. Roscoe's first reaction was to bend down to pick it up. When he grabbed the bag, Roscoe noticed that instead of money, the bag contained a bunch of dirty clothes. "Say, Dirty Red, what the—"

Roscoe's speech was cut off as Oscar dropped his bottle of beer and began choking him from behind. Roscoe struggled and tried to scream for help, but Oscar was too strong. Roscoe gasped for air as he wiggled out of the chair and onto the kitchen floor. He looked up several seconds later to see Dirty Red crouching before him and his eyes grew wide when he saw Dirty Red pull out a switch blade.

"You wanna threaten me and my people, bitch? You don't fuckin' know us at *all*, nigga! You ain't *shit* ta' me, Roscoe! And I ain't ya' fuckin' friend!" Dirty Red explained as he drove the blade repeatedly into Roscoe's chest and stomach.

Roscoe screamed in pain, but it was muffled as Oscar still had a death grip around his neck. Blood began running from his nose and mouth and down through Oscar's fingers as Dirty Red stabbed him over and over again whilst staring him directly in the eyes. After several minutes, Roscoe's arms grew limp and his body began to twitch. Dirty Red, who was by now out of breath, passed the knife to Oscar, and Oscar quickly slit Roscoe's throat, almost decapitating his head.

As Roscoe lay dead on his kitchen floor, Dirty Red and Oscar went and cleaned themselves up in the sink. Oscar had just dried his arms and hands and had relit Roscoe's blunt when he and Dirty Red heard keys unlocking the front door.

"Baby," a female called out happily as she opened the door. "Tell me that ain't your cleans ass Lamb out there!"

Oscar and Dirty Red eyed one another in dumbfounded disbelief. Snuggles, Roscoe's twenty-three year old girlfriend had come home.

"Talk about good timing," Oscar whispered to Dirty Red as he sat the blunt down and walked out of the kitchen and met Snuggles in the living room.

Snuggles was barely five feet tall. She was a dark-skinned voluptuous young woman with Betty Boo eyes, an onion butt and wide hips. She always had a fresh hairdo and smelled sweet as well. Oscar often eyed Snuggles whenever he saw her out with Roscoe; and his glances always made her feel uneasy. She jumped when she saw Oscar standing in the threshold separating the kitchen from the living room with a beer in his hand and she quickly asked for Roscoe.

"What's up, Snuggles? Roscoe in the kitchen," Oscar replied with a wry smile on his face. "Hey, Roscoe, your ole lady here, nigga." he called out.

Snuggles walked around Oscar and called Roscoe's name again as she entered the kitchen. She saw Dirty Red leaning against the sink staring back at her with his arms folded across his chest and a look on his face that said, *"You done fucked up now, bitch."*

Snuggles paused in her tracks because she'd suddenly taken on an uneasy feeling. She didn't see Roscoe's body on the floor because she hadn't traveled that far into the kitchen; but she knew something wasn't right. The house was dead silent, and it wasn't all that big either. Snuggles had called out for Roscoe twice and he hadn't answered her as of yet. Gut instincts were now telling Snuggles that something was wrong and she should just leave. "I left my doors unlocked on my car," she said to no one in particular. "I'm a go lock it and be right back."

Oscar curled his lips to the side and stuck his arm out and blocked Snuggles from leaving the kitchen as he stared down at her with that same wry smile he had on display when she'd first encountered him standing in the threshold. At that moment, Snuggles knew what was up. She had walked in on her boyfriend's murder and his killers were still in the house. "Oscar, please," she said as she began to cry. "Please. I ain't gonna say nothin'. Just let me go, please. I'm beggin', please."

She pleaded as tears began to roll from the corners of her eyes.

Dirty Red knew what was about to go down. Oscar had been having a thing for Snuggles for the longest and he knew his boy was not about to pass up this opportunity. He sipped his beer and watched as Oscar grabbed Snuggles and hugged her, "You gone be okay, baby," Oscar said lovingly.

"Oscar, no! Please!" Snuggles pleaded as she hugged Oscar back, trying her best to be compliant in order to have her life spared.

"You gone let me fuck, bitch?" Oscar said as he lifted Snuggles's chin and gazed into her big, round eyes.

Snuggles burst into tears at that moment. "Please," she said as she turned towards Dirty Red. "Y'all, y'all just let me go! Let me go!" Snuggles pleaded.

"That nigga over there ain't gone help you so stop beggin'," Oscar snapped coldly. "You knew what that nigga Roscoe was into! Shit was all good just a week ago, huh? Don't cry now!"

Snuggles tried to power her way through Oscar and run for the front door, but she failed. He grabbed her firmly around the neck and shoved her down the hallway towards the master bedroom. "Oscar, no! No please, sir! Please!"

"Sir? Don't call me sir! Just shut the fuck up and take your shit off!" Oscar commanded as he shoved Snuggles into the bedroom and closed the door.

Dirty Red could hear the scuffle unfolding through the closed door. He walked and stood in threshold where Oscar was standing as he finished his beer whilst listening to Snuggles's horrifying screams. Dirty Red began wondering what came over Oscar whenever the crew was pulling off a hit and a woman was around. Oscar had done this countless times; and it seemed to stem from the night he'd raped the female that was with Sebas back in 1991. Dirty Red had stopped Oscar from raping a female only once, which was back in March of 1992, when he was preparing to rape and murder a childhood friend of his. No one, not even Manny, had known that Dirty Red had

let someone live during one of their home invasions.

Amidst Oscar's grunts, and Snuggles's pleas to live, Dirty Red thought about the female he saved that night and wondered what had become of her because he had not a clue. The only thing he was certain of was the fact that the female didn't rat him out. She could've given up Dirty Red easily because she knew who he was; but the crew hadn't been harassed about the three murders they'd committed that night back in '92 and the female hadn't been seen or heard from again.

"She probably dead." Dirty Red said to himself just as Oscar emerged from the room covered in sweat.

"You done, nigga?" Dirty Red asked as he downed the last remnants of his beer.

"Boy, that bitch had some good pussy!" Oscar said as he went into the kitchen.

"Nigga, is you done?" Dirty Red asked through a smile as he shook in head.

"Right after I cut this bitch throat, homeboy." Oscar replied as he walked out of the kitchen with a long butcher knife in his left hand.

Oscar entered the room where Snuggles lay on her back unconscious on the bed and naked from the waist down. He'd strangled her into silence after completing himself and was now back in order to finish the job. He straddled Snuggles's body and tilted her neck up and slit her throat from ear to ear. She bled out on the mattress before Oscar had even left room.

After Oscar cleaned himself up for a second time, he and Dirty Red finished off the blunt that Roscoe had been smoking and called Swanson and Montgomery to clean up the mess that they would leave behind. The two men walked out of the house and saw that everything on the block was just as normal as before they entered into Roscoe's house and perpetrated a double homicide.

Roscoe's murder set the crew free from all ties to major

dealers in the city. The Miami boys, in turn, never even bothered to find out what happened to Roscoe. They were planning on getting rid of him anyway. Somebody had merely done them a favor. The crew received their first shipment from Damenga the following morning and the wheels were set in motion for the crew to begin counting down to the day that they could walk away from the game.

CHAPTER TWENTY-EIGHT

BUSINESS IS BOOMIN'

It was now mid-May, a month after the boys had made their connection with Damenga and freed themselves of Roscoe. The crew had gotten a firm grip on two-thirds of the city's drug market and was rapidly expanding throughout the remaining territories. The Ninth Ward belonged to the Ben Holland Gang as they came to be known. The Third, Sixth, Tenth and Seventeenth Wards belonged to them as well. People all across town knew and respected the boys. They also knew that the gang was not to be played with on any level. Rumors of the crew's bloody feuds abounded on the streets of New Orleans; and many people came to fear the gang because of their violent lifestyle. It was fair to say that the Ben Holland Gang's violent reputation preceded them.

The gang's reign over the city was a prosperous one; peace abounded, prices were low, and murders had subsided. All was well on the streets; but within the organization, problems were beginning to arise.

After Dirty Red and Oscar eliminated Roscoe, Burtell and Jarell faded into the background, but, once again, they were beginning to cause problems.

Two weeks earlier, Derrick told Jason that Kim had been going behind Jermaine's back with the twins again. Jason then told Jermaine to his face that Kim was nothing but trouble and he should just let her go on her way. Jermaine, however, loved the short, slender nineteen year-old with all his heart. Jason and Lamont, and even Dirty Red and Katrina, tried repeatedly to get Jermaine to leave Kim alone. He would tell them that they were through; but Jason and Lamont, as well as everybody else, knew better. The hard truth was, no matter how hard a stance Jermaine took in front of the crew concerning the matter, everybody knew that he was weak behind Kim.

Jermaine was a real good earner though; and he wasn't afraid to kill a man and he was down for his boys at all times. That, along with the indubitable fact that they were like brothers, was the only reason the boys didn't cut Jermaine loose. Kim, however, was no longer welcome at *Par 6* or any of the dope houses the boys ran throughout the city. Whenever she came to a party that the boys were throwing inside one of the city's many nightclubs, the crew, including Katrina, acted as if she weren't even there.

Jermaine, meanwhile, even though he loved Kim, had begun running around with Jason and Lamont. The two of them had turned Jermaine on to Tanaka and Alicia the day after their senior prom, which was a week ago, after Kim had gotten upset and stunted on Jermaine on front of a crowd. The night of the prom, Jermaine was standing beside his jeep in a peach tuxedo, sporting a fresh, low cut fade and two three-quarter karat diamond earrings in his left ear. Kim, who wore a tight fitting peach evening gown and peach shoes with her hair finger waved in the front and braided in the back, looked stunning that warm spring night as the crew, minus Katrina, Tanaka, and Alicia, all stood out in front of the Sheraton Hotel on Canal Street watching as students from G. W. Carver Senior High School strolled into the hotel's ballroom.

Later that night, Kim began pestering Jermaine inside the ballroom about him buying her a car for her graduation. She began bothering him once she saw Katrina pull up into the

hotel's valet lot in a brand new '00 yellow convertible Mustang on 19" chrome rims and all white interior. The crew had all chipped in to buy Katrina a graduating and parting gift because she had earned an Academic Scholarship to Arizona State University. The eighteen year-old jumped for joy the night of the prom when Dirty Red and Oscar presented her with the keys to the car. She thanked them both and they, in turn, told her that they were proud of her earning that scholarship and knew she would make the whole Ninth Ward proud.

When Katrina pulled up to the hotel's valet section and got out of her new Mustang and proudly stepped towards Jason, Lamont, Dana, Kim and Jermaine, Kim told her that it was a nice rental she had picked. Katrina announced that the car was hers and she could see the envy growing in Kim's eyes. She simply loved to see Kim get jealous. She smiled to herself as Kim promptly walked off and headed towards the restrooms. When Kim returned, she saw about fifty people in the hotel's valet section admiring a bubble gum blue, 1973 Chevrolet convertible Impala. The car had white interior with bubble gum blue trimming to match the outside paint; the system was killer with two 18" woofers and eight, 6x9 speakers in the doors and dash.

Kim walked to the side of the car and saw Tanaka driving and Alicia sitting in the front seat beside her. Tanaka had the music up loud, playing *Turn off the Lights* by World Class Wreckin' Cru. Kim again turned green with envy as Lamont parted the crowd and announced that the two girls were driving his new toy that night. Everyone gave Lamont his props on the ride, which he called, "The Heavy Chevy", as he walked into the ballroom with Tanaka on one arm, and Alicia on the other.

It was then that Kim decided that Jermaine should buy her a car for her graduation, even though she was attending a GED program at Delgado Community College and wasn't scheduled to graduate for another month.

"You can buy me a fuckin' car, Jermaine! All the resta these hoes pullin' up in Mustangs and drop top Chevy's and shit, and here I am still ridin' on the side of you!" Kim nagged as she

followed Jermaine into the ballroom.

"Dana don't have a car." Jermaine responded as he paused just inside the ballroom's doorway.

"Fuck Dana! I'm talkin' about me! I'm supposed ta' be your woman and you treatin' me like shit!" Kim argued as scores of prom-goers looked on and eyed the situation.

"When you decide ta' stop actin' like a li'l hoe and change ya' fuckin' attitude, you might be in a position ta' get that car, but as of today, no. Fuck no!"

Kim took the bouquet of flowers she held in her hand and threw them at Jermaine. She then pushed him in the chest and yelled aloud, "You know what? You know what, Jermaine? Fuck you! You a weak ass nigga! Look at me! It's a lotta niggas out there that'll love ta' take care of me! I don't *need* or *want* your weak ass no fuckin' more!"

Kim had embarrassed Jermaine in front of half of the senior class. He looked around at the people as they stood in shock, waiting to see his reaction. Kim had always talked disrespectfully to him, and he always accepted the verbal abuse —but only in private. Not wanting to show weakness in front of his peers, Jermaine hauled off and slapped Kim in the face, knocking her to the ground. He then picked her up by one arm and escorted her out of the hotel. Kim spat at him and walked hurriedly down Canal Street.

When Jermaine walked back into the ballroom without Kim on his side, Jason, Lamont, and Katrina gave him his props for handling the situation. Jermaine, however, felt remorse for the way he had treated Kim that night. He had put up almost five-thousand dollars to help the crew buy Katrina's Mustang, but he didn't want to buy even a used car for his girlfriend. He figured that Kim, as conniving as she was, may have had a point that night. He called and apologized to her after he left the prom and secretly agreed to buy her a vehicle—but only if she stopped sleeping with the twins.

Kim agreed, but Jermaine told her that she would have to

prove it to him. Kim knew if she made Jermaine feel comfortable, she would be able to persuade him into buying her a vehicle. They agreed to see each other in secret to keep the crew from finding out. Kim had a serious hold on Jermaine, and he loved her dearly, no matter how many times she hurt his heart or talked down to him. Jermaine hung up the phone with Kim just as he pulled into *Houston's*, an upscale restaurant in New Orleans's Garden District.

The crew was scheduled to meet Dirty Red, Anna, JoAnne, and Oscar for dinner. The four felt they were too old to attend a high school prom so they offered to buy dinner to honor Katrina, Dana, Tanaka, and Alicia, the only ones out of the entire crew who were actually graduating. The gang all ate and talked for a while. When Katrina brought up what happened between Jermaine and Kim that night, Jermaine played it off and told the crew that he was finished with her, even though he had apologized to her on the phone for almost thirty minutes. The crew had no choice but to take Jermaine at his word; but after dinner, when the teens left to go to the club to see Non-Stop perform, Jermaine told them that he was going back to *Par 6* to relax and clear his head.

The crew all knew right then and there that Jermaine was going to see Kim. No one said a word of protest however; they had all washed their hands with Jermaine and Kim's turbulent relationship that very night. The teens all left and Dirty Red and Oscar, along with Anna and JoAnne, had stayed behind and ordered adult beverages and discussed Jermaine's troubling situation over glasses of cognac.

"Hey, why you think this nigga won't leave that no good bitch alone?" Oscar asked JoAnne.

"Love, man! The same reason I can't leave your no good ass alone!" JoAnne remarked as she shook her legs rapidly and stirred her drink, whilst looking over the crowd inside the restaurant.

"I'm serious, JoAnne!"

"Me too, nigga!" JoAnne replied as she faced Oscar and

looked him square in the eyes.

"She might've put some voodoo on Jermaine or something." Anna remarked, breaking the silence that was beginning to turn into tension between JoAnne and Oscar.

Anna shifted her eyes rapidly back and forth to Oscar and that got Dirty Red's attention. He looked over to Oscar, who looked as if he was preparing to throw his drink in Joanne's face. JoAnne, in turn, was staring back hard at Oscar preparing to do the same. Not wanting an embarrassing altercation to unfold inside the booth, Dirty Red gave his diagnosis of the situation in order to redirect his two friends' mounting animosity. "Jermaine don't believe in voodoo, Anna." He quickly remarked. "You gotta believe in voodoo in order for that shit ta' work. So if Kim *did* put a spell on 'Maine, it ain't gone work 'cause 'Maine don't believe in voodoo. I think she just got some fire ass pussy."

"Well, I know my pussy the bomb and I don't see you losing your mind behind me, Ben. And how you know so much about voodoo?" Anna asked, taking Dirty Red's lead.

"I read about that when I was younger. And I got a spell on you, Anna," Dirty Red said as he waved his hands in front of Anna in a sort of mystic motion.

Anna laughed aloud and said, "That ain't gone work 'cause I don't believe in voodoo. You just said that the person that has a spell cast on them has to believe in voodoo. I don't."

"See? You believe everything I say. You already under my spell," Dirty Red stated as everybody laughed. "Seriously, though, Kim just, I think she just crazy. What you think, Big O?" Dirty Red then asked, satisfied that he had broken the tension between Oscar and JoAnne.

"Say, brer? You know they say that crazy women have the best pussy? I remember hearing that somewhere!" Oscar said.

JoAnne waved her hands from side to side in disagreement and said, "Man, none of what y'all sayin' apply ta' Jermaine. He just in love with the wrong woman, and that right there can

be deadly. I hope for his sake he gets control of his emotions. Once a woman finds out that ya' weak for her, she will eat your ass alive and spit out the pieces."

"All women ain't the same, Jo." Anna chimed in. "If Ben was weak for me, I'd see him as a sweet young man, not a weak one. Some women want a knight in shining armor to come along and sweep 'em off their feet. And I would be his beautiful princess."

"Yea?" Dirty Red chimed in, "well that nigga there better be riding a big pretty ass horse and have a lotta gold coin in his knapsack or the beautiful princess gone turn into the wicked witch of the west. A pretty face don't mean shit now-a-days. You gotta get inside a chick's head and find out where she coming from. 'Cause even the strongest man can fall weak behind a woman. Remember Samson and Delilah? Look how Manny fell. If he woulda chose a woman that wasn't a part of the game, he probably still be alive." He said somberly.

"You right about that, my nig, but it won't be too long before we out this game. Jermaine gone be all right." Oscar remarked.

"Yea." Dirty Red answered lowly as he stared into his glass while making small circles around the sides of the glass with his fingertips.

"There you go again, Dirty Red." Oscar quipped through laughter.

"Go again with what, dog?"

"Makin' them circles and shit with your fingertips. What's that about?"

"Shit, I don't know," Dirty Red replied. "It's just a habit I guess, brer."

"That's a funny habit, dog. You been doing that for years. Anyway, you don't sound too happy with the way things goin'." Oscar stated.

"Nahh, it's not that, Big O. It's just that shit going too good for us right now."

"Shit going just the way we planned it, brer. We running damn near the whole city. We got respect, and Damenga happy with the arrangement. It don't get no better than this!"

"I know, but we on one helluva run, brer. I don't think nobody ever made it this far from nothing. Ten years we been in the game, causin' havoc and making major loot."

"We caused havoc 'cause we got police on the payroll and some real niggas behind us. Most crews don't have that."

"Right, right, but everything come with a price. After the Memphis job, we lost Manny. Now we done took over all these hoods and took down so many gangsters—Sebas, Rico, Haywood, Roscoe."

"Them niggas had that comin'!" Oscar remarked as he poured another glass of cognac and quickly gulped it down.

"You true in everything you saying O, but I just got a feeling its gone get worse before it get better. Our history, I'm talking 'bout the history of our crew, history taught me that. I just hope when it's time to pay, the price don't exceed the effort, ya' feel me?"

"Business is boomin', dog! It's fuckin' boomin'! The way I feel right now, we gone go out on toppa' the game and look back on all we done and feel justified for everything that's done happened, and for everything that will happen."

"I'm feeling that, O." Dirty Red said as the crew got up to prepare to leave.

Dirty Red left one-thousand dollars on the table and he, Oscar, Anna, and JoAnne left the restaurant and headed out to *Par 6* to continue their evening together.

"Like I say," Dirty Red replied as the group walked away from the table, "if ever that day should arise, I hope the price for our success ain't too high a price ta' pay."

CHAPTER TWENTY-NINE

HOOK, LINE, AND SINKER

"Say, brer, why the fuck you keep comin' on this set?" Lamont asked Kim in an agitated tone.

Kim had been hanging in the Seventeenth Ward where her cousins resided, which was down the block from where Jermaine and Lamont ran the dope house in the apartment over "Ma's" store with Sean and Hottie, two seventeen year-olds. Sean and Hottie were scoring a quarter-kilo a week from the crew at the out-set. When the boys saw how well they were holding down their block, they asked them if they wanted to move up in the game by joining the crew as soldiers. Sean and Hottie agreed and were hired to work at the dope house to stand guard for Lamont and Jermaine whilst they repackaged their product and sold weight ranging from ounces to kilograms.

Kim had been coming around the store the entire week. Even though she would try and stay on the side of the corner store out of Lamont, Sean and Hottie's site, her presence would agitate Lamont to the point that he would ask her to leave. This day was no different.

"Go on 'bout your business, brer!" Lamont snapped towards

Kim.

"Nigga, I'm waiting on Jermaine. And until he ask me ta' leave, I ain't leavin'!" Kim retorted.

"You make a nigga wanna bat the piss out your li'l funky ass!" Lamont stated angrily as he, Sean and Hottie walked off and stood in front "Ma's" store just as Jermaine exited the building and walked towards the corner to meet Kim.

Kim had just earned her GED and she was getting worried that Jermaine wasn't going to purchase a car like he had promised a month ago. Katrina, Dana, Alicia and Tanaka had all graduated as well. It was now the second week of June in the year 1999. Kim wanted so badly to join in on the girls' fun. She wanted a car so she could pull up alongside Katrina's Mustang, or the Heavy Chevy that Lamont would let Tanaka and Alicia use at their leisure. She was trying hard to regain Jermaine's trust. Although they agreed to keep their relationship under wraps, word eventually got out that the two were talking again. The crew didn't care, however, as they had grown tired of Jermaine and Kimberly's on-again-off-again relationship. All they asked was that Kim not show herself around the crew anymore. She complied most times, but when Jermaine was at "Ma's" store, she would sometimes unintentionally agitate Lamont. That's the reason the two passed words on this day. The crew, although they had washed their hands of their affiliation with Kim, didn't like what was going on between her and Jermaine; but they weren't going to interfere.

Dirty Red had even asked Derrick, who knew the twins well, about Kim and the twins. Derrick told him that, as far as he knew, Kim really did stop messing around with Burtell and Jarell, so the crew decided to let Jermaine deal with Kim on his own.

Lamont had again asked Kim to leave. He got in her face this time. "Didn't I tell you to get the fuck from 'round here?" Lamont lamented as Kimberly calmly backed away and looked at Jermaine.

"Look," Jermaine said, "go down by ya' cousin and I'm a hollar at ya' when I'm done down here."

"Alright, baby," Kim replied in a soft voice. "I can't wait to see you later. I'm happy we back together, Jermaine. I missed you so bad." Kim said sweetly as she hugged her man and placed her head on his chest. She looked into Jermaine's eyes and kissed him fully on the mouth and turned and began to walk slowly down the block.

With hungry eyes, Jermaine watched as Kim's dark-brown, petite frame sashayed down the side walk. He admired the slim and sexy nineteen year-old's firm behind and shapely, bowed legs. Kim smiled and waved at Jermaine before she crossed the street and turned onto her cousin's block. The eighteen year-old smiled and headed back into "Ma's" store to rejoin Hottie, Sean, and Lamont.

When Kim was out of the store's site, she got on her cell phone and dialed a number.

"Hello?" The voice answered.

"I need a li'l bit more time with Jermaine, man." Kim stated as she stood on the sidewalk in front of her cousin's house.

"That's cool. We 'bouta get ready to do that other thing anyway in a li'l while so be ready. I'm a hit ya' back later."

A few hours had gone by and the sun had been down for almost an hour now. Katrina had been hanging around the dope house in the Ninth Ward all day long with Jason, Dana, Torre` and Derrick. She and Jason had been flirting with one another in secret the entire evening, and when the sun went down, Dana left to go to her parents' home to study for her college entrance exam. Katrina and Jason soon found themselves in the den of the dope house engaged in a heated sex session. The two lay in each other's arms afterwards, kissing each other passionately as they lay naked on the sofa side by side in a tight embrace.

"I love you so much, Jason. I wish I woulda never brought you and Dana together because I feel guilty every time *we* get

together. Dana my friend, but I just can't stay away from you. You got me hooked on your love, boy."

"Yea, I am a bad mutherfucka," Jason replied as he smiled and rubbed his chin.

"I'm serious, Jason. I'm in love with you. Not having you to myself is killing me, brer. I know we can't keep doin' this 'cause if Dana found out, it'll kill her."

"Ya' know, I been having feelings for you for a long time, Kay Kay. And ta' be honest, I know we wrong. We both wrong for this shit. I want you bad, but Dana don't deserve this right here."

"What we gone do, Jay? 'Cause I don't wanna let go either." Katrina remarked lowly as she laid her head atop Jason's chest.

Jason raised Katrina's head and kissed her lips gently. He then got up from the sofa and put on his Girbaud jeans, grabbed his .44 automatic and headed towards the bathroom. Before he left the den, Jason told Katrina, whose heart was pounding with love and passion, that he loved her, but he wasn't in love, and it was time to make a decision. "You know we ain't right, Kay Kay. As much as I wanna to be with you, I can't, nahh, *we* can't keep playing Dana like this. I gotta man up and do right by Dana, baby. I can fuck with any other bitch out there, but what me and you doin', you and I both know we wrong. We can't keep playing Dana. She one person that don't deserve this shit right here." Jason reiterated as he stood in the doorway and stared at Katrina.

Katrina's eyes began to well up. She knew this night would be the last time she and Jason would ever make love. As much as she hated to let him go, Katrina knew it was the right thing to do as she had always considered herself a loyal friend of Dana's. Katrina knew that if she were to keep sleeping with Jason behind Dana's back, it would prevent her from being the "real bitch" she prided herself on being. Above all else, Katrina knew that if Dana found out about her and Jason, it would prove Kim right; and that was something Katrina could not let happen. She agreed with Jason solemnly and relented

her love and quickly began to search for ways within herself to stop loving him as much as she did. It would be a task Katrina knew she was capable of conquering, but would find all-so difficult none-the-less.

Tanaka Romaire, meanwhile, was over to Alicia's house in the Desire Project braiding her friend's hair when her cell phone rang.

"Hello?"

"Remember what we did that night on the boat in Daytona?" The voice spoke lowly.

"Who this is?" Tanaka asked inquisitively.

"Katrina, girl!"

"Do I remember Daytona? How could I forget that, Kay Kay?"

"Okay, good. 'Cause I wanna do it again!"

Tanaka had been steadily fantasizing about Katrina ever since they had left Daytona in April. She thought Katrina was just experimenting with lesbianism, but when she heard her voice on the other end, her Chinese eyes lit up and she cracked a smile, parting her thin lips and biting the lower one.

"Where you at?" Tanaka then asked with a wide smile.

"I'm by Jason right 'round the corner. Come get me in the Heavy Chevy!"

"You can just ride around here in ya' 'Stang. When I'm done with Alicia hair, we can ride out!"

"No. I'm 'bouta let Jason use it to run in the Seventeenth by Ma's. You know he ain't gone let me use the Caddy, girl. Just come pick me up right quick. When you done with Alicia hair, we can all ride out together in the Heavy Chevy and have some fun. I'm so fuckin' horny right now!"

"You right 'round the corner you say?"

"Right here by Jay waiting on you."

"Okay," Tanaka said in a soft, low voice as she hung up the cell phone and grabbed the keys to Lamont's Chevy.

Tanaka told Alicia that she was going to pick up Katrina right quick and after she finished her hair, the three of them were going to have a little fun.

"What kind of fun?" Alicia asked in a shocked and excited manner as she turned around in her chair to face Tanaka.

Tanaka stuck out her tongue and flicked it rapidly.

"Nooo!" Alicia said in a surprised manner.

"Umm hmm! I told ya', girl! You do it right and they gone just keep comin' back! You game?"

"Hell yea, bitch! Hurry up and go get her so you can finish my hair and we can ride out!" Alicia replied as she turned and checked her half-done hair in the mirror.

Tanaka jumped into the Heavy Chevy, let the top down, and put in R. Kelly's CD and selected the song *What I Feel* off his album titled *R*. She was feeling real good about being with Katrina again and she began to nod her head slowly to the music coming from the car's stereo as she thought of ways to please Katrina once more.

As she approached the intersection of Piety and Benefit streets, about three blocks from the dope house, Tanaka stopped at the stop sign, and then pulled slowly into the intersection. When she did, gunshots began to echo from the side of one of the houses that lined Piety Street. Tanaka didn't hear the gunshots because the music was too loud, but when she felt a bullet graze her right shoulder, she screamed and turned to her right in time to see someone shooting at her. She pressed the gas, but another gunman ran in front of the car. Tanaka slammed the car into park and attempted to get out and run, but before she could clear the door, she was shot two more times in her side and back. As she lay on the concrete in between the driver's side door and the body of the Chevy,

Tanaka begged for her life as the two gunman approached.

"What did I do?" Tanaka asked in a panic-stricken manner as she lay up against the car.

The gunmen said nothing as they pointed their guns at Tanaka.

"Y'all don't kill me! Please! I ain't do nothin'! I ain't fuckin' do nothin'! What I did?" Tanaka cried aloud.

Tanaka then screamed for help, but it was in vain. One of the gunmen shot her two times in the head and both gunmen fled the scene.

Eighteen year-old Tanaka Romaire's body lay on its side on the concrete in the middle of the intersection as R. Kelly's song continued to play inside the Chevy. Finally, someone looked out of a window and saw a young girl in tight-fitting black jeans and a red tank top lying in a pool of blood and decided to call an ambulance.

Word of somebody being shot spread quickly throughout the neighborhood. As Katrina and Jason stepped onto the porch, they saw people running towards the intersection in droves.

"What happened?" Jason asked loudly.

"Somebody got shot on the corner down the street!" Torre` answered as he and Derrick ran from the dope house towards the intersection under the moon-lit sky.

Jason locked the dope house and he and Katrina headed towards the crime scene. When they got there, they saw Lamont's Chevy in the middle of the intersection with scores of onlookers, along with the police, who had just arrived on the scene. Jason began screaming Lamont's name as he and Katrina rushed through the crowd.

"Lamont!" Katrina yelled hysterically.

"Not my fuckin' dog! Tell me that ain't my nigga laid out like that!" Jason yelled towards Alicia, who merely stared at the scene in a state of shock as Tanaka's mother wept

uncontrollably as the police held her back to prevent her from running towards her daughter's corpse.

"Lamont! What happened?" Katrina asked as she approached the crowd.

"Bitch, that ain't no motherfuckin' Lamont! You know who tha' fuck that is!" Alicia yelled as she charged at Katrina and began to throw punches at her.

Jason grabbed Alicia's arms and asked her what the problem was. The eighteen year-old told Jason that Katrina had called Tanaka right before she got shot to come and pick her up so they could hang out.

"What?" Katrina and Jason said at the same time.

"Hold up," said Jason. "Let me call Lamont so he can get his ass down here and see 'bout Tanaka and his fuckin' car. I need ta' call Dirty Red, too."

"Hello?" Lamont inquired as he answered his cell phone.

"Lamont, ya' need ta' get down in the Ninth Ward quick like, my nig!"

"What's wrong, J-Dog?"

"Just, just come right now, brer. It's fuckin' bad, brer, Tanaka, ya' Chevy. Look like Tanaka was—"

"I'm on my way, nigga!" Lamont said, cutting Jason off before he hung up the phone and jumped up from the table and began to run towards the staircase leading back down to the first floor of "Ma's" store.

"Where ya' going, dog?" Jermaine asked as he sat at the table with Hottie and Sean, counting money from the day's sales.

Lamont figured his car was wrecked so he told Jermaine, Hottie and Sean to finish counting the money and he'd be right back. He didn't know Tanaka was dead until he got to the scene. He broke down when he saw her sheet-clad body and he kept saying over and over that the bullets that Tanaka had

taken were meant for him.

Dirty Red, along with Anna, meanwhile, had made it over to the scene from *Par 6*, and Jason explained to him what Alicia had told him when he and Katrina arrived on the scene. "But that can't be true." Jason stated.

"How you know?" Dirty Red asked.

"Man, first of all, you know just as well as I do, that Katrina wouldn't pull no shit like that on Tanaka. Second," Jason said as he looked Alicia directly in the eyes, "me and Katrina been fuckin' for the last forty-five minutes and I know damn well she ain't make no phone call. Look like somebody set Tanaka up."

"Who would do that to her? And why?" Alicia asked with tears in her eyes.

"That's the sixty-four thousand dollar question right there, Alicia." Dirty Red remarked.

Around that time, the phone rang over at "Ma's" store in the Seventeenth Ward. "Ma" answered the phone and a female voice asked for Lamont. "Ma" told the female that Lamont had stepped away and asked to take a message. The person refused and politely thanked "Ma" before she hung up the phone.

As Jermaine sat at the table with Hottie and Sean, rubber-banding about two-hundred and thirty-seven thousand dollars, his cell phone rang. Jermaine answered his phone, got up from the table and chatted lowly for a few minutes and headed towards the stairs.

"Eh! Where you going, mutherfucka? We ain't even finish countin' this shit!" Hottie yelled.

"I be right back, brer! I'm just going check somethin' right quick! Bag what we got counted and I'm a band up the rest when I get back. I know how much it is already!" Jermaine remarked as he ran down the stairs into the store where he saw "Ma" counting her day's earnings.

"Ma" asked Jermaine if the boys were finished for the day

when she saw him heading towards the bolted front door.

"No, Sean and Hottie still upstairs baggin' what we got counted. I'm just gone hollar at somebody right outside real quick. I be right back." Jermaine replied.

"Ma" knew Lamont never unlocked the door until the boys were ready to leave her store. She reminded Jermaine of that fact, but he insisted on stepping outside of the store for a few seconds. "Ma" reluctantly handed Jermaine the keys and he unlocked the door and stepped onto the sidewalk. As "Ma" bent down behind her counter to unlock her safe and deposit her earnings, she just didn't feel comfortable with Jermaine having the door unlocked. She cautiously knelt behind the counter for a minute or so, but not before making sure Jermaine was still in front of the door. When she arose not even two minutes later, she saw that Jermaine was gone. "Ma" shook her head and was about to go and check on Jermaine when Hottie came down the stairs complaining aloud that Jermaine was trying to make him and Sean count all the money by themselves.

"We gotta get this money counted and drop it off to Dirty Red in the next hour! Lamont done jetted and this nigga here fuckin' around!" Hottie stated angrily to "Ma" as he walked up the aisle from the back of the store headed towards the front door.

"He disappear! Check and see if he out there!" "Ma" remarked as she walked back behind the counter and began cleaning her grill, satisfied that Hottie was in control of the situation.

"Don't worry about it, Ma! I'm 'bouta get this pussy-whipped nigga straight!" Hottie remarked just as he reached the front door.

Hottie was calling Jermaine's name loudly and repeatedly as he approached the front door and snatched it open. When he did so, he was blasted in the face with a .45 automatic. His body collapsed and lay trembling on the floor of "Ma's" store as the old Chinese lady screamed in terror.

The lone gunman, who wore a black tee shirt, black jeans, and a black ski-mask ran down the middle aisle of the store headed towards the stairs, but he was greeted by Sean, who stood at the top of the stairs blasting an SKS automatic assault rifle. The gunman turned, ran back up the aisle and jumped over Hottie's trembling corpse and fled the store. Seconds later, "Ma" and Sean heard screeching tires coming from a car that was obviously speeding away from the scene.

Neither "Ma" nor Sean had seen the car because they waited a few minutes to make sure no one else would enter the store. Sean looked at his dead friend and stepped slowly out the front door onto the sidewalk and saw Jermaine's light blue North Carolina hat and cell phone lying on the sidewalk in front of the store and feared the worst as "Ma" franticly dialed 911 to get an ambulance for Hottie. Sean knew it was too late for Hottie, though; his head had been blown open by the gun shot blast that penetrated his skull. He stared at his dead friend in a state of disbelief as the seventeen year-old light-skinned male lay dead with his eyes open. Sean kept his focus in spite of the heart-stopping drama that had unfolded, and the gruesome scene that lay before his eyes. He hid the money and the guns just before the police arrived because he knew the store would be searched and he and "Ma" would be questioned concerning what actually happened. Sean also kept in mind not to mention that Jermaine had suddenly disappeared and he quietly told "Ma" to do the same as the police began to place yellow tape around the front of the store.

Dirty Red, Jason, Torre` and Katrina meanwhile, were headed back towards the dope house to finish their discussion. Derrick and Lamont stayed at the scene with Alicia, who cried silently into Lamont's chest as she stared at her childhood friend's lifeless corpse. Tanaka looked as if she were asleep, but the bloody sheet that covered her body, and the amount of blood that soaked the portion of the sheet that covered her skull let it be known to everyone that Tanaka Romaire was gone forever.

Meanwhile, as Dirty Red and company walked down the sidewalk towards the dope house, they began their

conversation again concerning what Alicia had said when Jason and Katrina first arrived on the scene. "Man, I can't figure that out for nothing in the world," Katrina said. "Why would somebody wanna kill Tanaka? I mean, she wasn't 'bout no drama or nothing! She wasn't even 'bout that!"

Just then Dirty Red's cell phone rang. It was Jermaine's voice that he heard when he picked up. "Hey! Yo, Ben, I fucked up, brer. They—"

Jermaine was cutoff as another male voice began to speak, "Yea, nigga! We gotcha' fuckin' boy!"

"What?" Dirty Red asked as he stopped in his tracks and pressed the phone tighter to his ear.

"You heard me, bitch! I said we got Jermaine! You want this nigga back alive? Bring one-hundred g's to the fuckin' table! You got two hours ta' get my money! I say when and where! Answer ya' phone when I call too, or ya' boy gone be takin' a long ass nap, whoaday!" The voice ended just before the phone call dropped.

Dirty Red looked as if he had seen a ghost. He stood frozen on the sidewalk in front of the dope house with a thousand yard stare. He was about to throw the phone up against the house until he remembered he needed it to receive the next phone call from the kidnapper. "Mutherfucka!" He yelled aloud.

"What the prob?" Jason asked as he, Anna, Katrina, and Torre` surrounded Dirty Red.

"The price startin' ta' exceed the effort," Dirty Red remarked calmly.

"What ya' mean, Dirty Red?" Torre` asked inquisitively.

"Somebody kidnapped Jermaine."

CHAPTER THIRTY

SHOULDA SEEN IT COMING

Dirty Red, Jason, Torre` and Katrina, along with Anna, sat in the dope house discussing who could be behind Jermaine's kidnapping and awaiting the phone call. Dirty Red had talked to Sean after he was let go by the police. Sean had told him that Hottie was dead and he had two-hundred and thirty-seven thousand dollars for the crew. Dirty Red had Sean under suspicion briefly; but hearing the young gangster speak set Sean free of his impending rampage. Sean couldn't be involved. Dirty Red knew how much money the crew usually took in over to "Ma's" and Sean was right on point with the money count. On top of that, Hottie was dead. Dirty Red knew Sean would not kill Hottie to set up a jack-play, and he would not be willing to turn over the crew's cash if he was involved.

Derrick and Torre` had not the capacity to mount such an act of disrespect. Lil Earl was bed-ridden for a few days, unable to move as he was fighting a bout of gonorrhea. Not to mention he had been loyal to Dirty Red for years. On top of that, Lil Earl, Derrick and Torre` always kept the crew abreast of any mounting tensions they knew of in order to keep making money themselves. Dirty Red quickly eliminated those three as being suspects.

The next possibility for Dirty Red was his own boys, who were down from day one; but Dirty Red knew all-too-well that Oscar, Jason and Lamont were dead solid. Jermaine would not stage his own kidnapping; but whoever came at the crew hit them in their weak-spot—which was Jermaine Duplessis. Whoever hit the crew, had ties to Jermaine, at least that's what Dirty Red had surmised.

Satisfied that none of his boys were staging a coup, Dirty Red sent Oscar to pick up the money and to take Sean and "Ma" to a hotel for a couple of days.

Dirty Red, Anna, Jason, Torre` and Katrina all sat at the dining room table in silentce while Dirty Red and Jason loaded shells into three SKS assault rifles and a Glock .45 semi-automatic. Anna began chatting with Dirty Red, asking him what they were planning to do. Dirty Red told the four that he had an idea who was behind Hottie's murder and Jermaine's kidnapping, and if he was right, they were going to retaliate this very night. The crew began talking in low tones at the dining room table, repeatedly saying that they couldn't believe what had happened.

"What about Tanaka?" Anna asked Dirty Red.

"What about her?"

"You think her murder had something to do with all of this stuff that's goin' down?"

Just then Dirty Red's cell phone rang. He answered and a male voice told him to put Jermaine's ransom money in a blue dumpster beside the Winn-Dixie grocery store on Almonaster Boulevard in one hour.

Anna and Dirty Red then moved to the bedroom so that he could retrieve one-hundred thousand dollars from the safe in the floor. He answered the question she had posed to him in the dining room by telling her that he didn't know how Tanaka's murder fit into what was going down, but he was sure it had something to do with what was taking place this night.

Anna was worried that Dirty Red, Torre` and Jason were

316

going to get themselves hurt, or worse. "You should let the police deal with it," she said softly as she watched Dirty Red place stacks of money onto the wooden table inside the bedroom.

Dirty Red looked up from the safe and said, "What I'm a tell 'em Anna? That my boy got kidnapped from a dope house and the kidnappers want a hundred g's for his ransom? You know what it is. I can't let that shit go down like that!"

"Maybe the police can—"

"Fuck the police! This shit started in the streets and its gone end right there! In the mutherfuckin' streets!"

"What about me, Ben? Do I have a say so in all this?"

"Yea, just say you understand why I gotta do what I'm doin'." Dirty Red replied as he began stuffing the stacks of money into a leather duffel bag.

"I do understand, Ben. I do, but I don't wanna see you go down behind this." Anna said as she walked slowly towards the man she loved.

"I ever fucked up before? I know what I'm doin' Anna! And I ain't changin' my mind—period!"

"Can I go?"

"This game ain't for you and you know that. Besides that, you ain't have nothin' to do with this shit. This between me, Katrina, Jason and Torre`. Everybody else tied up right now. Us four gotta do it."

Anna rubbed her hands across Dirty Red's face as she stared intensely into his eyes. "What ever happened to that warm-hearted fifteen year-old young man I fell in love with?" She asked in a compassionate tone of voice.

"He met a dude named Manny and jumped in the game. Head first! When all this over, you might see 'em again, if you still around." Dirty Red remarked as he headed back into the dining room, but not before Anna grabbed him and pulled him back

and hugged his neck tightly.

"I ain't goin' nowhere, Ben," she said in a loving manner as she stared into his eyes.

"That's what I need ta' hear comin' from my woman." Dirty Red remarked as he headed into the dining room with a black duffel bag stuffed with one-hundred thousand dollars and rejoined Jason, Torre` and Katrina, who were finishing up loading the guns.

They each sipped a glass of cognac as they went over what they were planning to do. "If I'm right about this, we should be okay. If not, we regroup and go after them niggas from another angle." Dirty Red remarked as he grabbed one of the SKS rifles and slid in a clip.

Katrina sat at the table silently as she sipped her cognac and swayed back and forth in her dining room chair. She knew, without the boys even telling her, that she would be a part of what was to take place this night. Jermaine was her dog, her childhood friend, and Katrina was not going to let anybody fuck over Jermaine without her having a say in the matter. Even if the boys didn't want her to go, she was going anyway. When the boys got up from the table, Katrina grabbed the Glock .45 and followed closely.

Anna stood in the living room and watched as the four walked out of the dope house and headed towards Jason's Cadillac. Dirty Red placed the money inside the car and went back to Anna, who was standing alone in the living room, "I got a loaded nine millimeter in the glove box in the Benz," he said as he hugged Anna tightly. "You know how to shoot, baby, so do so if ya' gotta. I want you to go on home to Par 6. If you believe anybody, you hear me? If you feel anybody trialing you, call me and drive over to the Winn-Dixie on Almonaster. When you get to Par 6, call me, alright?"

Anna nodded and kissed Dirty Red and hugged him tightly before she left out of the dope house with Jason guiding her towards Dirty Red's Mercedes.

Dirty Red had gotten the keys to Anna's black 1998 four door Nissan Maxima whilst she took his Mercedes back to *Par 6*. The crew then went over to JoAnne's house in the Eighth Ward, and dropped off some cocaine and gathered a few more firearms. Dirty Red and Katrina then drove Anna's car to the grocery store with Jason and Torre` following close behind in Jason's Cadillac.

After Dirty Red dropped the money into the dumpster, the four of them sat in their cars across the street and down the block from the grocery store within eyesight of the dumpster. Dirty Red had received a call from Anna as he walked back towards her car. She had made it to Par 6, much to his relief.

There was a Chinese store across the street from the dumpster and its parking lot was filled with young black males and females. Dirty Red had a pair of binoculars and he watched each individual closely as he sat in the passenger seat of Anna's car. He paused when he saw one teen in particular looking over towards the dumpster. The teenager stood about 5' 7" and weighed about one-hundred and fifty-five pounds and wore Rastafarian dreadlocks in his head. The young teen looked at his watch, waited about five minutes and then walked over to the dumpster and retrieved the duffel bag. He then made a call on his cell phone and waited at the edge of the parking lot with the duffel bag on his shoulder.

Dirty Red called Jason and had him and Torre` focus in on the suspect.

Jason and Torre` sat smoking a blunt as they watched the scene unfold on this hot and muggy night in June. "Who you think behind this shit, Jay?" Torre` asked as he coughed after taking a toke.

Jason took the blunt from Torre`, eyed the Rastafarian and said, "That nigga there, I think I seen him with Roscoe a few times. But Roscoe dead. Might be the Miami boys."

"Really?" Torre` asked. "Behind that bitch ass nigga Roscoe?"

319

"Niggas done retaliated over a lot less, T-Dog." Jason replied as he hit the blunt two times and passed it back to Torre`.

"You right, my nig. But I'm ready for war, ya' heard me?" Torre` responded. "Hey, that's that nigga Non-Stop on the radio," he then said as he turned up the music slightly.

Dirty Red and Katrina, who sat behind the wheel of Anna's Maxima, sipped cognac as they watched the Rastafarian. "Seems like old times, huh, Dirty Red?" Katrina asked as she looked out the window.

Dirty Red smiled over to Katrina, revealing his ten gold teeth. The two of them then had a good laugh about what happened that night with Rico. Just then, an old 1986, four door, dark grey Oldsmobile pulled up in front of the Chinese store and the Rastafarian got into the backseat.

The four followed the Oldsmobile until it pulled into a gas station on the corners of Chef Mentuer Highway and Louisa Street, where, after about ten minutes, the Rastafarian got out of the back seat and headed towards the driver's side door of the Oldsmobile. The driver of the Oldsmobile got out as well, and the four could see for the first time that it was Burtell who was driving the car.

Jarell got out of the passenger's side and the three men shook hands and began laughing to themselves. The four, who were parked across the street in a McDonald's parking lot, peered from the side of the building at the three young men until their Expedition pulled into the parking lot. Dirty Red figured the twins were behind Jermaine's kidnapping, but everybody got the shock of their lives when the Expedition's tinted windows rolled down and Kim began yelling the twins' names.

"I shoulda seen this one coming!" Dirty Red swore as he tapped Katrina on the back and before the four headed back to their cars.

"They 'bouta split up." Dirty Red remarked as they all walked back to their vehicles.

"Me and Kay Kay gone follow that nigga in the Olds. Y'all

two follow the twins and Kim, but don't do nothin' 'til ya' hear from me, understand?"

Jason and Torre` nodded and went back to Jason's car and trailed the twins, staying a good distance behind so as not to be seen. Torre` had placed his SKS rifle on his lap and slowly puffed on another blunt as the two gangsters discussed the maliciousness of Kim's betrayal.

"I can't believe that bitch did some shit like this brer." Jason said somberly.

"I knew Kim was devious. But ta' set ya' own nigga up for a kidnap?" Torre` exclaimed.

Meanwhile, Dirty Red and Katrina had trailed the Rastafarian until he pulled up to a house behind Southern University (SUNO) in Ponchartrain Park, a predominately Black middle-class, often quiet neighborhood. He quickly exited the vehicle with his share of the money, unlocked his door and entered the house. Dirty Red and Katrina sat in the Maxima as Dirty Red locked and loaded his SKS rifle.

"You want me ta' go in with you?" Katrina asked.

"Nah, I can handle this nigga myself."

"Bu they might have more people in there."

"Maybe, but all the lights was off. He right there in the kitchen. I can get him, and be able ta' see anybody else comin'. I'm a call you on the cell when I get this nigga straight."

Dirty Red exited the vehicle, and ran up to the front door of the house toting his SKS rifle. He jumped in the air, kicked the door and it flung open. The Rastafarian was sitting at the kitchen table with the money spread out across the entire area of the table top, along with a set of steak knives. He tried to grab for his gun, but Dirty Red had the ups on him. He sat back in his chair with his hands in the air and Dirty Red hit him with the barrel of the gun and knocked him out cold.

Dirty Red went and checked the back door and saw that it was still locked from the inside, letting him know that no one

fled out the back of the home. He then checked the windows to make sure they were still closed and quickly searched the two bedrooms inside the house to make sure no one was hiding under the beds or inside one of the closets. Satisfied that the house was void of any other persons, Dirty Red called Katrina and told her the coast was clear.

When Katrina walked into the house, she saw Dirty Red tying up the Rastafarian as he lay on the floor. He then poured a glass of water onto his head to awaken him. When the Rastafarian awoke he was staring down the barrel of Katrina's . 45 semi-automatic. When Dirty Red asked what was going down, the young man immediately began to tell what happened.

He told Dirty Red and Katrina that Jermaine was tied up at a hotel in New Orleans East and he was scheduled to release him later in the night. He then told the two that Kim had grown impatient when Jermaine wouldn't buy her a car. She had complained to the twins and the twins told her that she could get more than a car if she played it right and gave them a cut. The Rastafarian then told Dirty Red and Katrina that the twins knew Lamont would not let Jermaine open the door as long as he was at "Ma's", so they had Kim, who stated that she knew how to get Lamont to leave the store, call and pretend she was Katrina to get Tanaka to leave the house. "Kim said she was gone set Tanaka up for my cousins so they could beat her up real bad and get somebody to call Lamont. That was the plan from the get go—to get Lamont to leave the store," he said as he lay on the floor with his hands tied behind his back.

"Them niggas ain't just beat Tanaka, brer. They killed her." Dirty Red stated as he held on to the rifle.

"Aww, man. If I knew they was gone kill her, I wouldna teamed up with them niggas, brer. For real. I ain't bout killin' nobody. All I was supposed to do was pick up the money."

"It's all good, dog. That's how the game go, ya' dig? What else happened?" Dirty Red asked calmly as he held his SKS rifle on the young man.

"They knew Lamont would go and check on his ole lady. They was only planning to rob Ma's store, but when Hottie came out, it fucked it up for 'em. They couldn't sneak into the store. Burtell still tried, but that other nigga at the toppa' the stairs started blastin'. We already had Jermaine in the car so we sped off when Burtell ran out the store. We took 'em to a hotel and hit 'em with a dose of heroin to keep him quiet."

Dirty Red got on his cell phone and called Oscar and had him ride out to the hotel where Jermaine was supposedly being held. He and Katrina waited patiently for word from Oscar. Their attitude was serious as they sat at the table and kept a close eye on their captive and looking out of the windows on occasion to see if anybody was coming towards the house.

When Oscar got to the hotel, he convinced the clerk to give him an extra key to the door. He entered the room and saw Jermaine lying on the bed on his back.

"Eh yo, 'Maine you straight?"

Jermaine didn't answer.

"Jermaine! Get up fool, we gotcha nigga!" Oscar said as he walked towards Jermaine whilst smiling.

The closer Oscar got to the bed, however, he could see that something was wrong. His smile dropped and his eyes began to well up with tears as memories of his finding Manny dead on the bedroom floor of Shawonda's house resurfaced. He sat on the side of the bed and silently wept for Jermaine when he realized that his friend was dead. Jermaine had foam around his mouth and a rubber tube tied around his left arm. There was an empty packet of aluminum foil on the night stand next to the bed also. Oscar then called Dirty Red and told him that Jermaine was dead.

Dirty Red figured early on that Jermaine was already dead. He saw the steak knives on the table; he also knew no kidnapper in his right mind would leave his hostage in a hotel alone. He figured the Rastafarian was going to cut Jermaine into pieces and discard his body. Dirty Red prevented that, but

he couldn't save his friend's life. He stood up and aimed his rifle at the young man and released a hail of bullets. He shot the young man a total of thirty times, leaving his body riddled with bullets and chunks of his skull and other parts of his body splattered on the kitchen floor. He and Katrina grabbed the money off the table, stepped over the lifeless body, hopped into the black Maxima and sped away.

Dirty Red then contacted Jason and Torre`, who were still parked outside of the twins' apartment in the Seventh Ward, and told them he was on his way after learning their location.

The twins, along with Kim, were holed up inside their duplex not too far from City Park. Jason and Torre` waited patiently until Dirty Red and Katrina arrived. Oscar was there with them, too, as well as Lamont, who had returned from the police crime lab after signing papers to have his car processed for evidence relating to Tanaka's homicide.

The crew was all together now; full of anger and sadness as Dirty Red and Oscar had broken the news concerning Jermaine to everyone. This time however, the crew knew the very same night what had happened and their minds were set on revenge. Emotions ran deep. Tears were shed by all. Lamont took it the hardest. He felt that he should have never let Kim keep coming around "Ma's" store. Everyone secretly blamed him or herself for Jermaine's death and they all openly expressed their desire to avenge his death.

The crew all gathered their weapons: SKS assault rifles, AK-47's, and Katrina with her Glock .45. She pulled her hair back into a French twist and tightened her tennis shoes. They split into threes and took Jason's Cadillac and Anna's Maxima and drove slowly up the block towards the twins' duplex. The cars came to a slow halt and the two front doors on Anna's Maxima flung open. All four doors on Jason's Cadillac flung open at the same time. Everybody hopped out of the cars with guns in hand and the six all merged and ran towards the front door of the duplex like a small platoon of World War II Soldiers closing in on a small pocket of Nazis.

The six crossed the yard and rushed up to the front door while

looking at the figures inside the apartment. They could see Kim through the slats on the blinds covering the windows as she sat on the lap of one of the twins facing him with a bottle of champagne in her hand, laughing and gyrating sexily to Outkasts' song *Spotieottiedopalicious,* reminiscent of an exotic floor technician that was giving a lap dance inside of a raunchy strip club.

The three were having a good time right up until the front door flew open with a loud crash. Burtell threw Kim off his lap and ran towards the back door but he was quickly gunned down by Dirty Red. Jarell jumped from the sofa and stood frozen with his hands in the air as Kim dropped to her knees and began crawling towards Dirty Red as she pleaded with him.

"Get the fuck up!" Dirty Red yelled over the music as he shoved a groveling Kim away from him with his right foot.

"Dirty Red! I'm glad y'all here! They was holdin' me hostage while they was kidnapping Jermaine!" Kim stated as she sat up on her heels.

"Bitch, please! You the whole reason all this shit happenin'," Dirty Red remarked coldly.

"They made me do it, Dirty Red!" Kim pleaded as she crawled towards Dirty Red once more.

Dirty Red had seen Kim sitting on Burtell's lap having a good time and it didn't look like she was being held hostage then. Besides, he had gotten the truth from the Rastafarian. Even more, Jermaine was dead. So everyone had to pay regardless.

"Y'all kill the other twin and grab the money." Dirty Red ordered as he picked Kim up off the floor and he, Jason and Katrina rushed her to Anna's Maxima.

The three heard Jarell scream for his life just before a barrage of gunshots was let loose. Everything then went silent as Torre`, Oscar, and Lamont jogged out of the duplex with their rifles at their side, leaving the door wide open and the music steadily playing in the background.

Kim was now flanked by Jason and Dirty Red in the backseat of the Maxima as Katrina drove towards Manchac, Louisiana, which was a rural area northwest of New Orleans that was surrounded by swampland off Interstate-55. The rest of the crew had split up and headed back to *Par 6* to await their return.

Kim was feeling pure terror. She pleaded over and over again for the crew to let her go, promising not to tell what they had done to Burtell, Jarell and their cousin. Dirty Red had heard all of the begging before and he was now numb to the pleas of his victims. He punched Kim in the face and she turned and banged on the rear window of the car as she screamed aloud, trying desperately to get other motorists' attention. Other motorist couldn't see through the tinted windows, however; and Katrina had the stereo up loud in the car to drown out Kim's pleas of mercy.

Katrina drove to Manchac and headed down a narrow dirt road that led to a secluded clearing surrounded by bald cypress trees that lined a small bayou filled with black murky water. She pulled the Maxima to the edge of the bayou and slammed it into park and exited the vehicle along with Jason and Dirty Red.

The two young men struggled with Kimberly as she kicked and screamed in terror, knowing full well what would happen to her if she was pulled out of the vehicle. Dirty Red grabbed Kim's ankles tightly and began yanking her furiously, demanding that she let go of the seats; but Kim held on for dear life. She let out a blood-curdling scream just as her grip slipped and she was pulled out onto the dirt. This was the moment of truth for Kim. She knew she was facing her comeuppance. She tried to get up and run through the darkness of the swamp, but Jason threw a fury of punches to her head that forced her to the ground. The three then began beating Kim ferociously over a ten minute period. Jason picked Kim up and held her from behind in order to allow Katrina to punch her repeatedly in the face. Kim was begging for her life as Katrina pounded her face and body without mercy. Dirty Red then held Kim and she was slapped repeatedly in the face by

Jason, steadily begging to be left alone and apologizing for Jermaine's death.

Katrina then held Kim and she was choked by Dirty Red until she went silent. Katrina and Dirty Red released Kim from their clutches and she fell to the ground and tried to crawl away whilst calling out for help. The three then took turns kicking Kim until she was unable to move nor scream any longer. With her eyes half closed and blood running from the corners of her mouth, Kim was kicked in the head one last time by Katrina and forced onto her back. Katrina then walked back to the car and grabbed the .45 off the front seat and returned and stood over Kim's small frame and aimed the gun as Dirty Red and Jason stepped back to watch the scene unfold.

"I told you a long time ago, bitch—you fuck with mine, I was gone kill you! Didn't I say that, hoe?" Katrina yelled angrily as she tightened her grip on the pistol.

Kim nodded her head to say yes and with tears in her eyes, she looked directly at Katrina and whispered through her busted lips that she was sorry for what happened to Jermaine. "I didn't mean for him to die," she whispered through her swollen and busted lips.

Katrina looked Kimberly square in the eyes, bit her bottom lip, and fired four rounds into Kim's skull and ended her life. The boys then stripped off Kim's clothes and threw her badly bruised and bullet-stricken body into the murky waters of the bayou. As Katrina backed away from the bayou, alligators were seen entering the murky waters on the opposite bank; their eyes reflecting a devilish red hue in the car's headlights as they swam towards Kim's lifeless corpse. The three then headed to the airport where they burned Kim's clothes, cleaned Anna's car and headed back to *Par 6* to rejoin the rest of the crew. It had been a bloody, violent-filled night indeed; but for the crew, it was time well spent.

CHAPTER THIRTY-ONE

TIME FOR CHANGE

It was five days after the murders of Jermaine and Tanaka. The crew had helped in the planning and paying of their friends' funerals and they were on their way to attend the services. Both Jermaine and Tanaka were being buried at Gertrude Gettys Funeral Home on North Claiborne Avenue, not too far from the very park where Jermaine had first met Kimberly Pollard. It was June 21, 1999, the first day of summer, and there were at least three-hundred people on hand to pay respects this day, mostly from the Ninth Ward.

Other hustlers and players, including major players from the Third, Seventh, and Seventeenth Wards, came out to show love to Jermaine and the rest of the crew. Damenga and Alphonso had even ridden into town to show love on this day.

It was a festive sight indeed, as gangsters throughout various neighborhoods and wards of the city turned out in rare form to bring the underworld to light. The people who were on the scene were behind much of the violence that permeated the streets of New Orleans during the year of '99. To outsiders, Jermaine and Tanaka were just two teenagers who died on the streets. For people who knew the truth, however, there was a reason for the two homicides. If you explained everything to

the police, they might have understood why the twins and the Rastafarian were found shot up in their homes. They would understand why a young man nick-named Hottie was killed in the Seventeenth Ward, and why a young lady by the name of Kimberly Pollard was reported missing by her family. The police, however, would never make those connections. In their eyes, the six homicides and the missing person's case were more of the senseless violence and bravado that consumed the inner city's youth.

As Dirty Red, Oscar, Jason, Lamont, Derrick, Lil Earl and Torre` stood in front of the funeral home, they accepted handshakes and condolences from various thugs. When Damenga and Alphonso exited their stretch hummer and walked up to the crew and shook Dirty Red's hand, other game players knew for certain that the crew was at the top of the cocaine drug trade in the city.

"I feel your pain, amigo," Damenga said. "But I hope your friends' deaths won't interfere in our arrangements."

"Not at all." Dirty Red replied.

"Good. Because I brought eighty more kilograms with me. We can make an exchange at your hangar after the services. It's been a while since I've attended one of these God-forsaken events." Damenga stated as he stretched and pulled out a Havana Cigar.

"You lost a friend to the game?" Dirty Red asked.

Damenga nodded as he lit his cigar and took a series of quick puffs. "I've lost many friends to this shit business. Each time they were buried, it was always a beautiful day. Just like this morning. It is the first day of summer. There's a clear blue sky. It is beautiful out. All of these people make you feel as if you're at a huge picnic with friends all around. Instead, we all gather to say good bye to people who have lost their lives," he said as he offered Dirty Red a cigar.

Dirty Red declined and said, "You know, I always knew that somewhere down the road, something real fucked up would

happen. I wish you could've met Manny, brer. He was one of the realest to play the game. He, too, just like Jermaine, fell behind a woman. I always thought when the grim reaper came for me or somebody out my crew, it would be in a hail of bullets. Some Armageddon type shit, you know? Instead, my people died in silence and I couldn't even protect them."

"Don't blame yourself, hermano. It's not your fault. Women have been man's downfall from the beginning of time. Look at Adam and Eve, Samson and Delilah." Damenga remarked as Dirty Red chuckled to himself.

"What's funny, hermano?" Damenga then asked.

"I said almost exactly the same thing not too long ago when me and Oscar talked about how Manny died."

"Well, I guess great minds think alike, amigo. Manny, huh?" Damenga then asked through light laughter. "Look, Ben," he then stated seriously, "I have a few things to look into while I'm down here. Alphonso will meet you at the hangar later and do the drop. My condolences, amigo. Talk to you later."

As Damenga and several of his soldiers headed back towards his double-parked Hummer, many people attending the services began filing into the funeral home to pay their final respects to Jermaine and Tanaka. The two lay side by side in pearl white coffins trimmed in fourteen karat gold. People walked by the two coffins, shaking their heads in disgust and disbelief. When Alicia walked in front of Tanaka's coffin, she cried openly for her deceased, lifelong friend.

"Why you?" Alicia asked silently as tears streamed down her face.

Alicia had worn her hair half pressed and half braided, the same way Tanaka had left it the night she was killed. She could still feel Tanaka's fingertips coursing through her skull and it made her cry even harder because she knew that night, would be the last living memory she would ever have of her friend before she was taken away. She placed a bouquet of flowers inside of Tanaka and Jermaine's caskets and said a

prayer before taking her seat on the second row next to Katrina and Dana who were themselves overcome with sadness. Dirty Red, Lamont, Oscar, and Jason went in after the service and sat alone with their dead friends for about thirty minutes. They joked about the silly things Tanaka used to do and say. And they said good bye to a fallen soldier whose only flaw, was loving the wrong woman.

As the group rode to the burial site, Dirty Red, Jason, Oscar, Lamont, and Katrina sat quietly in the limousine listening to Ms. Joyce preach to them about their lives. The forty-two year-old, dark-skinned, thick-thighed woman sat with her legs crossed as she spoke with tears in her eyes. "I remember when y'all was just kids running around in the courtyard on Benefit, playing football and cheerleading," she said through tears of anger. "Now ten years later, it's like y'all just racing each other ta' see who can get ta' heaven first! Or maybe hell! Because the life y'all leading ain't that of angels!"

Ms. Joyce was trying to put something in the crew's minds. She talked about how depressed she had gotten after Manny's death and how she contemplated suicide because she couldn't bear the pain of losing her only son.

"Ben, I talked to you a long time ago about this shit! But it just went in one ear and came right out the other!" Ms. Joyce snapped.

"I heard you, Ms. Joyce." Dirty Red replied in a low tone.

"No, ya' didn't! Ain't shit change, Ben! It's been three months since Manny died. Three months! And you only managed to dig a deeper hole for ya' self and the ones that's with you! And Katrina you lucky to even be alive after all the shit you done been through! I tell ya', y'all becoming worse than the children of the corn! And y'all young black males and females are bringing a lot of grief and shame to your parents and the entire African-American community. But y'all don't see it," Ms. Joyce said, as she rocked to and fro and wept louder. "Y'all young children today—y'all just don't see it!" The woman cried. "Jermaine and Tanaka was good kids at the out-set—but they got caught up in the street life and the streets killed 'em. If

y'all not careful, I'm a be goin' to *all of y'all's* funeral someday! Think about that fact!"

Ms. Joyce preached the whole trip to the cemetery and the crew felt somewhat remorseful as they stepped out of the limousine. Ms. Joyce had brought reality home to the crew. She knew what they were doing and she urged them to change their ways. Five days ago, they had done some terrible things to the people who were involved in their friends' deaths, but they all felt justified for what they had done at the time; still, the fact remained that Jermaine and Tanaka were dead at the young age of eighteen. At a point and time in their life when they were supposed to be preparing themselves for adulthood, Jermaine Duplessis and Tanaka Romaire were cut down by the corruption and deceit that ran profusely through the drug game like an unchecked running faucet.

What happened to the crew would play out on the streets of New Orleans, Atlanta, Houston, Memphis, Miami, and every other city throughout the south and all over the U.S. and the entire globe. No one on Earth can stop it. Who can tell someone who once had nothing, that life in the streets is not the way when it was the streets that had given that person wealth beyond measure, and respect and admiration from the same people who once ridiculed and belittled that person? When faced with the hard fact that "if I don't do somethin'— I'm a die out here on these streets," what is a person to do? When all one has is the streets and the people from the 'hood backing everyone up like they were family, because one's own blood betrayed him or her, a person is naturally compelled to turn towards those who show love.

With help from Manny and Oscar, Ben Holland became one of the best at what he did. Maybe in some utopian society, Ben Holland could've been an ace mechanic, a restauranteur, or a legitimate businessman, but those dreams aren't always recognized in the Ninth Ward; or any other ghetto for that matter. For Ben Holland and the rest of the boys, the cocaine came before the scholarships, and the bottom line was that, for them, it was too late. They couldn't turn back. The boys had a good thing going with Damenga and the hard truth was that, no

matter what Ms. Joyce had said this day inside the limousine, they weren't going to change their ways no time soon.

As for Katrina, she took what Ms. Joyce said to heart. After Tanaka and Jermaine's funeral, she, Dana and Alicia stayed away from the dope house. The two females focused on preparing themselves for college and Alicia was now looking for a job. In the weeks following Jermaine and Tanaka's sudden departure, Katrina had taken a couple of trips to Tempe, Arizona to visit Arizona State University.

Eighteen year-old Katrina Sanders was leaving her past behind. She was now changing her life for the better. She gave up on Jason completely and began dating a sophomore basketball player she had met on one of her tours at Arizona State named Timothy McMillan. Katrina would write Tim daily while relaxing at *Par 6*, patiently waiting until her classes started in late September when she would be with Tim full time.

The boys, meanwhile, continued to rise to the top of the game. Despite the loss of Jermaine and Hottie, the crew was still feared throughout the city. They were inside of a year now, and the time was passing just as quickly as the money and cocaine exchanged hands.

CHAPTER THIRTY-TWO

WHEN REAL ONES TURN FAKE

Dirty Red and the crew were at Kantrell's Beauty Salon getting haircuts and just kicking back for the day in early September of '99. Twenty-six year-old Kantrell Luckett was cool with the boys. Whenever they came through, the boys always ordered lunch—seafood, boxes of Popeye's chicken, pizza or whatever, for Kantrell and her customers. In turn, the boys would get free haircuts, manicures and neck massages. On top of that, they would always get up on some females that they could get with later that night over to the three-bedroom suite they had purchased, which was right beside the Super Dome inside the Hyatt Hotel. The boys had bought the place a couple of weeks after Jermaine's death.

Dirty Red was sitting in the lounge watching the L.S.U. Football game while eating a Shrimp Po-boy when his cell phone rang. "Hello?"

"Where you at, fool?" It was Sherman, Manny's cousin from Memphis.

"I'm in the N.O.!"

"That's what I'm sayin'! Where you at? I'm in the city myself!

335

I came down ta' chill for few days!"

"I'm in the Ninth Ward. Jump on Saint Claude and head across the canal and ya' gone see our cars out front the shop right past Flood street." Dirty Red replied with a hint of suspicion.

Sherman made his way over to the beauty salon and parked his '99 Grand Cherokee in the parking lot and walked into the salon and greeted Dirty Red, Jason, Lamont and Oscar before he grabbed a seat beside Dirty Red in the lounge. Dirty Red offered Sherman a Po-Boy and he reached over into a basket containing numerous shrimp sandwiches along with ham, roast beef, and hot sausage and grabbed a roast beef sandwich.

Things were going well for the boys now. The violence in the city had seemed to subside for a while and the crew hadn't killed anyone since their rampage the night they killed the twins and Kim. The boys were mainly concentrating on moving the now fifty kilos a week that Damenga was shipping to them from Houston, and hooking up with women they met inside the salon on weekends. They were doing well and staying under the radar. Dirty Red had also increased his monthly payments to Swanson and Montgomery and the detectives kept the crew abreast of any potential dangers, and that coveted information was now keeping the crew trouble free and out of jail.

As the two sat eating, Sherman soon began talking openly to Dirty Red about the job the crew did in Memphis six months ago in front of Kantrell. Dirty Red quickly pulled him to the side and told him not to say nothing about Memphis or any other job the crew had ever done.

"Man, I'm just saying man, y'all niggas handled y'all business that night, brer!" Sherman stated lowly as he and Dirty Red stood in the back of the salon's lounge.

"Why the fuck you talkin' bout that shit?" Dirty Red asked in a near whisper.

"You right, dog. I ain't gone bring that up no mo'. They got a

war goin' on up in Memphis on the north side, though."

"What the fuck that gotta do with us?" Dirty Red asked as he and Sherman exited the salon and stood outside beside Sherman's jeep.

"I think some niggas out ta' get me, dog. I just need a place ta' chill for a few days ta' get my head right." Sherman replied as he lit up a blunt.

"Say, brer, we just come out some shit not too long ago. We lost Jermaine and another one of our soldiers, a young nigga name Hottie. Not ta' mention a li'l chick we been knowing since back in the day named Tanaka. Me and my people don't need ta' be jumpin' into no shit that's gone heat up these streets again. It's been quiet down here for a good while and I plan on keepin' it that way for as long as possible. I can set ya' up at a hotel out in Kenner, but ya' gotta lay low until ya' ready ta' ride back up to Tennessee, ya' dig?"

Sherman said he understood what Dirty Red had told him; but after four days had gone by, he found his way over to the boys' dope house in the Ninth Ward. When Dirty Red saw Sherman's jeep pull onto the block, he immediately stepped out onto the porch and walked quickly to the street and stopped Sherman from entering the front yard.

"What the fuck you doin' 'round this mutherfucka, brer?" Dirty Red asked as he got up in Sherman's face.

"I just came ta' chill for a minute, brer! Y'all got dope? Put a nigga ta' work while I'm down here, shit! What you, what you workin' with, cousin?"

Dirty Red was already suspicious as to why Sherman had come to New Orleans unannounced from day one. His instincts were telling him that something wasn't right with the dude. Sherman had come down and tried to get Dirty Red to talk about the Memphis job over to Kantrell's salon. Now he was around in the 'hood asking him about dope. It was as if Sherman was trying to get him to talk about the illegal things he was involved in and the crimes that he had committed;

crimes in which Sherman knew about. Dirty Red ripped off Sherman's tee shirt and saw that he was wearing a wire. His suspicions were right.

"You, you F-E-D nigga? You workin' for the mutherfuckin' feds?" Dirty Red asked in disbelief as he stood in the middle of the street staring at the wire tap Sherman was wearing.

Jason, who'd watched the entire scenario unfold, along with Torre' and Derrick, rushed to Dirty Red's side. The boys immediately began to pounce on Sherman and the four of them beat him savagely until he lay on the ground begging them to stop. As they continued stomping Sherman, Dirty Red told everybody on the block to leave.

"Just get the fuck! Everybody just get the fuck!" Dirty Red yelled as he kicked Sherman in the face.

People began to run off in different directions and peel out in their cars. Dirty Red told his boys to grab the cocaine, the guns and the money before they all scattered to their own rides. They all knew they couldn't kill Sherman because they feared police knew that Dirty Red had found the wire.

In less than three minutes, the entire block was empty. The crew had left Sherman swollen and bruised in the middle of the street and headed over to JoAnne's house where they dropped off fourteen kilograms and one hundred and eight thousand dollars that was neatly rubber-banded into thousand dollar stacks. Dirty Red then called Swanson and Montgomery and they met the boys at their airport hangar a couple of hours later, just as the sun began to set. The men all discussed the amount of damage Sherman had done to the crew.

"This is fuckin' bad, boys, let me tell ya'." Swanson said in between puffs of his cigarette as he shook his head from side to side in disbelief.

"We know that," responded Oscar. "How we gone go about fixin' this shit?"

"We can't." Swanson replied.

"What the fuck you mean 'we can't'!" Jason asked angrily.

"What fuckin' part y'all gangsters don't understand," Montgomery then said in frustration. "We talkin' about the FBI! Ya' man crossed state lines with a wire! You know just as well as I do that when the feds get involved, it ain't no tellin' how far-reaching this shit can be! We not talkin' about ya' local task force anymore! This is bigger than us!"

"If he came from outta' town with a wire, then it has to be over something that happened in another state that he knows about. Y'all ever done business with him?" Swanson asked.

Dirty Red didn't know who to trust. He wasn't about to speak on no crime he committed to no one. He answered Swan's question with a quick nod to say yes.

The two detectives looked at one another and simultaneously shook their heads from side to side. "It's best you all get lawyers." Montgomery stated as he rubbed his eyebrows. "We're umm, we're gonna look into this shit. But don't contact us, we'll contact you," he ended as he and Swan walked out of the hangar.

Sherman had brought the crew's entire operation to a grinding halt. The possible charges could be severe: murder, transporting drugs and guns across state lines, bribery, and who knows what else Sherman would bring to the table.

As the crew sat in the office of *Par 6*, later on in the night, anticipating a phone call from the detectives confirming the indictments, Dirty Red got a call from Damenga. He told Dirty Red that his money was being held up in the bank, so it would be about three weeks before he could make another payment. That was coded talk to let Dirty Red know that Damenga's cocaine was held up in Valle Hermoso, a small Mexican town about thirty miles south of Brownsville, Texas; he wouldn't be able to make a drop for three weeks.

Dirty Red was relieved to hear the news from Damenga. It was good news for the crew. They could lay low and wait until Swanson and Montgomery could use their resources to find out

exactly how much damage Sherman had done.

Several hours later, just before dawn, Sherman was back in Memphis, Tennessee. He was being held in the downtown precinct having just finished talking to FBI agents and vice-squad cops working the case against Dirty Red and the boys. The agents held Sherman in custody for over five hours after his debriefing. Sherman thought it to be unusual, as the agents had never held him in custody for this extended period of time. He watched as the cops made phone calls and wrote down notes, all the while acting as if they didn't even know him.

"Sweetwater," Sherman called out aloud to one of the vice-squad agents.

The agent looked over to Sherman for a few seconds before turning his attention back to his paperwork.

"That's how you gone play me, Gilbert? You know I done came through. The least you can do is give me a call, Sweetwater. Let a nigga make a call."

The agent Sherman was talking to got up and unlocked his cell and walked Sherman down the hall towards a small room that had a phone sitting atop a small wooden table.

"You got five minutes."

"Good looking out, Sweetwater." Sherman said as he walked briskly towards the phone.

"I know you trying to be funny by calling me Sweetwater, but we'll see who has the last laugh." The agent said before he walked out of the threshold.

"Okay," Sherman responded. "I see how y'all do around here." He ended as he picked up the receiver.

Sherman called his girlfriend, Shelia, back over to his apartment. When she picked up, Sherman told her to pack her bags immediately. As she packed her bags, Sherman had Shelia call her sister Verna on three-way. He instructed Verna to mail an old newspaper article that he kept hidden at her house to Kantrell's Beauty Salon back in New Orleans as

Kantrell's salon was the only address he remembered back in the city.

"Do that before you pick up Shelia and my daughter." Sherman requested of Verna.

"Okay. Where y'all going?" Verna asked.

"To the airport." Sherman replied.

"Y'all crazy. I wouldn't never fly in no plane. Okay. I'm on my way." Verna replied as she hung up the phone and began searching for the newspaper article.

The cops released Sherman three hours later and he hurried home to retrieve about fifty-five thousand dollars he had hidden in his closet. He was planning on meeting Shelia and his baby girl, along with Verna, at the airport and purchase tickets for the next available flight no matter where it was going; but it had to be a flight within the U.S. Sherman's intended destination was the Jamaican Islands; but he knew he wasn't going to be able to catch a direct flight there. He knew, however, that he could catch a last minute flight on a plane that had open seats. Once he landed in another city, he would promptly work his way down to Jamaica and settle in and wait it out until things blew over with Dirty Red and the feds.

Sherman was putting the final touches on his plan as he rode home in his jeep. He would open a bank account and deposit nine thousand dollars for starters. He would keep eight grand on him and have Verna wire the rest of the money to Jamaica once he touched down. *"I know Verna gone wanna get paid for doing all this for me, but it's cool, sister-in-law birthday gone hit while I'm down in there anyway."* Sherman thought to himself as he turned into his apartment complex.

Sherman was surprised when he reached his apartment and saw Verna's car still sitting in the parking lot. He sucked his teeth as he exited his vehicle and walked quickly towards the building and unlocked the door, entered the apartment and called out for Shelia. When she didn't answer, he called out for Verna. He still hadn't received a reply as he walked past the

kitchen towards the bedroom to retrieve his money.

When Sherman got to his bedroom, he was greeted with a . 9mm semi-automatic handgun that was aimed directly at his forehead. Three men were in the room. The man with the gun on Sherman motioned him to the bed. The other two grabbed duct tape and rope as they guided Sherman towards an empty chair that was positioned beside Shelia and Verna. The two females were gagged and tied to the chairs, crying and trembling in fear. Sherman's four year-old daughter was sitting on her knees before her family in a corner facing the wall. She was crying uncontrollably and calling for her mother, and now her father.

The men tied Sherman to the chair and began to place silencers onto the barrels of their pistols as they stood in front of him, Shelia and Verna.

"I ain't know about that shit, brer. That wasn't on me!" Sherman told the men.

"That still don't make it right," the man in the middle remarked.

"Well, let my people go, man. They ain't have shit ta' do with this!" Sherman pleaded.

"You knew early on and you didn't tell me. You didn't tell because you were involved," the man standing in the middle replied as he leaned against the dresser and screwed the silencer onto the barrel of his gun.

"I swear I ain't set that shit up! I ain't have nothing to do with that! Man, my daughter! I got a family, man!"

"So do I. And I love them just as much as you loved yours," the man in the middle replied as he and his two henchmen opened fire on Shelia and Verna, killing them both in an instant.

Sherman cried as he stared at the corpses of his dead girlfriend and her sister. He begged for mercy as one of the soldiers went and stood over his four year-old little girl, who

began to cry as she turned and faced the killers of her mother and aunt while calling out to her father. "Daddy, don't let them kill me like they did momma and Auntie Verna!" The little girl screamed.

"Come on, man! She, she only four, man! Don't kill my baby, please!" Sherman pleaded.

The man leaning against the dresser took a puff of his cigar and walked over and looked Sherman in the eyes as he aimed the .9mm at the top of his daughter's skull. The little girl covered her head and screamed aloud just as the man fired two muffled gunshots. The little girl fell back into the corner and died instantly, her tiny body now drenched in her own blood. Sherman was begging to be killed after what he had just witnessed. His daughter had just been blown away in front of his eyes, and his child's mother had been killed along with her sister. He could bear no more. One of the soldiers placed the gun to Sherman's left eye and fired one shot. The man then shot Sherman in the other eye, and all three men walked out of the room.

"Why you kill the baby, boss," one of the soldiers asked.

"She wouldn't have amounted to shit without her parents. I did the poor bastard a favor." The man replied matter-of-factly as the three men walked out the front door.

CHAPTER THIRTY-THREE

CONSEQUENCES AND REPERCUSSIONS

It was two days after Sherman's murder. His and his family's remains were found late in the evening by Sherman's mother and uncle, but no one in Memphis had bothered to contact the crew down in New Orleans. Damenga had called Dirty Red from Houston and informed him of another delay. He had flown to Denver the week before and had received bad news regarding his sister Carmella. He didn't know the exact date in which he would resume shipping product. Dirty Red was now on standby so he decided to take the opportunity and the extra time afforded him to take the crew on a trip to Arizona with Katrina to visit the city of Phoenix. From there, the crew was going to head to Las Vegas and kick back at *Caesar's Palace Casino and Resort.*

Lamont, upon hearing the news of the trip, had decided to purchase an expensive ring for Alicia, whose 19th birthday would arrive during the time the crew was on their trip to Arizona. He was planning to give it to her in Phoenix on the day of her birthday. Problem was, Lamont wasn't sure about what type of ring to purchase, so he asked Katrina, who was a connoisseur of jewelry, to help him pick out a special ring for his beau.

The two met in front of the Canal Place Shopping Mall in downtown New Orleans on Canal Street on this hot and steamy late summer day. As Katrina stepped from her Mustang parked in front of the mall, she slid down her Gucci sun shades and looked around for Lamont, who hadn't made it yet. He arrived a few minutes later and parked his car behind Katrina's and stepped out of his Chevy. The two entered the mall and rode the elevator up to the third floor and headed towards the jewelry store. The pristine mall was quiet this day as it was a weekday in the early afternoon hours.

Katrina and Lamont walked into the upscale jewelry store and were greeted by a mid-forties, petite white woman with frost white hair. "Can I help you two with something?" She asked politely.

"Yea, we wanna see some nice rings y'all got up in here." Lamont answered.

Lamont and Katrina were standing in front of a display case that held rings in the price range of $999 to $2500 dollars. The lady chuckled and cleared her throat and suggested that Lamont and Katrina look at another set of rings. The two kindly followed the lady as they made small talk about how fancy the store looked. When the lady stopped, she was in front of a display case that held rings ranging from $89 to $199 dollars. She then hurriedly walked off just as an older white couple walked into the jewelry store. The sales lady immediately guided the white couple over to the display case that Lamont and Katrina had been inspecting. The two looked at one another in shock as they couldn't believe what had just transpired.

Lamont looked at Katrina with his jaw agape.

Katrina, on the other hand, was smiling from ear to ear because she knew Lamont was about to explode.

"She, she tryna play a nigga?" Lamont whispered to Katrina.

Katrina began shaking her head up and down in rapid motion, egging Lamont on. "No doubt! No doubt, L-dog! She tryna say

you a po' somebody!"

"She must don't know who the fuck I am!"

"She *can't* know who in the fuck you are! You know what? You should just go over there and tell her just who in the fuck you are!" Katrina responded, barely able to keep from laughing.

Lamont began walking towards the sales lady, and as he did so, he reached into his front pockets. His actions caused the woman to begin panicking.

"How you gone send me over there to them cheap ass rings and let these mutherfuckas stand were I was? You think I can't buy them rings in that window or somethin'?" Lamont asked angrily.

"I don't want any trouble, mister. Please don't hurt us!" The sales lady replied as she raised her hands into the air as if she were getting robbed.

Lamont removed his hands from his pockets and looked around briefly before he stared angrily at the woman. "Put, put ya' fuckin' hands down! This ain't a damn robbery! I came ta' *buy* a fuckin' ring! But yo' stankin' ass gone imply that I can't afford shit in here," he stated as he shook his head in disgust and disbelief.

"In *this* day and age!" Katrina chimed as she tapped Lamont on the shoulder. "In *this* day and age, they still got people who act like that towards the *black* man!"

"It's gone be pandemonium and severe ruckus if I don't get some justice up in this mutherfucka!" Lamont stated as he looked around the store in search of another salesperson to come to his aide.

"We want justice! Equal rights! Shit like that!" Katrina spoke in a loud tone as she giggled to herself.

Just then, a tall, slender black woman emerged from a backroom and asked in a pleasant voice and pretty smile if she could help Lamont and Katrina.

Lamont calmed down and told the lady he wanted to look at some nice rings.

"You have a price range in mind, sir?" The lady asked nicely with a smile.

"Yea, whatever this can buy!" Lamont replied as he put his hands back into his front pockets and brought out two stacks of hundred dollar bills, each about four inches thick.

He tossed both stacks of money towards the slender black woman and she caught them both and widened her eyes. She then put on a pair of eyeglasses and began to walk the two towards the showroom in the rear of the store. As Lamont and Katrina walked off with the lady, they both eyed the white sales lady and the white couple seriously and just shook their heads.

"Excuse us," Katrina then said lowly as she tip-toed past the white couple, "y'all two have fun with the bigot. Us colored folk goin' look at the good shit in the back!" She ended as she snickered.

Lamont and Katrina sat and chatted in friendly low tones with the sales lady as they looked at different rings and necklaces that she presented to them. The lady had also brought the two a glass of alcohol-free champagne and had given them a plate containing crackers and cheese as she showed them the various ring styles and different types of gems the store offered as they sat before a small vanity.

Lamont and Katrina eyed some beautiful pearls, rubies, diamonds, and the like until they came across a two karat diamond and sapphire princess cut ring worth about six-thousand dollars. Lamont paid the lady in cash and gave her a six hundred dollar tip for the pleasant and unbiased service.

As the two walked out of the store, they walked pass the white sales lady and her two customers who were now standing in front of the same display case that she had guided Lamont and Katrina to the first time. The two burst into laughter as they headed out of the store. "Wonder what your

commission gone be offa that." Lamont said just before he left the store.

When the two exited the mall, they stood and talked for a few minutes. Katrina had offered to buy Lamont a daiquiri from the daiquiri shop in the Ninth Ward stating that she was headed over that way to meet JoAnne and Anna, but Lamont declined, telling Katrina he was headed back to *Par 6* to hide the gift that he had just bought for Alicia.

"Alright then, homeboy! Hit me up when you get out to Par Six." Katrina said as she let the top down on her Mustang and pulled off and made a right turn onto North Peters Street in order to take the scenic route through the the French Quarters on her way to the daiquiri shop.

Lamont said he would as he, too, let the top down on his Chevy and pulled off, but not before taking one last look at the huge ring he had gotten for Alicia. *"Alicia gone love this here, no doubt!"* Lamont thought to himself as he stuffed the ring into his jeans pocket.

Lamont proudly cruised down Canal Street in his convertible bumping The Big Tymers' song, *How You Luv That* from his stereo system and enjoying the hot summer sun. He approached Canal and Bourbon Streets and blew his horn at a couple of females he knew that were standing out in front of Foot Locker on the corner of the intersection on his right. He continued cruising down Canal admiring the scenery, the street cars riding down the center of the median, people out looking good and just chilling, shopping, and spending time with their friends and family. It was a nice day out. Lamont saw nice-looking young lady walking beside a young man around his own age while pushing a baby in a stroller as he turned onto Basin Street and headed towards the intersection of Orleans and Claiborne Avenues.

The couple looked happy. Lamont pictured him and Alicia doing the same thing someday as he reached the intersection of Orleans and Claiborne Avenues and spoke to a few more people he knew who were hanging in front of the liquor store that sat on the corner, again to his right.

As Lamont waited patiently at the intersection just below the elevated section of Interstate-10, bobbing his head to the music, and really thinking hard about marrying Alicia and starting a family, a black Navigator pulled up alongside him on the left. The back passenger window was let down and the barrel of an automatic twelve gauge was pointed in Lamont's direction. Lamont saw the play about to go down, and with a sense of urgency, he reached for his Glock .45, which was tucked under his seat. When he bent down to grab his weapon, however, he was blasted in the back and in the left side by buckshot.

Lamont scrambled towards the passenger side door in a panic-stricken state of mind, leaving a trail of blood on the front seat in the process. He knew he had no time to reach his gun, so he was now attempting to open the passenger side door in order to flee. As he fumbled with the door handle inside the car, the gunman in the Navigator quickly jumped out of the back passenger seat and shot him two more times in the back and once more at nearly point blank range, completely blowing off the back of Lamont's skull. The pristine Chevy slowly rolled forward and crashed into a traffic signal as Lamont's killers hurriedly sped off, leaving a crowd of onlookers who were in front of the liquor store, and several people who were standing at the bus stop in a state of shock. They had just witnessed one of the most well-liked members of the Ben Holland Gang get gunned down in broad daylight.

Lamont's death came as a shock to everybody and word spread quickly. The crew had rushed to the scene only to see Lamont's body draped across the front seat of the car and covered with a blood-stained sheet; the passenger side door was still open as well. The entire intersection had been shut down and traffic was being rerouted. Katrina was numb. She was just kicking it with Lamont not even an hour ago and now he was dead. It all happened too fast for her. She desperately wished that she was dreaming and she would wake up at *Par 6* and see Lamont sitting in the living room watching TV. But it was all-too-real for Katrina and the entire crew. The gang had suffered another devastating loss, but unlike Jermaine's death, Lamont's killers were unknown.

The trip to Arizona was becoming more and more appealing to Dirty Red. He went and handed the blood-covered jewelry box to Alicia after he retrieved it from one of the coroner office's personnel who'd seen the ring protruding from the jeans pocket of Lamont's bloodied corpse as he lay across the front seat in a twisted, bloody mass. Dirty Red tipped the woman a thousand dollars because he knew many coroners would have simply kept the ring.

Alicia wailed openly as she placed the last item she would ever receive from her dead lover onto her middle left finger. She felt in her heart that Lamont was going to ask her to marry her when she saw the ring. And she would have said yes—yes indeed. Alicia loved Lamont; she really wanted to be his wife and have his child, or children. She had come close, but her dream had been taken away on this very day.

Dirty Red was even more convinced that the crew should take some time off until Damenga could get his shipments back on-line. The boys had plenty of money to spend and he was now under the belief that the crew's inactivity was one of the reasons why they were being knocked off. Without their cocaine on the streets, the city was going through a major drought. Dope was hard to come by, and because of that fact, the streets were getting restless and violent once more.

Whenever they had cocaine, the crew always stayed low key and focused, and violence was kept to a minimum; but with no cocaine on the streets, or very little, Dirty Red believed that his crew was becoming the targets of bottom feeders because of their wealth and power. And with so much free time on their hands, the boys were beginning to become more open with their money, spending freely. Dirty Red didn't think New Orleans was the place for the crew to parlay because the streets of New Orleans were full of armed jackers and jealous type of players. The time spent in Arizona could be used for the crew to regain their focus, and return to their real business: slanging cocaine.

Dirty Red told his boys that another war was about to get underway; but immediately following Lamont's funeral, they

would leave for Arizona. And when he and the rest of the crew returned, they would deal with Lamont's killers and anyone else who was a threat to the crew's survival.

CHAPTER THIRTY-FOUR

ARMAGEDDON

The funeral services for Lamont was over; the crew was now outside of the small red-brick Baptist church in the Ninth Ward on a warm, sunny, autumn Monday morning. Dirty Red had suggested that the funeral be a small, private affair, but Lamont's family had ignored the suggestion and invited any and everyone who knew Lamont to come out and commemorate their loved one's life. Word spread quickly where the gangster's funeral was being held and scores of people showed up that morning to pay homage to another fallen comrade from the Ninth Ward. They all spoke kind words to the crew, telling them that the streets still respected them despite losing Lamont and Jermaine in a relatively short span of time.

While Dirty Red was standing on the stairs of the small church watching the crowd, his cell phone rang. At the same time, Kantrell, the young lady who owns the salon where the crew frequently got haircuts, was running up the sidewalk waving an envelope screaming his name. Dirty Red answered the phone to hear Swanson's voice. "Ben!" Swanson yelled over the phone just as Kantrell approached him.

"Dirty Red, I got this envelope and—" Kantrell was silenced

353

by Dirty Red as he began to converse with Swanson, so she placed the envelope in Dirty Red's hand and announced that she wanted to go in and pay her respects to Lamont.

Dirty Red listened vaguely to Swanson as he opened the envelope and found an old newspaper article from Memphis titled, "*3 Killed, 1 Injured in Home Invasion*". The date on the paper was March 11; two days after the crew had done the job in Memphis.

"I thought it was four." Dirty Red whispered to Oscar.

"What happened?" Oscar, who was standing beside him, asked calmly.

"Ben! You listening to me?"

"What ya' got? What's up?" Ben replied, ignoring Oscar's inquiry.

"Ya' man Sherman and his daughter, girlfriend and sister-in-law was killed last week."

"By who?"

"Don't know. But we found out about the wire."

"What's up with the feds? How much they know?"

"Sherman didn't wear a wire for the feds," Swanson said as he paused to take a drag off of his cigarette, "he wore a wire for Damenga. The feds in Memphis are on the Columbian's payroll. Do you even know how connected this man is? Whatever happened in Memphis is causing a lot of trouble for you and your people. I suggest you stay away from Damenga, my friend. That guy's dangerous."

The whole time he talked to Swanson, Dirty Red had never taken his eyes off the article. He was looking for names. He was slowly beginning to put the pieces together about what was transpiring with his crew. He flipped the pages quickly, not seeing the three light-skinned men in black trench coats and grey silk suits approaching the front of the church where the entire crew stood openly chatting with people from the

neighborhood who had attended the funeral services. The three men walked slowly and quietly through the crowd, never taking their sunshade-covered eyes off the front of the church.

The crew was in a somewhat festive mood this morning; they had mourned for Lamont for almost a week and now the trip to Arizona was in high anticipation. They couldn't wait to leave. Immediately after Lamont was buried, the crew would have dinner with his family, enjoy a second-line through the Desire Project, and hop into their cars and caravan towards the southwest. They had all agreed to drive, as it would give them time to reflect on the past and all the events that had gotten them to this particular juncture of their young lives. They were going to spend a night in San Antonio, Texas and have dinner. They would do the same in El Paso, Texas and Tucson, Arizona before they made it to Phoenix. The trip would be relaxing, slow-paced, and would be a nice change of scenery.

Katrina looked forward to going to college in Tempe, just outside of Phoenix; and as she stood at the bottom of the stairs talking to Dana, Jason and Alicia, she expressed her excitement.

"You got all ya' shit packed, girl?" Jason asked with a smile on his face.

"You know it! My mustang right across the street. I got the money that Dirty Red gave me set up in several different banks out there, and a fine ass nigga that's waiting for me too! I'm glad y'all comin' out for a while. Y'all can help me furnish my apartment."

"I know, girl," Alicia smiled. "I wish Tanaka was still alive so she could join us."

"Ummhmm," Dana sighed in a joking manner, "she probably looking down from heaven wishin' she could trade in her wings to come with us. Especially when we get ta' Vegas. You know whatever happens in Vegas stays in Vegas. And I plan on gettin' loose before I start my classes next month."

"How loose?" Jason asked.

"You'll find out soon enough, lover boy." Dana answered as she wrapped her arms around Jason and the two stood in a warm embrace under the warm autumn sun.

"Hey! Y'all ready ta' bring my homeboy out and send 'em off right?" Jason yelled towards Dirty Red and Oscar, who were both now standing at the top of the church stairs with Anna and JoAnne.

"Come on man, let's go get our dog and send 'em home." Oscar said to Dirty Red.

Dirty Red, however, was entrenched in the article that Kantrell had handed to him. He knew there were supposed to be four dead people inside the house in Memphis. When he got to the name of the survivor, he yelled out for his crew just as gunfire erupted from the three men who had walked up the sidewalk towards the front of the church.

Dirty Red looked up to see Katrina get blasted in the stomach with twelve gauge buckshot. The gun blast knocked her backwards. She landed against the concrete wall that lined the stairs of the church and screamed aloud before she fell to the ground on her left side and began coughing up blood.

Bystanders began running for cover as Jason, who was about thirty feet away from the gunmen, began blasting with his .45. Dana and Alicia, who were standing behind Jason, dropped to the ground and began screaming uncontrollably as they covered their ears. Jason hit one of the soldiers, killing him, as Dirty Red and Oscar began shooting at the remaining two gunmen. Lil Earl, Torre`, and Sean opened fire on the soldiers as well. The bullets coming from Dirty Red, Oscar, Jason, and the other soldiers' guns cut the remaining two soldiers down in front of the church.

People were still trying to figure out what was going on when a black Jaguar, loaded with three more assassins, pulled up and began shooting automatic twelve gauges at the front of the church while the boys were reloading their guns. Lil Earl, Torre`, Sean and Jason had to take cover to reload. And that left Dirty Red and Oscar exposed at the top of the stairs.

Dirty Red grabbed Anna and hid behind a concrete wall as Oscar continued to exchange gunfire with the gunmen as their car remained parked in front of the church. JoAnne, meanwhile, had run back into the church.

Dirty Red had tried to get Anna to run with JoAnne, but she was struck with fear. "Anna you need to go in the church. You need to get inside while we hold these dudes off." Dirty Red said as adrenaline rushed through his veins.

"I'm scared!" Anna yelled.

"Just don't look back. You can make it just like JoAnne just did. Run, baby." Dirty Red pleaded.

Dirty Red kept urging Anna until two of the gunmen got out of the car and started running towards the church, heading directly towards him and Anna. Oscar was reloading his pistol and Dirty Red was getting ready to fire his weapon, when Anna saw the men approaching. Terrified, she broke free from Dirty Red and finally tried to run back into the church. Dirty Red called aloud for her to come back, knowing it was too late for Anna to run, but Anna just kept running. When she got to the front door, one of the gunmen aimed his twelve gauge and blasted Anna four times in the back just as she opened the door to enter the Lord's House.

Dirty Red's eyes grew wide as he watched his future bride's body slide down the front of the church doors and onto the concrete. Oscar opened fired on the two gunmen and they began running back towards the black Jaguar from which they had come as they fired upon the crew on the ground. The two gunmen were killed in a hail of gunfire by Torre`, Lil Earl and Sean before they could return to their vehicle. The driver quickly sped away after witnessing his cohorts get gunned down in a failed attempt to kill Dirty Red and make it back to the car.

Dirty Red stood up after the gunfire ceased and walked slowly over to Anna. His childhood sweetheart lay dead with her eyes open in a huge pool of blood that was beginning to flow down the stairs of the church. Dirty Red stood silently for

a minute before he knelt down and swooped Anna up into his arms and hugged her tightly.

"I'm sorry, Anna," Dirty Red said as he closed his eyes and cried, "Not you, baby, shouldna, shouldna *never* been you." He whispered through his tears as he gently laid Anna down and closed her eyes. The reverend, a few ushers and numerous funeral attendees tried to help Anna by placing their suit jackets and scarves over her wounds and applying pressure, but Dirty Red knew Anna had died on the steps before he'd even picked her up into his arms.

Dirty Red then stood up slowly and turned towards Katrina, who by now, was surrounded by JoAnne, Dana, Alicia, and dozens of other people. He walked slowly towards the crowd. People stepped to the side as he let his .44 automatic fall from his right hand and dropped to his knees in front of his lifelong friend, his sister, the one person he wanted to see make it in life.

Katrina wasn't moving or no longer screaming; but her eyes were still open. Blood ran down the corners of her mouth and covered her chin. She called out for her mother from time to time. Dirty Red once again was seeing the little girl from Benefit Street. He wished he could make everything alright, but the reality of the situation was that his friend lay dying in front of his eyes and he was helpless to do anything about it. Katrina shifted her eyes towards Dirty Red and she tried to speak.

"Don't talk baby girl, the ambulance comin'! We gone be all right!" JoAnne said with tears in her eyes as she held Katrina's hand. "We gone be all right!"

"I'm, I'm sssorry, Ben." Katrina said through her pain.

Katrina then heaved, coughed up more blood, and passed out, her body going limp in the process.

"It's not your fault!" Dirty Red yelled as he knelt down beside Katrina and grabbed her hand away from JoAnne. "You hear me! It's not your fault! Katrina!" Dirty Red said as he began to

cry. "Katrina!" He called out again.

When Katrina didn't answer, Dirty Red broke down. This one here really hit home. Anna and Katrina, two of the most important people in Ben Holland's life had just been shot before his very eyes. Anna was already gone, and things didn't look too favorable for Katrina at this point.

Ambulances soon arrived on the scene. Katrina was quickly placed on a gurney and loaded into a unit and it sped away towards Charity Hospital in downtown New Orleans. The crew quickly scrambled to cars to get to the hospital to be with Katrina in her neediest hour.

Dirty Red jumped up from the stairs and he and Jason, along with Oscar, jumped into his Mercedes and quickly caught up to the speeding ambulance and followed close behind. Dana, JoAnne and Alicia followed the boys and the ambulance in Jason's Cadillac.

Lil Earl, Torre`, Sean and Derrick had gathered the guns left on the ground and calmly fled the scene; even though the police were present. Lamont's funeral was ruined. The church was now empty, except for Lamont's closed casket, his family members, the reverend and the ushers.

Anna's body was covered with a blood-stained white sheet. She lay alone at the top of the stairs while the police asked around for any witnesses. No one knew who the people were that opened fire on the crowd, however; so the police had very little to go on.

Meanwhile, as he trailed the ambulance, Dirty Red began to explain what was going down. "I know what happened." He said as he drove, keeping speed with the ambulance.

"Run it down, nigga." Oscar said as he lit a blunt to calm his nerves.

Dirty Red told Oscar and Jason that it was Damenga who'd killed Lamont and pulled the hit in front of the church. He also told them that Damenga had killed Sherman in Memphis.

"How you know all that?" Oscar asked as he passed the blunt to Jason.

"Why would Damenga wanna do some shit like that after we cut a deal with that mutherfucka not too long ago?" Jason asked before he took a toke of the blunt.

Dirty Red said, "Sherman got busted in Memphis. He told the feds about the job we did ta' try and cut a deal. But he didn't know the feds was working for Damenga."

"So what?" Oscar said.

Dirty Red handed Oscar the newspaper and he, too, read the title and proclaimed that there was supposed to be four dead people in the house.

"There was one survivor on that jack-play in Memphis, brer." Dirty Red said as he continued to follow the ambulance that held Katrina's life in its hands.

"Who?" Jason and Oscar asked simultaneously.

Dirty Red looked at Oscar, shook his head briefly, stared straight ahead and said, "Carmella Lapiente`. Can you believe that shit? The bitch that was in the house up in Memphis that night was Damenga's sister! How the fuck she survived two bullets to the skull from a three-fifty-seven magnum is a fuckin' miracle!" He said as he repeatedly banged his right fist on the steering wheel in frustration.

"How she knew it was us?" Oscar asked.

"Sherman had to tell the feds our names. They had to be the ones who gave our names to Damenga. I'm thinking Damenga wasn't sure, so he waited until his sister pulled through. When she did, I'm guessing she had ta' say somebody named Manny done it. Put that with what Sherman bitch ass told the feds, and there ya' go. Everybody name was made known."

"Damn. We *did* say Manny name in the living room that night." Oscar said somberly.

"It wasn't a coincidence that Manny ran with some niggas

named Oscar, Dirty Red and Jermaine. I said Manny's name myself at Jermaine's funeral. Damenga knew the whole time what he was doin'. He slowed down the shipments and set the whole crew up. That bitch ass nigga Sherman sold us out, brer." Dirty Red said in disbelief as the boys exited the car and walked into the emergency room and awaited word from the doctors regarding Katrina's condition.

After about an hour, one of the surgeons came into the waiting room and spoke to the crew. JoAnne had called Ms. Joyce on the way to the hospital and she had been on the phone ever since. She listened over her phone as she rode in a cab headed south on Interstate-75/85 headed towards Hartsfield International to catch a jump flight from Atlanta to New Orleans. Ms. Joyce was on assignment at Grady Memorial Hospital, but she got someone to cover for her stating she had a family emergency. Ms. Joyce was extremely worried about Katrina, praying that she wouldn't die. Katrina was supposed to be on her way to college, not laid up in the ICU fighting for her life.

Everybody listened as the lead surgeon gave her prognosis. "Miss Sanders has suffered severe gastrointestinal and digestive tract injuries," she said. "She has severe stomach lacerations and what appears to be a collapsed lung and she's might have lost the ability to bear children because her right fallopian tube is barely recognizable. We've sewn up what we can, but we still have a lot of work to do. We just need her to keep fighting. If she can hang in there until we can get a digestive tract specialist into the operating room from nearby L.S.U. Medical Center, it'll greatly increase her chances of survival."

"How long? Ask them how long before the specialist arrives." Ms. Joyce requested of JoAnne.

JoAnne asked the doctor Ms. Joyce's question and she answered by saying a doctor was en route and should be on the premises within the hour. Ms. Joyce knew Katrina's situation was life-threatening. She hung up the phone with JoAnne and entered the airport and headed towards the ticket counter. Ms.

Joyce figured she would be at the hospital in New Orleans in three and a half hours. She hoped that when she got there, Katrina would still be alive.

Back at the hospital, another doctor tending to Katrina was asking if Katrina had any next of kin and Dirty Red told her they were her family. The doctor asked them to wait in the lobby and he would update them as frequently as he could during and after the surgery and up until he got off duty.

"Can we see her?" Dirty Red asked.

"She's heavily sedated right now," the man said. "She can hear you intermittently, but she can't move nor speak. She's in really bad shape, her condition is critical. I would advise against it; but you're all welcome to go in for just a few short minutes so long as you remain quiet."

Everybody went in to see Katrina. They wished they had listened to the doctor when they saw the shape she was in, however; she lay in the bed with her eyes swollen shut. A breathing tube was inserted into her esophagus and there were four IV's pumping various chemicals into her body to numb the pain and fight infection. Katrina's stomach was heavily bandaged, her arms were spread-eagle and her legs were elevated above her head with straps that hung from the ceiling. An EKG machine was on her side to monitor her heart rate. Katrina Sanders, the once happy-go-lucky eight year-old little girl from Benefit Street, was now, at the age of eighteen, fighting for her life in the ICU of Charity Hospital. Her fate uncertain.

As the gang all sat in the lobby of the hospital in stunned silence over the way the last week had played out, Oscar's cell phone rang. He answered and handed the phone to Dirty Red. "Ben, it's Swan."

Dirty Red snatched the phone from Oscar, "Where you been?" He asked in frustration.

"Trying to find out about the feds for ya'. I did. And it's not good, Ben. Look, me and Montgomery leaving town on a

private jet to nowhere, understand? The indictments have come down and the FBI has issued warrants for you and Oscar's arrest for racketeering, money laundering and conspiracy to distribute cocaine in New Orleans. You and Oscar are also suspected of committing a triple murder in Memphis based on Sherman's statements. They have enough to send you guys to death row. I'm sorry, Ben."

After hearing Swanson speak, Dirty Red began thinking about putting together a hit squad in order to go after Damenga on his home turf. Damenga had told him early on that if he wanted to kill him, he would do it on his own turf so Dirty Red was now planning to beat Damenga` to the draw. He was facing a possible death sentence anyway, so he might as well go all out. As Dirty Red contemplated his next move, knowing he may not survive the episode, he couldn't help but to express his grief and anxiety. "Ain't shit left, Swan. Anna dead. Katrina dying. And this nigga Damenga want me and my entire crew dead."

"I'm sorry about Katrina. Your future wife too, Ben. Anna was a very fine young woman. I know you want revenge, so I'm a give it to ya', my friend. Before I destroyed my computer, I thought it to be a good idea to check and search the airport departures and the names as well. You won't believe this—Damenga's in town. I been trying to call you to let you know that."

"I lost my phone at the church."

"Here's the deal, it's twelve-thirty right now. Damenga's flight leaves in an hour and fifteen minutes from Louis Armstrong airport at gate seven. I guess he came personally to see that the job was handled. He didn't get what he wanted, and you can believe this man will never rest until he sees your bloody corpse. You want retribution, there you go; but this is where me and Isaac get off. Take care of yourself, Ben Holland. It was a fantastic ride."

Swan hung up the cell phone and threw it into the waters of Lake Ponchartrain before he and Montgomery boarded their private jet. The two former narcotics agents would later appear

on *America's Most Wanted.*

"What he say?" Oscar asked lowly once Ben hung up the phone.

"We looking at death row, man. But Damenga at the airport." Ben replied as he eyed Oscar seriously, the both of them thinking the same thing.

"Well, let's go, shit!" Jason said as he started to move.

Dirty Red stopped Jason by placing his hand out onto his chest, "Nahh, Jay. The FBI only looking for me and Oscar, dog. We facing death row, brer. You home free, young blood. You should stay here with Dana, Alicia and JoAnne and take care of Kay Kay."

"Fuck that shit! That nigga killed Lamont in cold blood over some shit he didn't even do? You met him after the fact! And he still went ahead and tried ta' kill us all! I can't let that ride, brer!"

"You know what's 'bouta go down, Jay?" Oscar asked quietly.

"The game all I know, brer, and for my people, I ride!"

"Fuck it! Let's move on this nigga then." Dirty Red said as he headed towards the exit doors.

"Y'all ain't gone make it outta there!" JoAnne yelled as Dana began to scream for Jason not to go.

"Don't care 'bout that shit, JoAnne," Dirty Red said in quiet anger. "We had the fuckin' world. Livin' good like a mutherfucka, and this nigga done came and took everything. Everything! I ain't got nothin' left. And I be damn if Damenga gone fly off into the sunset." He said as he continued walking towards the exit.

JoAnne knew there was no talking to Dirty Red. "Oscar, baby, please," she said in desperation as she grabbed him. "It's you and me! You ain't gotta do this! Let's stay here with Katrina!" She said as her eyes began to fill with tears.

"You seen Anna body all tore up on them church steps? You saw Katrina in that fuckin' room back there?" Oscar asked through tears. "She got busted up guts, fucked up lungs, can't have children. Ben lost his wife? Like Jason said, I can't let that shit ride, Jo."

JoAnne grabbed Oscar and hugged him tightly as she hid her face in his chest and continued to beg him to stay.

"Somebody has ta' say enough is enough!" Alicia suddenly said through her tears, causing Dirty Red to turn and face her. "Y'all just gone keep killing each other? You got beaucoup money for a lawyer, Ben! Just let it go for now and we can still leave the city together!"

Dirty Red, who was now leaning against the wall, looked over to Alicia. "I couldn't live with myself knowing I let somebody hurt family. And to turn and run? That's not me, Alicia. You should know me by now." He said somberly as he resumed walking towards the exit doors with Oscar and Jason following close behind.

JoAnne, Dana, and Alicia wept openly and begged the boys not to go. Alicia and JoAnne tugged on Dirty Red's cream colored, blood-stained Armani suit as Dana tugged on Jason in his black tailor made Gucci suit. JoAnne soon left Dirty Red and grabbed Oscar's dark grey silk Armani suit jacket and tried to hold him back, but he shoved her aside, as did Jason towards Dana, and Dirty Red towards Alicia.

As the boys walked out of the double doors of the emergency room, people sitting in the lobby watched as the girls trotted behind the young men, crying and begging them not to go after Damenga.

"Jason, *please!*" Dana cried out as she fell to her knees in the middle of the emergency room's lobby. "What about our future? Don't do this 'cause you gone ruin it! Please! Stay with me! Just stay with *me!*" Dana pleaded as she rested on her knees and clasped her hangs together.

Jason merely stared back at Dana. He knew how much she

loved him; but Lamont's murder at the behest of Damenga could not be forgiven by him. Jason felt that he had to go along with Dirty Red and Oscar on this one, even if there was no coming back. He placed a pair of sunglasses over his eyes, blew a kiss to Dana, and headed out the door, jogging slightly in order to catch up to Oscar and Dirty Red.

Dana placed her head into her hands and wept openly on the emergency room floor, screaming to the top of her lungs, worried sick that she would never see Jason again.

"That's our next generation," an old black man said aloud. "That gangster stuff is gonna destroy all of our young kids." He ended before he sipped a can of soda.

People sitting in the emergency room nodded their heads in agreement as they began to chat amongst themselves. They knew who Ben Holland was and they knew what he was about. Word of the shootout had spread quickly throughout the city, and when they heard that Katrina had been shot, multitudes of people from the Ninth Ward gathered in front of the hospital to await word of her status.

The crowd standing outside of the emergency room grew quiet when Dirty Red, his face and clothes stained with Katrina and Anna's blood, walked down the sidewalk with Oscar and Jason following close behind. The crowd wondered what the boys were up to; and no one dared to ask about Katrina because they were too afraid. Dirty Red had a look in his eyes that told everyone around to not say shit to him. They all watched in silence as the three young men went to the trunk of Dirty Red's Mercedes and pulled out a calico and two SKS rifles, quickly hopped into the car and sped away.

The boys were shell-shocked by what had transpired on this tragic day. Blinded by rage and set on revenge, all the rules were now tossed aside. To get Damenga at all costs was their mission. The ride to the airport was somber; the boys didn't speak one word to one another. The only sound being made was that of bullets being loaded into extra clips. Dirty Red, who was behind the steering wheel, lit up the blunt Oscar and Jason were smoking earlier and pulled out a half full bottle of

cognac from under the front seat and the boys smoked and drank all the way to the airport as they listened to the remix of Ghetto Mafia's song *On The Grind* repeatedly.

Dirty Red slammed the car into park directly in front of the main entrance to the huge airport and he, Jason, and Oscar quickly hopped out of the Mercedes, leaving the doors on the car wide open. With guns in hand, they ran through the airport terminal, setting off metal detectors and shoving people aside in a desperate attempt to get to the drug lord who had destroyed all that they had built together.

Airport security and state police got wind of what was going down and they began heading in the boys' direction just as they approached gate seven. Dirty Red recognized the slim, lanky frame in an all-white suit and the stouter figure beside him. Swanson's tip had paid off. Not only did the boys catch Damenga, they caught his younger brother Alphonso as well.

"What's up now?" Dirty Red yelled aloud as he stood in the gateway aiming his rifle at the two brothers, who were just about to board their flight.

Damenga turned around amidst the chaos as people dropped to the ground and ran from the gateway to avoid being shot. Damenga took off his shades and his eyes widened when he saw the three young men aiming rifles at him. He and Alphonso tried to run towards the plane, but the two brothers were immediately gunned down by Dirty Red, Oscar and Jason before they could even turn and run. The Lapiente` brothers thought that by catching a commercial flight they would be safe from retaliation within the city; but they were wrong in their assumption.

Damenga and Alphonso fell dead from the hail of bullets released by Dirty Red and his boys, and the three quickly turned and began running out of the gateway trying to make it back to the Mercedes. They were met at the end of the hall by airport security and state troopers who immediately opened fire on the crew, however; Oscar's brains were blown against the walls of the gateway and he collapsed to the ground, dying before he hit the carpeted floor.

Dirty Red attempted to fire, but his gun jammed. He caught a bullet in the shoulder that knocked him to the floor.

Jason opened fire, but he was severely outnumbered. His body was riddled with bullets, but as he fell to the floor, he continued squeezing the trigger on his calico, killing a state trooper and wounding an airport security guard before he, too, expired on the gate way floor.

Dirty Red was still alive. He was handcuffed and carted away to Oschner Hospital in Jefferson Parish, just outside of New Orleans within minutes.

The Louis Armstrong International Airport shootout had stunned the city. Never before had the violence been so brazen. The boys had gone all out. They knew they had bought a one way ticket the moment they agreed to go after Damenga, but it didn't prevent either of the three from not going through with their mission.

The crew's reign was officially over. A newspaper article the following day, which had pictures of Ben Holland, Oscar Henderson, and Jason Witherspoon displayed boldly on the front page read, *"She Has Fallen! The Ben Holland Gang Has Fallen!"* which was a spin-off of Revelations Chapter 18:2 which describes the fall of Babylon the Great. It was a befitting title for the crew since Dirty Red always believed that his downfall would be along the level of an Armageddon-type affair.

The police would hold Dirty Red in custody without bail until his trial. As he lay in the Jefferson Parish jailhouse infirmary, he wondered how Katrina was doing. No one came to see him, nor did he receive word from the street. The federal government was also moving his trial to Shreveport, Louisiana to avoid publicity and no one, not even Ms. Joyce, had bothered to contact him.

All Dirty Red knew was that the feds had confiscated everything. *Par 6* was no more, the dope houses and all the cars were seized by the government. The federal government had confiscated a net total of $9.5 million dollars in cash and

another $3,000,000 in assets from the now defunct Ben Holland Gang.

At his trial, in late November of 1999, a trial in which he plead not guilty to all charges, Dirty Red was found guilty on five counts of murder, the three in Memphis during the home invasion, and the two Lapiente` murders inside Louis Armstrong International Airport, murders that had been recorded on live camera. Ben Holland was also charged with racketeering, drug smuggling and money laundering. The feds had a good case. They had Sherman on tape admitting that Dirty Red had orchestrated the triple murder in Memphis and that landed his conviction on those charges. Most of all, they had him red-handed for the murder of Damenga Lapiente` and his brother Alphonso. Ben Holland was lucky not to receive the death penalty. He was sent to a federal penitentiary in the state of Colorado in February of 2000 with a life sentence. Far from home, and out of touch with everyone who ever mattered in life, Ben Holland would not be eligible for parole for seventy-five years. By then, he would be one hundred years old—Ben Holland was going to die behind bars.

For all that he had done, Dirty Red had merely become another black man behind bars. People back home moved on. There would be another crew that would soon arise and fill the shoes that the Ben Holland Gang had left behind. Dirty Red was now penniless and had lost over thirty pounds; he no longer looked like himself. He worried so much about the friends he had lost that his health began to be affected. He'd developed a serious case of stomach ulcers which required frequent trips to the infirmary. He was once light-skinned, but bad eating habits, regret, and despair had darkened his skin. He shaved all of his hair off and began chain smoking cigarettes, all the while longing for his friends.

The day before they shipped him to Colorado, a security guard at the prison in Shreveport, Louisiana where Dirty Red was being held before his departure, seemed as if he was glad to tell him that Katrina Sanders had died two months ago, right around the time he was being sentenced. The news had devastated Ben. He went to Colorado a heartbroken and grief-

stricken individual longing to die.

CHAPTER THIRTY-FIVE

MERCY ON YOUR SOUL

Dirty Red had now been living in Colorado's federal penitentiary for over a year. It was now March of 2001. When he first got to Colorado's Federal Complex in February of 2000, the twenty-five year-old former big-timer had just about given up on life. Although he read the Bible, something he hadn't done since his parents were killed in January of 1984, it did little to ease the pain. The man thought constantly about the life and the people he had lost and left behind. The people in the facility were nice to Dirty Red, though; they liked him, and their kindness had begun to cause changes within Ben Holland.

Despite all his troubles, Ben became a model prisoner shortly after his arrival. The day of his twenty-sixth birthday, in April of 2000, Ben shed his nick-name. No longer was he a gangster called Dirty Red, he was now a young man by the name of Benjamin Holland, Ben for short. Ben also became friends with a Native American prisoner who had a lot of power within the facility early on in the year of 2001. Ben had opened up to the man in February of 2001, a year into his stay at the facility. Having been missing his parents all of a sudden, and thinking about his past, Ben told the Native American his

whole life's story.

The Native American, whose name was Yiska Hoka, quickly took Ben under his wing and began tutoring him on the spiritual aspects of life. He taught Ben how to pray to God properly with humility and reverential awe. He let him know that jail was not the end of his life, but the beginning of a new journey. As they sat and talked in Dirty Red's cell one late night in March of 2001, Ben had finally released all the pinned up emotions he had carried with him ever since the day of Lamont's funeral. Ben felt responsible for everything that went wrong. His friends were dead because of him, he believed.

"It wasn't your fault, Ben. Everybody was along for the ride." Yiska said lowly.

"Yeah, but I was the one driving, Yis. I could've steered that car towards a more less than hostile pasture and still come out on top. I wanted fast money. We all did. And they all followed my lead—right to their own deaths. Those that died got off easy though; I'm forced to live with this regret for the rest of my life. If I could turn back time man…" Ben said as he let his voice trail off as he looked to the floor and rested his arms on his knees and shook his head from side to side slowly.

Yiska could feel the love that Ben had for his people. But he knew if he didn't get over his past, Ben would lose his sanity inside the facility. "You must get past the regret you have inside you, Ben. We all make mistakes. It's not your fault they're dead. Truth is, many men indulge themselves into a way of life that ultimately forces them to become slaves to the very world they seek to conquer." Yiska stated lowly as he sat beside Ben on his cot.

Ben repeated Yiska's statement. "Many men indulge themselves into a way of life that ultimately forces them to become slaves to the very world they seek to conquer. I like that, Yis. I'm feelin' that creed," he said.

Ben Holland took what Yiska had said to him at that exact moment and he vowed to make that slogan the main focus of his life. It was one of the most profound statements he had ever

heard. Ben finally realized that once upon a time, he had the world in his hands, but by trying to keep it, he, in effect, became a slave to it. He loved his friends dearly; they had become his family over time, and he wanted them all to be successful at the out-set and they were; but they had gone about it the wrong way.

Ben often sat with Yiska and talked about life in general and how much he wanted to change for the positive. The Indian had a genuine interest in what Ben had to say and gave him positive advice.

"You'll get another chance, Ben. You're gonna be just fine." Yiska would always say.

Ben didn't believe he had a chance of ever getting out; still he could at least live a productive life behind bars. Maybe prevent other young people from making the mistakes he made. Life was now routine for Ben, but he had a certain measure of freedom by being associated with Yiska; and the Indian's constant prayers and positivity towards Ben would begin to bring forth blessings in Ben's life as he would soon come to realize.

Ben had come in from working in the penitentiary's mechanic shop on a hot spring day in May of 2001 and had just dozed off when Yiska knocked on his cell and pulled open the small steel door that encompassed the small window, waking Ben from his short nap in the process.

"You must come and see!" The Indian said with glee in his eyes as he peeked through the small opening.

"What's going on?" Ben asked as his cell door was unlocked.

"You have a visitor!"

Puzzled, Ben eased up from his bed and walked to a huge vista window in the gangway that overlooked the highway that ran in front of the prison.

"They say no visitors for you right now, but I have people that can fix that in time." Yiska stated as he handed the

correctional officer a billfold of twenties.

The officer placed the money in his pockets and handed Ben an envelope and a pair of binoculars.

"Aim the binoculars there!" Yiska said excitedly, pointing towards the prison's parking lot.

Ben put the binoculars to his eyes. When he focused them, he laughed aloud in delight and said, "I'm dreaming and I'm about ta' wake up," before he removed the binoculars from his eyes and wiped them, waiting for the moment when he would awaken in his cell.

"Ben, you are not dreaming!" Yiska replied happily.

Ben put the binoculars to his eyes again and focused, and to his delight the image was still there. He watched the parking lot through the binoculars as the correctional officer flashed his flashlight repeatedly until a poster board that read, *HELLO FROM ARIZONA! I LOVE YOU!* was flashed before his eyes.

It was Katrina Sanders. She had survived after all.

The guards back in Louisiana had played a cruel trick on Ben. They wanted to see him suffer. They accomplished that goal, but only for a little while. Ben had held on long enough, and, with the help of Yiska Hoka, his faithful Native American friend, he remained mentally sound enough to see his childhood friend once more and see with his own eyes that she was okay.

Ben couldn't hear it, but as Katrina stood before her Mustang holding the poster board, she was playing a song by Rome and Daneesha Starr titled, *As Long As I Live.* She stood before the car with her eyes closed, rocking slightly as she held onto the poster board while singing Daneesha's lyrics, *"I don't wanna live... without you baby... 'cause we've been through...so much together...I wanna tell you...that my heart needs you so...and my love baby...is still the same..."* All of the memories, from the day she first met Ben on Ms. Joyce's front porch, up until the day she was shot at Lamont's funeral, came flooding back on Katrina. She couldn't help but to cry at this

moment as she listened to the song.

Katrina was twenty pounds heavier as she was pregnant with her first child for the now junior basketball player she was engaged to. The young man had a good chance of reaching the NBA.

Katrina was planning on opening a New Orleans style café with two-hundred thousand dollars that Ben had given her for college. The café was destined to become a huge hit in downtown Phoenix as people were already inquiring about its opening date. Katrina's future seemed secure.

It was time for Katrina to go, but Yiska assured Ben that, in due time, he would be able to have conjugal visits with Katrina. He returned to his cell in a joyful state and read the letter that the guard had given him from Katrina.

Katrina wrote to Ben and told him that JoAnne Clemmons was doing well. She was a teacher's aide at a middle school back in New Orleans.

Dana Shelby was working in her parents' pharmacy and attending Xavier University in order to become a pharmacist.

Alicia Mason had purchased her own home and was working at a large retail store inside of Clearview Shopping Mall.

Sean was killed in a botched home invasion shortly after Ben was moved to Colorado, and Lil Earl was back in jail with a thirty year sentence for armed robbery after he was apprehended while fleeing a bank with a sack full of money and a loaded pistol.

Torre` and Derrick had moved to Atlanta, Georgia and formed a record label and the two of them, along with Non-Stop, were beginning to get serious recognition within the record industry by collaborating with popular artists in the city, including Lil Jon and the Eastside Boys, Ludacris, and Pastor Troy.

The news was heartwarming for Ben. He was glad to know that most of his friends had chosen to do something

worthwhile with their lives after all of the turmoil and chaos.

Katrina Sanders, the little girl from Benefit Street, had become a successful young lady. And this young lady, on this day, would give Ben Holland the best gift he had ever received: the will to continue on with the remainder of his life. At the time, however, neither Ben nor Katrina knew just how far their newly reformed rapport would take them, because for what should have been the end of Ben Holland's story—was only the beginning.

In December of 2004, Katrina had written Ben a letter,

Hey, baby, I have some good news! First, The New Orleans Cafe` is the talk of the town! I own two now! I'm doing just fine, Ben, and I hope you are as well. What I really have to tell you though is that I've found a lawyer for us! He's a beast, Ben! It's a long shot I know, but at least I can give you a chance. I owe you so much, baby. Stay strong, and I'll give you all the details when I visit you next year. I would like to come sooner but I'm busy with this lawyer and my marriage, if that's what you want to call it. Anyway, I have a wonderful Christmas gift for you, well, besides finding this lawyer. The guards are going to allow me to bake you and Yiska a turkey and send it to you along with some fancy wine. I'm sending you some spicy boiled crawfish too. It's costing, but it's worth it. I just wanna give you a taste of home. Like it was back in the day, because I believe you have brighter days ahead. Yiska believes that as well. He's a good friend, Ben. Keep him close. Looking forward to seeing you soon.

Love always,

Katrina Sanders

Ben smiled as he folded the letter; but he believed in his heart that he would never see daylight again. Katrina was willing to put money up to buy him a lawyer, but Ben told himself that he would not let her waste her money.

Ben wrote Katrina back and told her not to waste her time or money as the situation was futile; but Katrina quickly sent a

reply and insisted that they at least try. Ben gave in, and Katrina continued on with her plans. She would have done so anyway; no matter what Ben had said to her. Katrina was fighting hard for Ben, and he grew to appreciate that fact. The two were close again, having had many a conversation and conjugal visits over the last three years or so.

Katrina was Ben's only connection to the outside world; although he would receive a letter from JoAnne from time to time and he would see Torre` and Derrick on TV on occasion, Ben wasn't mad that the majority of his friends weren't coming to visit him. To them, especially for JoAnne, Dana, and Alicia, who hadn't been anywhere outside of New Orleans, except for the trip to Daytona, Colorado might as well have been on the other side of the world.

Ben asked no one for nothing and held no grudges. The letters from JoAnne were cool, although they were few and far between, and he never expected Dana or Alicia to write or visit. Ben also understood that Derrick and Torre` were busy with their business even if they did send a shot out to their "homeboy Dirty Red" as they were often heard yelling on TV. Besides, Ben knew if he ever needed them, Katrina knew how to get in touch with everybody.

In January of 2005, Katrina was on her computer in her home office booking a flight from Phoenix, Arizona, to Boston, Massachusetts. At the same time, hundreds of miles away, a woman had just hung up the phone in her home after booking a flight from New Orleans, Louisiana, to Denver, Colorado. These two moves by two totally different women, who didn't know one another personally at the time, would become moves that would put Ben Holland's life on a different path and shed further light on The Holland Family Saga.

Before she boarded her flight to Colorado, the woman in New Orleans requested that the taxi driver stop by Saint Louis Cemetery Number 3 near Bayou Saint John before he took her to the airport. The woman walked slowly through the graveyard and stopped in front of a white marble mausoleum. She stood staring at the marble wall before she laid flowers at

its base. She then eyed the names on the graves: Samson Holland, Gabriella Holland, and Samantha Holland.

The woman's eyes began to well up as she tentatively reached out and touched the marble structure. "We lost three angels the day you all left," she said through her tears. "And I foolishly turned one into a demon. But I've found him again, Gabriella. I found him. He shall know all there is to know about you. About us. I'm so sorry for what I've done to him," the woman said as tears ran down her cheeks. "Forgive me, Gabriella. Please, forgive me. I love you. And, and Ben will learn who he is, and where he comes from, I promise you that. I can't let him go through life not knowing who you truly were. And he deserves to know who he is, where he comes from, and who he was truly meant to be." The woman ended as she wept silently in front of the mausoleum before backing away and walking back to the taxi.

With tears streaming down her face, the woman rode to the airport to catch her flight....To Be Continued

Made in United States
Orlando, FL
02 March 2024

44251618R10212